MIKE EVANS

THE
SAMSON OPTION

A NOVEL

TimeWorthy
·B·O·O·K·S·

P.O. Box 30000, Phoenix, AZ 85046

Published by TimeWorthy Books
P. O. Box 30000
Phoenix, AZ 85046

GameChanger: The Samson Option
Copyright 2010 by Time Worthy Books
P. O. Box 30000
Phoenix, AZ 85046

Design: Lookout Design, Inc.

Hardcover ISBN: 978-0-935199-15-4
Paperback ISBN: 978-0-935199-16-1

1

EGYPT, NEAR THE GAZA BORDER

NASSER HAMID STEPPED OUT from beneath the tent and checked his watch. It was almost four o'clock. They should have heard something by now.

Overhead, the afternoon sun beat down with a scorching heat. Around him, Hamid saw nothing but the rolling sand dunes of the Egyptian desert. He scanned the western sky and focused on the horizon—anyone approaching from that direction would stand out like a dark silhouette against the stark background. He watched a moment, carefully surveying the line where sky and sand met.

Behind him, the top of the tent made a flapping sound as a breeze blew up from the east. Hamid glanced in that direction, then looked up at the clear blue sky. When he saw nothing but the vast expanse of the heavens, he closed his eyes and listened intently for the telltale sound of an unmanned drone. Yet all he heard was the eerie silence of the desert.

Footsteps hurried toward him. He opened his eyes and spun in that direction to see Salim, who was carrying a small shortwave radio. "They did it!" Salim shouted, his young eyes alive with excitement. "They did it."

Hamid's heart skipped a beat. "It really happened?"

"Yes." Salim thrust the radio toward Hamid. "Listen for yourself."

Hamid took the receiver and adjusted a knob on the side to increase the volume. His heart pounded as he raised the antennae and turned it toward the east. The voice came in loud and clear. "This is Radio Iran."

The first reports from America indicated the missile from the *Panama Clipper* had done its job. It had traveled in a perfect arc from the ship's deck southwestward toward Washington, D.C. All available information indicated it had detonated at an altitude of one hundred twenty miles above DuPont Circle, exactly as planned. In spite of his usual cynicism, Hamid's chest swelled with pride as he thought of what he'd done and what had happened when the warhead exploded.

Salim stepped closer. "Those arrogant Americans. Now they will know what it is like to live in the desert." Hamid motioned for silence and once more adjusted the position of the antennae.

As originally conceived, missiles from three carefully constructed ships, each carrying specially designed cargo containers, were to steam within range of the American continent—the *Panama Clipper* and the *Amazon Cloud* approaching from the Atlantic side, the *Santiago* from the Pacific. As planned, the first missile, launched from the *Panama Clipper*, would detonate a nuclear warhead high above the nation's capital, creating an electromagnetic pulse that would take out the government's technological capability. Then, while the mighty American military was blind to the world, the other two ships would launch their missiles striking targets on the ground—the *Santiago* hitting Los Angeles and the *Amazon Cloud* obliterating Washington, D.C.

Hamid listened a moment longer, then switched off the radio. Salim smiled at him. "Now we can do it?" He gestured over his shoulder. "We can launch our own missile?"

Parked beneath the tent a few feet away was a Russian-made

MAZ 534 missile launcher like the ones that had been loaded on the ships. Resting on it was an Iranian Shahab-3 missile. Just days earlier, the tent had been filled with engineers and technicians working feverishly to make final adjustments to the missile and its payload, a five-megaton nuclear warhead. Now the tent was empty and silent as the missile rested there, awaiting the launch codes and coordinates for the real target of the plan—Israel.

"No," Hamid said, shaking his head. "We must wait."

"For what?"

"For confirmation that the others have launched their missiles."

"But they have," Salim protested. "Did you not hear? Up and down the East Coast the electrical power is out. The United States is in the dark."

"The eastern half is in the dark," Hamid corrected. "That was the result of the first missile. We have no report of the other two."

"How will we know?"

"I will know."

"But how?"

"Bring me the radio in one hour." Hamid handed the radio to Salim. "One hour," he repeated. "And do not turn it on until then. We must not run down the batteries."

Hamid turned away and folded his arms across his chest. He pulled his robe up over the back of his neck and scrunched his shoulders. What they were attempting was far more daring than anything conceived by the 9-11 martyrs. Others had tried, but they had all fallen victim to the myriad details and logistical complexity of a global effort, and Hamid knew more than anyone else that there was ample reason to worry this attempt might fail, too.

At first, everything had gone according to plan. The ships had established a record of service as legitimate cargo vessels, calling on ports in the Atlantic, Pacific, and Indian oceans, establishing a paper trail that made them seem like all the other container ships plying trade routes in the East. Then, as the time approached, they each had reached their assigned ports precisely as directed. The *Panama Clipper* in Bremerhaven, Germany, and the *Amazon Cloud* in Aden, Yemen, had taken their cargo and proceeded on schedule. The third ship, the *Santiago*, reached the port of Guangzhou, China, where it was loading as planned, and then the trouble began.

"Wu and his stupid temper," Hamid growled to himself. He wrapped his arms tighter across his chest. "The Chinese are more arrogant than the Americans."

If Wu had held his temper, the ship would have reached its destination, and Los Angeles would be a wasteland. But no, Wu could not wait. He had to vent his anger. When the authorities discovered the FBI agent's body, it was a simple matter to work backward through his day and figure out that he had been at the port. Their investigation delayed the ship two days while the Americans and their Chinese counterparts determined the details of how the agent died. Now the *Santiago* was somewhere in the Pacific and no one knew for sure what the crew would do. The missile could strike from three thousand miles away, but communicating with the crew was nearly impossible. Once the ships were underway, Adnan Karroubi had forbidden the use of cell phones and satellite phones for fear the Americans and their allies might intercept the conversation. Instead, all of the crews, including Hamid, were relegated to information broadcast over traditional shortwave frequencies using coded language embedded in scheduled news reports.

"I should have thought of this," Hamid castigated himself. "I should have made certain everyone knew to launch at the appointed time, regardless of their location." Still, there was the chance they would do it anyway. Perhaps Allah would remind them.

At five that evening, Salim returned with the radio. Hamid

flipped the switch to turn it on and punched in the numbers for the correct frequency. A moment later, he heard the familiar voice of the newscaster from Tehran. Hamid listened intently, but all he heard were more reports of the blackout along the American East Coast. "They are having trouble." His face turned serious. "But there is no news of a strike against Los Angeles. And nothing of a direct hit on Washington."

Salim's face lit up. "Perhaps they do not have a report about Washington because no one can call out with news of it."

Hamid smiled. "I like your optimism. But by now there should have been news about Los Angeles. And we should have—" The voice on the radio interrupted him.

Salim looked worried. "What is it?"

Hamid ignored him and lifted the radio to his ear. He listened a moment, then shook his head. "They are expecting a statement from Karroubi later this evening."

"Adnan Karroubi? Why not the president?"

"Karroubi is head of the Assembly of Experts."

Salim looked puzzled. "But he is not the president."

"No."

"This is not good." Salim spoke with a hint of resignation in his voice.

"No," Hamid shook his head. "That is not good."

"What will happen now?"

"We must wait and see."

Hamid glanced at his watch. It would soon be six in the evening in the desert. He calculated in his head. *Almost noon in Washington, D.C.,* he thought. There was still time to strike the other targets in America, but the window of opportunity was rapidly closing. He was not certain Karroubi understood the precarious position they faced.

With the shortwave radio in his hand, Hamid walked to a tent on the far side of the compound, a hundred yards from the one that held the missile. Inside he found technicians lounging near a worktable. Karim Atef, the senior physicist in the group, looked up as Hamid approached. "You are ready to launch?"

"No." Hamid shook his head. "Not yet."

Atef rose from his place at the table and pulled Hamid aside. "This waiting is not good." He gestured over his shoulder to the others at the table. "These are the best minds Iran has to offer. Why are they still sitting here? All this waiting is putting them at risk."

"Karroubi will issue a statement this evening."

Atef ran his hand over his forehead. "This is insane."

Under other circumstances, Karim Atef would have spent his career teaching physics in America at a prestigious university like MIT or Stanford. Instead, after completing his education he returned to Iran, where he became the father of Iran's indigenous missile program. An ardent follower of Shi'a Islam, he was singularly focused on Jihad against infidels that threatened the spread of the faith, once even beating his cousin to death for converting to Christianity. He demanded complete devotion for himself and had little patience for those who did not display the same.

"We cannot just sit here waiting. Send them away. All of them," Atef gestured to the others in the tent. "We do not need them. Send them now. You do not need them to launch the missile. Send them now."

Hamid glanced down at his feet as if contemplating the request. It made sense. The men sitting around the table beneath the tent represented the heart and soul of Iran's technological community. They were essential to Iran's continuing effort to achieve a viable defense system. And they should have been gone from the compound long before now. Once again, Hamid excoriated himself for not thinking of it. "Yes." He lifted his head and nodded. "You are right. Tell them to go."

"Good," Atef nodded. "Good." He turned away to tell the others. Hamid called after him, "Not all at once."

2

LANGLEY, VIRGINIA

THE SKY WAS DARK when David Hoag and Dennis Kinlaw reached the outskirts of Washington. They steered the old pickup truck carefully through stalled traffic on the Beltway and made their way toward the Langley exit. Around them, all was still, quiet, and dark. Here and there, the glow of a campfire pushed back the darkness, but neighborhoods that just a day earlier were vibrant and alive now seemed deserted and empty.

"This is life before electricity," Hoag sighed.

"Life as it was at the beginning of the twentieth century," Kinlaw added. "But I imagine we'll get things up and running faster than people expect."

"You really think that? Or are you just trying to be optimistic?"

"I'm saying, things never turn out as bad as they seem at first."

"I hope you're right. 'Cause right now things are looking pretty bleak. It's November. No running water. No toilets that flush. No electricity. With two days of this, people are going to be cold, hungry, and miserable."

A sign for the Langley exit appeared. Hoag steered the truck from the highway. In a few minutes, they reached the main gate at CIA headquarters. Unlike the dark countryside around them, lights across the campus glowed brightly.

Hoag glanced out the window. "I guess Operations Support did their job."

"Looks like they kept the lights on," Kinlaw added.

The son of a wealthy Ohio banker, Hoag had attended Yale, where he earned a degree in Near Eastern History. He had also obtained a proficiency in Arabic and ancient Hebrew. Following graduation, he enrolled with his friend Dennis Kinlaw at Harvard Law School. A CIA recruiter found them during their first year. Six months after graduation, they were sent overseas where they worked as field officers from the embassy in Istanbul, then served together in London and Paris. Each at the ripe old age of thirty-five, they were placed on loan to Georgetown University and worked for the CIA on a part-time basis. They had been in New York trying to piece together clues about Nasser Hamid when the warhead detonated over Washington, D.C.

Hoag brought the truck to a stop at the gate. A guard came from the guardhouse. "May I help you?"

Kinlaw handed the guard his building pass. "I'm Dennis Kinlaw." He pointed across the seat. "This is David Hoag." After a check of their identification, the guard waved them forward. To their amazement the gate opened under its own power.

When they reached the building, a security officer stationed at the front entrance recognized them at once. "Winston Smith is waiting for you. He's in the conference room down the hall to the right."

Kinlaw and Hoag crossed the lobby and started down the hall. They found Winston in the Operations Support conference room seated at the far end of a long table, surrounded by stacks of papers and books. A phone bank sat to one side but it had been relegated to propping up a technical manual, which Winston hastily scanned. He glanced up as they entered. "Gentlemen." He pushed back his chair and stood. "You finally decided to join us?"

"We know who did it," Kinlaw blurted out. "We've got to get word to the president. We can't let them—"

"I know," Winston interrupted. "A missile launched from a cargo ship. The *Panama Clipper*. Twenty-five miles off New York Harbor."

"How did you know?"

"Jenny told us."

"Jenny?"

"Yeah. She told us about it and the other two ships."

Kinlaw was puzzled. "Other ships?"

"The *Amazon Cloud* and the *Santiago*. The director thinks this was the work of Al-Qa'ida."

"Al-Qa'ida?" Kinlaw frowned. "Why would he think Al-Qa'ida did it?"

"Those cargo ships are owned by Pakistan Shipping. Nabhi Osmani controls the company. Al-Qa'ida controls Osmani."

"Maybe so, but the missiles were Iranian. Does he really think Al-Qa'ida built nuclear warheads in his Afghan cave?"

"No." Winston had a sobering look. "He thinks they came from Pakistan."

"That's crazy," Kinlaw protested. "We gotta stop them. Where's the director?"

"Omaha."

"Omaha?" Kinlaw felt deflated. "What's he doing in Omaha?"

"Everybody's headed that way. President Hedges set up a command center at Offutt Air Force Base. Congress is moving out there. Supreme Court. Entire government will be located there by next month."

"Why?"

"In case you haven't noticed, other than this compound, nothing works anymore."

Kinlaw pulled a chair from the table and flopped down on it.

"Then why are you here?"

"Somebody had to stay behind to run things here."

Kinlaw sighed. "Is this a permanent move?"

"East Coast will be inoperable for a long time. Your kids will be grandparents before this gets fixed. If at all."

Hoag spoke up. "Is Jenny with them?"

"No." Winston shook his head. "She's in her office. Most of us have been living here the past two days. She's got a—" By then, Hoag was already at the door. "Take the stairs," Winston called. "The elevator doesn't work."

The daughter of a prominent New York attorney, Jenny Freed grew up in Manhattan, where she lived a privileged life. She attended Yale with Hoag and Kinlaw, then joined the CIA as an analyst. She and Hoag had dated on and off since meeting during their first year in college. Their relationship was back on when the attack occurred.

Hoag made his way downstairs and walked quietly to Jenny's office. He stood at the door and watched her sorting through stacks of files that covered her desk. Cardboard boxes were stacked on the floor nearby. "I'll have some boxes for you in a minute," she said without looking up. Hoag leaned against the doorframe and waited. Still unaware of his presence, Jenny closed the file on her desk and turned to shove it in a box. When she looked up, she gasped.

"Hello, Jenny," he said softly.

For a moment she stared at him as if unable to comprehend what she was seeing. Then slowly she stood. Hoag leaned away from the doorframe and stepped forward. She moved from behind the desk and slipped her arms around his waist.

"I wasn't sure I'd ever see you again, and the next minute I was certain you'd show up. And then I was—" she began to cry.

Hoag leaned over and kissed her, then kissed her again. "I wasn't sure you'd see me, either," he whispered. "Are you all right?"

"Yes," she nodded. "And you?"

"I'm fine." She leaned away and wiped her eyes. "I went back and looked at the tapes. I found two more ships. This is what you were working on, isn't it? Missiles launched from cargo ships."

"Yes." He pulled her close and kissed her once more. "I love you," he whispered.

Jenny buried her face in his chest. "I love you, too."

"You weren't hurt?"

"No." She shook her head. "We didn't even feel the explosion."

"What about radiation? Has anyone checked the radiation levels?"

"They've been monitoring as best they can, but the air samplers don't work."

Hoag sighed. "Nothing works." He guided her back to her seat at the desk, then pulled a chair next to hers and sat down. Jenny rested her head on his shoulder and looked up at him. "What was New York like without electricity?"

"There were cars everywhere. Just stopped in the street. We were the only thing moving. Coming out of the city we passed cars parked all the way across the bridge but not a person in sight. It was like they had all vanished. I began to wonder if what Dennis had said wasn't true."

"What?"

"About the Rapture and all that." Hoag squeezed her shoulder. "I thought maybe it had happened, and you'd be gone."

Jenny draped her arm across his chest. "I'm still here."

"When we got down to Philadelphia, it was like taking a trip in a horror movie. Cars abandoned on the highway. People running around like lunatics. Fighting. Stealing. When they saw the truck was running, they turned on us. Then I was sure the Rapture had come."

"But David," Jenny chuckled. "Dennis was with you."

"Yeah. I guess so," he sighed. "I didn't think about that. I just didn't want to be without you. I realized what a mess I'd made of things, and I didn't want to be like that anymore."

Jenny squeezed him even closer. "I was praying."

"I know," he whispered.

Hoag scooted a trash can from beneath the desk and propped his feet on it. "But we're here, and the Rapture hasn't come yet, which means there's still time to do something."

"Yes," Jenny nodded. "There's still hope."

"You found three ships?"

Jenny sat up and wiped her eyes again. "We already knew about the *Panama Clipper*. That's where the missile came from that caused this. But they also loaded the same kind of containers on two other ships. The *Amazon Cloud* and the *Santiago*. *Amazon Cloud* left Yemen for Newport, Virginia. I'm sure it's out there in the Atlantic, just waiting. The *Santiago* is apparently headed for the West Coast."

"Does anyone know about this?"

"I told Winston. He took me to the director, and they sent the information to the president." Her shoulders sagged. "But they think this was Al-Qa'ida, using missiles from Iran and warheads from Pakistan."

"That's crazy." Hoag sat up, suddenly alert. "We have to tell them."

"We have one secure line that works, from the situation room on the third floor."

"We could send a message from there?"

"I tried. We sent them a memo detailing how this was more likely an attack backed by Iran and not Pakistan, but I don't think anyone's listening."

"We need to get out there to Omaha."

"Which reminds me ..." Jenny paused and gave him a questioning look. "How did you and Dennis get here?"

"A pickup truck," Hoag grinned.

"A pickup truck? You found a truck that actually worked?"

"It's old. Doesn't have a computer. Dennis hot-wired it off the street."

"That's funny." Jenny leaned back in her chair and laughed. "Dennis Kinlaw hot-wiring a pickup truck." She took a breath and then looked at Hoag. "So, what do we do now?"

"I don't know. If we have to hit back at someone, Pakistan might not be that bad ... I mean, it would be bad, but they aren't strategic partners with anyone. China would protest, but they wouldn't retaliate. But if we hit Iran, the world could just come unglued."

"You want to go to Omaha? Almost everyone else is there."

Hoag took her hand. "I want to stay right here with you."

"But you want to be in the middle of this."

"Maybe history reached this point before, where the end was about to happen, and someone stepped up and did the right thing. They averted the end, at least for a little longer."

"Maybe," Jenny smiled. "You never talked like this before. You aren't the same person who left for New York the other day."

"No." Hoag sighed. "I'm not."

"I like this David better than the one you used to be."

He pulled her close. "I do, too."

3

EGYPT, NEAR THE GAZA BORDER

ALL THROUGH THE NIGHT, Hamid watched as technicians and assistants trickled out of the compound and disappeared into the desert. Traveling in groups of two or three, and dressed as goat herders and wandering nomads, some rode on camels that the Bedouins kept tethered near the first large dune. Others left in the trucks that Hamid had procured for hauling supplies and parts. Some simply walked away. Saying good-bye proved to be a distraction as each of them came by the tent for a word of blessing and to assure him they would all meet again. Hamid would have rather they simply left with no acknowledgement at all. He cared little for their personal relationships, and spending time with them meant he was only able to check the radio reports intermittently until well past midnight.

Around two in the morning he caught an hourly news broadcast. Atef, one of the few men remaining in the compound, sat by the radio with Hamid. They listened as the report led with the statement from Karroubi: "Sources have confirmed that the American navy is patrolling the sea lanes, stopping ships even on the high seas. Some of those ships are carrying Iranian cargo. Iranian citizens living lawfully in foreign countries are being detained and questioned by American authorities, without regard for legal standards or human rights. Because of these disturbing developments, we are advising all citizens traveling on Iranian passports to exercise extreme caution. If at all possible, residents of Iran should refrain from traveling abroad and those who are abroad should make every effort to return home."

Atef glanced over at Hamid. "What was that about? What did he mean?"

"It is nothing. Just a travel advisory." Hamid switched off the radio and set it aside.

Atef grasped Hamid's forearm. Their eyes met. "It *wasn't* nothing. The Assembly of Experts doesn't issue travel advisories. What does it mean?"

Hamid pulled his arm free of Atef's grasp. "It was nothing. Everyone has left?" Atef dropped his hands to his side. "Only the three of us remain. You, me, and Salim."

"There is one truck remaining?"

"Yes," Atef replied. "And the missile."

"Take Salim with you in the truck."

"You are going to drive the launcher?"

"I will take care of it."

"You will not succeed."

"I will be fine."

"They will see you," Atef insisted. "Believe me. Their satellites are still functioning. We did not disable them with that single blast."

"I am aware of the effect our missile had."

"They will see that missile on a launcher, riding down a desert road. It will show up as bright as the city lights. They will see it and they will ..." A look of realization swept over Atef's face. "You do not intend to destroy the missile." Hamid looked away. Atef took hold of his arm once more, his face alive with anticipation. "You are going to launch it."

Hamid seemed not to listen. "Take Salim and go."

"That message meant you were to return. They do not want you to launch the missile."

Hamid looked him in the eye. "Perhaps I misunderstood."

"They will not like it."

"You must go now."

"Very well," Atef sighed. "I will go." He leaned forward and embraced Hamid, grasping him by the shoulders with both hands. "Allah Akbar," he whispered.

Hamid nodded. "Allah Akbar."

Salim entered the tent. "Has there been a new report?"

Hamid backed away from Atef's grasp. "Karroubi has issued a statement."

Salim looked eager. "What did he say?"

"All persons traveling on an Iranian passport should return home at once."

For a moment, Salim's eyes searched Hamid's face for a clue about what the statement meant. Then a knowing look came over him. He shook his head from side to side. "No," he said emphatically. "I will not leave without you."

Hamid moved near him. "You must."

"I will stay and help you."

"I am taking the missile from here." Hamid's eyes darted to Atef, but he spoke to Salim. "We are not launching it."

"Not launching it? Why not?"

"This is the way Karroubi wants it. This was his decision."

"Where will you take it? What will you do?"

"I am not certain."

"You will need help. I can help you drive. I can help you unload it or hide it in the sand," Salim spoke quickly. "That is what we can do. We can hide it in the sand. Mark the coordinates. Come back later to get it. I will help you."

"No, Allah has spoken. I have to accomplish my assigned task," he said quietly. "You must go with Atef." He took Salim by the shoulders. "I will find you in Tehran when this is finished."

Salim saw the truth in Hamid's eyes and clutched him tightly. The missile would be deployed, not abandoned in the desert. "I do not think you will get far."

Hamid pulled free and stepped back. "We shall see," he smiled. "We shall see."

By then, Atef was at the doorway. He pushed back the tent flap and held it while Salim moved past, then he glanced back at Hamid. "I will see that he stays with me." Atef had a wan smile. "You know where to find us in Tehran."

"I will come to you soon," Hamid nodded.

"You will give us a head start?"

"Yes."

"We will need an hour."

"I understand."

Atef patted him on the shoulder. "I will see you in Tehran." And with that he disappeared into the night.

From inside the tent Hamid listened as the truck doors banged closed. He heard the engine start and a moment later heard it whine as the truck made its way across the sand to the road. A sense of sadness swept over him as the sound faded into the distance, but he pushed it aside and ducked out from beneath the tent.

Above him the sky was filled with tiny specks of light that seemed so thick they almost touched. He tipped back his head and stared up at them, turning slowly in a circle as his eyes moved from one constellation to the next. His father had been interested in the stars and did his best to teach Hamid the Zoroastrian constellations. *"These are the ancient teachings of our people,"* he had said. *"From long before Mohammed. The ancient teachings of the stars that show us signs and messages from the heavens."* As a boy, Hamid had endured those sessions out of respect for his father, but he could never see the figures outlined in the stars that others found so fascinating. Now he wished he'd paid more attention.

An hour later, Hamid sauntered back to the tent that housed the missile. A single lantern burned near the front wheel of the cab. He moved quickly to it and turned it off, then dropped to the ground and leaned his head back against the truck tire. Atef had asked for an hour's head start, but that was far too short. Those traveling into the desert would need longer. They would need a day.

4

LANGLEY, VIRGINIA

EARLY THE NEXT MORNING Hoag and Jenny met Winston in the court-yard behind the headquarters building. They sat on a wooden bench near the fishpond watching the sun as it rose over the horizon. "I love to watch the sunrise from here," Winston mused. "Nothing like working all night, then coming out here with a cup of coffee to see a new day arrive." He turned sideways and looked down the bench at them. "The Air Force is sending in a couple of C-17s. They'll be land-ing at Dulles in an hour. Bringing in generators, trucks, and fuel."

"Good," Hoag replied. "Want me to help?"

Winston glanced at Jenny, then back to Hoag. "I want the two of you to get down there to Dulles and fly out to Omaha when those planes return."

"What about Dennis?"

"I sent him home last night. He's with his wife. I'll find a place for him if he wants to go, but right now he needs to look after his family."

Hoag felt sad at the thought of leaving his friend behind, but he was excited about going to Omaha, especially with Jenny. "So, what will we do in Omaha?"

"The director is assembling a team of analysts. I told him I'd send the two of you out there to help."

"What about you? Aren't you coming?"

"No," Winston shook his head. "For right now, I'll stay here."

Hoag didn't like the idea of operating without Winston as his cover. Winston had been more than a supervisor. He had been mentor, friend, and shield against the rough and tumble politics that often marred the agency. The thought of having to work without his protection was troubling. Winston gave Hoag a knowing look. "I'll be around. You won't get rid of me that easily."

"Maybe I could work from here. We have one line that functions. Operations is already working on another."

Winston shook his head again. "They'll get the lights on in a few places, fire up the Capitol and the White House for morale, but life on this end of the country will be primitive for a long time to come. If you and Jenny are going to have a future, it'll be somewhere west of the Mississippi." He stood and patted Hoag on the shoulder. "Get moving. I need you two on that plane. They won't wait."

As Winston started across the courtyard, someone called from the building entrance. "Come quick. The EU is making a statement."

Hoag and Jenny hurried after Winston. They rushed inside and down the hall to the conference room where a crowd had already gathered around a shortwave radio that sat on the table. Winston glanced at a man to his left. "What have they said?"

"Mueller, the German chancellor, is speaking. European Council met. He's been talking about the extent of damage we've incurred."

The voice on the radio continued. "We regret that our friends in America face such a difficult hour, but the consequences of that difficulty fall not only on them but on us, as well. We in Europe, and citizens of every country, face an uncertain future. In the past we looked to America to address situations like this. It was they who brought stability to our lives and gave us relief for our fears. Now America can no longer respond. No one knows for certain if that great nation shall ever return to its former glory. Meanwhile, life goes on and we must, too.

"Today, the European Union, in concert with the great nations of China and Russia, has taken the unprecedented step of assuring the world's financial markets that our economic life will proceed in an orderly and efficient manner. We in the European community remain economically strong and financially sound. Germany, in particular, had little exposure to American debt. Consequently, Germany and its fellow EU member countries have agreed to inject sufficient amounts of capital into both the Russian and Chinese financial systems to insure that losses on U.S. debt obligations will not cripple their economies.

"In addition, we have agreed to purchase sufficient quantities of oil on the open market to maintain stable supplies throughout Europe. We regret that events have brought us to this point, and we extend our best wishes and deepest sympathies to the people of America, but we cannot sit idly by while the world and our future crumble." There was a rustling sound, and then an EU spokesman took the microphone for questions.

Those listening in the conference room began to murmur. Someone spoke up. "Josef Mueller is a traitor."

"He had no choice."

"We saved Germany when they were devastated."

"That was a long time ago. They've repaid us many times over."

Jenny leaned close to Hoag. "What does this mean?"

"Josef Mueller is making his play."

"His play?"

"We're out. Germany sees a chance to step up."

"Step up for what?"

"World leadership."

She looked troubled. "A crisis is a great opportunity. He can control the world."

"I didn't think about it like that." Hoag raised an eyebrow. "We talked about this with Vic Hamilton."

"We?"

"Dennis and I."

"You talked about Germany?"

"No. About the Four Horsemen of the Apocalypse."

Winston gave Hoag a nudge. "You two better get moving. There's a truck waiting out front."

"We have trucks?"

"Old ones. Like the one you and Kinlaw drove from New York." Winston nodded toward the door. "Get moving. I want you both on that plane." Hoag felt a lump in his throat. Winston's eyes were misty. "I'll be in touch."

Hoag took Jenny's hand. "Come on. We better go."

Jenny tossed Winston a wave and turned to leave. As she and Hoag walked out the door she looked up at him. "So, what do they mean?"

"What does what mean?"

"The Four Horsemen. What does that mean?"

At the front entrance Hoag pushed open the door and held it for her as they stepped outside. "They aren't creatures, literally. They represent—"

A guard met them at the steps. "Winston Smith said you needed a ride to Dulles."

"Yes."

"Right this way."

Jenny tugged on Hoag's arm. "But, what does it mean?"

"Let's get in the truck. I'll tell you on the way."

5

EGYPT, NEAR THE GAZA BORDER

HAMID SPENT THE SECOND DAY in the desert recounting the many steps it had taken to get this far. There had been endless meetings in Karachi with Nabhi Osmani about the design of the ships. Then more meetings to work out the contracts for their construction. Locating oversized cargo containers and positioning them at the correct ports, all the while attending to details necessary to keep the nuclear program moving forward, and still they had not achieved their original goal. *But we did what no one thought we could do,* he grinned. *The Americans are eating by the campfire in New York, if they are eating at all.*

When the day grew hot, Hamid unrolled a sleeping mat and stretched out on the hard-packed sand next to the launcher. He stared up at the roof of the tent billowing in the afternoon breeze and daydreamed of home until sleep overtook him. Finally, after hours of reflection and a long, restful nap, he rose from the mat and checked his watch to find it was seven o'clock. He would have preferred to strike with the missile on the day before, timing the explosion with the afternoon rush hour, but that had not been possible. *This might work out better. The explosion would come in the night. There would be mass confusion until morning. All the news channels would cover it. The world would cower in fear.*

Hamid rolled up the sleeping mat and tossed it aside, then walked to the cab of the truck and opened the door. He reached inside and took a green webbed belt from the seat. A smile spread across his face as he read the words, "A. Kirkland, U.S. Army," printed in plain block letters on the inside.

Taken from a dead American soldier, the belt had been a trophy presented to him by the sniper team guarding Iran's nuclear test site high in the Zagros Mountains near Al-Akbar. Hamid had carried the belt since then, preserving it for this occasion. He strapped it around his waist over the top of his white thawb and cinched it tight, then climbed in behind the steering wheel and pressed a button to start the engine. The truck roared to life, belching thick black diesel smoke that rolled in a dark cloud beneath the top of the tent. Hamid pressed the clutch pedal and moved the shifter into gear. The truck lurched once as he slowly released the pedal, then it rolled forward. Through the reflection in the mirror he saw the missile as it inched its way past the edge of the tent.

Thirty yards across the sand, he brought the truck to a stop and set the brake. He climbed from the cab and walked to the back of the launcher trailer. A control panel was located near the rear wheels. He removed the cover from it and pressed a button to extend the trailer stabilizers. Hydraulic pumps whined as the legs extended on either side. When they were in place, he moved to the front of the trailer and pulled a lever to unlock the latch that kept the launch rack fixed in place against the trailer frame. Satisfied the clasp was free of the frame, he returned to the control panel and pressed a second button. The truck's engine coughed and sputtered, then picked up speed as a second hydraulic pump extended the piston that raised the launch rack into the air with the missile. Hamid smiled as it slowly rose to a vertical position. When it was in place, resting firmly on the launch pad at the end of the trailer, he dropped the rack back to the trailer frame.

He returned to the cab of the truck once more and retrieved a laptop. Using a USB cable, he connected it to a port on the control box and logged in to the missile's guidance system. With a few clicks of the keyboard he opened a program on the computer and entered the coordinates for Tel Aviv. There was a brief delay while the laptop synchronized the coordinates to the missile's system.

When that was loaded, he switched the laptop to the launch system and checked his watch. It was past seven. *No point in waiting any longer.* He set the program to launch in two minutes, then pressed a key to enter the time. After a moment, the program uploaded the information. A message box appeared indicating it had been accepted. Then a second window opened showing the time as it ticked down, second by second.

As the clock moved below fifty-eight seconds, a clicking sound came from inside the missile. Hamid set the laptop aside and retreated to a spot beyond the last tent. He had a clear view of the missile, but was far enough away to avoid the heat of the blast.

Seconds went by slowly, then a hissing sound came from the bottom of the missile. Steam and smoke boiled from between the control fins. An instant later, fire shot out the bottom of the launch stand, scorching the sand beneath. Then the missile erupted from the launch pad and shot straight into the sky. Hamid watched it race toward the heavens, then slowly arc toward the north. In less than a minute it was out of sight.

With the missile on its way, Hamid wasted little time. He walked quickly past the tents toward the first line of dunes. After the dust had settled around the ruins of Tel Aviv, the Americans would step in with their satellite imagery and sophisticated technology. They would plot the missile's path in reverse and comb the desert for the launch site. But by then he intended to be far away.

6

SOMEWHERE OVER
THE AMERICAN MIDWEST

WHEN THE C-17S LANDED AT DULLES, the loadmasters and their crews quickly removed the cargo. In less than two hours, they emptied the planes and reconfigured the cargo bays to hold a full load of passengers. Hoag and Jenny trooped aboard with department executives, senior staffers, and several cabinet officers. Moments later they were airborne.

As the plane leveled off at its cruising altitude, Jenny leaned next to Hoag. "Okay," she began. "What did you and Dennis talk about with Vic Hamilton?"

"We had been working over the idea of ships and cargo containers. What if this, what if that."

"Right."

"And then we found those containers that had the symbol on the door. The crescent moon with the circle."

"The circle that doesn't quite close."

"Yeah. So Dennis kept telling me we needed to think about prophecy and the idea that the threat we were investigating had some connection to end-time events."

"And you didn't think much of that idea."

"That was before they turned out the lights on the East Coast."

"So, you went to see Vic Hamilton?" Jenny asked.

"Yeah. And he started talking about *Revelation* in a way I'd never heard before."

"Like what?"

"Like at the beginning, there were letters to seven churches. All of those churches were located in what is now Turkey. And the letters contain a warning of a pending judgment. 'Do this or I will remove you completely.'"

"That's interesting," she replied. "Because none of those churches exist today."

"Right. That's what Vic said. They're all gone. But do you know why they don't exist?"

"Not really."

"After World War I, the Allies occupied most of Turkey. But by then, Turkey had been through a civil war. The young Turks were in charge and they wanted the foreign armies out. So in 1923, the Turks and the Allies negotiated the Treaty of Lausanne. By the terms of that treaty, all Greeks living in Turkey were sent back to Greece and all Turks living in Greece were sent back to Turkey. It was one of the largest repatriations in the history of the world."

"And what does that mean?"

"The Turks implemented the treaty by deciding that all Christians were Greeks. If you were Christian, they deported you to Greece."

Jenny frowned. "I've never heard of that."

"When the treaty was fully implemented, Turkey was ninety-nine percent Muslim. The most Muslim country of any in the Middle East."

"And what about the Four Horsemen?"

"I asked Vic the same question. Most people think of them as animals or beasts or spiritual beings. He said, 'What if they aren't actually beings but countries?'"

"Countries?"

"Yeah. A plain reading of the verses makes it seem like they're talking about a rider on a horse, something with a spiritual meaning. But when you look at the descriptions, it makes sense to see them as countries, and it fits better with what happens later."

"What happens later?"

"There's a big war. It makes better sense if the horses are actually countries."

"How so?"

"Countries go to war." He gave her a tight smile. "Horses don't."

"Interesting theory."

"Yeah. We're still working on it. White horse, stately and composed, a kingdom out to regain its former glory. The red horse, brutal and unruly. The black horse, a grain merchant. He has something to sell, but he's demanding a high price for it. And the pale horse, a country willing to risk complete annihilation of the human race by the most horrible means available." He paused for a moment, thinking. "It's actually a …" Suddenly he realized Jenny was no longer talking. He glanced to his left to see her eyes were closed and her jaw was slack. The sight of her sleeping with her head on his shoulder made him feel good. He rested his arms across his lap and closed his eyes, too.

7

MOSSAD OPERATIONS CENTER ASHDOD, ISRAEL

TZIPI LEVANON SAT AT HER DESK in the operations center and stared at the monitor. For the past thirty minutes she'd been watching satellite images of a house in the West Bank. Long suspected of being a meeting place for an Al-Aqsa terrorist cell, the satellite had been retasked to a geosynchronous orbit five days earlier. Hovering directly overhead, it fed a steady stream of up-to-date information about activities on the ground at the house and in the surrounding region.

Suddenly, an alarm sounded. Levanon glanced up at one of the screens lining the wall directly opposite her desk. She pressed a button on the console before her and slipped on a headset. "We have an alert," she said in a curt, businesslike tone. "Sensors indicate a missile launch."

Almost before the words had left her lips the door to the room burst open and Efraim Hofi, the Mossad director, rushed in. "What is it?"

"Missile launch, sir. Telemetry indicates it is carrying a nuclear warhead."

"From where?"

"The Egyptian desert." Levanon pressed a button on her keypad and pointed. A second screen at the far end of the room showed a map with the missile trajectory plotted in red.

Hofi studied it a moment. "What is the target?"

"Tel Aviv."

"Time to impact?"

"Approximately five minutes."

Hofi moved to a nearby desk, snatched up a telephone receiver, and began barking orders. "Get me the watch commander at Hatzerim Air Base." Within seconds, the watch commander answered the call. Hofi's voice was loud but measured and controlled. "This is Ashdod Operations. We are tracking a missile inbound from south of your position. Targeted on Tel Aviv. Possibly carrying a nuclear warhead. Activate all defense systems and put your troops at defense condition four. This is not a drill. I repeat; this is not a drill."

Without waiting for a response, he switched to another phone line. "I need the prime minister." Moments later, the prime minister was on the line. "Mr. Prime Minister, we are tracking a missile possibly carrying a nuclear warhead. It was launched from the Egyptian desert. The target is Tel Aviv."

"You have ordered the necessary measures?"

"Yes."

"Should we do anything more?"

"If we cannot knock it down, the missile will strike in less than five minutes."

"Very well."

Hofi slammed down the receiver and turned to those in the room. "What is our status?"

An operator seated across the room called out, "Iron Dome and Arrow systems have come online."

Someone else shouted, "Patriot missile batteries have been activated in Hatzor and Ramon."

"Do they have the target?"

"No, sir. Not yet."

Hofi's voice grew louder. "Why not?"

"Iron Dome and Arrow are searching for it. The Patriot batteries are still coming online."

"We have no time to wait."

"We have planes in the air," someone shouted, continuing to update the status of forces. "Ground troops are on alert. Ships at sea have been notified."

An image on the screen continued to track the missile as it arced toward Tel Aviv. Moment by moment the line grew longer as it inched toward the target. Data appeared in a box along the edge of the screen showing speed, altitude, distance from launch, and distance to target. Hofi stood silently in the center of the room, watching, hoping, waiting. "Come on," he growled. "Where are the missile batteries?"

Levanon spoke up. "One minute to warhead release."

"Any report from Hatzor or Ramon?"

"Nothing from—"

"Target acquired," someone shouted. "The battery at Ramon has acquired the target."

Icons on the screen lit up in red indicating the missile batteries at Ramon were active and launching their missiles. Moments later, the missiles at Hatzor went active, too.

8

OFFUTT AIR FORCE BASE
OMAHA, NEBRASKA

HIGH ABOVE THE PLAINS OF NEBRASKA, the C-17's engines throttled back to a slower speed. The change in pitch roused Hoag from sleep. He glanced out the window and watched as the city of Omaha slowly inched closer. Jenny shifted positions against his shoulder. "Something wrong?"

"We're approaching Offutt."

She sat up and rubbed her eyes. "I had a good nap. How about you?"

"I slept some."

"You were snoring."

He glanced at her with a smile. "You were, too."

"I think we were more tired than we realized."

"Tense couple of days."

The plane continued its descent, then banked in a lazy arc to the south. Before long, the runway came into view. The pilot touched down softly and taxied to a stop in front of a large gray hangar.

Hoag and Jenny slipped from their seats to the aisle and followed the others down the steps from the plane into the hangar. Staff members met them there and methodically guided each of them through the registration process. Hoag was standing in line waiting to receive security credentials for the base when a young woman approached.

"David Hoag? Jenny Freed?"

"Yes."

"I am Donna Bynum." She had an olive complexion with almond eyes and dark, straight hair that fell just above her shoulders. "The director would like to see you. He's waiting for you in the situation room."

"What's up?"

Jenny gave him a knowing look. "I think they'll tell us when we get there."

Hoag pointed to the suitcase at his feet. "What about this?"

"Bring it with you," Donna turned away and started toward the exit. "We'll find a place for it." Jenny walked with her. Before they reached the far side of the building, they were already in an animated conversation.

Hoag called after them, "What about credentials and housing and all that?"

"Don't worry about it," Donna replied without looking back. Jenny turned in his direction without breaking stride and motioned for him to follow.

Reluctantly, Hoag picked up the suitcase and hurried after them. "I was looking forward to a hot shower," he grumbled.

In the parking lot outside the hangar, Jenny and Hoag stuffed their suitcases in the trunk of a gray Chevrolet sedan, then climbed inside. Jenny sat up front with Donna. Hoag got in the back.

Donna steered the car from the lot. Streets on the base were jammed with traffic but she paid it little attention. The engine whined as they weaved back and forth around cars, trucks and buses. First speeding up, then jerking to a stop. "Come on," she complained, and pressed the horn. "We don't have much time."

"What's going on?"

"There's a situation developing in Israel. I don't know much about it. They just said you'd be on the plane and they sent me to get you. I'm supposed to bring you up there as soon as possible." She turned the wheel sharply to the left and pressed the gas pedal.

Hoag held on to the armrest with one hand and braced the other against the seat. "Is it always this busy?"

"We have most of the department executives out here now," Donna explained. "Interior is in that building." She pointed out the window to the left. "They don't like being way out here, but defense and national security have priority right now. They're in the building with the president." A little farther down the street she pointed to the right. "Treasury is operating from that building." Hoag looked out at a three-story brick building. "They already have most of their essential staff in place."

Minutes later, Donna turned the car into a driveway that led up to a gleaming six-story steel and glass structure. They came to a stop at the front entrance. Air Police stationed at the front entrance stepped forward and opened the car doors. Donna got out and made her way around to the curb.

Hoag stepped from the car. "What about the suitcases?"

"Will you stop with the suitcases? They need us inside."

"I just want to—"

"It's okay," Donna interrupted. "I'll have someone deliver them to your quarters." She turned away and started up the steps. Jenny walked with her. Hoag followed.

Inside the building, Donna led them down the hall to an elevator and pressed a button for the basement. Moments later, the door opened to a corridor filled with overstuffed filing cabinets and people who seemed to be rushing in every direction. A cacophony of voices filled the air. Hoag looked bewildered. "What is this?"

"Analysis section. Come this way." Donna walked up the hall to the right, her steps quickening as they went. "We need to hurry." She glanced at her watch. "It may be over by now."

At the end of the hall they came to a door with two Marine Corps guards posted outside. A biometric screen was mounted on the wall. Donna pressed her palm against it and held it there while the screen scanned her prints, then the lock on the door clicked. A guard opened the door. She glanced at him and pointed over her shoulder. "They're with me." Hoag and Jenny stepped inside. The door closed behind them.

Much like the situation room in the basement at CIA head-quarters, large LCD screens covered the walls. Workstations were arranged around the room facing the screens. An operator's console occupied the center of the room. Civilian employees and military officers were crammed shoulder to shoulder into the remaining space.

With Hoag and Jenny in tow, Donna worked her way across the room to an Army colonel standing near a desk. She whispered something to him, then turned to Hoag. "This is Colonel Whiston. He'll bring you up-to-date on what's happened so far. I'll catch up with you later." She backed away and disappeared out the door.

Whiston shook hands with Hoag. "Fifteen minutes ago NORAD picked up a signal from a missile in the Egyptian desert."

"What kind of signal?"

"When the missile's guidance system went active it acquired a data link with a Pakistani satellite. We intercepted the telemetry between them."

"What's the target?"

"Tel Aviv."

"What's happening now?"

"Not sure. Israeli missile defense batteries locked onto it two minutes into its flight. It disappeared from our screen at three."

"Think they got it?"

"Don't know yet."

Hoag glanced around the room. Hoyt Moore, the CIA director, stood to the right. Their eyes met and he acknowledged Hoag with a nod. A few feet in front of Moore the president, Jack Hedges, leaned over a console and watched the images on an operator's monitor. Across the room, Secretary of State Lauren Lehman stood next to Braxton Kittrell, the president's chief of staff. While Hoag checked for others, the door opened and Carl Coulliette, the Secretary of Defense, entered. With him came Russ Williams, the national security adviser. Hoag leaned close to Jenny. "Didn't know this many egos could fit in one room."

"Hush." She jabbed him with an elbow. "This is serious."

"I know it's serious. And I know if the Israelis didn't shoot down that missile, there's nothing we can do about it."

An operator spoke up. "Mr. President, we have confirmed the hit."

"They got it?"

"Yes, the Ashdod Operations Center has informed us their Patriot battery took it out."

Cheers went up from the room. Hedges smiled and nodded as he shook hands with those standing near him. After a moment, he turned to the room. "Okay, okay," he said, waving for quiet. "We dodged a bullet with that one. But we need to know whether there are any more of these attacks to come and who is behind them."

"It's not the Egyptians," Lehman offered.

A colonel standing a few feet away chimed in. "Are we certain we can rule that out?"

Another voice came from the opposite side of the room. "The missile's guidance system used a Pakistani satellite."

"So what are you saying?"

"That we ought to take a serious look at Pakistan."

"The missile that hit us was launched from a ship owned by a Pakistani company."

"Exactly."

"Sir," Russ Williams interjected. "Our best intelligence estimates indicate elements within Pakistan have been sponsoring these attacks. It's the only theory that accounts for the information we now have."

A voice from across the room countered, "But the missile that hit us was an Iranian Shahab-3."

"They could have gotten that missile from any of a dozen different places. We know Iran has sold them in the region. But think about the evidence." Williams ticked off the points with his fingers. "Missiles fired from ships owned by a Pakistani company that, in turn, is owned by someone who had deep ties to Osama bin Laden and his successors. Target acquisition data provided by a Pakistani satellite."

Lehman shook her head. "But we don't know that for sure. They have no reason to attack us."

"What about the other two ships, the one off Virginia and the one headed toward California? Aren't they both owned by the same company?"

"Are we searching for them?"

"That would be a waste of time, money, and effort. Nothing indicates those ships pose any threat."

"Waste of time?" someone shouted. "Are you kidding me? We have planes flying up and down the coast right now looking for the one off Virginia. We can't afford *not* to look for it."

"All right, all right." Hedges held up his hand for silence and turned to the operator at the center console. "What do we have in the area?"

"Virginia?"

"No," Hedges snapped. "Israel."

"A couple of missile cruisers in the immediate area. And two littoral combat ships."

"Give the Israelis all the assistance they request. And offer them anything we have." He looked across the room at the secretary of defense. "Carl, I need options for a response. And a better mechanism for analyzing these situations. We can't stand around here arguing back and forth. We need a genuine policy apparatus."

"Yes, Mr. President."

Hedges turned and made his way from the room. Cabinet officers followed him out the door. Hoyt Moore caught Hoag's eye and made his way toward him.

9

BERLIN, GERMANY

JOSEF MUELLER SAT AT THE DESK in his private study at the Chancellery. After a long and busy day, he'd had a quiet dinner alone and looked forward to spending the remainder of the evening reading. Since his speech to the European Union two days before, accolades had continued to arrive from heads of state on every continent. He spent most of his time responding to them and addressing details of the new, emerging order of nations. The world, it seemed, was finally turning to Germany. He took a sip from a glass that sat on his desk and leaned back in his chair. A smile crept over his face. All was going according to plan, and soon the real prize would be within his grasp.

Mueller had arrived on the political scene ten years earlier in a race to choose Bavaria's next governor. He campaigned on a platform that stressed a more prominent leadership role for Germany in world affairs. The landslide victory that followed coincided with a resurgence of German nationalism. After his two terms as governor, Bavaria was at the height of economic prosperity. Mueller's overwhelming popularity assured him of an easy move to the office of chancellor. Then, a week after the German parliament elected him to that office Mueller gave a speech in Munich. As he concluded his remarks a disgruntled Czech extremist stepped forward on the pretense of shaking Mueller's hand. Before anyone could react, he fired three gunshots into Mueller's abdomen. Gravely injured, Mueller lingered on the verge of death until Gregor von Bettinger paid him a visit.

A mysterious figure, Bettinger practiced a heretical blend of Orthodox Christianity and an ancient Germanic religion that led the Orthodox prelate to defrock him. Bettinger visited Mueller in the hospital and prayed for him. Almost immediately Mueller began to improve. His rapid and full recovery was widely viewed as a miracle.

In the days that followed, Bettinger became a regular visitor at the Chancellery, where he schooled Mueller on the ancient Germanic arts. Those sessions energized Mueller's growing sense of Germanic identity and pride. During one of their sessions, Bettinger gave Mueller a small sun wheel medallion as a gift. About the size of a two-Euro coin, it had an open circle in the center with ten spokes that extended in jagged lines to an outer rim. Mueller carried the medallion in his pocket as a reminder of the destiny Bettinger assured him was his.

While he took another sip from his drink, he slid his left hand into his pants pocket and curled his fingers around the medallion. His index finger traced lightly over the spokes. Ten spokes, representing the ten nations of the European Union. He was serving a term as EU president now. Others thought it an appropriate position for such a prominent figure. Little did they know that if the words of Bettinger were true, Mueller would be their final president.

Just then the door to Mueller's study flew open and six armed security guards rushed into the room. Mueller turned toward them, his eyes wide with a look of anxious surprise. "What is the meaning of this?"

Werner Beck, the agent in charge of the detail, stepped to Mueller's desk. "Sir, we have an emergency." Security guards took up positions around the room. Werner came behind the desk and took Mueller by the arm. "You must step away from the window and come with us."

"How dare you." Mueller pulled away in protest. "What are you trying to do?"

"We must get you to the situation room."

Franz Heinrich, Mueller's special assistant, appeared at the door. "Sir, we need to get downstairs."

Born in Munich, Heinrich was Mueller's lifelong friend. They had grown up on the same street, attended the same schools, and went to university together. After graduation they began their professional careers in the same investment banking firm. When Mueller first entertained the notion of entering politics, Heinrich had been his lone supporter. Now, in office, he was Mueller's closest adviser.

"There has been another attack," Heinrich explained.

Mueller had a questioning look. "There was a second missile?" The words had special meaning for them and touched a secret about which only a privileged few were aware.

"Yes." Heinrich gestured with his hand for Mueller to hurry. "They need us in the situation room right away."

Mueller continued to talk as he started toward the door. "This one was against the Americans, too?"

"No." Heinrich shook his head as they emerged from the study. "This time it was a launch against Israel."

With Heinrich in the lead, they hurried downstairs to the basement. The situation room was located on the opposite end of the building from his residence. Security guards fanned out ahead of them, clearing the hallway. Guards opened the door as they approached.

At the far end of the room was a large projection screen. Television monitors were mounted on either side. The main screen showed a map of the world. News from Berlin, New York, and London played on the monitors.

A conference table occupied the center of the room. Around it were seated Georg Scheel, the Foreign Office minister, and representatives from the German Army, Navy, Air Force, and the Federal Police. They all came to attention as Mueller entered. He acknowledged them with a nod and pulled a chair from the end of the table. "Take a seat, please." Everyone sat. Mueller looked around at them. "I understand we have a situation."

General Erhard, commander of the German Air Force, stood. "Twenty minutes ago, our satellites detected the launch of a missile from the Egyptian desert."

"What kind of missile?"

"We are not certain, but from the telemetry we intercepted it appears to have been a nuclear missile that was armed at launch."

"What is the target?"

"Tel Aviv."

Mueller's eyes darted to Heinrich, then back to the others. "Has it struck yet?"

"No."

The large screen at the far end of the room displayed a map of the Middle East with the missile's projected trajectory outlined in blue. Its actual progress in flight traced along that same course in red. At the crest of the arc, the red line disappeared. Mueller pointed to the screen. "I see the arc of the projected trajectory, but the flight path of the missile is not moving."

"They shot it down, sir."

"We are certain?"

Georg Scheel answered. "As sure as we can be at this time."

"They have missile defense capability?" Mueller looked around the room. "We knew this?"

"It was the American system," Scheel replied. "Operated by Israeli soldiers, but provided by the Americans."

"Patriot missiles."

"Yes." Erhard picked up the conversation. "And at least two other more advanced systems."

"The Arrow?"

Erhard nodded. "And Iron Dome."

"But the Israelis operated them?"

"We are fairly certain the Americans provided active support. They have many ships and planes and satellites. None of them were affected by the recent attack."

"Yes. Well." Mueller paused a moment as he collected his thoughts. "Of course they helped them." He cleared his throat. "Has Israel responded?"

"No, sir," Scheel replied.

"Has there been any other movement in the Egyptian desert?"

"No, sir."

"And this was not an attack by the Egyptians?"

"Highly unlikely."

"We have people in Israel?"

"Yes."

"Find out what is going on and get me a report as soon as possible."

"Certainly, sir."

"Any threats to Germany?"

Hermann Schroeder, head of the Federal Police, stood. "None, sir."

"Mr. Chancellor," Scheel said, interrupting. "As current president of the EU, perhaps you should issue a statement condemning the attack."

"Perhaps." Mueller had a curt smile. "But not yet." He looked across the table at Heinrich. "Contact the EU chiefs, arrange a conference call."

Mueller pushed back from the table and stood. Those at the table stood, as well. Mueller turned toward the door. "We shall reconvene in one hour to assess the situation further." He spoke without looking back. "Alert me immediately if there are new developments." By the time the last words slipped from his lips, the door was open and he was in the hall.

10

BEIJING, CHINA

MING SHAO LAY FAST ASLEEP IN HIS BED in the Zhongnanhai compound. Located near the Forbidden City, the compound was composed of six residences arranged around a man-made lake. Most of the structures were completed before the year 1500, when the site was first constructed as an imperial garden. More recently, two modern office buildings were added when the area became the official state residence for China's most important leaders.

Since the attack on the United States, most of Ming's time and energy had been devoted to endless meetings designed to calm fears about the potential for economic collapse from the loss of trade with America. At the same time, hardliners were worried about the potential for social unrest. They were urging him to put troops on the street as a show of force, both to dispel any who might be planning to protest and as a way of showing the world that China was fully capable of defending itself. Ming had worked hard to resist them.

Ming was elected president of China five years earlier and elevated to chairman of the Communist Party a year after that. Attaining those positions required cunning, design, and intrigue. Maintaining his grip on power depended solely on ensuring China's economic prosperity. Doing that was already taking a toll on Ming's physical stamina. He had gone to bed early that evening in hopes of obtaining much-needed rest.

From somewhere in a dreamless sleep, Ming felt a hand shake his foot. He opened his eyes to see his aide, Yong Shu, standing beside the bed. "Mr. President," Yong said quietly. "They asked me to wake you."

"What is it?"

"The military council has detected a missile launch."

Ming threw back the covers and rolled to a sitting position with his legs over the edge of the bed. "Why did they do this?" he seethed through clinched teeth. "I will reduce Taiwan to a bad memory. How long until impact?"

"No, no, no," Yong said, waving his hand. "It is not an attack against us."

"What, then? Why did you wake me?" Ming looked over at Yong with a piercing glare. "Who is the attack against?"

"I do not know." Yong took a satin robe from a chair near the bed and held it open. "Come," he urged politely. "They will give you all the details."

Ming slipped on the robe and tied the sash around his waist. He hurried across the bedroom and out the door to a sitting area. Hu Chang, commander of the People's Liberation Army, was waiting there and snapped to attention. Ming acknowledged him with a quick nod. "Relax." Ming took a pair of glasses from the pocket of his robe and slipped them on. "What has happened?"

"Aerospace Command has detected the launch of a missile from a location in the Egyptian desert, near Gaza."

"What is the target?"

"Tel Aviv."

Ming had a troubled frown. "Egypt is attacking Israel?"

"It does not appear to be an attack from Egypt. We suspect this was the work of Muslim extremists."

Ming took a seat on a sofa. He gestured to a chair that sat nearby. Hu took a seat. Ming looked over at Hu. "This changes things."

"Yes," Hu nodded. "I should think so."

The door opened and Quan Ji, chief of foreign intelligence, entered the room. He bowed to Ming, then took a seat. "General Hu has told you?"

"Yes," Ming agreed. "You have new information?"

"No, sir." Quan shook his head. "But this is not good." He wagged his finger for emphasis. "It will upset the balance of the German plan."

"Yes," Ming replied. "With an attack on the U.S., even multiple attacks, their plan remained harmonious, symmetrical, balanced. But with Israel now involved, the balance and symmetry are destroyed."

"Well said," Hu nodded. "Germany cannot control Israel, and they cannot manipulate the United States into doing so, either. Not now."

Ming glanced at them both. "You two must find out what the Germans are planning."

Quan looked perplexed. "You mean the Israelis?"

"The Israelis are of no importance to us," Ming scoffed. "The Germans are the key to this situation." He had a determined look. "You have agents in Berlin who can learn of these things?"

"Yes," Quan nodded.

"Good." Ming closed his eyes and rested his head on the back of the sofa. "Find out their response. I do not trust the Germans, especially in light of this new development."

11

OFFUTT AIR FORCE BASE
OMAHA, NEBRASKA

AS THE SITUATION ROOM EMPTIED, Hoyt Moore made his way toward Hoag and Jenny. He greeted them with a smile. "Sorry to drop you into the middle of this without a chance to get settled first."

"That's quite all right." Hoag and Moore shook hands.

Moore turned to Jenny. "Miss Freed, I read your analysis on those ships. We have every available crew searching for them now."

"Good. From the conversation just now, I wasn't sure we were doing anything to locate them."

"Ahh," he said with a wave of his hand. "Being out here like this, with everybody thrown together in makeshift facilities—makes it a little crazy." He looked over at Hoag. "I call it 'empowered ignorance.'"

"Yes, sir." Hoag nodded. "And they're completely wrong about Pakistan, by the way."

"You think so?"

"Yes."

"How's my friend Winston Smith?"

"He's doing great."

"I suppose things are a little Spartan back there."

"Yes, sir. But they're starting to dig out."

"Winston is a good man. That's why I wanted him in charge."

Moore led them from the situation room and down the hall toward his office in the opposite corner of the basement. As they worked their way around filing cabinets and people, Moore looked back at Jenny. "I've circulated your report. State, DoD, NSC. I believe the president saw it, too. Everyone was impressed."

Jenny was glad for the positive response but cringed at the thought of so many people reading her work. "That would be more impressive if we actually found those other two ships."

"As I said," Moore reiterated, "we're working on it."

As they turned down the back hallway they passed an office that had boxes stacked to the ceiling, leaving just enough space in the center of the room for a worktable. On it were twelve piles of documents. Staff members were huddled around the table, sorting papers into each of the stacks. Boxes in the room bore the seal of the U.S. Treasury Department. Hoag caught Moore's eye. "I thought Treasury was in a different building."

"They are, but right now they're in a huge race against time."

"For what?"

"T-Bill auction," Moore replied.

"An auction?"

"Yeah."

"Didn't the market for T-Bills take a hit?"

"Yes," Moore nodded. "But we don't have much choice. Because short-term interest rates were so low for so long, most of our national debt was placed on a short maturity schedule. About sixty percent of it has to be refinanced every eighteen months. The eighteen-month deadline is only days away." Someone darted from the room and pushed past Hoag. Moore saw him coming and stepped aside to let him pass. "We have part of their refinance team in here so they can stay up on the latest events."

"Seems like an impossible task."

"How's that?"

"Auctioning T-Bills. I can't imagine anyone would want them."

"Get the price right, someone will want them." Moore looked grim. "There's a lot riding on it."

"We've never defaulted on our debt."

"Right. But it's bigger than that."

"Bigger?"

"We have a lot of rebuilding to do. This auction is the rest of the world's vote on whether they think we can pull it off. If they buy our bonds, we're in business. If not, we're in serious trouble."

At the end of the hall they came to Moore's office. Windowless, and much smaller than the one he had at Langley, it was nevertheless neat, orderly, and efficient. As they stepped inside, Peter Burke appeared in the hallway behind them. Tall, broad-shouldered and athletic, he was a little younger than Hoag. Moore waved him in and introduced Hoag and Jenny.

"Peter is deputy director for Middle East Analysis." Moore looked at Hoag and Jenny. "He's in charge of the team I told Winston about."

Burke was impeccably dressed in a business suit that lay smooth and flat across his shoulders. With it, he wore a custom-made cotton shirt that had been starched and pressed stiff enough to stand on its own. The collar points of the shirt lay in exactly the right spot, concealing all but a hint of the knot of his silk tie. His shoes had a bright shine and his hair was neatly trimmed. He looked to Hoag as if he'd stepped from the cover of GQ.

"Glad to have you with us," Burke said as they shook hands. "We can use the help."

"We're still getting things organized out here." Moore took a seat behind the desk. "The structure chart is a little confused. You work for me, but when you aren't doing anything else, you'll report to Peter."

"We have offices for you both in a building across the street." Burke glanced at his watch. "I need to check in on a meeting over there right now." His eyes darted to Jenny for an instant too long. Hoag cleared his throat. Burke gave him a smile. "Why don't you two join me? I'll introduce you and take you to your office." He looked back at Moore. "If that's all right with you."

"Fine with me, but wait a minute before you leave. I think Donna has something for them." Moore pressed a button on his phone.

Donna Bynum appeared at the office door. "I had all your things delivered to your apartments. You both have a one-bedroom. And you'll need these." She handed them each an ID card and base credentials. "These will get you where you need to go on the base." She looked over at Hoag. "If you need anything, give me a call."

"What about a key to the apartment?"

Donna stepped to a desk across the hall and returned with keys. "This should do it."

——— (((———

Burke led Hoag and Jenny from Moore's office. They retraced their steps down the hall and made their way to the elevator. He pressed the button and turned to Jenny. "I understand your parents live in New York."

"Yes."

"Manhattan?"

"Yes," she replied. "Midtown."

"Have you heard from them?"

"No. I tried to reach them a couple of times before we left, but all the lines were down."

The elevator door opened. Burke held it as Jenny and Hoag stepped inside. He followed them inside and pressed a button for the lobby. "Perhaps we can make a few calls."

"You can get through?" Jenny looked puzzled.

"There are a couple of lines open," he smiled. "To the police department, a few other agencies."

Hoag spoke up. "How bad is it?"

"On the East Coast?"

"Yeah."

"Not as bad as we thought, but still rough. The Northeast was hit the hardest. Most of the power grid up there will have to be rebuilt. The Southeast is without power, but most of that is because of the way the load switched when the Northeast went down. That didn't work exactly right and it pulled them off-line."

"They'll get back up?"

"Eventually. Have to bring it up one section at a time. Make sure nothing's damaged." The elevator stopped and the door opened. Burke gave Hoag a wry smile. "But what do I know? I'm just an analyst."

They walked off the elevator and followed Burke outside. He waited for them to catch up, then walked next to Jenny. Hoag trailed behind. "Everything in this part of the country is operating pretty much as normal. They've had an influx of people, but not as many refugees as they expected." He glanced back at Hoag. "At least not yet."

"The more areas they can bring online with the electrical grid, the better."

"Right." Burke turned back to Jenny. "Out there," he pointed, "life goes on as normal. Restaurants. Movies." He smiled at her. "Maybe after you're settled we could check it out."

Jenny grinned and slowed her pace to let Hoag catch up. She slipped her arm in the crook of Hoag's elbow and looked Burke in the eye. "We'd love to see it." She smiled up at Hoag. "Wouldn't we?"

"Yeah," Hoag nodded. "Sure."

Burke turned quickly away and led them on across the street to a two-story building. A sign out front identified it as the Adams Office Annex. Built of concrete blocks, it was one of the older buildings on the base. They entered through a side door and started down the hall. Burke pointed to the left. "The stairs are over here." He jerked open a heavy steel door that led into the stairway. "No elevator in this building."

As they stepped onto the second floor, they were greeted by the echo of voices from down the hall. Burke glanced over his shoulder at Hoag and Jenny. "I see they got the meeting started without us."

"That's your meeting?"

"Yours too."

"What are they discussing?"

"Options. The president wanted an analysis with options. That's what we're trying to give him."

At the far end of the hall they came to a conference room. A long table ran down the center of the room with cheap office chairs clustered around it. Folding chairs lined the walls and filled every other available space. Burke squeezed in between two chairs at the end of the table. "Okay," he called in a loud voice. "Listen up." He pointed over his shoulder. "This is Jenny Freed and David Hoag. They came out here from Langley."

Hoag glanced around the room. Several of the faces were familiar.

"They're here to help us figure this out," Burke continued. "Jenny did the analysis on the ships. I think you all saw her report." Several around the table nodded in response. Burke continued. "David Hoag was in New York when the blast took place. He and Dennis Kinlaw have been conducting research into many of the leads we've been following. He has some pretty good stuff on a group they think might have been behind the attack."

"A group that *was* behind the attack," Hoag corrected.

"Yes. Well. That remains to be seen." Burke looked around the room. "Where are we?"

Someone answered from the opposite end of the table. "We were discussing whether the missiles and ships had been arranged with the help of the Pakistani government."

A voice from the right chimed in. "The ships *were* registered in Panama."

"Almost every ship is registered in Panama."

A voice chimed in from the back of the room, "They might have been registered there, but they were owned by a Pakistani corporation with ties to Al-Qa'ida"

Someone pointed to Hoag and Jenny. "These two actually did the work."

"Then they know what I'm talking about."

"Well," Hoag began. "It is true that the ships are registered in Panama. And they are owned by a shipping company in Karachi. But that doesn't mean Pakistan had anything to do with the attack."

"Give me a break," answered a voice with a snarky tone. "NORAD and NSC have already identified the missile as a Shahab-3. This isn't that difficult. Just connect the dots."

The conversation picked up again and everyone began talking at once. Hoag held up his hand for quiet. "Wait." The conversation faded. He looked around the room. "How many of you went to law school?" Several hands went up. "And how many of you remember the phrase, '*post hoc, ergo propter hoc*'?"

A woman at the end of the table replied, "After this, therefore because of this."

"Exactly," Hoag acknowledged. "Proximity in time does not mean causation. And in this case, proximity in location doesn't mean it, either."

"Then who did it?"

"I think we have to look at who has the capability and who has the motivation."

"They all have the motivation."

"Yes," Hoag nodded. "But begin with capability."

"Pakistan."

"Okay. But who else?"

"Iran."

"Right. Anyone else?"

"Egypt."

A man seated to the left threw up his hands in frustration. "And that's exactly where the strike against Israel came from."

"Right," Hoag agreed. "So, we could apply your earlier analysis now and say this was all a plot from Egypt."

"But they have nothing to gain."

"And neither does Pakistan."

"Except that they might think they could get us out of the way."

Hoag gave them a skeptical look. "Do you really think that's what happened? They launched a nuclear attack against us, with no second-strike capability, just to get us to leave them alone?"

"What do you mean?"

"If we knew for certain that the missile strike against us was orchestrated by Pakistan, what kind of response would we give them?"

"An all-out attack on every known nuclear site in their country."

"Exactly." Hoag had a confident smile. "And I think even the Pakistanis could figure out that much."

"So what, then?"

"We haven't discussed whether these two attacks are related."

"What two attacks?"

"Israel and the one against us."

"You think they are related?"

"I think those are the dots you need to connect."

Burke caught Hoag's eye and nodded toward the door. He and Jenny followed Burke to the hallway. Hoag shook his head. "They are so far off base."

"Tell me about it."

Hoag had a pained expression. "Do they know anything about what they're doing?"

"Most of them are mid-level or below."

"Where's the team from the basement at Langley?"

"Back at Langley, working on data recovery and trying to make certain their files weren't compromised by the blast. Many of them are older, with families. Difficult to relocate them quickly." Burke pointed back at the room. "That's why the director asked Winston Smith to send the two of you out here. Your job is to make a team out of them."

Jenny was skeptical. "You want us to train them?"

"We want *you* to do that," Burke replied, pointing at her.

"This is worse than I thought."

"Right," Burke agreed. "You'll have to rebuild it from the ground up." He looked over at Hoag. "We have something else for you."

"Like what?"

"Come to my office and we'll talk about it."

12

LAS VEGAS, NEVADA

TWO LEVELS BENEATH THE PARKING LOT of a single-story building on the western edge of town, Pete Rios stood in the NEST command center. Created in 1985, NEST was an obscure Federal agency charged with the responsibility of monitoring and responding to nuclear threats against the United States. For that purpose, Rios had at his disposal a cadre of scientists and technicians from both the public and private sector. When force was needed, he could draw on any asset necessary. The command center had been operating night and day since the missile from the *Panama Clipper* struck Washington, D.C.

Unlike the situation room at the Pentagon, the NEST command center wasn't built to accommodate casual observers. This was a working room, built to allow analysts to monitor ongoing events in real time without interruption. Workstations with monitors, keyboards, and laptops filled every square inch of floor space. Large, flat screens covered the walls. In the center of the room was an operator's console that functioned as its nerve center, but those who worked there often operated in a freewheeling frenzy of activity, shouting back and forth, often handling more than one incident at a time.

A screen on the wall displayed a map of the eastern Mediterranean. Rios and others in the room watched as the track of a missile rose from the Egyptian desert, arced toward Israel, and disappeared. Rios turned away. "We have confirmation?"

"Yes, sir," the operator replied. "A Patriot missile battery took it out."

"Good," Richard Weavil chortled. "Maybe now someone in Congress will listen when we talk about a missile-defense shield."

"I doubt it," someone offered.

"I do, too," Rios agreed. "Do we have the telemetry from the missile?"

"Yes, sir," Ken Aycock spoke up.

"What was it?"

"An Iranian Shahab-3 missile armed with a nuclear warhead."

"The warhead was active?"

"From the moment it was launched."

"And the target was Tel Aviv? We know that for a fact?"

"Yes, sir," Aycock nodded. "The missile was taking its bearings from a Pakistani satellite. We have the telemetry. Tel Aviv was the target."

"Anyone listening to the Pakistanis?"

Jeff Howell was seated across the room to the right. "I don't think they knew about this."

"About the satellite? How could they not know?" Rios argued. "Whoever launched that missile had to enter the access codes into the guidance system to let it log on."

"Right. But the way they're talking about it, I don't think they knew this beforehand."

"What are you listening to?"

"Telephone and radio traffic from Inter-Services Intelligence."

"Well." Rios rubbed his chin. "Pass that off to the FBI in New Orleans. If someone hacked their system, maybe they left a trail. The Fibbies have people who can follow that."

"You want me to ask them to assist us?"

"Tell them this is a NEST priority and give them your information. We need to stay focused on our primary task, which is figuring out where the bomb that struck D.C. came from. And for that we need a radioactive signature. Anybody got any ideas on how to get enough of a fallout sample so we can run some tests?"

"It was a high-altitude detonation," Weavil answered. "We have no fallout."

"None in the immediate area," Howell suggested.

"What do you mean?"

"The explosion occurred in the upper reaches of the atmosphere," Howell explained. "But it produced fallout and that fallout will drift down to earth. It won't disappear. It'll hit the ground somewhere, eventually."

Rios was intrigued. "How eventually?"

"Depends on the weather."

Rios turned to the operator at the console in the center of the room. "What was the weather like that day?"

She typed in a command. An image appeared on the monitor at her desk. "Clear and sunny in Washington, D.C. New York was clear. There was a snowstorm moving through New England."

"Prevailing winds to the east?"

"Surface winds on and offshore along the coast. Prevailing winds to the north-northeast." She pressed a button on the console. A map of wind direction appeared on a screen to the right. She pointed in that direction. "There's a tendency for a more northerly direction."

Someone explained. "That's because heat differentials along the coast divert it in that direction."

As Rios studied the map, Randall Morris entered the room. Easily the oldest person in the Las Vegas office, Morris was NEST's deputy director in charge of daily operations and had been with the agency since the beginning. He came and stood at Rios' side. "Checking for fallout drift?"

"Thinking about it."

"Not a bad idea," Morris nodded. "There's snow on the Adirondack Mountains by now. Certainly in the high-peaks region. Mount Marcy is almost a mile high. Could have something on the southern face."

Rios stared at the screen a moment longer, then turned back to the operator. "I want a field team in upstate New York. Send them to Mount Marcy." He glanced back at Morris. "It's a long shot, but maybe we'll catch a break."

"It's been almost a week," Aycock said, making no attempt to hide his skepticism.

"The half-life isn't that short," Weavil countered. "If it hit the ground, it'll still be there."

Rios moved to the operator's console. "What about those airborne detection units?"

"Still patrolling off Long Island."

"We need them to work farther down the coast. At least as far as North Carolina."

"No wind in that direction."

"The Carolina coast is inside the blast circle," Rios explained. "Might catch some airborne particles along the coast."

"But will it be enough for analysis?"

"I don't know." Rios' voice had a hint of frustration. "I'm just reaching for anything we can find." He took a deep breath and tried to relax. "Won't take much more than a trace. If we can get a signature on the bomb's makeup, maybe we can track it back to a known reactor." He shot a glance in Morris' direction. "Maybe."

13

OFFUTT AIR FORCE BASE OMAHA, NEBRASKA

BURKE'S OFFICE WAS LOCATED on the ground floor of the building opposite the central complex. It was smaller than Moore's but equally neat and orderly. Hoag took a seat in a chair to the right of the desk. Jenny sat a few feet to his left. Burke hung his jacket on a coatrack in the corner and sat down in the chair behind his desk.

"So," Hoag began, "you said you had something for me to do."

"Yeah." Burke scooted the chair back and crossed his legs. "We're searching for the other two ships right now, but we've located the one that carried the missile and launcher. The *Panama Clipper*."

Hoag slid forward on the chair. "Where was it?"

"About twenty-five miles east of Long Island." Burke grinned. "The blast knocked out its electronics. They were dead in the water."

Hoag laughed. "Who found it?"

"Satellite locked on to it the minute they launched the missile. Took a little while for everyone to catch up. Coast Guard boarded it before you got back to Langley. It's being towed down to a facility at Kings Bay Naval Base in Georgia."

"Why Georgia?"

"Nearest base not affected by the blackout. It's just north of Jacksonville, Florida, so it's fully functional. Sophisticated communications system. The works."

"What about the crew?"

"Right now they're secured onboard the vessel." Burke gave Hoag a questioning look. "Are you interested in talking to them?"

"Yes." Hoag nodded. "Of course."

"Good. They should arrive in port sometime tonight. I want you to get down there as soon as possible and interview them. Look over the ship. See what you can find out."

"Great. When do we leave?"

Burke moved his feet forward and leaned over the desk. "Listen, I know you two enjoy working together, and you came out here together, but you'll probably not be working together right now."

Hoag felt unsettled. "I need Jenny to help me. We learned what we know about these guys by working together."

"She can help you from back here." Burke leaned away from the desk. "But right now we need her to pick up the analysis she was working on, help us locate the two remaining ships." He gave Hoag a smug look. "You know what I mean?"

"Yes." Hoag stood. "I think I do." He glanced at Jenny. "Are you okay with that?"

"I'll be fine," she smiled. "You saw the group in that room a while ago. They need some help."

"Great!" Burke exclaimed. "We'll get you started working with them right away."

14

MOSSAD OPERATIONS CENTER
ASHDOD, ISRAEL

EFRAIM HOFI TOOK A HANDKERCHIEF from his pocket and wiped his brow. "Are we certain the missile is down?" He spoke with his eyes fixed on a map that filled the screen at the end of the room.

"Yes," Levanon replied. "Our radar system has confirmed the hit. And SIGINT indicates the missile stopped transmitting telemetry."

"Did we get the trajectory data from the Americans?"

"It is downloading now."

"Have you checked our own system?"

She nodded. "The missile was launched from a site in the Egyptian desert, but our system is unable to give an exact location."

When the file finished loading, Levanon typed a command from the keyboard on her desk. A map appeared on her monitor. Moments later, a small red box appeared, superimposed over the map. Hofi leaned over her shoulder and pointed to the box. "That is the location?"

"The launch site is within that box."

"How large is the area?"

"Less than twenty meters square. The actual site is that dot in the center of the box."

"These are pinpoint coordinates?"

"The coordinates we have received from the American satellite give us the exact location of the launch."

"Put it on the screen."

The map appeared on the wall screen. Hofi pointed to it as he turned to face the others in the room. "This is the location from which the missile was launched. Is there any other movement in the area?"

Yossi Avidan, an analyst, spoke up. "None, sir."

"Have Egyptian forces gone on alert?"

"They went on alert at the same time we did."

"But not before?"

Avidan shook his head. "Nothing unusual to that point."

"And there has been no repositioning of their units?"

"Apparently they went on alert in response to the launch, just as we did."

Hofi stepped near Avidan's workstation. "You are certain of this?" Hofi's eyes bore in. "Certain enough to risk the fate of the nation on your conclusion?"

"Yes," Avidan nodded. "I know what I have seen. They are in a defensive position. Troops are in the barracks. A dozen planes are in the air, but they are confined to patrols over urban areas. The remainder of their air wing is on the tarmac. Engines cool. No activity reported."

"Good." Hofi nodded. He backed away from Avidan and turned toward the others once again. "Then we must ask ourselves, 'Who did this?' "

From across the room, Uri Einstein answered, "There is only one country in the region with this capability."

Hofi wheeled around to face him. "And who is that?"

"Iran."

"And are you certain of this?" Hofi stepped close to Uri's workstation. "Certain enough to order an attack on them? An all-out attack with our own nuclear weapons? Assuring the deaths of millions?"

"Yes," Uri nodded.

"So certain that you would unleash the Samson Option?"

"I am," Uri nodded. "I am that certain."

"Well." Hofi backed away. His shoulders sagged and he dropped his gaze to the floor. "I am not as certain as either of you." He folded his hands behind his back. "I am not certain enough about Egypt to let down our guard, and not so convinced of Iran's culpability. We must have confirmation."

"And how do you propose we get that?"

Hofi looked up at Uri and pointed toward his eyes. "With these," he smiled as he turned to face Levanon at the center console. "Send two response teams to the launch site."

Levanon hesitated. "The launch site?"

"That location," Hofi shouted, pointing to the map on the screen. With three long strides he reached the wall and jabbed the coordinate box on the map with his finger. "That location right there."

"That location is inside Egypt's borders." Levanon looked perplexed. "Should we not ask for permission?"

"Permission for what?"

"We will be sending a military unit across the border into Egyptian territory. Will they see that as an act of war?"

"We have been attacked by a missile launched from Egyptian soil." Hofi's voice was loud and abrasive. "Have they contacted us? Have they offered an explanation or assistance in determining who is behind it? The missile launch was an act of war. We are merely responding, and in the least aggressive means possible. We did not launch a counterstrike against Egypt. We are merely sending a small team to investigate the launch site. If Egypt was not involved, they have no reason to protest." Hofi paused and took a deep breath. He lowered his voice. "Time is of the essence. Our teams must reach the site before anyone has time to tamper with it. Send them at once. I will notify the prime minister. He can decide whether to tell the Egyptians what we have done."

15

BREMERHAVEN, GERMANY

MANFRED ROSLER SAT AT THE KITCHEN TABLE, sipping a cup of coffee. Crumbs were scattered here and there on the tabletop, the final traces of the evening meal. Across the room to the right, Eva, his wife, leaned over the sink, scrubbing the dishes. A small television sat at the end of the counter. Rosler took a pack of cigarettes from his shirt pocket and tapped the end against his finger. A cigarette slid from the pack.

"Not in here," Eva sighed without looking back.

"What?" Rosler gave her a perplexed frown. "You are standing with your back to me. You have no idea what I am doing."

"For almost forty years I have lived with you. I know exactly what you are doing." She came from the sink with a washcloth to wipe the table. "Every night the same thing. Dinner, news, smoke a cigarette." The cloth left a trail of moisture in front of Rosler.

"So you have lived with me all this time," he said in a flat monotone, "why are you just now telling me not to smoke in the house?"

Eva dropped the washcloth in the sink and turned to face him. "Because I no longer want to smell like smoke." She wiped her hands on a towel. "I am tired of the house smelling like smoke. And the clothes smelling like smoke. Sometimes I think the food smells like it, too."

"Sometimes I do not understand you." Rosler shook his head. "What brought this on?"

"Nothing." She poured a cup of coffee, brought it to the table, and took a seat. "Anything new about Israel?"

"Just more double-talk from the politicians. Everybody knows who did it, but no one is willing to say."

"So, who did it?"

"Same people who did it to the Americans." His voice grew louder. "It is the same thing ... the same people."

She looked over at him. "You have the night shift tonight?"

"Yes. Why?"

"You are dressed for work? I was just wondering, since you worked until this morning already."

"We need all the work I can get."

"The shift does not start for four hours. You could take a nap. I will wake you."

"I must go in early." Rosler took a sip of coffee and swallowed. "I have to meet someone."

A frown wrinkled Eva's forehead. "You have to meet someone? Since when do you go out at night to meet someone?"

"Since now."

"Who are you meeting?"

"A reporter."

"A reporter? Why? You are a dockworker. What—"

"A foreman," he said, interrupting. "I am a foreman at Europe's busiest seaport."

"You work on the docks," she countered. "Loading ships. What do you have to say that a reporter would want to hear?"

"I know lots of things."

She took a sip of coffee. "Like what?"

"I cannot tell you what I know." He arched an eyebrow and

lowered his voice. "But I know."

"You can tell a reporter, but not me." She took another sip. "You sound like a crazy man."

"I sound like a man who woke up from a deep sleep."

"What do you mean?"

"I mean the country is changing. Since they put Mueller in as chancellor, nothing has been the same."

"You are just upset because the trouble in America means fewer ships to load." She patted the back of his hand. "We will be fine. They will not cut your job. And if they do, we will find a way to make it work. We have always found a way to make things work."

"No," he snapped. "It is not about the work." He turned to face her. "I am tired, Eva ... tired of sitting here every night, watching the news, waiting for someone else to do something." He pushed his chair back from the table and stood. "Tonight, I do something myself instead."

Eva had a worried look on her face. "What are you going to do?"

"I have already done it."

"Done what?"

"I called that reporter."

She took his hand. "Tell me what you are going to tell him."

"You do not want to know."

"Manfred." She had a stricken look. "If you really know something, is it something you are not supposed to know?" She pushed back her chair and stood. Her hand touched his side. "Those who want to keep it secret will make certain it never gets told. Tell me first, then we will decide about the reporter."

He paused a moment, thinking. Then he looked her in the eye. "They knew about it. Before it happened, they knew about it."

"Knew about what?"

"The attack on America."

"What do you mean?" She gave him a skeptical look. "How do you know this? How could you know such a thing?"

"Checking the cargo."

"What does that mean—'checking the cargo'?"

"Ever since the attacks in New York. The first attack with the planes flying into the buildings. I have been checking the cargo containers."

"Checking them for what?"

"Radioactive materials."

A grin broke across her face. "What are you talking about?" She put her hand to her mouth to stifle a laugh. "You know nothing about radioactive materials."

"Before," he continued, ignoring her response, "when the police suspected the North Koreans of shipping things to Iran, they gave us a dosimeter."

"They put in a scanner. You told me. For the trucks."

"No." He shook his head. "This was before that. Three … four years ago. With the North Koreans."

"And?"

"They gave us a dosimeter. A handheld dosimeter. Not much bigger than that." He gestured with his palm to indicate the size. "I kept it in my locker all this time and every day since then, at the beginning of the shift, I walk around the stacks with it."

She wasn't laughing anymore. "They let you do that?"

"I am the foreman. Who is going to stop me?"

"Konrad knew about this?"

"Yes," he nodded. "Konrad Bohl knew all about it. That is why he is not there."

"Are you sure about this?"

"Listen to me," he said sharply. "One day, I was out with the dosimeter and it started to beep. I told Bohl about it. He made a call.

A little while later, the Federal Police arrived."

"And what did they find?"

"They opened the cargo container and found a missile inside."

Eva's mouth fell open. "What kind of missile?"

"I do not know. A big one. And two weeks later a missile hit the United States."

She leaned back against the table. "You do not know that it was the same one."

He gave her a confident nod. "The container was loaded onto the *Panama Clipper*. Bound for New York." He turned aside and took his coat from a peg by the back door. "That is what I am going to tell the reporter." He slipped on the coat and grabbed his cap.

"No, Manfred," Eva protested. She reached for him and clutched at his arm.

"I must." Rosler pushed her hand away. "I was silent before, and look what happened." They stared at each other a moment, then he leaned over and gave her a kiss. "Do not wait up for me." And with that, he opened the back door and stepped outside.

16

BERLIN, GERMANY

FRANZ HEINRICH GLANCED OUT THE WINDOW from the backseat of a black Mercedes sedan and watched as the buildings moved past, enshrouded in darkness. Just beyond the Hotel Adlon, they drove through the Brandenburg Gate and into the government compound. A few blocks farther, the car turned right and came to a stop beneath the canopy at the rear entrance to the Chancellery. The driver hopped out and opened the rear door. Heinrich stepped from the car and made his way inside the building.

A guard cleared him through the security checkpoint and he walked quickly down the hall to the elevator. Moments later, he arrived at the door to the chancellor's residence. He tapped lightly and waited. Seconds later, Mueller opened it just far enough to see out.

"This better be good." He was dressed in a silk robe tied at his waist with a sash. As his eyes met Heinrich's, a smile turned up the corners of his mouth. "It better be very good."

Through the opening past the door, Heinrich saw a young woman hurry across the room, a sheet draped around her shoulders. Heinrich glanced over at Mueller. "Helen did not return this afternoon?"

"She was delayed in Paris for an extra day."

"So I see."

"I assume you came here because you actually needed something." Behind them a door closed. At the sound of it, Mueller's shoulders sagged. "You might as well come in now." He gestured with a wave of his hand and backed away from the door. "But be quick about it."

"You said we should keep you informed." Heinrich stepped inside the bedroom as he spoke. "About the missile and the Israelis."

Mueller looked impatient. "And?"

"We were finally able to confirm that the Israelis shot it down."

"This could not have waited until morning?"

"You wanted to know when we reached a conclusion."

"Yes. I did," Mueller replied. He put his hand to his chin as if in thought. "The Americans must have helped them do it. Those Jews would have never been able to do it on their own."

"Perhaps."

"Any indication of who launched it?"

"The defense missiles?"

"No. The attack. The missile that took off from Egypt."

"Not yet," Heinrich replied, "but our analysts reviewed its electronic signature. They say it was almost certainly an Iranian Shahab-3 missile."

Mueller nodded as if he already knew. "And how did an Iranian missile arrive undetected in the Egyptian desert?"

"No one knows that yet."

"Have the Israelis responded?"

"No."

Mueller stepped to the nightstand and picked up a glass. "I want you to arrange a meeting with Kermani."

Heinrich was puzzled. "The president of Iran?"

"Yes."

"You cannot meet with him," Heinrich argued. "Not now. Not after all this."

"I am not meeting with him." Mueller pointed with a smile. "You are."

"Me?" Heinrich was taken aback.

"Yes." Mueller took another sip from the glass. "You."

"But they are almost certainly the ones behind these attacks. First on the Americans and now on Israel."

"I know." Mueller nodded. "And that is why you must meet with them." He slipped an arm across Heinrich's shoulder. "We must use these incidents to our advantage."

"What will we accomplish?"

"We will offer them our protection in exchange for their oil."

"They already sell us their oil."

"No," Mueller wagged his finger. "Not all of it. They also sell oil to China."

"We do not want them to sell oil to China?"

"No," Mueller said, shaking his head.

"Why not? I thought we had an arrangement with the Chinese."

"If Iran sells oil to China, China will have the ability to respond to incidents like the one we have seen today. They will have the ability to invade Pakistan, Afghanistan, the entire Middle East."

"If Iran does not sell to China, China will invade anyway."

"Perhaps," Mueller smiled. "But first things first."

"How will we pay for it? That is almost an incalculable amount."

"We will not actually pay for it. We will become oil marketers to the world. With Russian and Iranian supplies under our control, we will dominate the market." He glanced at Heinrich. "Control the oil and we can control the world. But first you must convince Iran we will protect them and that they are better off trusting us than the Chinese."

"How will I do that?"

"You will remind our friends in Iran that the Chinese hold a tremendous amount of U.S. debt, which has suffered a serious drop in value and will very soon be completely worthless. And after that, they will have no way to pay for the oil."

"Worthless? American debt instruments have taken a hit on the world markets, but they are not yet worthless. What are you talking about?"

"More than half of America's outstanding debt will be up for refinancing in a week. When it's offered at auction, they will not be able to find any buyers. And the Chinese economy will collapse right along with it."

"You know this for a fact?"

"That the Chinese economy will collapse? Certainly. They hold so much U.S. debt, they cannot possibly survive the economic loss."

"No. I mean, you are certain no one will participate in the U.S. debt auction?"

"Trust me."

"I do not know," Heinrich sighed. "What if the Iranians are more worried about the Israelis?"

"You must tell them their secret is safe with us. We know what they did. We saw their missile when it was in Bremerhaven."

"You want me to tell them that?"

"In so many words," Mueller shrugged.

"And if Israel attacks them, what do we do?"

"If they attack, we will crush those stupid Jews once and for all." Mueller paused to take another sip from the glass. "But they will not attack. They can only do that with American help, and the Americans will not help them now."

"America may be looking for a way to attack Iran without having to do it themselves."

"No." Mueller shook his head. "The Americans are looking elsewhere. They think the attack came from Al-Qa'ida, using Iranian missiles with warheads from Pakistan's arsenal." Mueller tipped up the glass once more and drained it dry. "Get moving. We have a small window. We must cut off the Chinese while we still have the opportunity." Mueller paused a moment, his eyes fixed on Heinrich. "Are you with me on this, Franz? If not, I need to know now."

They stared at each other for what seemed like a long time. "Yes," Heinrich said finally. His gaze fell to the floor. "I am with you."

—— (((——

A block from the Chancellery, Tang Daoming and Chen Guo sat in a van parked in an alley off a side street. The van bore the markings of the German Federal Police. From a small opening in the side of the van, they had a clear view of a window in Mueller's bedroom. Using a laser microphone they listened to the conversation between Mueller and Heinrich. Reels on a tape recorder turned slowly, capturing every word they said.

While they listened, the driver's door opened. A man dressed in a Federal Police uniform climbed in behind the steering wheel. He held a Styrofoam cup of coffee. Daoming looked up at him. "Heinrich is leaving now."

The driver glanced over his shoulder. "Do we follow him or stay here?"

"We will follow." Guo jabbed the air with his finger. "And this time, we must not lose him."

"That was not my fault."

"Just drive," Guo snarled.

"He will come out right there," the driver said, pointing. "There is only one way out of the compound."

Just then a black Mercedes sedan appeared. At the end of the street it turned left, toward the Brandenburg Gate.

"There he is," Daoming pointed excitedly. "There he is."

"Hurry," Guo added. "We are going to lose him."

"Hush." The driver put the van in gear. "I see him. I am not going to lose him." He steered the van from the alley and started up the street. At the corner, he turned left and followed at a safe distance.

17

BERLIN, GERMANY

HERMANN SCHROEDER WALKED DOWNSTAIRS to a control room in the Interior Ministry building. As he opened the door, images from a video camera appeared on a screen that hung on the wall. Schroeder stepped inside the room and eased the door closed, then moved quietly to the left and watched from the corner.

Paul Kruger, a supervisor, stood near the center of the room, arms folded across his chest. "Okay," Kruger called out. "Listen! I need you all to pay attention." A grainy image on the screen followed Manfred Rosler as he stepped from a bus in Bremerhaven. Kruger turned to an analyst seated near the screen. "Where are we getting these images?"

"A traffic camera at the corner."

"We are controlling it?"

"Yes."

On the screen, Rosler glanced to the left and right, as if checking, then started down the sidewalk. In the center of the block, he veered to the left and entered the Lichthaus Café. A camera mounted inside followed him as he crossed the room to a table in back. A man was seated there already. He looked up as Rosler approached.

Kruger snapped his fingers. "Do we have confirmation on the man at the table?"

Someone called out, "It is Martin Doring. Freelance reporter with *Der Spiegel*."

"We are certain?"

An analyst replied, "He won several awards last year. His picture is everywhere." A photo of Doring appeared in a box on the screen next to images from the café. "This is a picture of him."

"Do we have audio?"

"Coming up now."

A voice crackled from a speaker in the control room. "Mr. Rosler. I was not sure you were coming."

They shook hands. Rosler took a seat. "My wife," he smiled. "She loves to talk."

"Trouble?"

"No. Just the trouble every wife gives her husband."

A waiter appeared. Doring looked over at Rosler. "You want something?"

"A beer, perhaps."

The waiter stepped away from the table. Doring leaned forward and propped his elbows on the tabletop. "You said on the phone you had something important to talk about."

"Yes."

"What was it?"

Rosler took a deep breath. His eyes seemed to stare past Doring for a moment. Then he began. "You know about the explosion in America?"

"Of course," Doring replied. "We were all upset. The whole world is upset by it."

"They used a missile," Rosler continued.

"Yes. I understand." Doring's voice had an edge. "It is all over the news. Everyone knows this. Did you call me here to tell me that?"

"The missile came through this port." Rosler tapped the tabletop with his finger. "Right here in Bremerhaven."

The waiter returned with two steins, set them on the table, and then stepped away. When he was gone, Doring continued. This time his voice was much lower and less cynical than before. "You know this for certain?"

"Yes," Rosler's voice rumbled up from his chest. "I helped load it."

Doring leaned back from the table and reached inside his jacket for a small notebook. He took it from his pocket and laid it on the table. "What was the name of the ship?"

"The *Panama Clipper*."

Doring scribbled in the notebook as he continued. "And it was docked at Bremerhaven."

"It is a container ship. We loaded it with containers."

"Are you telling me you think one of those containers held a missile?"

"I know it did."

For the next fifteen minutes, Rosler gave Doring details about how he came to have a handheld dosimeter and how he discovered radiation leaking from the cargo container. Doring listened with his head down, his eyes focused on the notebook, scribbling notes as Rosler talked.

"And you reported the radiation levels?"

Rosler nodded. "I told my supervisor and he called the police."

"Local police?"

"I do not know if he called the Bremerhaven police," Rosler shrugged. "I did not see them out there and I am not sure they can come to the docks."

"You mean it is not their jurisdiction?"

"The port has its own police."

"Did they respond?"

"The Federal Police sent a special team. We stacked containers in front of the one I found. To block the view. And then they went inside the box."

"The Federal Police entered the cargo container you identified from the readings on the dosimeter?"

"Yes."

"And what did they find?"

Rosler took a sip of his drink and swallowed. "I did not see it. They made us move away to the other end of the dock."

A frown appeared on Doring's brow. "Then how do you know it was a missile?"

Rosler leaned over the table. "It was an oversized box," he explained. "The police were there. They went inside it, waited around awhile, and then left."

"They did not take anything with them from the cargo box?"

"No." Rosler shook his head. "As they were leaving, one of them looked at me and said, 'Good work but it is not our call.' He patted me on the shoulder and then they left."

"So. They found something. It was radioactive. They left without removing it. What makes you think there was a missile in that cargo container?"

"Radiation levels were extremely high. It was loaded onto the *Panama Clipper*. The ship departed for New York. Two weeks later, a missile was launched from it against America."

"And you are suggesting the government knew about it."

"I am telling you they knew it for a fact, and they let it go." Rosler glanced around, his eyes darting nervously from table to table. "I have already been in here too long."

"What do you mean?"

"They are watching."

Doring looked up from the table and let his eyes scan the room.

"I do not see anyone that looks like anyone."

"They are always watching. They warned me not to talk."

"Warned you?" Doring looked concerned. "Who warned you?"

"I cannot say. But they know when you talk. Konrad Bohl talked, and they got to him."

"Who is Konrad Bohl?"

"My supervisor."

"Who did he talk to?"

"His supervisor. And then he tried to go even higher. They said he had a problem with his back, but there was nothing wrong with him. He left work one day at the end of his shift, fine as you and me sitting here, and the next day he did not come back. When I asked, they said he got hurt on the job the day before, and he was at home. Next thing I knew, he was dismissed. Put on permanent disability. I knew he was not injured. I rode the bus home with him the last day he worked. He was fine." Rosler took another sip of beer and glanced around the room. "I really cannot say more than that."

"They have the manifest at the dock? The one for the *Panama Clipper*?"

Rosler nodded. "I am sure they do."

"Think you could get a copy for me?"

"Why do you need it?"

"To check what else the ship was carrying. Maybe see who was sending the cargo container."

"I will see if I can find it." Rosler glanced at his watch. "It is late. I have to go. My shift starts soon." He pushed back the chair and stood. "I will call you."

Other voices came from the speaker in the control room as operatives at the café went to work. "He is moving toward the door. Can you see him?"

On the screen, Rosler reached the front door and stepped outside.

A grainy image from the traffic camera on the street showed him as he walked up the sidewalk toward the corner. Then the image on the screen switched back to the camera inside the café. Doring was still seated at the table.

A voice came from the speaker. "This is One. I have the subject. I can see him through the glass."

Doring took another sip from his glass, then pushed back his chair and stood. He tossed some money on the table, picked up his notebook, and walked toward the kitchen door.

"Castle, this is Lombard." The voice was clear, even, and businesslike. "Subject is mobile."

The analyst at the console near the screen looked over at Kruger as he answered the operative. "Lombard, this is Castle. We see him on the screen. Stand by."

Another voice broke in. "This is Lombard Six, subject is coming out the back door. I have him in the alley. Moving toward the corner."

A live feed from a camera mounted on an operative's pistol appeared on the screen in the control room.

"Castle, this is Lombard. We need confirmation of the order."

The analyst looked up once more. Kruger nodded. The analyst pressed a button on the console. "Lombard, you have a green light."

"Affirmative. Lombard has a green light."

In the alley behind the café, two men approached Doring. They were breathing heavily as they moved quickly up the alley. Then there was the faint sound of a shot from a silenced automatic pistol. Doring's body crumpled to the ground.

On the screen, a man appeared from the left. He held an automatic pistol, which he pointed at Doring's head. He squeezed off another round. Doring's body jumped as the bullet tore through his skull. Seconds later, blood trickled from his forehead, leaving a crimson trail down the bridge of his nose.

The man with the pistol knelt at Doring's side and opened his jacket. He searched through the pockets, taking out the notebook, a cell phone, and a wallet.

Schroeder spoke up from his place in the corner of the room, "Where is Rosler?"

"He is waiting at the bus stop." Kruger turned in Schroeder's direction. "You want him, too?"

"I want this cleaned up." Schroeder started toward the door. "Call me when it is finished."

18

BREMERHAVEN, GERMANY

MIRKO KIEFER, AN AGENT WITH THE FEDERAL POLICE, stood in the shadows and watched as Manfred Rosler entered the employee locker room at the port facility. Kiefer turned his head and spoke into a microphone that was tucked beneath the collar of his shirt. "Subject is in the building." He listened for a response through a tiny bud concealed in his ear.

Joscha Lang replied, "I have him."

"You are inside?"

"Yes."

Dressed as a dockworker, Lang sat on a bench near a row of lockers and tied the laces on his work boots. A white hardhat sat beside him.

Rosler appeared at the corner. He made his way to a locker nearby and twisted the dial on the combination lock. His eyes darted in Lang's direction. "I do not remember seeing you here before."

Lang nodded. "First night." He straightened the cuff of his pants and stood.

"They are hiring now?"

"I guess," Lang shrugged. "I applied. They hired."

"I thought with all the trouble, maybe they would be cutting back."

"I think everything has worked in the opposite direction." Lang picked up his hardhat. "With all the trouble in America and now in the Middle East, Europe is the most stable continent in the world." He smiled proudly. "And Germany is the strongest of all."

"Yes," Rosler mumbled. "I guess we shall see." He took a jacket from the locker and slipped it on. Then he removed the dosimeter from a shelf and dropped it into his pocket. "Where did they assign you?"

"Wharf 31."

Rosler's eyes lit up. "That is my wharf." He nodded, pointing to others in the room. "They should all be as lucky as you, to work with me on their first night. You might actually learn a few things." He closed the locker door. "Come on. I will show you around."

Rosler made his way across the locker room to a door that led out to the wharfs. Lang followed, doing his best to sound and act like a new employee. "You like working the night shift?"

"I do not mind."

"Not too rough? I mean, living on a schedule that is different from everyone else?"

"Gets me out of the house at night and I sleep all day."

"I have not done this before."

"What? You have never worked at night?"

"Never worked at night." Lang had a nervous smile. "Never worked on a dock."

"There is nothing to it. Machines do all the work. We spend most of our time staying out of the way."

"And sleeping in the day really is no problem?"

Rosler smiled over at Lang. "With nobody home, it is quieter in the day than it is at night."

As they moved across the wharf, Lang listened through his ear bud as Kiefer talked to the crew. "Anybody got a clear view?"

Steffen Richter whispered in response, "They are about five feet away from my position."

Lang cut his eyes to the right and saw Richter sitting in the cab of a pickup truck. As they passed by, Richter turned to look in the opposite direction.

Directly in front of them, tied at the wharf, was the container ship *Rotterdam*. To the left was a row of cargo containers. Stacked three boxes high, they extended a quarter of a mile down the wharf. A smaller row stood to the right. Rosler pointed to the left. "Those boxes go on the ship."

"I thought we were unloading."

"We are." Rosler pointed to the cargo boxes on the right. "Those are the containers coming from the ship. But after we get them all off, we have to load something on it. We do not send an empty ship to sea."

Near the bow of the ship, an overhead crane lifted a cargo container from the deck. Lang stopped to watch as it dangled in the air above the wharf, then came to rest on a chassis frame. Rosler pointed in that direction. "You see that man wearing the orange hat?"

"Yes," Lang nodded. "What about him?"

"Report to him. Tell him I sent you. He will assign you to the lift. Probably have you watching from the other side."

"There is a job of 'watching'?"

"The crane takes the cargo containers from the ship and sets them on the chassis frame so the truck can pull them to the stack. The containers lock in place automatically on the chassis, but someone has to make certain everything works properly." He tapped Lang on the chest. "It is a job for a new-hire."

Lang nodded with a grin. "The guys with orange hats."

"Yes. Let me know how it goes."

Rosler turned away and started toward the row of containers to the left that were waiting to be loaded on the ship. As he came near the stack, he took the dosimeter from his pocket and checked to make certain it was working. Then, holding it out to his side, he walked slowly down the line.

While Rosler checked the row of cargo containers, Lang walked toward the overhead crane. Halfway there, a top-pick loader came by carrying a cargo container. It passed in front of Lang and continued to his right toward the stack of containers that had been taken from the ship. Lang turned in that direction and walked quickly, using the loader to shield him from view.

"He is just starting now," Lang said quietly.

"Let us know when he gets near the end."

Lang reached the first row in the stack to the right. Two odd-sized containers stood at the end. Longer than the others, they stuck out ten feet past the edge of the row. Lang ducked around the corner and hid in the space beside them.

A few minutes later, he glanced out from his hiding place to see Rosler as he arrived at the far end of the stack. Lang whispered, "He is at the end. Turning toward the water."

A moment later, Richter passed in the pickup truck. On the far side of the container rows he turned left, let the truck idle across the wharf, and brought it to a stop near the stern of the ship. He opened the driver's door and climbed from the truck, then reached behind the seat and took out a steel bar about eighteen inches in length. With the bar in hand he made his way to the edge of the wharf. When Rosler came into view at the end of the container stack, Richter waved his arms excitedly. "Come here! Come here!" he shouted.

Rosler hurried toward him. He was panting when he arrived. "What is all the trouble about?"

"There," Richter pointed toward the water.

Rosler moved around the end of the truck and came up the driver's side. With the truck shielding them from view, Richter wasted little time. He moved behind Rosler, brought the steel bar around quickly, and struck Rosler with a resounding blow to the head. Stunned by the blow, Rosler's eyes rolled back in his head and his body pitched forward. Using both hands, Richter gave him a shove toward the edge of the wharf. Seconds later, Rosler splashed into the water and floated facedown. Richter wiped the steel bar with the tail of his jacket, then tossed it into the water. He heard it splash twenty yards to the left as he climbed into the cab of the pickup.

19

BERLIN, GERMANY

HERMANN SCHROEDER LOOKED UP FROM THE REPORT in his hand and glanced at the clock on his desk. It was late, very late. He rocked his chair back and propped his feet on the desktop. He should have heard something by now. Kruger's teams in Bremerhaven should have finished the operation hours ago. "Maybe I should have given this to—"

A knock at the door interrupted him. The door opened slowly and Ernst Klaus appeared. Schroeder looked up at him. "You have some news?"

"Just now. From the control room. They told me to tell you the problem in Bremerhaven has been solved."

"Where is Kruger?"

"He will be up to see you tomorrow."

"No," Schroeder said sharply. "I want to see him now. Is he still in the building?"

"I will have security stop him and send him up."

Klaus backed away and closed the door. When he was gone, Schroeder swung his feet to the floor and stood. On the far side of the room a decanter sat on a cabinet next to a silver tray stacked with heavy crystal glasses. He made his way to it and poured himself a drink. He'd taken three sips when Kruger arrived.

Schroeder stared at him over the rim of the glass. "Have they found the reporter's body?"

"Bremerhaven police are at the scene now."

Schroeder held the glass in his hand and swirled the liquid around inside. "Anything for them to find?"

"No." Kruger shook his head. "Our men did a clean job."

"There were no witnesses?"

"None."

"You have the reporter's notes?"

"Yes."

"Bring them to me as soon as they arrive." Schroeder took another sip from his glass. "Rosler's body had better not be found!"

"His co-workers have reported him missing. They are looking for him now. I do not think they will find him. The current is very strong there."

"What do they think happened?"

"No one knows."

"Are they suspicious? Did they see anything?"

"There were no witnesses. They saw nothing. Sir, I assure you, these matters were dealt with in a most professional manner. There will be no repercussions."

Schroeder seemed unmoved by the assurances. "Rosler had a supervisor."

"Yes, Konrad Bohl."

"You have someone watching him?"

"Around the clock."

"Has anyone tried to contact him?"

"No, sir."

"Very well." Schroeder turned away. "You may go now. But bring that notebook to me as soon as it arrives."

When he was gone, Schroeder returned to his desk, picked up

the phone, and placed a call. Moments later, Mueller was on the line.

"Mr. Chancellor. I am sorry to call so late, but you wanted to know about the operations in Bremerhaven."

"You have good news to report?" In spite of the late hour, Mueller sounded wide awake.

"Yes," Schroeder replied. "It is finished."

"You are certain?"

"Yes."

"There can be no more leaks."

"I understand." The phone clicked as Mueller ended the call. Schroeder hung up the phone and reached for the decanter.

20

OFFUTT AIR FORCE BASE OMAHA, NEBRASKA

HOAG AND JENNY SAT ON THE STEPS outside the apartment building. They'd been sitting there since just before sunset, watching as the last rays of light faded from the western horizon. With the sun now gone, the night air was cool, even brisk.

Jenny leaned against Hoag's shoulder. "So how does this fit with prophecy?"

"How does what fit?"

"The attack on Tel Aviv. Is this one more step to the end?"

"These are the locusts," he replied.

"The attacks are the locusts?"

"Not the attacks, but the terrorists behind them," Hoag explained. "They are the locusts of chapter nine."

"In *Revelation*?"

"Yes."

"We're already that far?"

"At the end of chapter three, the pending judgment was executed on the churches in Turkey. That happened at the end of World War II. Chapter six, the Horsemen are identified."

"The four countries."

"Right. They are held up while Israel is established in chapter seven. Then the locusts appear in chapter nine."

"What makes you think the locusts are the terrorists?"

"In the prophecy, the locusts are desert locusts. They come from the desert and attack humans—something they aren't supposed to do. Locusts aren't carnivorous. And they have the power to sting, but cannot destroy." Hoag shrugged. "I know it's anecdotal, but I think that's what it means."

"So, they can attack, but they can't actually succeed in what they are trying to do."

"Right."

"Not sure this crowd would ever believe that."

"That's what the prophecy says, too."

Jenny looked puzzled. "What do you mean?"

"In spite of all that happens, no one will believe."

She snuggled closer and slipped her hand between his arm and side. They sat in silence a few moments, neither of them saying a word. Then finally he turned to her. "You have everything you need for now?"

"Yes." She squeezed his arm. "I don't want you to go. We just got here."

"I won't be gone long. But you're safe, and you have running water."

"Yeah."

He gestured with his thumb over his shoulder, toward the east. "A few hundred miles in that direction, people are living like they did in the 1800s."

"I hope my parents are okay."

"Did you try to reach them this afternoon?"

"I did."

"Didn't get through?"

She shook her head. "They said some calls do get through, but the capacity is very limited. And almost no one in the east has equipment that works anymore."

Hoag sighed. "I tried to reach someone, too, and was told the same thing."

"Are you sure you have to go? Can't they send someone else down there to interview the crew?"

"They could, but I don't think they would know what to ask."

"You're probably right."

He changed the subject. "Get your office set up?"

"Sort of. Not much to it—just a cubicle with a monitor and keyboard. But I started looking at photographs and reviewing security video this afternoon."

"Think you can find those other ships before they find us?"

"Finding the *Amazon Cloud* ought to be easy. It should be out there near where the *Panama Clipper* was. And if the *Clipper* was disabled, then it probably is, too. Which means it's adrift."

"What about the other one? The *Santiago*."

"So far, we don't have anything. And it could be anywhere. The Pacific Ocean covers a huge area."

"They can get you all you need?"

She nodded. "Actually, with everyone right here together, there's a lot better cooperation. Sort of a pitch-in, can-do attitude right now."

"Those analysts in that meeting today didn't seem up to the task."

"I talked to some of them later." Jenny had an accommodating tone. "They're actually better than it sounded. They were supposed to do that. That's how the meeting was arranged. Like a bigger version of you and Dennis tossing out ideas and chasing them as far as they go."

"Dennis ... we need him out here. I wonder what he's doing now."

"I don't know. I was thinking about him and Debby earlier today. Think they're okay?"

"Yeah. Why?"

"Winston seemed really protective of them."

"That's Winston."

They talked awhile longer, then the conversation lagged. Finally, Hoag turned to face her. "Look. We need to … We can't wait …"

Jenny looked worried. "What is it, David? Is something wrong?"

"No. Nothing's wrong. It's just … us."

"Us?" She looked alarmed. "What about us? David, what are you trying to say?"

"It's not like this is our first date. We've known each other a long time."

"I know."

"I mean, I want us to be together, in the future, for the future. I mean, I don't want to go into whatever's going to happen without you."

She looked away. "You have me."

"You know what I mean."

"I know," she sighed.

He took her chin in his hand and gently turned her head in his direction. "That's not exactly the reaction I was expecting."

She had a weak smile. "It's not the reaction I was expecting, either—at least not when we were in D.C."

"What's changed?"

"I don't know." She pulled her knees up and rested her chin against them. "There's just a lot of uncertainty … about our circumstances and … everything."

"I didn't know you felt that way," Hoag said dejectedly.

"I didn't, either. I'm just afraid."

"Of me?"

"That things will turn out like they did before."

"I'm not like that anymore." His tone was more argumentative than he intended.

"I know you're different, but still. I just thought we would take a little time."

"Is there someone else?"

"No." She tugged on his arm. "You know better than that."

"Will you at least pray about it?"

"Yes." She kissed him lightly on the lips. "I already am."

They sat quietly again, staring blankly at the night sky. Then Hoag stood. "Come on." He helped her to her feet. "It's getting late. We should get inside." They walked together to the top of the stairs and down to her apartment. When they reached the door, she turned to him and took a cell phone from her pocket. "You'll need this." She handed him the phone. "Your old one was fried."

"Where did you get this?" he grinned.

"I asked around. You'd be surprised what you can get with the right forms."

He held the phone in his hand and looked over at her. "Do you have one?"

She took a second phone from her other pocket. "Already programmed our numbers in both of them."

He leaned forward and kissed her. "See you when I get back," he whispered.

"I'll be waiting." She kissed him again, then stepped inside and closed the door. Hoag turned away and started up the corridor to his own apartment.

21

KINGS BAY NAVAL BASE
ST. MARYS, GEORGIA

EARLY IN THE MORNING, Hoag arrived at Kings Bay Naval Base. He was met at the plane by Paul Ellis, a Navy lieutenant from the public affairs office. "Do you want to see the ship first, or the men?"

"I suppose the ship," Hoag replied.

"Very well. Right this way." Ellis led him to an SUV parked on the tarmac. From there they drove to a facility north of the submarine berths. "When did they get here?"

"Yesterday."

"Has anyone searched the ship?"

"FBI is going over it now."

"Who's in charge of that?"

"Some guy named Mike Stewart."

Ellis turned the SUV onto a side street that led toward the docks. In the distance Hoag could see the superstructure of a ship. "Is that it?"

"Yes, sir. That's the *Panama Clipper*."

Ellis brought the SUV to a stop near the gangway. Two armed guards in U.S. Navy uniforms stood at either side. As Hoag and Ellis stepped out, they were met by a man wearing a yellow vest with "FBI" emblazoned on the front. "Mr. Ellis," the agent nodded. "I need to see some ID for your friend." He gestured toward Hoag.

Hoag took an ID card from his wallet and handed to him. The agent checked it and handed it back. "Very well." He gestured toward the gangplank. "Make sure you don't touch anything without asking first."

"Sure thing."

Ellis led Hoag up to the main deck of the ship. A missile launcher and truck sat there, surrounded by a dozen FBI agents and at least as many pieces of equipment. The launch rack was in the vertical position with one end raised high in the air. Hoag started toward it. Ellis held out his hand to stop him. Hoag glanced in his direction. "Something wrong?"

"These guys are really touchy about their crime scene."

"Isn't this ship in Navy custody?"

"Yes, well, it may be our ship," Ellis explained, "but it's their crime scene."

Hoag pushed past Ellis and continued toward the launcher. When he was a few feet away, he heard someone shout, "Hey! Stand back!" Hoag wheeled around in the direction of the voice and saw a man coming toward him. His face was red and he pumped his arms in time with his long, deliberate strides.

"This is a crime scene." He jabbed the air with his finger to emphasize each word. "It's not some tourist attraction."

"Good," Hoag smiled. "I'm glad to see you're keeping things in order."

The agent was taken aback by Hoag's response. His face softened. "Who are you?"

"David Hoag."

"Oh." A glimmer of a smile lifted one corner of the agent's mouth. "They told me you were coming." He stuck out his hand. "Lancer Smith. Atlanta field office." The two men shook hands. "Sorry for the outburst. We've had all kinds of people in and out of here today.

Most of them just wanting to gawk."

Hoag nodded toward the launcher. "What have you found so far?"

"This is a Russian-made launcher. They call it an MAZ 534." Smith led Hoag closer. "You can look, but I'd rather you didn't touch anything until we get finished."

"Sure."

Smith pointed toward the cab. "There was a laptop computer sitting on the front seat of the truck."

"Anybody examine it yet?"

"We have our people going through it now. I haven't heard from them about what they might have found."

Hoag gestured toward the trailer. "Is it sitting in the same place from where they launched?"

"Yes," Smith nodded. "Come back here and you can see." He led Hoag to the rear of the trailer and pointed to a blackened area on the ship's deck. "That's where the missile scorched the surface. We took samples of the residue. The lab will get us a breakdown on the fuel content."

"Any indication what kind of missile they launched?"

"No. Not from the evidence here. I suspect they used the laptop to program the guidance system. That should give us some clues. But NSA and NORAD already identified it as a Shahab-3 missile."

Hoag nodded thoughtfully. "And this is the kind of launcher they would use."

"Yes. Iranian government bought a number of these from the Russians for that very purpose. Bought the launchers and designed their own rocket to work with it."

"Cut down production time and allowed them to devote their resources to producing an indigenous missile system."

"Right," Smith agreed. "They could get the launchers, but a

missile is something they would have a difficult time purchasing on the world market."

"Find anything else?"

"When we searched the captain's quarters we found a book. Had a note tucked inside it. The note was written in Arabic. Not sure what it was about."

"Where is it now?"

"We sent them both to the lab."

"The letter and the book were both in Arabic?"

"Yes."

"Anything else?"

"Just the log data from the ship. Ports where it called. Freight it was hauling. That sort of thing."

"What was it hauling?"

"Mostly clothes from China and electronics from India."

"Didn't the ship sail from Bremerhaven?"

"Yes, but it had docked in other places and they usually stack these things four and five containers high on the deck. When they found this one, the deck was cleared. From what we can tell, they dropped most of the cargo that was on the deck into the ocean."

"Anything below us, in the hold?"

"It's full of cargo containers."

"Did you check them?"

"We haven't opened them. But we had some technicians go through it, checking for radiation, to make sure we're safe."

Hoag gestured toward the cab. "You took prints from the truck?"

"Lifted some fingerprints," Smith nodded. "Vacuumed the interior."

"Any results?"

"We got a match on three of the prints."

"Think I could get a report on them?"

"Sure. We set up a temporary command post down on the dock." He turned toward shore and pointed. "See that trailer down there between the warehouses?"

"Yeah."

"That's it. Man in charge down there is Boots Mallory. He can tell you what you want to know."

"Boots?"

"Real name is Richard," Smith explained.

Hoag shook Smith's hand and thanked him, then walked back across the deck toward the gangway. Ellis met him there. He leaned near Hoag and lowered his voice. "I heard him telling you about the prints."

"He said they had a hit on three."

"That's not exactly right."

"What do you mean?"

"They got hits on six. Three of them they told us about. Three of them they buried."

"How do you know that?"

"I have a friend at Quantico—in the FBI lab. He told me about it."

"Their lab is functioning?"

"Yes. New lab. Shielded electronics. State of the art. Went to backup power as soon as the grid failed. Worked flawlessly."

"So, what about the three prints they buried?"

"They were 'excluded.'"

"What does that mean?"

"FBI knows who they are, but they aren't telling." They reached the foot of the gangway and stepped onto the dock. Ellis glanced back at Hoag. "You want to see the crew?"

"Yeah. Sure." Hoag followed Ellis to the SUV. "You got those prints?"

"Which ones?"

"The ones that were excluded. Do you have a copy of them?"

"Yes. Why?"

"Give them to me. I'll get someone to check on them."

"They're in my office. I'll get them for you after we see the crew."

"If you get them for me now, I can get them started. Might have something by the time I'm finished with the crew."

"Okay, but we'll have to go back to my office for it."

"Good," Hoag nodded. "Let's take care of that and come back to see the FBI. I want to get someone working on those fingerprints."

22

EGYPTIAN DESERT
NEAR GAZA

COLONEL DEGAN STARED OUT THE WINDOW of a Blackhawk helicopter and scanned the Egyptian desert. Flying at less than a hundred fifty meters above the ground, the hot sand below whipped by in a blur, but he did his best to search for clues—a hint, a shadow—anything to tell him they might be flying into a trap. After twenty years in the Israeli Army, he had learned to be cautious and deliberate. If something or someone was waiting for them, he wanted to know about it in advance. Watching the terrain for clues had served him well in the past.

A few minutes later, the pilot spoke through Degan's headset. "Less than a kilometer to target."

"Anything suspicious?"

"No, sir."

"Swing around to the west and come in with the sun at our back."

"Yes, sir."

The helicopter banked sharply away from the target area. A few minutes later, it turned then dropped even lower. Now only twenty meters above the sand, the helicopter rose and fell with the terrain in a nauseating roller-coaster ride. Unfazed by it all, Degan turned away from the window and looked at his men.

"Check your weapons. We will arrive at the site in less than a minute."

Lior Fortis, seated along the back wall, flipped the switch on his rifle to automatic. A man sitting next to him did the same. Seconds later, the pilot spoke again. "There is the spot."

Degan turned to look out the front windshield. Ahead of them were three large tents set in a flat spot with dunes on either side. The helicopter pulled up short and hovered a hundred meters away. Everyone stared at the tent fabric, flapping in the prop wash.

To the left was the empty frame of a missile launcher. Normally hooked to a truck that pulled it, the launch trailer sat abandoned on the sand. Degan keyed the microphone on his headset. "Anything on the radar?"

"No, sir," the pilot replied.

"Put us down."

The helicopter settled onto the sand and the side doors opened. Team members jumped out. Crouching low and moving quickly, they hurried toward the first tent. With Fortis giving directions, they took up positions at either corner. Then, on Fortis' signal, they snatched back the tent fabric and rushed inside to find it empty.

Fortis looked over at two of his men. "Raz, Yossi," he whispered, "stay here and make sure no one comes up behind us. The rest of you, follow me."

While Fortis and the team checked the tents, Degan walked over to the launcher. Heinz Bernard, a radioman, went with him. He stopped and stared. "This is it?"

Degan gave him a questioning look. "Is there a problem?"

"It is a Russian launcher. Is it not, sir?"

"Yes, it is." Degan moved to the rear of the trailer and pointed to the ground. "Look at that."

Bernard came to his side and glanced down at the blackened sand. "It has been scorched by the heat."

"Touch it with your fingers."

Bernard knelt and dug his fingers into the sand. The top was hard and crusted over. "Flames from the launch must have been really hot."

"Not quite hot enough to turn it to glass, but enough to crust over the top."

"So." Bernard had a perplexed frown. "The Russians did this?"

"No. Not the Russians," Degan shook his head. "The Iranians did this."

"How do you know?"

Degan pointed to the trailer wheels. "Goldstone tires."

Bernard frowned once again. "What about them?"

"Goldstone is Iran's largest private tire manufacturer." He gestured toward the radio Bernard was carrying. "Do you have a secure uplink?"

Bernard brought the radio pouch around from his shoulder and checked the screen. "Yes."

"Then tell them what we have found."

23

EL-ARISH, EGYPT

NASSER HAMID SAT ATOP A CAMEL as it loped along at a steady pace. From high above, the afternoon sun beat down mercilessly, scorching the back of his neck. His cheeks and the backs of his hands were burned from it and his head throbbed from the glare. For two days ... or was it three ... he couldn't remember ... he'd been plodding his way from the launch sight, moving south and west, gauging his progress by the stars at night as best he could, and by the sun during the day.

Then, at last, the buildings of a city appeared on the horizon. A breeze picked up from the north and with it, a pungent aroma. Hamid drew back on the reins and brought the animal to a stop. He sniffed the air and his face wrinkled in a scowl. The smell was awful. He turned his head to one side and listened. From behind the next sand dune he heard the sound of shouts and cheers.

Hamid tapped his heels against the camel's side, forcing it to kneel. When it was resting safely on the sand, he dismounted and let go of the reins, then made his way up the dune. As he reached the crest, a paved road came into view. Cars and trucks were parked alongside it. Fifty meters away, a crowd clustered around a racecourse that had been laid out in the sand, marked by ropes strung from pole to pole. On the course, they were holding camel races. The sight of it made Hamid grin as he stood there watching.

When the race ended, he stumbled back down the dune and mounted his camel. With a jiggle of the reins, it rose from a kneeling position and started forward. Hamid guided it up the steep incline of the dune, then down the other side. He arrived at the edge of the crowd as a new race was beginning. No one paid him any attention.

Camels not in the race were tethered to a line strung from a palm tree at one end to the rear bumper of a pickup truck parked twenty meters away. Hamid dismounted his camel and tethered the reins to the line. He dusted the sand from his robe and moved toward the crowd. A few minutes later, he was standing with them as they cheered the end of the race.

When the race was over, he left the camel and caught a ride into town with newfound friends he'd met while enjoying the race. By then he was just another spectator, dusty and grimy from an after-noon at the races. They dropped him off on Ramsis Street, a few blocks from the waterfront. As the truck drove away, Hamid crossed the street to a three-story apartment building. He climbed the steps to the landing on the second floor, took a key from beneath his robe, and unlocked the door.

Inside was a one-bedroom apartment with a bathroom and kitchen in back. A sitting area overlooked the street. He peeled off the robe and dropped it on the floor. Five minutes later he was stand-ing in the shower. The warm water felt good as it splashed over his skin. He stood there and let it rejuvenate his body.

Half an hour later, showered and dressed, he came to the kitchen. He took a kettle from the stove, filled it with water, and turned on the flame. While it heated, he returned to the bedroom and took a duffel bag from beneath the bed. In it he found a cell phone and ten thousand dollars in crisp, new U.S. twenty-dollar bills. He stuffed the cell phone and a stack of twenties in his pocket, then returned the duffel bag to its place.

Just then the kettle on the stove whistled. He started for it and took the cell phone from his pocket while he walked. A turn of the switch on the stove extinguished the flame and the kettle grew quiet. He took a teapot from the kitchen shelf and spooned loose tea into it from a can by the sink. Steam rose from the spout as he filled the teapot with boiling water. While the tea steeped, he turned on the cell phone and placed a call. It was answered on the third ring.

"We need to meet," Hamid said without introduction. "Do you have it?"

"Yes."

"Good. Pick a place."

24

BEIJING, CHINA

MING SHAO SAT IN THE PRESIDENT'S BOX at Mei Lanfang Theater.
Seated to his left were his wife and daughter. In front of him were
three American businessmen. Behind him were two Chinese bank-
ers. They had been meeting all day, conducting negotiations for
construction of an aircraft manufacturing facility in Guangdong
Province. Their meetings were the culmination of a long and ardu-
ous process that had taken several years to orchestrate. World Trade
Organization approval rested on the structure of the deal and they
were very close to reaching an agreement. Ming was certain a delight-
ful evening of entertainment would induce the Americans to get past
their final hurdles.

On the stage below, the Czech National Theater Ballet performed
Sinfonietta, a ballet choreographed especially for them by Jiri Kylian,
the Czech Republic's most famous ballet dancer. Early in the first act,
Ming's aide, Yong Shu, stepped into the box and tapped Ming on the
shoulder. "Quan Ji would like a word with you."

"Now?" Ming disliked the interruption.

"Yes," Yong nodded.

"But we are in the middle of the first act," Ming whispered. "Can
it not wait?"

"He said it was important that he see you right away."

"Where is he?"

"Downstairs. In one of the rooms off the main lobby."

Reluctantly, Ming rose from his seat and stepped out to the hall-way. Two men from the security detail joined them. Together they followed Yong down a winding staircase to the first floor. The main lobby was located to the right. Yong took them down a hallway to the left. At the far side of the building they came to an unmarked door. Yong pushed it open. Ming followed him inside. Quan was already there.

Bodyguards swept past him and quickly scanned the room. Satisfied it was safe, they retreated to the hallway. When they were gone, Ming turned to Quan, "What is so urgent that you could not wait a few hours to tell me?" He had an anguished look on his face. "My guests are in the box. My absence will not go unnoticed."

"Mr. President." He bowed. "We have some news."

"But it could not wait?"

"I was certain you would want to hear it immediately."

"Very well. What have you learned?"

As briefly as he could, Quan summarized the conversation his agents had intercepted from Mueller's bedroom in Berlin. Ming shook his head in disgust as the details became clear. "They intend to double-cross us," he seethed.

"Yes, Mr. President. There can be no doubt."

The door opened and General Hu Chang, commander of the army, entered. "Mr. President." He bowed as he stepped toward them.

"General." Ming acknowledged him with nod. "You have heard this news?"

"Yes, Mr. President. I was briefed earlier. I was the one who insisted we come here now."

"Well, since you have had time to think this over," Ming gave him a curious look, "how do you think we should respond?"

"We should strike now," Hu insisted. "While we have the fuel to spare."

"Strike now?" Ming was skeptical. "Against Germany?"

"No." Hu shook his head. "Against Iran."

"I do not think we should rush," Quan suggested. "We should wait until the outcome of Franz Heinrich's trip to Tehran."

Ming turned to face him. "You do not think he will be successful?"

"I do not think Kermani will meet with him."

"Why not?"

"Kermani is president," Quan explained. "Heinrich is a president's messenger. The distinction will not be lost on Kermani. I think Heinrich will have to meet someone of his own stature. And that will delay things."

"We cannot wait," Hu argued. "We only have a short supply of oil. Iran is our largest foreign source of oil. Our economy, our lifestyle, all that the generations before us have sacrificed to attain, depends upon a steady supply of oil. Without it, we have nothing."

"I do not agree." Quan's cheeks glowed red as he stepped closer to Hu. "You are suggesting we attack without provocation?"

"They have provoked us," Hu countered.

"But to support that position we would have to disclose our agreement with Germany."

"To whom are we required to offer justification for our intentions?"

Quan refused to concede the argument. "The nations of the world will demand that we offer some reason for such a bold military operation."

"We owe them no explanation."

Quan turned to Ming. "Mr. President, such an action would be based solely on the breach of a secret agreement, the intent of which was to undermine the American economic position. If we reveal that agreement now, we will be seen as the enemy of the United States, at a time when they are poised to purchase even larger quantities from us as they rebuild their country."

Ming held up his hand in a gesture for silence. He turned away, arms folded across his chest. The fingers of his left hand stroked his chin in thought. After a moment, he turned to Hu. "How long will it take to quietly assemble the Central Military Commission?"

"They could be here tomorrow."

"Without attracting special attention?"

"Yes."

"Then do it. This meeting is of the utmost importance, but I do not want to raise alarm by suggesting it was called in haste. Tell them to come with anonymity. We must use this time judiciously."

Quan spoke up. "Mr. President, I think you should consider the—"

Ming cut him off with a wave of his hand. "The Commission will meet tomorrow. I fully expect to authorize the planning process at that time."

Quan looked perplexed. "Planning process for what?"

"For the greatest, most efficient military operation the world has ever seen." Ming brushed passed them both. "Now, I would like to get back to my guests." Yong opened the door and followed him out to the hall.

25

OFFUTT AIR FORCE BASE
OMAHA, NEBRASKA

JENNY SAT AT HER DESK and stared at the computer monitor. Once more, she moved the cursor across the screen to an icon and clicked the Send key. But as she had seen for the past half hour, nothing happened. "Why doesn't this work?" she groused.

A woman appeared at her cubicle. "Having trouble?"

"I can't get this to work."

She smiled at Jenny. "I'm Susan Todd. I work down the hall."

"I'm Jenny Freed." She gestured toward the monitor. "I can't seem to get this machine to cooperate."

Susan moved behind Jenny and leaned over her shoulder. "You're trying to send something to the FBI?"

"Yes."

"This system isn't like the one you had at Langley," Susan explained. "Theirs had a direct link to the FBI lab and it ran a program that automatically formatted the file for you. All you had to do was hit Send."

"Right."

"This one isn't like that. With this one, you have to format it first."

"How do you do that?"

"You go here." Susan moved the cursor to a different icon,

formatted the file, and returned to the first screen. "Now it's ready."

Jenny pressed the Send key. A message box appeared on the screen indicating the file had been sent. She looked up at Susan. "Thanks. I've been trying for an hour to do that."

"You came out with David Hoag?"

"Yes. You know him?"

"Vaguely," Susan replied. "We did a couple of conferences together. He worked a lot with another guy. I can't remember his name."

"Dennis Kinlaw."

"Yeah. What's Dennis doing?"

"He's back in D.C. with his wife. They may be out later."

"Good," Susan smiled. "I liked the way the two of them worked together. One's eccentricities offset the other's."

"You know them well."

"Not really. Just a couple of conferences."

Jenny pointed to the monitor. "Anything else different from the system at Langley?"

"There's more available," Susan offered. "With a password, you can get into the Department of Defense's system and then you can get to a ton of sites and databases."

"I can go right into DoD's system?"

"Yes. Do you have a password for their system?"

"No," Jenny shook her head. "How do I get that?"

"You see me for it." Susan gave Jenny a nudge. "Get up and let me sit there. I'll take care of it."

Assigning a user name and password only took a few minutes. Jenny did her best to wait patiently while Susan completed the task. She was glad for the help but anxious to get a report on the fingerprints before the end of the day.

When Susan was finished, Jenny returned to her desk and uploaded the fingerprints to the CIA system. Langley wasn't yet operational, but the agency had backup systems at alternative sites around the world. Those servers were fully functional. She requested a report on each of the prints and turned to the issue of locating the two remaining ships.

Using the Department of Defense's system, Jenny was able to log on to Defense databases that were off limits to direct access from the CIA. One of those held raw information acquired by the National Geospatial-Intelligence Agency.

An obscure agency within the Department of Defense, Geospatial-Intelligence employed a network of satellites and nontraditional sources to acquire pictures from all over the world. It used that information to create maps and generate threat assessments in support of military operations. Their system proved a treasure trove of images.

By midmorning, Jenny had compiled a video history of the *Amazon Cloud* that traced its journey from loading in Yemen to passage through the Suez Canal. Sharp, vivid images showed the faces of crew members manning the rail as the ship departed Aden. Others showed the crew from the opposite side of the ship as they passed through the Great Bitter Lake portion of the canal.

Jenny studied them closely, searching for identifiable details. "If I could get these pictures to the FBI," she said to herself, "they could process them through their face-recognition software. We might get a match on their identities." She captured three of the best images, formatted them to meet FBI requirements, and sent them to the FBI lab.

Similar images were available for the *Santiago*, showing the ship as it steamed from Guangzhou. After a brief stop in Hong Kong, surveillance aircraft operated by the U.S. Navy tracked it across the open water of the South China Sea. There, it seemed to disappear. A check of ports in Taiwan and Japan showed nothing. Then, a little before lunch, she located video from the port of Singapore showing the ship at berth there three days after it had left Guangzhou.

"This isn't right," Jenny mumbled to herself. "This ship left China bound for Los Angeles." She took a copy of the ship's manifest from a file on her desk and checked it to make certain. "It shouldn't be in Singapore. That's three days in the wrong direction."

She spent the remainder of the morning searching for additional images of the ship, but found none. Not even security footage from Singapore showing the ship as it maneuvered away from the docks. "This is not right." Jenny leaned back in her chair and closed her eyes.

If the *Santiago* carried a missile similar to the *Panama Clipper*, and it made a stop in Singapore, that missile could be anywhere. Every country in the region, from Singapore to Saudi Arabia, on both sides of the Indian Ocean and the Persian Gulf, harbored active radical Muslim sects. All of them operated with enough sophistication to easily conceal a missile on a mobile launcher.

At noon, Jenny took a break for lunch. She walked down the hall to Susan's desk, thinking they might eat together, but Susan was already gone. As Jenny stepped outside, she thought of David and their discussion the night before. Loneliness settled over her like a dark cloud. *I shouldn't have said those things. I know how I feel about him. I was just ... being stupid.* She crossed the street to the central office complex and made her way inside. A cafeteria was located on the first floor. She ate at a table of Air Force officers and listened to them complain about the civilians who crowded the base. By the time she returned to her office, she was feeling sad and dejected.

That afternoon, she continued to search for the *Santiago*, but a methodical review of the databases proved fruitless. As the afternoon grew late, she turned to random searches of commercial sites and newspaper files, using terms like *Santiago, ship, sailing,* and *security* in simple Boolean language. One of those attempts produced a Reuter's news article about Peter Burke. Curious to know how it came up, she clicked on the link and found two pictures of Burke at a meeting in Santiago, Chile. The meeting, a conference on security issues facing South American countries, took place three months earlier. One of the pictures showed Burke standing alone at the podium, addressing the audience. The other was a casual photograph of Burke standing with someone identified as Franz Heinrich. A quick review of files for that name told her Heinrich was special assistant to Josef Mueller, the German chancellor.

Jenny stared at the picture and whispered to herself, "Why was the German chancellor's special assistant at a conference on security for the South American hemisphere?"

26

KINGS BAY NAVAL BASE
ST. MARYS, GEORGIA

AFTER A BRIEF STOP AT THE FBI'S makeshift operations center, Hoag and Ellis drove across the base to interview the ship's crew. Ellis steered the SUV away from the docks toward a row of single-story buildings. "Who do you want to start with?"

"The captain, I guess." Hoag glanced down at the legal pad resting on his lap. "Hakim Murad. And then we'll talk to the three men the FBI identified from the fingerprints on the launcher."

"Ephraim Zaheden, Sajjad Hadi and Abu Hezaan."

"Yeah." Hoag glanced out the windshield. "Are they all being held together?"

"Those three and the captain are being held at the CCU."

"The what?"

"Criminal Containment Unit," Ellis explained. "The brig."

"And they're all in there together?"

"Not in the same cell but in the same facility."

"How large is it?"

"Not very. I think it has six cells."

Hoag shook his head. "That's not good."

"Why not?" Ellis had a concerned look. "What's wrong with that?"

"If it's that small, they can talk to each other, even if they're in separate cells."

"It was the best we could do," Ellis shrugged. "This is a submarine base. We don't have much trouble here. It's not built to hold an entire ship's crew. It's only there for the occasional drunk and disorderly sailor. It's empty most of the time. But it's secure."

"Where are the others?"

"In a fenced area near the motor pool."

Hoag looked at him in disbelief. "They're in a pen?"

"It's not that bad. Seabees cleaned it up and put in some tents. Guards patrol it. But since we knew Murad was the captain, and we identified the other three with the launcher, FBI didn't want to put them into the general population."

"Has anyone interviewed them?"

"Those three guys?"

"Yeah."

"The FBI talked to them."

Hoag shot Ellis a look. "When did they do that?"

"Yesterday. I don't think they got much out of them."

"They didn't mention anything about it when we were in the office just now. And they didn't give me a report on it."

Ellis arched an eyebrow. "Welcome to the federal government."

"Did they tell you what they learned?"

"They don't tell anybody anything. But I hear things sometimes. That's why I don't think they got anywhere with them. They're sending in an interrogation team. They'll be here tonight."

"Good thing I got here when I did."

Ellis brought the SUV to a stop outside a single-story building. Hoag stepped out and followed him inside. A guard cleared them through the front entrance and led them to a conference room. "You can wait in here. I'll bring the captain to you."

The room was small with just enough space for a table and four chairs. A narrow window was located on the wall and a fluorescent light hung from the ceiling.

Hoag tossed his legal pad on the table and glanced over at Ellis. "Do they speak Arabic?"

"Murad speaks English," Ellis replied. "I'm not sure about the others. Do you need a translator?"

"I'll see how it goes. If they speak Arabic, we'll be fine."

Hoag slid a chair back from the table and took a seat. In a few minutes, the door opened and the guard appeared. With him was a slender man of medium height. He had dark hair and an olive complexion. Ellis gestured with his right hand. "David Hoag, this is Hakim Murad."

Hoag stood and reached out to shake hands. He drew back when he realized Murad's wrists were cuffed. He gestured instead toward a chair at the table. "Have a seat."

Ellis caught Hoag's eye. "You want me in here, or out?"

"Let me talk to him alone, if you don't mind."

"No problem. Just bang on the door when you're ready for the next one."

Ellis and the guard stepped outside. When they were gone, Hoag looked over at Murad. "Captain, I'd like to ask you a few questions."

"How are my men?"

"They are well, I think," Hoag replied. "I inquired about them earlier. I think they're fine."

"They are being fed?"

"As far as I know," Hoag nodded.

"And treated well?"

"Yes."

"Good." Murad seemed to relax. "We hear many stories about American soldiers. Most of the stories are not good."

"This is the Navy," Hoag quipped. "And you're on American soil.

I think they'll treat you decently." He took a pen from his pocket and positioned the legal pad at a comfortable place on the table. "What can you tell me about Ephraim Zaheden, Sajjad Hadi and Abu Hezaan?"

"Who told you they were on my ship?"

"What can you tell me about them?"

"I asked the FBI how they knew, and they would not tell me, either."

"What can you tell me about them?"

"Hezaan was quiet. Did his work. Kept to himself. But Hadi," he shook his head in disgust. "I think Hadi is crazy. I did not want him on my ship and when he tried to board, I refused to take him. But Zaheden insisted. So I let him aboard. But I told Zaheden he was responsible for him."

"Why didn't you want him on the ship?"

"He was on my ship before. Not a good worker. We had many arguments."

"At what port did he board the ship?"

"Karachi, I think." Murad's eyes darted away. "I can't remember exactly. It could have been in Singapore."

They talked for half an hour, most of it about procedures on the ship, the route they took, and the weather they encountered while crossing the Atlantic. Then Hoag turned to the real point of their meeting.

"Captain Murad, your ship, the *Panama Clipper*, is tied up at the wharf not far from here."

"Yes," Murad nodded. "They brought us down here on it. Miserable trip."

"There's a mobile rocket launcher sitting on the deck." Murad was silent. Hoag continued. "Tell me how that launcher came to be sitting there."

"I do not know."

"What about the containers that were stacked on your deck? What happened to them?"

Murad shook his head. "I do not know."

"Captain." Hoag gave him a disapproving look. "You've told me many details about your trip from Bremerhaven to New York, and you don't know what happened to the cargo containers that were on your deck, or how a rocket launcher got there?"

Murad leaned forward and hunched over the table, his face just inches from Hoag's. "They will kill me," he whispered. "If I tell you what you want to know, they will kill me."

"Who will kill you?"

"Zaheden and Sajjad Hadi." Murad slid back in his chair. He nodded at Hoag and made a slicing gesture with the edge of his hand across his throat.

Hoag continued. "I know there was a missile on the launcher. And I know it was launched. We've seen where the flames from the engine scorched the deck. And we know that Zaheden, Hadi, and Hezaan were at the launcher."

"Fingerprints." Murad's eyes lit up. "That's how you know. You have their fingerprints. And that's how the FBI knew they were on my ship." He had a satisfied grin. "Took me a while, but I figured it out."

"Did you talk to the FBI about this?"

"They asked me the same things you ask me, but I tell them nothing. They know nothing of the sea, or ships, or the men who sail them." He pointed at Hoag. "But I can see in your eyes. You enjoy the water." Hoag found it impossible to suppress a smile. "See," Murad chuckled. "I was right. You are a man of the water."

Hoag grinned in response. "Tell me what you know, Captain."

"It is true what you say." Murad's voice was soft and low. "They were the ones who did it. I do not know where the containers they used came from, or when they were loaded. But they were the ones who launched the missile." He paused a moment to look Hoag in the eye. "And if you tell them I said so, they will kill me before morning."

"What happened to the containers that were stacked on the deck?"

"We threw them in the water."

"The crane operator moved them?"

"Yes."

"What is his name?"

"Hosni Nikzad."

"Where is he?"

"With the others, I suppose. He was on the ship. They took him off with everyone else."

They talked awhile longer, then Hoag asked for Sajjad Hadi. As Murad had suggested, he was a difficult case.

"You are Sajjad Hadi?"

"I am nothing to an infidel like you," Hadi replied. "You cannot possibly comprehend what I might say to you."

"You were onboard the *Panama Clipper*?"

"Yes. I was on the crew. And I demand to be treated according to the laws and treaties of the sea."

"There's a missile launcher sitting on the deck of your ship. What can you tell me about it?"

"I can tell you nothing you will understand."

Their session continued for an hour, but Hoag got little more from Hadi than he obtained in their first five minutes together. Talking to Hezaan, however, proved even more futile, as he simply sat in silence and stared straight ahead.

Finally, Hoag asked for Zaheden. Slender and wiry, he appeared confident and sure of himself. And in spite of all that had happened, he had a winsome smile. Hoag gestured toward a chair at the table. "Have a seat," Hoag said in English. When Zaheden hesitated, he repeated the sentence in Arabic.

Zaheden smiled at Hoag. "I know what you said."

Hoag raised an eyebrow. "You speak English."

"Yes."

"You were on the—"

Zaheden interrupted him. "I suppose you saw the missile launcher on the ship."

"Yes," Hoag replied. "What do you know about that?"

"It's a Russian MAZ 534."

"Used to tow and launch Iranian-made Shahab-3 missiles."

"Among others," Zaheden nodded.

"We know the missile was fired from the ship. And we know it came from that launcher. And we know—"

"You know nothing."

"I know you did it," Hoag said, pressing the point.

"You can never stop us."

"Why is that?"

"We are on a mission for God. Allah is with us." Zaheden leaned back and folded his arms confidently across his chest. "You can lock us up. You can beat us and treat us like animals, but you cannot stop us. We will keep coming and coming until all of you are dead."

27

MOSSAD OPERATIONS CENTER
ASHDOD, ISRAEL

EFRAIM HOFI SAT AT HIS DESK, reviewing satellite data for the missile launched from the Egyptian desert. A map was spread across his desk with telemetry transmissions plotted in red. Coordinating the two, he was certain the missile had exploded over an area north of Kiryat Gat. He checked the map once more. "North of Kiryat Gat, but south of Yinon." He plotted the speed against the trajectory. "Which means," he mumbled to himself, "the debris field should be west of Highway 6." He stepped back and studied the map from a distance. "That narrows it down. But it is still a large area." Just then his cell phone rang. He took it from his pocket and glanced at the screen. The call was from Eli Tishby, one of the agents coordinating the search.

"We found it!" Tishby's voice was excited. "The debris field is in Gedera."

"Gedera." Hofi located the town on the map. It was squarely within the area his calculations predicted. "And the warhead?"

"Not yet. But with the debris here, the warhead must be very close."

"Where are you in Gedera?"

"Yasmin Street."

Hofi placed his index finger on the map at Gedera and spread his fingers apart so that his little finger landed on Tel Aviv. "That was close," he sighed. "Too close to Tel Aviv."

Tishby agreed. "I think we caught it just at the top of its trajectory. The momentum scattered the pieces forward."

"Seal off the area." Hofi came from behind his desk as he continued to talk. "I am on my way."

"Seal it off? With what?"

"Whatever you can find." Hofi took his jacket from a chair by the door. "We must collect all the pieces."

"We are talking about an area covering twenty square kilometers."

Hofi stepped from his office into the hallway. "Even if it covers the entire city," he barked, "seal it off. Secure the site. We must collect as much of it as possible. The world will never believe us if we do not show them the missile."

"There must be a million fragments." Tishby's voice was tense with frustration.

"Stay there," Hofi said finally. "I am on my way." He ended the call and shoved the phone into his pocket.

Farther down the hall, Hofi was joined by security agents, who followed him outside. They climbed into a waiting SUV and raced down the drive toward the street. Traffic screeched to a halt as they turned and sped across town.

Thirty minutes later they arrived in Gedera and made their way to Yasmin Street. Hofi groaned as the neighborhood came into sight. "Just as I feared," he sighed.

The driver glanced over at him. "Is there a problem?"

"Houses." Hofi gestured out the window. "Families. With children."

Six army trucks were parked along the street. Soldiers, armed and dressed for battle, loitered on the pavement and in the yards of the surrounding homes. The SUV came to a stop behind one of the trucks. Hofi opened the passenger door and stepped out. Tishby met him on the sidewalk.

"The biggest pieces appear to be right here," Tishby pointed. "In this four-block area."

Hofi glanced around. A man and three women stood across the street. Small children were gathered at their side. At the house next door, a woman peered out from behind a curtain at the front window. *They look scared,* Hofi thought to himself. *But is it the missile, or the soldiers?*

Down the street near the corner, another man appeared on the sidewalk. He carried a large piece of twisted metal. He had a big grin on his face as he hurried toward them with short, choppy steps. A soldier walked out to intercept him, but the man ignored him and hurried toward Hofi.

"I found this on the roof of my house," he called. "There are many more where this came from." He offered it to Hofi with a triumphant smile. "I knew you would want it." One side of the piece was painted white and on it was a phrase written in Arabic. The man pointed to it. "See. Arabic writing. It says, 'Revolutionary Guard.'"

Hofi took the piece of metal from him, being careful to avoid the jagged edges. "You are a true patriot. We appreciate your cooperation."

"I am glad to be of service."

"You live around here?"

He pointed over his shoulder. "Just a few blocks."

Hofi handed the piece to Tishby, then turned back to the man and placed his arm over his shoulder. "What is the name of your street?"

"Rotem Street." He pointed to the right. "A few blocks over."

"Can you show us where?"

"Yes," the man nodded. "Come, I will take you there."

Hofi turned back to Tishby. "Have some men take one of the trucks and drive him to his home. Have them check the site and make certain it is secure."

Tishby gestured to the soldiers standing nearby. They helped the man into the truck, then climbed in after him. When they were gone, Hofi glanced over at Tishby. "Who is in charge of the soldiers?"

"Colonel Rosen."

"We need more men. And more trucks." Hofi gestured toward the surrounding houses. "We need to have trucks patrolling the neighborhood. Looking for debris. Collecting it from the civilians."

"If we involve people from the neighborhood in the search, they could get hurt."

"I think they are involved now anyway. And besides, we need their help to locate the pieces."

"What shall we do with the pieces when we find them?"

"I will locate a warehouse." Hofi turned toward the SUV. "You get busy picking up the pieces. As many as you can find." He pointed to the people standing across the street. "Get them to help you. We need everything ... no matter how small." Hofi opened the door and climbed into the SUV. As the driver turned it around in the street, Hofi leaned out the window. "Remember. Pick up every piece. No matter how small. We need all of them."

28

KINGS BAY NAVAL BASE
ST. MARYS, GEORGIA

LATE THAT AFTERNOON, Hoag received a call from Jenny. She reached him on his cell phone as he was finishing the interview with Zaheden. He stepped outside the building to take the call.

"Were you able to find anything on those prints?"

"I re-sent all three sets to the FBI lab," she explained. "I thought maybe they would respond differently if the request came from us."

"Let me guess." Hoag knew what to expect. "They came back excluded."

"Yes. They gave us the same report they gave the Navy. So I went around them."

Hoag was glad, but not surprised. "How did you do that?"

"The computers we're using have Air Force software in them. They just loaded our system on with theirs. I can access the Department of Defense network without going through Langley, or Operations, or anyone."

"That opens up a lot of possibilities. What did you find?"

"One set of prints is not in any database."

"Meaning?"

"INTERPOL doesn't have them. Defense Intelligence Agency doesn't have them. And neither do the British or the French. Not even NATO has a file on them."

"That's interesting," Hoag smiled. "You really can do a lot from there. What did you find on the other two prints?"

"INTERPOL says they are agents from the German Federal Police."

"What are their names?"

"Dieter Eppler and Rolf Kaiser."

"Where are they located?"

"Bremerhaven."

The news caught Hoag off guard and he fell silent.

"David?" Jenny's voice sounded worried. "Are you still there?"

"Yeah," he replied finally. "I'm here."

"The agents are from Bremerhaven. That's the last port the ship called on before sailing to New York."

"They were in the box," he said quietly.

"What are you talking about?"

"The agents. Those prints came from the missile launcher. If their prints were on the launcher, that means they touched it. And that means they were in the cargo container while it was on the dock at Bremerhaven. Before it was loaded on the ship."

Jenny's voice took a serious tone. "They knew about the missile."

"And they let it go."

"But that makes no sense. Why would they do that?"

"I don't know. But I'll need a flight to Bremerhaven to find out. Can you get me one?"

"That might be a problem."

"What do you mean?"

"I mean, Peter Burke will have to approve the flight and I don't think he'll do it."

"Work around him."

"It will take some time to figure out how to do that from here. We aren't at Langley and there's still not much flying yet, especially

134

from the East Coast."

"Ask Winston," Hoag suggested. "Maybe he can help."

"Okay, I'll do my best."

Ellis was waiting by the SUV when Hoag finished the call. "Everything okay?"

"Yeah, I think so."

"Did you want to talk to anyone else now?"

"No," Hoag shook his head. "Not now." He glanced up at the sky. "It's getting late."

"Yeah. Come on. I'll take you to your quarters."

They drove across the base to a facility reserved for visiting officers. Hoag took a few minutes to settle in the room, then left for dinner at the base mess hall. On the way back to the room, his cell phone rang. Caller ID indicated Jenny was on the line.

Hoag answered on the second ring. "You're working late."

"You'll have a Gulfstream waiting on the runway in the morning."

"Great. How'd you do that?"

Jenny chuckled. "A few phone calls and a little stretching of the truth."

"What truth did you stretch?"

"The part about this being an agency priority."

"Does anyone at the agency even know what I'm doing?"

"No."

"Good. The fewer the better."

The tone of Jenny's voice changed. "I'm a little worried about this trip."

"About getting the jet?"

"No. I don't care about that. I'm just not sure what you're going to find over there. But you'll be careful?"

"I'll do my best."

29

ADIRONDACK LODGE
LAKE PLACID, NEW YORK

IT WAS LATE WHEN JIM OWENS turned the van from the road into the parking lot at the Adirondack Lodge. An old traditional hotel, it sat high in the Adirondack Mountains of upstate New York, not far from the Canadian border. Owens, a physics professor at MIT, had been summoned by Pete Rios to assemble a team to climb Mount Marcy in search of radioactive fallout from the missile explosion. With him were two of the best nuclear physicists in the country—Tim Rehner, from Stanford, and Larry Davis, on loan from the Savannah River nuclear facility.

Owens brought the van to a stop in a parking space near the front entrance and glanced back at the others. Rehner was sound asleep, his head propped against the door. Davis was drowsy but awake.

"Okay, guys. We're here."

Davis slid open the van door. Cold air rushed inside. Rehner's eyes popped open. "What are you doing?"

"This isn't California," Davis smirked. "Get your gear and come on." He grabbed two bags and a case from the back and started for the hotel entrance. Owens did the same and followed close behind.

The front door was locked and the building was dark, but through a window Owens could see the glow of a fire in a fireplace.

He pressed his face against the glass for a better look. "It looks like a lobby. I think I see someone sleeping on that sofa."

Davis moved next to him. "Where?"

Owens pointed. "In front of the fireplace." He tapped on the window, but no one responded. Davis stepped to the front door and tugged on the handle. To his surprise, the door opened.

Rehner gave Owens a playful nudge. "Why didn't you try the door?"

"I did, but it didn't open." He and Rehner followed Davis inside.

Made of logs and rough pine timber, the lobby had a rustic appearance that had been aged to a rich luster by years of use. To the left was a huge stone fireplace with a wide hearth. Overstuffed chairs and a sofa were arranged in front of it. On the opposite side of the lobby was an oak bar with several stools. Bottles of liquor lined the wall behind it, reflecting flames from the fireplace. It all looked friendly and inviting, but other than the three of them, the hotel appeared to be empty.

"Hello," Owens called out. "Anybody here?"

A head popped over the back of the sofa. "Who are you?" There was the sound of a pistol cocking. "Speak up or I'll shoot."

"We're from the Nuclear Emergency Response Team," Owens explained. "Someone was supposed to contact you about our arrival."

"Nobody has any way to contact me about anything. Phones are down. No electricity. What do you want?"

"A place to spend the night."

There was a rustling sound, and then a man appeared from the left. "We aren't really open," he growled. As he came near, Owens could see he was short and thin with gray hair and hollow cheeks.

"Nothing's really open," Davis offered. "Which means everything is sort of open."

"Yes," the man sighed.

Owens shook his hand. "It's just the three of us. Do you have three rooms?"

"I have a hundred rooms. But no electricity. And no phones."

"That's okay," Owens chuckled. "We don't want to call anyone. We just want a place to sleep."

"Well, then take your pick." The man gestured toward the hallway. "We can write it up in the morning if you like." He paused and let his eyes focus on Owens with a questioning look. "Is the power out everywhere?"

"Yes," Owens nodded. "It is for most of the East Coast. South of Atlanta the power is coming back. But almost everyone east of the Mississippi River is in the dark tonight."

"Everyplace?"

"Everywhere. Chicago, Memphis, Atlanta, Pittsburgh, New York City. No one in any of those places has electricity."

"My, my, my." He shook his head. "I didn't know it was that bad." He bowed his head a moment, then turned away. "Take your pick of the rooms. If it gets too cold, you can sleep out here by the fireplace."

"Do we need a key?"

"The doors don't have that kind of lock," he called. "Got a bolt inside for privacy. But we've never had locks."

Owens turned to the others. "Come on," he chuckled. "Let's find our rooms."

"I need a bed," Rehner sighed.

"You slept all the way up here."

"I can't see."

Davis reached into one of the bags and took out a flashlight. The beam from it sliced through the darkness. "I thought of this at the last minute."

They gathered up their bags and started across the lobby. As they trudged toward the hallway, Owens spoke up. "We need to take a look at the maps and figure out what we're going to do tomorrow."

"You mean today," Rehner groused.

"Yeah." Owens glanced at his wrist and pressed a button on his watch to illuminate the face. "It's really late, so let's not waste any time. Just come on to my room and we'll take a look at it right now. Then we can get to sleep."

Down the hall from the lobby they found three rooms on the front side of the building. Owens claimed the first one, and the others followed him inside. Rehner collapsed in a chair near the window while Owens and Davis spread a map across the bed and propped the flashlight so they could see.

"This is the high-peaks region." Owens pointed to a spot on the map. "This is the hotel where we are right now."

Davis pointed. "And that's Mount Marcy. About seven miles southeast of us."

Rehner leaned forward to look at the map. "Those are some really drastic elevation lines on that map. We're gonna lug all our gear up there?"

"No way to avoid it."

Rehner ran his finger across the map, tracking the path to the summit. "That mountain is fifty-three hundred feet high."

"The tallest in New York State," Davis added.

"And one of the tallest on the eastern half of the continent," Owens nodded. "That's why we're here."

Rehner looked up at them. "At that height, the top will be above the tree line."

"And covered with snow," Davis grimaced.

"Which makes it ideal for what we need," Owens continued.

"We should try the southern face first." Rehner leaned back in the chair and closed his eyes. "That's the way the storms would have moved—from south to north. If there's any fallout trapped up there, it'll be on the south side."

"Okay," Owens continued. "There are two ways to the top from here. Take the trail from the parking lot out front and go up to the ridge—it's a little steep but it's quicker. Or, drive around to Keene Valley and come in from the north. It's longer but the slope is more gradual."

"I like the gradual slope," Rehner offered.

"If we do that," Davis explained, "we'll have to spend the night up there. I don't think we can get up there on that route, take the samples, and get back in a day. That's an eighteen-mile round trip, in the snow and ice."

Owens looked over at Rehner. "He's right. We can't do it in a day by taking the easier trail."

"Then leave from here," Rehner sighed. "I don't care."

"Good," Davis agreed. "No point in adding an extra day to the trip. We can start from the trailhead down here and be at the top before noon." He traced a line on the map with his finger. "It's not the easiest route, but it's the shortest. Won't take that long."

"Sounds like a plan." Rehner stood. "I'm going to bed, if I can find one."

"Make sure you check the gear," Owens cautioned. "We'll start at seven in the morning."

"It's already three."

"Okay," Owens chuckled. "Make it seven-thirty. We can sleep in." He pushed the door closed and felt his way across the room to the bed.

30

OFFUTT AIR FORCE BASE
OMAHA, NEBRASKA

THE SUN HAD JUST BEGUN to rise above the Nebraska horizon when Peter Burke steered the black SUV off the highway and turned toward the base. He was cleared through the main gate and drove around to a parking lot behind the Adams Office Annex building. As he climbed from the driver's seat, he picked up a cup of coffee that sat on the center console. Holding it with one hand, he grabbed a copy of the morning *Omaha World-Herald* from the passenger seat with the other. He read the headlines from the paper between sips as he walked toward the building.

When he reached the office, he set the cup and newspaper on his desk and hung his jacket on a coatrack near the door. With the jacket neatly in place, he returned to the desk and took a seat in front of the computer monitor. He tapped a key on the keyboard, and the computer came to life. While it loaded the operating system, he unfolded the newspaper and continued scanning through the articles.

A few minutes later, the computer was ready. He set the paper aside, moved the cursor to an icon on the screen, and clicked it to open a log showing the overnight activity of the agency's Middle East Analysis Group. He scrolled quickly down the screen. Satisfied that nothing there warranted his attention, he moved on to another menu and scrolled through the individual user logs for the group's

GAMECHANGER: THE SAMSON OPTION

members. An entry in the log for Jenny's account noted that she had been added as a user on the DoD system. He was curious to see what she had done with her day.

With a click of his mouse, he opened an extension of her log file that revealed the content of all her online activity. That she had spent most of the day in both the CIA and Defense networks bothered him not at all. But a third of the way down the page he came to an entry that indicated she'd contacted someone in the Support Division.

"Why did she do that?" Burke whispered to himself. "All contact with Support is supposed to come through me."

By clicking on the file name, he followed the trail and came to an email arranging a flight for Hoag. The flight would take him from Kings Bay Naval Base to Bremerhaven, Germany. Burke scrolled farther down the page and found another email chain that ran to a message she sent to Winston Smith asking for help in getting a flight for Hoag. Burke's eyes grew wide when he read the reason for the trip. "To follow up on leads involving agents with the GFP who may have known about the missile before it was loaded onto the ship."

"GFP," he mumbled. "German Federal Police."

Burke closed the file, opened a secure email browser, and typed a message. "Hoag will arrive in Bremerhaven today to interview your men. Make certain they do us no harm." When he'd finished typing it, he pressed a button to send the message, then leaned back in his chair and took a sip of coffee. *The Germans can deal with Hoag. But perhaps I can find a way to handle Jenny.*

31

ALEXANDRIA, EGYPT

ILAN GOODMAN SAT ON A BENCH across the street from the Kushari Bondo, a crowded café in the Smouha section of Alexandria. Located near the Mediterranean shore, the café was popular with tourists and locals alike. From his place on the bench, Goodman had a clear view of the street from the corner on the left all the way to the one on the right.

He'd been sitting there for an hour when a slender man appeared on the sidewalk, working his way through the crowd. Dressed in cotton twill pants and a loose-fitting white cotton shirt, he made his way up the sidewalk to the café door. He hesitated there and glanced through the large plate glass window. After a quick check, he went inside.

Goodman took a cell phone from his pocket and placed a call. Chaim Sharett answered.

"He is here," Dayan said quietly.

"Good. I was wondering when he would arrive."

Sharett stood in the kitchen over a boiling pot of couscous. He propped the phone between his head and shoulder, then used both hands to set the pot off the burner. With it out of the way, he wiped his hands on his apron and glanced over his shoulder. Through a window in the kitchen door he saw Hamid sitting at a table near the back of the café.

Goodman continued. "Can you—"

Sharett interrupted. "I see him."

"You are certain?"

"Yes."

Sharett reached up and moved the phone from his shoulder. He ended the call, shoved the phone into his pocket, and stepped to the end of the workspace. From there he had an unobstructed view of the dining room.

Seated across from Hamid was an older man, with graying hair and wrinkles that creased his face near the corners of his mouth. A plate sat in front of him with a half-eaten piece of pita bread and a dollop of hummus. He took a sip from a cup and smiled.

Hamid said something to him. They talked briefly. The older man nodded. Hamid said something else and smiled. Then he reached inside his jacket and took out a plain brown envelope. He laid it on the table and slid it across. The older man picked it up and peeled back the flap. Even from a distance Sharett could see it was filled with cash.

They talked a little more, then the older man tucked the envelope in his inside jacket pocket. He took another sip from the cup and leaned over to one side of his chair. For the first time, Sharett noticed a leather satchel resting at his feet. The older man reached inside, took out an envelope, and handed it across the table. Hamid glanced at it and smiled. Without saying more, the older man rose from his seat, picked up the leather satchel, and started toward the door.

When he was gone, Hamid opened the envelope. He stared inside a moment, then slipped out a small blue booklet not much larger than his hand. Just then a waiter appeared at the table. Hamid said something to him. The waiter smiled and nodded, then turned toward the order window at the kitchen.

As the waiter placed a ticket on the ledge, he whispered quietly to Sharett. "A U.S. passport."

"Ahh," Sharett smiled. "Just as we thought." He reached beneath his apron and took out the cell phone and placed a call. Goodman answered immediately.

"He has it." Without waiting for a reply, Sharett closed the phone and returned it to his pocket.

32

UPSTATE NEW YORK

BY MIDMORNING, JIM OWENS and the NEST team had made the climb up from the lodge to the ridge that led to the summit at Mount Marcy. Already above the tree line, the trail followed the crest in a southward direction as it rose steadily to the top. To the east was Ausable Lake and beyond that was Indian Mountain and Blake Peak. Table Top Mountain stood to the west, and beyond it was Heart Lake.

"This isn't so bad," Owens huffed as he plodded up the trail. "Snow's not too deep. Not any ice beneath it. At least, none we've found."

Davis, a step or two behind, adjusted his sunglasses and glanced up ahead. "I still think we should have packed the snowshoes." He pointed. "Looks like a bad section up there."

Owens looked up to see a section of pristine snow lying white and brilliant in the morning sun. "I think we'll be all right on the climb up. We'll have to get back down before it freezes over. Would be fun to slide back down on the return, though."

"Snowboarders do it all the time."

A few steps farther, Owens paused and turned toward them. "How you doing, Tim?"

Rehner was twenty yards behind. "I'll make it." Owens and Davis waited for him to catch up. "I was just thinking," Rehner said as he came to a stop alongside them, "this is probably a lot like what the first hikers saw."

Owens had a puzzled look. "What do you mean?"

Rehner pointed up the slope. "Not a footprint ahead of us."

They all turned to see the trail ahead. "I never noticed," Owens chuckled. "No one's been up here since the snow fell."

"Since the missile exploded," Davis corrected.

"Yeah."

"Too busy staying warm," Rehner laughed.

"Come to think of it," Davis mused, "we didn't meet a single car on the road up last night."

"Nobody has gas," Owens explained.

"And nobody has a car that will work," Rehner added.

"Which brings up an interesting question." Davis turned to Owens with a quizzical look. "Where'd you get the van?"

"It was parked in the lot at school," Owens shrugged. "I went in the office and found the key. No one was there so I left them a note and went out to see if it would start."

"And it cranked?"

"On the first try."

"And you just drove away."

"I'll straighten it out when I get back."

"Same old Jim," Rehner laughed. "You haven't changed a bit."

They continued up the slope and reached the top several hours later. Rehner slipped the backpack from his shoulders and let it slide to the ground. He propped it against a rock and took out a Sarlyn XR5 dosimeter. Slightly larger than the typical handheld device, it had a long cable attached to a probe at the end. The face of the device included an analog meter with a needle that gave readings on a scale. Above it was a digital display that provided readout levels detected by the machine's sensors. A port on the side allowed it to be connected to a computer.

Rehner flipped a switch on the side and changed the setting to detect alpha and beta particles. It beeped when the settings were complete.

Davis glanced in his direction. "You checking for particles or rays?"

"Particles. Gamma ray readings might be thrown off by the temperature. If we don't get a hit this way, we can always check for rays later."

A gust of wind blew across the mountain, kicking up snow as it swept over them. "It's cold," Davis shivered. He zipped up his jacket all the way to his chin. "Let's get to work so we can get out of here."

Rehner slipped the glove off his right hand. "I've been colder." He turned the dosimeter over and glanced at a chart printed on the back, then entered a series of numbers into the operating program to adjust for background radiation. "Owens and I were up here for the Olympics in 1980. My feet got so cold I couldn't feel 'em." The machine beeped again. "Okay," Rehner announced. "We're good to go." He slipped the glove back on his hand and moved around to the south face of the peak. Working methodically, he pushed the probe into the ice and snow as he moved back and forth near the top.

When half an hour had passed, Owens called over to him, "Getting anything?"

"Not yet."

Rehner finished the most promising sites on the southern face and moved around to the east. When he slid the probe into a clump of snow behind a rocky outcropping, the dosimeter beeped. "Got a little here." The others hurried to his side and leaned over his shoulder.

Owens raised his hand to shield the meter from the sunlight. "That's only slightly higher than background readings."

Rehner moved beyond the outcropping to a drift accumulated on the backside of a large rock. Before the probe touched the snow, the dosimeter squealed. "That's what we want," Rehner called.

Owens leaned over his shoulder once more. The needle on the meter was all the way to the right. He pointed to the digital readout at the top of the machine. "Nothing but nines on the screen."

"We've pegged the limits of the program." Rehner looked over at Owens. "Think we should be worried about exposure?"

"Take some more readings. We'll get a sample."

Davis took a sampling tool from his backpack and pressed it into the snow. Owens dropped his backpack and took out a cryogenic canister. Davis filled it with snow and closed the cap. "That enough?"

Owens nodded. "Enough to test."

As they placed the canister in Owens' backpack, Rehner returned with the dosimeter. "It's really hot right here in this corner. Found a little more on the eastern slope, but that's about it." He looked around, scanning the mountain peak. "Whoever thought of coming up here had a pretty good idea. I just hope that sample came from the missile."

"What do you mean?"

"We know it's radioactive. We don't know where it came from."

"That's for someone else to decide. Think we should get another sample?"

"I don't think we'll get any higher reading than what we already have."

"Good," Davis nodded. "Let's head for home."

Rehner moved to the ledge farther down the east side, where he'd left his backpack earlier. Instead of picking it up, he took a seat. Owens looked over at him. "Something wrong?"

"No." Rehner shook his head. "But don't you want to enjoy the view?" He pointed to the valley below. "We hiked all the way up here. Might as well sit for a minute and relax."

"I thought you were worried about exposure."

"Not here. I checked this spot already. Nothing but normal radiation here."

"I'd rather hit the trail. Sooner we leave, sooner we get home."

"To your big screen TV?"

"Furman is playing—" Davis stopped in midsentence. "I guess Furman isn't playing anyone today."

"And even if they are, you can't see it because the television doesn't work."

"You have a point."

Davis took a seat beside Rehner. Owens sat to the right. The three of them stared out at the valley and the mountains behind. After a few minutes, Owens gave Rehner a nudge. "Break out that coffee."

"What coffee?"

"I saw you fixing it before we left. Break it out."

Rehner opened his backpack and took out a thermos. "You guys owe me," he grinned.

"How are we going to drink it?" Davis scowled. "Share a common cup?"

Rehner reached inside the backpack and took out three cups. "Like I said," he smiled, "you guys owe me."

33

BREMERHAVEN, GERMANY

HOAG ARRIVED AT BREMERHAVEN and took a taxi to the Hotel Haverkamp. He checked in, walked to his room, and found a phone number for the German Federal Police office. After several futile attempts, he finally succeeded in reaching the voice mail account for Rolf Kaiser. "I'm looking for information about a cargo container. I believe you know something about it. Loaded aboard the *Panama Clipper*. Bound for New York City. You inspected the cargo before it was loaded at Bremerhaven. We should talk. I'll be in the lobby of the Hotel Haverkamp in one hour."

An hour later, Hoag rode the elevator to the lobby. He took a seat in an armchair opposite the clerk's desk and waited. In a few minutes, the front door opened and a man entered. About six feet tall, he had broad shoulders and a thick neck. Even with a jacket, Hoag could see he had an athletic build. The man surveyed the room, then his gaze fell on Hoag.

"Did you call me?"

"Perhaps," Hoag replied. "I was looking for information about a cargo container."

"And what makes you think I would know anything about that?"

Hoag gestured to a chair nearby. "Have a seat, Mr. Kaiser. Let's talk."

Reluctantly, Kaiser dropped onto the chair beside Hoag. He unbuttoned his jacket and crossed his legs. The grip of an automatic pistol protruded from a holster at his side. "Now, tell me, what is so interesting about a cargo container?"

Hoag rested his elbow on the armrest and leaned to one side. "A missile, with a warhead, loaded on a missile launcher. A few weeks ago, a cargo container reached the port here in Bremerhaven. You and at least one other agent from the Federal Police went inside the box."

Kaiser's eyes were wide. "What are you talking about?" He moved forward in the chair, as if to leave. "This conversation is over."

Hoag spoke up. "We have your prints."

Kaiser stood. "You have nothing."

"Then I suppose I'll have to talk to Dieter Eppler."

Kaiser took a seat. "Who are you?"

"David Hoag."

"And who do you work for?"

"An American agency with enough contacts to identify your prints, even though the FBI refused to give them to us."

"Look, I do not know what you plan to do with this, but whatever we did—if we did anything about any cargo container—whatever we did was authorized."

"By whom?"

"By whomever was supposed to authorize it."

"Who decided to send you into the container?"

"I cannot say."

"Was it a local idea or one that came from somewhere else?"

"We routinely inspect suspicious shipments on our own authority."

"Who reported it to you?"

"I cannot tell you."

"Who told you to let it go?"

"We do not decide whether a shipment leaves or stays. We do as we are instructed."

"You weren't just a little bit concerned when you saw the launcher and the truck?"

Kaiser's eyes darted around the room. "Are you out of your mind? Anyone can hear you."

"Were you out of your mind when you let them put that container on the ship?"

"Come with me." Kaiser rose from the chair and started toward the door. Hoag followed him outside. When they were on the street, Kaiser turned to him. "I will tell you this only once, as a professional courtesy. Forget about this and go home."

"I can't forget about it."

"Forget about it," Kaiser shouted. "And go home now. You have no idea what you are getting into." He turned and walked up the sidewalk.

34

BEIJING, CHINA

AS PLANNED, MING SHAO convened the Central Military Commission to consider a response to Germany's overtures to Iran. The Commission gathered in a conference room adjoining Ming's private residence. In order to avoid being noticed, members entered the building through an underground transportation corridor. They gathered around an ornate conference table made of teak and mahogany, a gift from peasant farmers to Dong Zhuo, third emperor of the Han Dynasty.

Comprised of key military officials, the eleven-member panel held power over the entire Chinese military apparatus and comprised the single most powerful entity in the Chinese government. In the modern era few men had risen to political prominence in China without serving a leadership role on the Commission.

When everyone was in place, Ming pushed back his chair from the table and stood. "I have called you here today to consider a most grave situation. As you are aware, the United States was hit by a high-altitude nuclear detonation that wreaked havoc on its eastern coast. Then, just days ago, Israel was the subject of an attack by a missile launched from the Egyptian desert. Each of you has been briefed on that situation. There is little doubt the attack was the work of the Iranians, using a Shahab-3 missile carrying a nuclear warhead."

Li Chengfei, commander of the Second Artillery, China's strategic missile arsenal, raised his hand. "Have the Americans acknowledged assisting Israel in destroying the missile that was launched against Tel Aviv?"

"The Americans have remained unusually silent on the matter."

Down the table, Quan Ji, chief of foreign intelligence, laughed out loud. "I'm sure they have other things to occupy their attention."

"Let me continue," Ming interjected. "Iran is our largest source of foreign oil. If that supply is interrupted, we face severe economic consequences."

"Do you think the Israelis will retaliate?"

"I am certain they will, if we do not move first."

"Then we should—"

"Please," Ming interrupted. "Let me get through this presentation and we will have plenty of time for discussion." He paused for a deep breath, then continued. "Our sources in Berlin have uncovered a plot by the Germans to convince Iran to divert all of its oil production from us to the European Union."

"All of their production?"

"Let them have it," another sneered. "Once Israel attacks, their oil fields will be worthless."

"Israel has not yet moved. There is still time for us to signal our intentions."

"Intentions for what?"

"That is the reason for this meeting." Ming pointed to Chengfei. "You have a plan to propose?"

"Yes, Mr. President." Chengfei stood. "Our Second Artillery Group was asked to assess a precisely targeted response to this new threat." He stepped to an easel and flipped back the cover, revealing a map of Europe and Asia. "If called upon to respond, we would propose striking strategic locations inside Germany and Israel, eliminating both the threat of a strike by Israel and the economic power of the Germans. As you can see, we could easily strike targets in Berlin and Frankfurt that would severely cripple their economy and eliminate their financial ability to disrupt the oil market. And we could hit locations in and around Beersheba, which is the site of Israel's own nuclear missiles, preventing them from destroying Iran's production capabilities."

"And millions would die," someone groaned.

"The world would hate us."

"The world would love us," Chengfei argued. "They hate the Jews and they despise the Germans, but they love oil and the power it brings."

"It matters not what the world thinks," Quan replied. "If we must do this to preserve our way of life, then that is what we must do."

Ming caught Chengfei's eye. "What about the American reaction?"

"They still have their navy, which is entirely intact and fully functional. As far as we can determine, none of their satellite capability was affected by the blast. Half their country is living in the dark and the other half is reeling from the psychological effects, but they would be fully capable of responding, at least strategically."

"With missiles."

"Yes, Mr. President," Chengfei nodded. "With missiles."

"They know that attacking us would invite a full-scale retaliation. Los Angeles would disappear in an instant."

"And we would deploy—"

Ming tapped the tabletop with his index finger. "Before we fully investigate that option, let us hear from Xian Linyao."

Admiral Linyao, commander of the navy, rose from his seat at the opposite end of the table. "A second option would be to simply impose a naval blockade of Iran. We could coordinate that with special operations units destroying the oil pipelines that transport Iran's oil overland into Europe and Russia. This would be an indirect way of forcing Iran to sell to us and no one else. It is the least-risky military operation."

"Do you think Iran will launch a nuclear missile at us, or attack our ships at sea?"

Chengfei rested his elbows on the table and laced his fingers together. "I think they know the kind of response they would receive to a missile attack against us."

"We have assessed the threat to our ships," Linyao continued. "I am confident we have the ability to defend our fleet. Iran has very limited naval capabilities."

As discussion of that plan faded, General Hu stood. "There is a third option. It is larger, more grandiose, but, as compared to the first two options, it has the real possibility of solving several problems at once and dramatically altering the balance of power in the region." Hu moved from his place at the table to the easel and pointed to the map Chengfei had used. "Our plan would involve a massive two-pronged invasion of Iran, using ground troops that would deploy through Pakistan and Afghanistan. One prong would take a southern route through Pakistan and seize the Iranian ports." He traced the path with his finger across the map. "A second prong would come by a more northerly route through Afghanistan, capturing Iran's oil fields intact." He smiled at them confidently. "That is the intended objective of any response we may choose."

"But how many troops would this require?"

"At least half a million initially, more to follow after that."

"How many more?"

"We cannot project a precise number until we get into the actual operation."

"What casualty rate will we encounter?"

"We expect a high depletion rate in the initial days of engagement with Iranian troops. Perhaps as many as one hundred thousand. But that will drop as the operation moves forward."

"And what of Pakistan? Will they allow us to cross their territory?"

"I do not think that will be a problem," Ming offered. "They are our longstanding ally. I believe they would be glad to have us in their country, as a deterrent to any opportunistic move by India."

"The Americans have one hundred thousand men in Afghanistan."

"Yes," Hu nodded, "and that is one reason why we would want to begin with the largest force possible—to let them know they are overwhelmed and that they should avoid any attempt to stop us."

"Slaughtering helpless Americans would make us appear barbaric. Invading to assure a supply of oil is something many would understand. Useless slaughter they would not."

"Confronting the Americans would mean an unnecessary delay," Hu continued. "We would attempt to simply ignore them. Hopefully, diplomatic contacts could convey our intentions in a way that would convince them to step aside."

Jin Ping, the minister of national defense, leaned forward and looked down the table at Hu. "How much time would you require to initiate this plan?"

"We can begin assembling our forces immediately and have five hundred thousand men crossing the Iranian border in one month, two at the most."

Jin continued. "What is our reserve strength?"

"We could easily place one million men on the Iranian plain without impeding our ability to maintain internal control. We have no external threats from our neighbors."

Jin pressed the point. "Our reserves, General."

"Our total ready reserve stands at three million."

"But many of them are poorly trained and ill-equipped. It will take time to bring all of them up to sufficient levels of readiness."

Hu bristled at the comment. "They will fight."

The discussion moved on to the advantages of each option. Finally, after an hour of discussion, Ming rose from his chair. "Gentlemen, I think we have reached a consensus." He looked down the table at General Hu. "Prepare timetables for a two-pronged attack. I shall need to see schedules for moving the troops and the proposed domestic measures you will need to insure tranquility during the buildup."

"Yes, general."

35

TEHRAN, IRAN

ADNAN KARROUBI WALKED ALONG the reflecting pool outside Golestan Palace. Hands behind his back, fingers laced together, he was lost in thought. As a powerful member of the Assembly of Experts, he had much about which to be concerned. Nasser Hamid had been his chosen operative, handpicked to lead the coordinated attack against America and Israel. His failure to succeed had placed Karroubi in great danger both from his fellow Assembly members and from the Ayatollah. For the first time in his long career, Karroubi feared for his life.

News that the *Panama Clipper* had been seized by the Americans had come as a shock. Nasser Hamid had assured them this would never happen. Then the *Amazon Cloud* went silent. Physicists at Tehran University told him the ship was probably adrift, its electrical system a victim of the electromagnetic pulse of the first detonation. Nabhi Osmani, who supplied the ships, had been instructed to make certain they could withstand the effects of the blast. Now he was missing. Rumors suggested he'd been taken into custody by the Pakistanis to prevent the FBI from arresting him. Yet even in light of these problems, and contrary to specific instructions, Hamid had launched the missile against Tel Aviv, handing the Israelis the victory of shooting it down.

Karroubi's pace slowed as he thought of everything that could have gone right, and all that went wrong. Now it was up to him to limit the repercussions and distance the government from its failures. Otherwise, fire would rain down on their heads. *And if the fire does not come, they will put a knife to my throat while I sleep.*

The sound of footsteps interrupted his thoughts. He looked behind him to see Hasan Dirbaz coming toward him. "They found him," Dirbaz said as he came alongside Karroubi. There was a big smile on his face. "They have located Nasser Hamid."

Karroubi's eyes opened wide in a look of surprise. "Where?"

"Alexandria."

"They are certain it is him?"

"Majid identified him. Goudarzi confirmed it from DNA left on a drinking glass."

"What was he doing there?"

"He acquired a passport."

"This is predictable," Karroubi nodded. "We had discussed this once before. In case something went wrong."

"It is an American passport."

Karroubi's eyes flashed. "American?"

"Yes."

"We had not discussed this. What would he do with a U.S. passport?"

"He would go anywhere he wants. Right now he has an airline reservation for Montenegro."

"Montenegro? Why?"

"My guess is they have no extradition agreement with the United States."

"My guess," Karroubi said, gesturing with his index finger, "is that he has a bank account there."

"I thought we were dealing with Switzerland for payment."

"We were. But once the money is deposited in the account, he could move it anywhere. Have we made the final payment?"

"Yes."

"Then I am sure his Swiss account is empty by now." Karroubi shook his head. "Any success in locating Osmani?"

"No."

"Are the rumors true?"

"We have been unable to confirm any news of him." Dirbaz glanced away. "What would you like our people to do with Hamid? We can stop him before he boards the plane."

"No," Karroubi said, shaking his head. "Tell them to follow him. See if they can locate the bank he is using." Dirbaz turned to leave. Karroubi called after him, "And tell them to be on alert. If we located him, I am sure the Americans and the Jews will find him, too."

36

GEDERA, ISRAEL

AFTER A QUICK SEARCH of the neighborhood, Efraim Hofi located a warehouse near the community center not far from the street where the missile debris had been found. Technicians were flown in by helicopter from Ashdod. Equipment stands and jacks came by truck from Jerusalem. With help from Colonel Rosen's unit, pieces of the missile began arriving in a steady stream. Technicians worked to reassemble them.

Hofi walked among them and watched as first the engine cone, then the main body, took shape. With each piece they added, he felt the anger growing inside. Iran, he was certain, had orchestrated the attack against Tel Aviv—as they had done against America—in a carefully calculated, intricately coordinated attempt to wipe Israel from the face of the earth.

While Hofi studied the addition of the latest pieces to the growing missile, his cell phone rang. He took it from his pocket and checked the screen. The call was from Tishby.

"We have located the warhead."

Hofi felt his pulse quicken. "Where?"

"Rotem Street. Just a few blocks from where we met before."

Hofi ended the call and rushed from the building toward an SUV parked nearby. The driver saw him coming and climbed in behind the steering wheel. They arrived at the Rotem Street address in a matter of minutes. Tishby was waiting for them.

"It is in the backyard." He gestured over his shoulder to a house that faced the street. "We moved the family and some of the neighbors to avoid radiation exposure. I was waiting for you before we evacuated the town."

"No," Hofi shook his head. "We dare not evacuate the town."

"Why not?"

"It will take too long. Panic will spread." Hofi placed his hands on his hips. "And the media will know. Others will find out. It will send the wrong strategic signal." He shook his head again. "We have to get the prime minister and diplomatic corps involved before anyone finds out we have it."

"It is a nuclear warhead," Tishby argued. "We cannot just leave it in the backyard."

"I know." Hofi ran his fingers through his hair as he gathered his thoughts. "Get the technicians in here and have them secure it. Is it leaking?"

"Yes. But not at critical levels."

"Make certain you monitor exposure levels. Where is Colonel Rosen?"

"Behind the house with his men."

"You have a plan?"

"Yes. Once the technicians are certain the warhead is stable enough to move, we will get a crane in to load it on a truck."

"Do we have a containment canister large enough for it?"

"Not as it sits."

"It would have to be taken apart?"

"Some of it. It is inside the rocket cone."

"The cone is intact?"

"Yes. To use a containment vessel, we would have to remove it from the cone."

Once more Hofi shook his head. "We cannot risk that here."

"No," Tishby agreed.

"Where will you take it?"

"To the base in Beersheba."

"Good. How long before you can confirm where it came from?"

"There is an Iranian flag on the cone."

"Show me."

Tishby led Hofi across the front yard and down the side of the house. They stood at the corner and stared across the backyard at it. "The flag is right there on the—"

"I see it," Hofi interrupted. The cone was partially buried from impact. Three technicians in hazmat suits huddled over it. Six or seven soldiers stood nearby. Hofi pointed to the soldiers. "Do you need them back here?"

"They were keeping the neighbors away."

"Move them back to the next house. They can secure the scene from there. And issue everyone a dosimeter badge. We want them to know how much exposure they have received. Maybe we should rotate the soldiers in and out."

"Badges are on the way."

Hofi stepped away from the house and started back toward the street. "We need to confirm the origin of the material inside the warhead."

Tishby had a skeptical look. "That may take a while. A day or two at least."

"We do not have a day or two. I need an answer in twelve hours."

"I will do my best."

37

OFFUTT AIR FORCE BASE OMAHA, NEBRASKA

LATE IN THE AFTERNOON, Peter Burke appeared at the doorway to Jenny's cubicle. "How's it going?" His voice surprised her. She jerked her head around to see.

"Sorry," he smiled. "Didn't mean to startle you."

"That's okay." Her shoulders relaxed as she leaned back from her desk. "I can use the break."

"Are you finding what you need?"

"Yes," she nodded. "I think so."

"We have access to systems here that you wouldn't have at Langley. So, take advantage of them."

"I will."

He folded his arms across his chest. "Weren't you looking for your parents earlier?"

"Yes."

"Any success in locating them?"

"No. Not yet. I'm sure they're all right. I'd just like to know."

"Of course," he nodded. "I understand your concern. I would want to know, too. Where do they live?"

"Manhattan."

"Right," he nodded again. "You told me that."

Jenny pushed her chair back from the desk and turned to face him. "What about your parents? Were they affected by the blast?"

"They're both deceased." Burke checked his watch. "Listen, I know this is rather abrupt, but would you like to have dinner with me tonight?"

"I don't know," she hesitated.

"I assure you," he gestured with both hands, "it's just dinner. You're new out here and David's off in Georgia. I know it's no fun eating by yourself."

"You don't have family out here?"

"No," he smiled. "Just me." He leaned against the doorway. "So, what do you say? It's been a stressful week for you. Might do you good to get away from things for a few minutes. See the town."

Jenny's face brightened. "The town?"

"Omaha."

"Wow." Her eyes were wider. "I forgot there could actually be a normal town out here."

"I don't know how normal it is," he chuckled. "But the restaurants are open and the steaks are on the grill."

"They have restaurants?"

"Of course they have restaurants." A frown creased his forehead. "What are you talking about?"

"I mean restaurants that are actually open."

"Yes." He looked amused.

She paused a moment to think, then smiled up at him. "Okay. That would be great."

"Good. We can go after work. I have a meeting that will take about an hour. I'll pick you up out front after that."

Burke turned away and walked up the hall. When he was gone, Susan Todd appeared at Jenny's cubicle. "Be careful," she warned.

"About what?"

"Peter Burke."

"Oh?" Jenny felt suddenly unsure about her decision. "You've had some experience with him?"

"No. But he gives me the creeps."

"Yeah." Jenny had a coy smile. "In a handsome sort of way."

"Nobody's hair is that perfect," Susan scowled.

38

BREMERHAVEN, GERMANY

THAT EVENING, HOAG WALKED from the hotel to the docks. He hid in the shadows near the gate and watched as trucks passed by on their way to and from the wharf. With each pass, he noted the procedure at the checkpoint. Trucks traveling in either direction stopped at the security stand and swiped a card through an electronic reader. A picture of the driver flashed on a screen outside by the reader, and on a monitor inside the guard shack. Hoag watched through a window as the guard inside checked the screen, then glanced up to confirm that the driver behind the steering wheel was the same as the person in the picture. Rarely did the guard seem to notice anything else. Cameras mounted above the gate provided a view of the truck on a separate monitor, but the guard gave that screen only cursory attention. After a few minutes, Hoag was confident he could beat the system and get inside.

A truck turned from the street and started toward the gate. As it moved past Hoag's position, it blocked the guard from his sight. Moving quickly, Hoag crossed the road and slipped into the shadows near the fence. When the truck stopped at the checkpoint, he slipped along the far side and stepped quickly past the gate, making certain to stay close enough to the fence to be out of the camera angle. Once past the gate, he tucked his hands in his pockets and acted as if he knew where he was going.

On the wharf, cargo containers were stacked to the left and right. A hundred yards farther, a ship was tied at the dock. An overhead crane positioned above it moved back and forth, lifting cargo containers from the ship's deck and setting them onto waiting trailer chassis. Most of the men working the ship wore blue hardhats. Only one wore a hat that was orange. He made his way in that direction. *Must be a supervisor.*

The man saw him coming and turned toward him. "Where is your hardhat?"

"Sorry." Hoag feigned a sheepish grin. "I don't have one."

The man glared at him. "You are not allowed out here without it."

"I was looking for the supervisor."

"I am the supervisor. Who are you?"

"I work for a freight forwarding company in New York." Hoag did his best to sound convincing. "They sent me over here to check on a missing container."

The supervisor looked perplexed. "They did what?"

"I know it sounds crazy," Hoag shrugged, "but I guess there was something important in that cargo box."

"How did you get in here?"

"Walked through the gate."

"If you work in the freight business, you know that is not allowed."

"I know. But I ..." Hoag forced an embarrassed smile. He leaned closer and lowered his voice. "I met someone earlier today. I'm supposed to see her again tomorrow. I was trying to take care of this quickly so I could have the day free tomorrow." He smiled plaintively. "With her, you know."

The supervisor had a sardonic smile. "What cargo container are you looking for?"

"It was supposed to be on a ship called the *Panama Clipper*. Left here a couple of weeks ago, bound for New York. The container never made it to the yard."

"You do not work for any freight forwarding company." The supervisor's face went cold. "And I know of no such ship."

"Look," Hoag argued, "we both know what's going on here. Now, I can go through the usual channels, get the embassy involved, and make a big deal about it. But I think it would be a lot simpler for both of us if we handled this between us." Hoag looked him in the eye. "I need the name of the supervisor on the shift that loaded the *Panama Clipper*. Think you could check that for me?"

"I told you–"

Hoag held up his hand to stop him. "Listen, I'm telling you—this will go much easier for both of us if you just check your records and tell me the name of the supervisor in charge of loading that ship. No one except you knows I'm here. There's no record of the visit. No video of me coming on the wharf. No paperwork or signatures." He paused for effect. "Just you and me."

"They will kill us both."

"Not if we keep our mouths shut."

The supervisor took a deep breath. His eyes darted away for a moment, then back to Hoag. "Come with me." Hoag followed him as they made their way to a building near the gate.

Inside, the supervisor tossed his hardhat on a table near the door and stepped across the room to a computer. "I am not supposed to do this."

"Somebody else put us in this position."

"Is that not always the case?" The supervisor pressed a key on the keyboard. A moment later, a screen appeared with a list of the cargo. He scrolled down to a line at the bottom. "Konrad Bohl," he said flatly. "Konrad Bohl was the supervisor on duty when that ship was loaded." He pressed a key and the screen went blank. "If you want any more than that, come back tomorrow and follow the rules." The supervisor moved toward the door and picked up his hardhat.

"Will Konrad Bohl be on duty tomorrow?"

"No," the supervisor replied. "He no longer works here."

"What happened to him?"

"He was sent home on disability."

"He was injured?"

The supervisor gave him a knowing look. "He was sent home on disability. I hope I fare as well if anyone finds out we talked."

"Do you have an address for him?"

"No. And if I did, I would not give it to you. I have told you all I can." Hoag gave him a wry smile. The supervisor put on his hardhat. "Bohl lives in Schiffdorf." He jerked open the door and gestured with an index finger. "Out."

Hoag stepped outside. "Where is Schiffdorf?"

"On the east side of town." The supervisor slammed the door closed and turned toward the wharf. Hoag made his way to the gate, waited for an approaching truck, and again slipped past the guard.

39

BERLIN, GERMANY

HERMANN SCHROEDER WAS SEATED at his office desk long after everyone else had gone home. As he flipped through a file, his telephone
rang. The call was from Rolf Kaiser.

"He is here."

"You met with him?"

"Yes. Earlier today."

"What did he want?"

"He was asking about a cargo container."

"How did he know to ask for you?"

"Fingerprints."

That news caught Schroeder by surprise. Their black-ops teams
were specially trained for these kinds of missions. Fingerprints in
a detectable location meant someone was careless. He resisted the
urge to pursue the issue and turned the conversation in a different
direction. "They have the container?"

"I think they have the truck."

"And the crew?"

"We did not discuss it."

"Where is Hoag now?"

"He is staying at the Hotel Haverkamp."

"Have someone follow him. I want to know where he goes, who

he sees, everyone he talks to." Schroeder ended the call and reached across the desk for a cell phone. Very quickly he typed in a text message. "A full report. David Hoag. American in country." He read it once to check for errors, then sent it.

When the phone indicated the transmission had been successful, he typed in a second text. "Place the Bremerhaven team on standby." He scrolled down the contacts list for Kaiser's number and pressed the button to send the message. Seconds later, the phone rang again. Schroeder laid the phone on the desk and leaned back in his chair.

He had been ready for Hoag's arrival, thanks to the email from Burke, but the presence of fingerprints was far more serious. Either Kaiser and Eppler were careless, or someone planted the prints to disclose their presence. Regardless, the incident had to be contained, and for that he needed approval. He leaned forward in his chair and picked up the phone.

40

BERLIN, GERMANY

FRANZ HEINRICH ENTERED THE DEN and took a seat in a chair near the window. His wife, Nadja, glanced up from the book she was reading. "You look tired."

"Long day," he sighed. A book rested on a small table that sat between them. He picked up the book and opened it to a page marked with a scrap of paper.

"You are ready for your trip?"

"Yes," he nodded, his eyes focused on the page.

She reached over and rested her hand on his. "Are you sure you are all right?"

"Yes." He gave a thin smile.

Two pages later, the telephone in the upstairs study rang. He glanced at his wife. "I should let it ring."

"You should answer it." She closed the book she was reading and set it on the table. "It might be important." She stood. "I will turn on the kettle for some tea. It will be ready when you come down."

Heinrich laid aside the book and rose from the chair. He lumbered across the room to the hallway and around to the stairs. The study was located at the end of the second-floor hall. The phone continued to ring as he hurried inside and moved behind the desk. He took an electronic smart card from his pocket and inserted it in a slot at the base of the telephone. A tiny red light near the slot flickered, then turned green. Heinrich lifted the handset. The call was from Schroeder.

"We need to meet."

"I am on my way out in the morning. Early."

"Someone has been asking about the cargo container."

"When?"

"Tonight. Just now."

"Where?"

"Bremerhaven."

"Who is it?"

"Not sure."

Heinrich was certain Schroeder knew full well the extent of the inquirer's identity. He was simply unwilling to share that information without first gauging Heinrich's reaction to the issue. Heinrich would have done the same. Every aspect of the government was divided into cliques and factions, each with their own agenda. One could not be too careful. "We need to find out who he is before we act."

"We need to stop him," Schroeder countered, "before he gets too far."

"No. Find out who he is, gather all the details. We will meet when I return."

"That may be too late."

"This is too important to make a hasty decision."

"I can end it right now."

"And we will have no way of knowing who sent him or who is behind his inquiries. Wait until I return." Heinrich hung up the phone, removed the smart card from the slot, and placed it in his pocket. He waited a moment while the light on the base changed from green to red, then walked out to the hall and closed the door. He arrived downstairs to find Nadja still in her chair, sipping from a cup of hot tea. A second cup sat on the table.

"Is everything all right?"

"Yes. Everything is fine."

She gestured to his chair. "Come, sit with me." She pointed to the table. "I made you a cup of tea." Heinrich took a seat beside her and lifted the cup to his lips. "There," she murmured, "is that not better?" She smiled at him. "You always get so worked up when that phone rings." He smiled back at her and took another sip.

41

OMAHA, NEBRASKA

AS PLANNED, LATE THAT AFTERNOON Peter Burke picked up Jenny outside the Adams Office Annex building. She got in on the passenger side and closed the door. Burke put the SUV in gear and started forward.

"Any more progress in locating those ships?"

"Not yet. I did find something interesting about the *Santiago*."

"That's the one that departed from China?"

"Yes. We have images of it crossing the South China Sea and arriving in Singapore."

Burke frowned. "Singapore?"

"Yes," Jenny nodded.

"I thought it was supposed to be headed for Los Angeles."

"That's what the manifest said."

They reached the main gate. Burke lifted his foot from the accelerator and slowed the SUV, anticipating a stop. A guard came from the building and waved them through. Burke pressed the pedal and the SUV picked up speed. He looked over at Jenny. "What happened to the ship after Singapore?"

"No one seems to know," she shrugged. "It just disappeared after that."

"Did you ask Singapore?"

"I sent them a request. They haven't replied."

"If you don't hear from them tomorrow, let me know. I'll get involved. We need to find that ship before it finds us."

In Omaha, Burke turned the SUV onto F Street and came to a stop outside Anthony's Steakhouse. He stepped out and tossed the keys to a parking valet. Jenny climbed out and waited for him. Together, they walked toward the entrance. An attendant opened the door and welcomed them inside.

An Omaha tradition for almost half a century, Anthony's was a throwback to an era when times were simpler and dining out was an occasion when old friends met to discuss the business of the day. Its brick and wood interior reminded Jenny of pictures she had seen of Toots Schor's, a restaurant in Manhattan where her parents celebrated special occasions. Toots Schor, the owner, always stopped by their table for a laugh with her dad. A wave of sadness swept over her and she wondered if she'd ever see her parents again.

A hostess took them to a table in back. When they were seated, a waiter appeared. Burke ordered for them both. "I hope you don't mind. They have the best filet in the world."

As they continued to talk, he asked about her apartment. She asked about the nature of their operations on the base. He wanted to know about her family. She wondered how long they might be at the base before they could return to Washington. In what seemed like a short time, the waiter returned with their steaks. Dinner was better than she imagined.

The room was crowded but Jenny had no trouble hearing Burke as they talked. She glanced around. "This isn't at all like what I expected."

"What did you expect?"

"Something a little more resembling the fact that we are fighting a war."

"You mean, you thought people would act like we're under siege?"

"Yes," she nodded. "A siege."

"Back east, they are under siege. I saw a report from Akron, Ohio, today that said—"

"You mean a television report?"

"Yeah. I'm not sure how they were able to do it, but the reporter was standing near the river. He said that Akron residents would be out of water in two days if electrical power is not restored to the pump and treatment facilities."

"I never thought about the treatment plants. They can't treat the waste."

"I don't think anyone is worrying about the waste water right now. It's the drinking part that has them concerned."

"I have been so into my work lately, I haven't even thought about how bad it is for everyone else." Jenny glanced around the room. "I wonder if this was what it was like during World War II."

"I don't know. With most of the government moving out here, Omaha has become a boomtown."

"I expected panic."

"Not here. Not even in the East. A few people are moving west but most are staying right where they've always been, making the best of it. Figuring out how to survive. It's really better for them that way. There's not any radioactive fallout to contend with. At least none we can find." Burke checked his watch. "You about finished?"

"Yes." She took a drink. "Are we in a hurry?"

"I need to stop by the office for a minute." Burke paid for their meal and ushered Jenny out to the sidewalk. The parking valet brought the SUV and they drove from the restaurant back to the base. Burke parked at the curb outside the building and led her down the hall to his office. Jenny felt uneasy, being there alone with him, but she didn't want to be rude.

In the office, Burke moved behind the desk and reached across to the phone. Without sitting, he lifted the receiver and glanced over at her. "Just this one call I have to take."

"I can wait outside." She gestured over her shoulder. "If you need the privacy."

"No. No," he wagged a finger insistently. "Stand right there. It's okay." He pressed a button and turned his attention to the phone. "Are you ready with that call?" He paused a moment, then handed her the phone. "I think this is for you."

"For me?" She was perplexed. "What is this about?" She took the phone and raised it to her ear. "Hello?"

"Jenny?" The sound of her father's voice brought tears to her eyes. "Jenny, is that you?"

"Hello, Dad." She wiped her cheeks with the palm of her hand. "Are you okay?"

"We're fine. Had a little trouble at first finding water, but we're all right now."

Burke stepped from the room as they continued to talk. After ten minutes, an operator came on the line to end the call. Jenny said good-bye and hung up. When she turned to leave, Burke was standing at the door.

"Everything okay?"

"Yes," she beamed. "Everything is fine." She slipped her arm around his waist and gave him a quick hug. "That is the nicest thing anyone has ever done for me. Thank you."

"No problem." He reached past the doorway and turned off the office light. "Come on." He offered her his arm. "I'll drive you home."

42

SCHIFFDORF, GERMANY

HOAG MADE HIS WAY FROM THE DOCKS back to the center of town and took a taxi to Schiffdorf. The driver let him out in front of Café Planet, an Internet sports bar. Hoag obtained a prepaid access card from the bartender and logged on to the Internet. With a simple Google search, he located an address for Konrad Bohl. A second taxi took him to the house. He walked to the front door and knocked. A woman answered the door.

"May I help you?"

"I'm looking for Konrad Bohl."

"And who are you?"

"David Hoag. I work for a shipping company. In America. I wanted to ask Mr. Bohl about a shipment."

"He no longer works on the docks."

"This is about a previous shipment."

A man appeared behind her. "I am Konrad Bohl." The woman walked away.

"I wanted to ask about a shipment," Hoag repeated.

"I heard." Bohl looked past Hoag, as if searching for something or someone. "As she told you, I no longer work on the docks."

"This was a cargo container. It was loaded on the *Panama Clipper*."

Bohl looked stricken. "You should not be here."

"We need to talk."

Bohl motioned for him to enter and Hoag stepped inside. Bohl closed the door and moved to the window. He pushed the curtain to one side and looked out. "Did anyone follow you?"

"I don't know," Hoag shrugged. "I don't think so. Why would anyone follow me?"

"I am being watched."

"Who?"

Bohl stepped away from the window. "The police."

"Why? What do they want with you?"

"I cannot say."

"What happened the day you found the cargo in that container?"

"I was not the one who found it."

"Who did?"

Bohl stared at Hoag. "Manfred Rosler, the man who found that cargo container, is now dead."

"What happened to him?"

"They found him down by the docks, floating in the water." Bohl led the way through the house to the kitchen. "Just after he got moved to the night shift." He took a coffeepot from the stove and filled a cup. "Would you care for coffee?"

"Sure."

Bohl took a cup from the cabinet and filled it. He slid it across the counter in Hoag's direction. "Rosler never liked the night shift. Hated sleeping during the day."

Hoag took a sip of coffee. The bitter taste stung his tongue but he swallowed anyway. "So, Rosler found the container and the Federal Police came to inspect it."

Bohl glared at Hoag. "How did you know about that?"

"Mr. Bohl, someone always knows, and people always talk."

Hoag took another sip of coffee. "Who authorized the shipment?"

"I do not know who was shipping it."

"No. That's not what I mean," Hoag said, shaking his head. "Someone had to let it pass. I've seen the men on the docks. They wouldn't do it. So, who gave the okay to load those containers on the ship?"

"I cannot give you a name." Bohl moved to the table and took a seat. He gestured to a chair on the opposite side. Hoag slid it from the table and sat down. Bohl took a paper napkin from a holder and found a pen on the counter. He scribbled a note on the napkin. Hoag picked it up and read it.

"They might be listening right now," it read. Hoag took the pen from Bohl and scrawled a reply. "I need a name."

Bohl took the pen. "I loved the waterfront," he said. "But being at home with my wife has been fun, too." While he talked, he wrote on the napkin the name "Hermann Schroeder." Hoag read the name and frowned. Bohl wrote on the napkin, "Berlin." Hoag felt his heart skip a beat. This wasn't an oversight. This was a deliberate decision by someone to let the missile pass. They knew where it was going, and they knew what would happen when it arrived.

Hoag left the house and walked up the sidewalk toward the corner. Talking to Bohl had made him both nervous and suspicious. He glanced over his shoulder to see if anyone was watching. *This is crazy. No one is watching his house.*

Just then a truck passed by. The beam from the headlights washed over a gray sedan parked across the street. In the glare, Hoag saw two men. The man on the passenger side held a radio in his hand. Fear stabbed at Hoag. Someone really was watching. Hoag ducked his head and quickened his pace.

At the corner near Bohl's house, Hoag caught a taxi and rode back to the Internet café. With the access card he'd used earlier, he logged on to a computer terminal. A Web browser appeared with a Google search page. He typed in the name "Hermann Schroeder" and pressed a button to enter the term. Instantly the results came back with a page full of references. Hermann Schroeder was head of the German Federal Police.

Hoag leaned back from the monitor. *Schroeder is a powerful man, but he would never make that decision on his own. And there's only one person above him who could.* He tapped his finger on the table. *Josef Mueller. The chancellor.* He sat there a moment, staring at the screen. *Surely Mueller would have realized that we would find out. Were they that brazen, or just that arrogant?* To answer those questions, he would have to talk to Schroeder face-to-face.

A check of the Web site for the Federal Police indicated Schroeder's office was located in Berlin at the Interior Ministry building not far from the Chancellery. A virtual tour of the site included photographs of the building's lobby, showing a security station just inside the door. Behind them, guards were visible at strategic locations on the first floor. *Getting past them might be a little difficult.*

He returned to the earlier search-results page. It listed newspaper articles about Schroeder. As he scrolled through the list he came to an article from the *Herald Tribune* about a seminar on global security. The meeting was being held at the International Conference Center in Berlin. Schroeder was scheduled to address the conference the following afternoon.

Hoag checked his watch. *If I take a train tonight, I can get there before Schroeder's session ends.* He logged off the computer, took the access card from the machine, and started toward the door. As he stepped out to the sidewalk, he saw the same gray sedan parked just up the street. Two men were seated inside.

43

ATLANTIC OCEAN
NEAR VIRGINIA BEACH, VIRGINIA

JOHN GLOVER SAT IN THE LEFT SEAT of a U.S. Coast Guard HC-144A airplane as it cruised over the Atlantic, just off the Virginia coast. Known as an Ocean Sentry, the plane was used to conduct search and rescue missions. That day, it was carrying radiation-detection equipment, which sampled the air in an attempt to track the range of fallout from the blast that had occurred over Washington, D.C. NEST authorized the mission in hopes it also would aid in locating the *Amazon Cloud*. If a missile was aboard the ship, it might leak enough radiation to be detectable from the air.

After thirty years with the Coast Guard, Glover had participated in hundreds of recovery operations and was well versed in a dozen different air-search methods. That day, he flew the plane in a pattern of ten-mile loops up and down the coast, each loop carrying it one mile farther out to sea. It was critical work, but mind-numbingly boring.

Seated next to Glover was Chris Stevens. With five years as a copilot, he was just beginning his career. He glanced out the window at the water below. "I can't imagine a container ship loitering this far south." He checked the instruments and the map in his lap. "We're all the way down to North Carolina now."

"You're probably right," Glover agreed. "But we gotta check, just to be sure. Never know what we'll find." He smiled at Stevens. "Might catch a break. Big cases always turn on a break."

"I thought it was hard work."

"That's right. You work hard and then you catch a break."

"You've been flying too long."

"Okay, wise guy. How did they catch the mastermind behind the first time they tried to bomb the Trade Center?"

"The first time?"

"The van with the bomb in the parking deck. 1993, I think."

"I don't know. But his name is Ramzi Yousef and we got him. He's sitting in a maximum-security prison somewhere."

"He's at Supermax in Colorado. And he's there because the guy who rented the van for him had to put down a deposit."

"A deposit," Stevens shrugged. "Nothing unusual about that. How'd that get them caught?"

"After the van blew up with the bomb, the guy reported it stolen."

"That was kind of stupid. If he'd actually been from here he would have known not to go to the police. Why did he do that?"

"Because he wanted to get the deposit back."

"So he filed a police report and then went back to get the deposit?"

"Right."

"Not Ramzi Yousef."

"No. Yousef was too smart for that. This was the other guy. Somebody who was ..." Glover paused a moment. "Hang on." He pressed a key for the microphone on his headset and spoke to the regional control center. "Roger, control. Turning left." The airplane banked to the left. When it leveled off, Glover resumed the conversation. "Yousef was long gone by then, but the guy who rented the van filed a report saying it was stolen. Then he went back to the rental office to get the deposit."

"And they caught him?"

"Clerk at the rental office got suspicious, put him off for a day. Said he had to check out the theft report. Then he called the FBI. And when the guy came back the next day for his money, he was greeted by an office full of FBI agents."

A crewman's voice broke in on the headset. "Sir, this is Franklin. We have a ship off the port side."

Glover glanced out the window. Below him was a container ship lying dead in the water. Cargo containers bobbed on the waves around it. "What do you know!" Glover pointed. "I think that's our ship." He banked the plane and put it in a circle to loiter over the site, then switched frequencies and called the base at Kings Bay.

44

OFFUTT AIR FORCE BASE
OMAHA, NEBRASKA

THAT AFTERNOON, PETER BURKE knocked on the door of Jenny's apartment, unannounced. She was dressed in jeans and a sweatshirt. They talked at the door.

"They found the *Amazon Cloud.*"

Jenny was surprised. "Where?"

"It was adrift off the Virginia coast."

"They're sure it's the *Amazon Cloud*?"

"Yes. They've boarded it. The electromagnetic pulse from the blast disabled the electronics. It had no power."

"That is hilarious," she laughed. "I guess they forgot the EMP would affect them, too."

"Good thing, too."

"How's that?"

"They had a missile with a nuclear warhead. If they'd been able to launch, it would have probably been an actual hit on Washington. Not another high-altitude detonation."

"There, or New York."

"Well, anyway, the Navy is towing the ship down to St. Marys. We'll know more in a day or two. If Hoag hasn't left, he could just stay down there and interview them, too."

"Yes." Her eyes darted away. "I suppose so."

"You did some good work on this."

"Thanks." Jenny stepped back from the doorway. "You want to come inside?"

Burke had a playful smile. "I was thinking maybe we could get away for a few hours. Everybody's excited about the ship but there really isn't anything to do until they get it to the dock. I know a place where we could go. I think you'll like it."

"I'm a mess." Jenny gestured with both hands at her clothes. "I'll have to get dressed."

"I'll wait."

45

BERLIN, GERMANY

EARLY IN THE EVENING, an assistant opened the door to Mueller's office. "Max Brody is here to see you."

"Good. Send him in."

Brody was born and reared in Hohenzollern, an area now part of Baden-Wurttemberg, a state in southwestern Germany. As president of Deutsche Bundesbank, Germany's central bank, he held the keys to Germany's financial success. Mueller needed Brody's cooperation for the next step of his plan.

A moment later, the door opened again and Brody entered. He glanced around as if searching. "Where is Heinrich? I have not seen him in a while." He pointed to an empty chair. "He is usually sitting right there."

"He is taking care of other things." Mueller gestured to a chair near the desk. "Sit."

Brody dropped onto the chair and crossed his legs. "Well, to what do I owe this interruption of my evening?"

Mueller despised Brody's arrogance but tolerated him because of the influence he wielded among prominent Germans, many of whom longed for the monarchy's return. Mueller wanted to tap into their sense of national pride. Brody was part of that plan. "We have decided to stop buying U.S. Treasury notes." He said it flatly, without inflection, then leaned back in his chair to gauge Brody's reaction.

The muscles in Brody's jaw flexed. "Not surprising, coming from a Bavarian." He rested his hands in his lap. "I assume you have made your decision and are not really asking for my opinion."

"We are committed to the policy. What would be the result?"

Brody's eyes darted to the left as he collected his thoughts. "The bonds have already declined in value." He seemed to be thinking while he talked. "This will hurt their value even more." His eyes focused on Mueller. "Perhaps even force their total collapse."

Mueller nodded. "I am certain you are correct."

"America is reeling from the effects of a nuclear attack."

"A high-altitude detonation," Mueller corrected.

"Still, it has brought them financial chaos. They are barely able to maintain the façade of solvency. This will push them over the edge."

"I am aware of that."

"Then why did you bring me all the way from Frankfurt? You could have phoned me for this much…." His voice trailed away. "Or sent me one of those bizarre emails you love to write."

"I wanted to hear your thoughts and to see the look on your face when you explained them to me."

"Glad to be here for your amusement." Brody moved his hands from his lap and shifted sideways in the chair. "You do realize, do you not, that if you pursue this policy, for the first time in history, the Americans will be forced to default on their national debt."

"Yes," Mueller nodded. "I am sure they will."

"And still you are willing to take such a drastic measure?"

"You think it is drastic?"

"We still live in a global economy. This is quite a provincial reaction."

"It is a necessary step."

Brody looked puzzled. "A necessary step to what?"

"To a sane and orderly world."

"You do understand that an American default will hurt everyone?"

"And by 'everyone' you mean...?"

"Our fellow EU members. Russia. China. Canada. The countries of South America and Africa. Every nation in the world holds U.S. Treasury notes."

Mueller propped his elbow on the armrest of the chair and ran his finger along his chin in a pensive gesture. "When our nation was reunified, after the collapse of the Soviet Union, our leaders took steps to dismantle the East German social welfare state. That was a hard and bitter time."

"Yes, it was," Brody nodded. "Though I cannot say it affected my own lifestyle."

"Many in our nation, who were not as fortunate as you, suffered from that decision. But the suffering was short-term. Prosperity followed."

"And you think this will produce prosperity?"

"I think we have carried the United States for many years. All those countries you mentioned—every country in the world—has sent its money to Washington to support a lavish lifestyle they have long since lost the means to afford. With our support, America became a great nation, perhaps the greatest in the current era. But now it is time for Germany to take her rightful place."

"So which is it now? We are cutting off the hand that fed us, or the hand we fed?"

"We should not prop up the value of those bonds. It does Germany no good."

"The bonds we hold will become worthless, right along with those held by every other country."

"We can absorb the loss." Mueller sat up straight. "The bonds are worthless now anyway. This would merely force the markets to reflect their current value."

"They are doing a pretty good job of that already. Have you seen today's closing numbers?"

"Do not worry," Mueller smiled. "It will all work out right."

"Well, you do not need my approval to do this. But you cannot implement new policy of this nature without the finance minister's consent."

"I have discussed this with Geerken already."

Brody arched an eyebrow. "And he is in agreement?"

"He will not oppose it."

Brody appeared skeptical. "You are certain of this?"

"Yes. I am quite confident of it, actually."

"Because I recall a discussion with him in which he argued quite decisively that our financial interests were intimately related to continued American success."

"That was before recent events occurred." Mueller stood as a signal the meeting was over. "We will meet with him together. I will call you when it is arranged."

"Well, then." Brody stood. "I shall await your call."

46

OMAHA, NEBRASKA

FROM HER APARTMENT on Offutt Air Force Base, Burke and Jenny drove toward the city. The afternoon was bright, clear, and cool. She felt guilty about being there with him. It felt like a date, and they were supposed to be tracking down major threats against the country. She looked across the seat at him. "Are you sure we shouldn't be at the office, working on the *Amazon Cloud* or trying to find the other ship?"

"There's nothing more to do about the *Amazon Cloud* until they get her into port." He looked over. "It'll be in St. Marys in a few days." His eyes brightened. "David should just stay there and wait for it, don't you think? He could interview that crew, too."

She looked away, unsure whether to tell him about David's trip. "But what about the *Santiago*?" She tried to sound spontaneous. "We still need to find it."

"We have satellites and ships combing the Pacific. Relax. Let your mind unwind. I don't think much will happen for a few hours."

"Where are we going?"

"You'll see."

An hour later, they turned into a parking lot off Tenth Street near the river. Jenny looked around, puzzled. "What is this?"

"Ameritrade Park."

She saw the entrance to the left. "A stadium? Why are we here?"

"Football."

"Football?" She looked astounded. "Half the country's living in the Stone Age, and they're playing football?"

Burke grinned. "Life goes on. And they aren't living in the Stone Age. They just don't have electricity. People out here can't stop living just because the East Coast is in the dark."

He parked the SUV near the stadium entrance and met her as she climbed out on the passenger side. They walked to the gate. Burke took two tickets from his pocket and handed them to an attendant, who pointed to the right. "Elevator is just over there."

Burke nodded and ushered Jenny past the turnstile. She looked back at him. "Why did he tell us about the elevator?"

"Only way to get to our seats."

"That seems strange. Where are they?"

"Upstairs. Come on." He rested his hand against the small of her back and guided her through the crowd. "It's around here."

A security guard saw them coming and pressed a button for the elevator. The door was open and waiting as they reached it. They stepped inside and rode to the next level.

Jenny managed a smile. "Who's playing football in Omaha?"

"The Omaha Nighthawks." Burke gave her a knowing look. "An appropriate name on any number of levels, don't you think?"

"I've never heard of them."

"United Football League," Burke explained. "It's a startup league. Google money, a few former NFL executives and coaches. There are plenty of good players who can't get on an NFL roster simply because of the numbers."

"The numbers?"

"Roster limits. Salary caps."

"You're a fan."

"Yes," he grinned. "I'm a fan."

The elevator doors opened and Burke led her out to a corridor. He guided her toward another door manned by security personnel. Someone opened it as they approached. They stepped inside to a luxury suite.

A buffet filled with food sat to the right. A wet bar stood to the left. Sliding glass doors looked out on the field below. Jenny turned to Burke. "You have got to be kidding!"

"Isn't this great?"

"It is, but it seems like … it's wrong."

"Wrong?" He pointed her toward the buffet. "What's wrong with it? The season was underway before the attack on Washington. If they cancel now, several thousand people will lose their jobs. Millions of dollars of economic activity will be lost. We need this. The country needs this. If we stop doing this, we'll cease to be Americans and the entire economy will grind to a halt." A friend came by. Burke paused to introduce him to Jenny. Before long, others gathered around.

They spent the afternoon watching the game, eating, and talking. Jenny found herself in a crowd that included the mayor of Omaha, team owners, and the president of Google. The game that day was played against the Las Vegas Locomotives. The mayor of Las Vegas dropped by at halftime and brought with him a number of popular entertainers. Jenny experienced a lifestyle she hadn't seen since her college days. At first she felt a tinge of guilt—indulging in excess while so many in the country were without the basics of modern life—the same way she'd felt earlier while riding in the SUV on the way into town—but before long she was caught up in the party atmosphere and spent the day laughing and enjoying herself in way she hadn't for quite some time.

When the game was over, they rode the elevator down to ground level and walked out to the parking lot. On the ride back to the base, they continued to laugh and joke about what they'd seen and heard. It was almost dark when they arrived at the apartment.

Burke parked the SUV in a space near the stairway and escorted her to the door. "I had a good time," he said.

"I had a great time," she smiled. "I haven't laughed that hard in years."

"You looked like you were happy."

"I was. I really was."

"Good." He stepped closer and took her hand. "I like it when you're happy." He leaned forward. Their lips touched. She withdrew, then leaned into him and closed her eyes as their lips met once more.

47

OMAHA, NEBRASKA

JENNY AWAKENED THE NEXT MORNING remembering the events of the day before. She tried to tell herself it was okay. *Nothing really happened.* She rolled out of bed and started toward the kitchen. *We just kissed.* She took the pot from the coffeemaker and rinsed it at the sink. *I'm not a schoolgirl. I can see other people.* She filled the basket with coffee, poured in the water, and turned on the machine. *I was honest with David. I didn't lead him on. I told him exactly what I was thinking and feeling.* She collapsed on the sofa and clutched a pillow against her chest. *Who am I kidding? I got swept up in the whole thing from the moment I got in the car.* She threw the pillow aside. *I've been aware of him since the first day.* She banged her fist against the cushion. *And he knew it.*

By then the coffee was made. She poured a cupful and drank it while sitting in front of the television. As she scanned through the news channels she realized it was Sunday. She checked the time. *Only nine. I can still make it to church.*

A phone book sat on a table at the end of the sofa. She opened the book and turned to the Yellow Pages. All the listings were for churches located off the base. A base directory lay on the kitchen counter. She retrieved it and found an address for the chapel. It was just a few blocks up the street. She refilled her coffee cup and sipped from it while she walked to the shower.

Thirty minutes later she was dressed and ready. She walked from the apartment to the sidewalk and started up the street. Susan Todd met her at the corner. They walked together to the service. When it was over, Susan took her to the officer's club for lunch.

"You seem rather subdued today," Susan said. "Something wrong?"

"I went to a football game with Peter Burke yesterday."

"Uh-oh." Susan had a worried look. "What happened?" Susan rested her fork on the edge of the plate. "Are you going to tell me what happened?"

"The entire East Coast is in the dark." Jenny threw her hands in the air. "And there I was with a stadium full of people, acting like nothing happened."

"And you were right there with them." Susan's tone became insistent. "What happened?"

"He kissed me."

Susan leaned forward. "What did you expect? Did you kiss him back?" Jenny looked away. Susan shook her head. "Was that all that happened?"

"What do you mean?"

"Was that all? Or was there more—after the kiss?"

"No," Jenny huffed. "I kissed him. That's all. That was it. Just one kiss. Then I felt so bad I turned away without saying good night and went inside."

Susan picked up her fork. "That's what I was trying to tell you."

"I know," Jenny sighed.

"How serious is your relationship with David?"

"I don't know. Not that serious. Well ... We talked about it before he left. I sort of put him off."

Susan tipped her head to one side in a disapproving manner.

"You don't just 'sort of' put someone off."

"I know."

"What do you want to do about it?"

Jenny made a pouty face with her lips. "Can I just go back to Manhattan?"

"No," Susan said, shaking her head. "That's not an option."

Jenny's shoulders sagged. "I messed up."

"Do you want to continue to see him?"

"No," Jenny shook her head.

"Are you sure?"

"Yes."

"Then make certain you let him know," Susan replied. "Peter Burke is not one of those guys who will automatically pick up on your mood." She took a drink of tea. "You'll have to make it obvious to him."

48

BERLIN, GERMANY

MUELLER REACHED ACROSS HIS DESK and picked up the phone. He pressed a button for his assistant. A moment later, she was on the line. "Ask Hermann Schroeder to come up here, please."

"Certainly, sir."

Within the hour, Schroeder stepped into Mueller's office. He took a seat in front of the desk. "What may I do for you, Chancellor?"

Mueller rested his arms on the desktop and leaned forward. His voice was low, but firm and resolved. "I am a little concerned about some of our people."

Schroeder's eyes were alert. "You think there is a traitor among us?"

"I think some are not as loyal as the times require."

"What do you propose?"

"I want you to keep an eye on them."

"Who are we talking about?"

"Max Brody."

Schroeder nodded. "Anyone else?"

"Our finance minister, Raimund Geerken." Mueller leaned back in his chair. "Will that be a problem for you?"

"He is a powerful figure."

Mueller nodded in agreement. "You will have to be discreet."

"How much do you want to know about them?"

"As much as you can give."

"Follow them?"

"Of course."

"Tap their phones?"

"Yes."

"You will authorize it?"

"I think I just did."

"You will sign a warrant?"

Mueller shook his head slowly. "I do not think either of us wants anything on paper about this discussion."

Schroeder cocked his chin at an angle. "But you will cover us?"

"Yes," Mueller replied. "But I will need a full package."

Schroeder looked puzzled. "A full package?"

"Bank accounts. Credit cards. Cell phones. Everything."

"Very well." Schroeder stood and turned to leave.

Mueller called after him, "And there is one more name. Add Franz Heinrich to the list."

Schroeder turned back toward the desk and arched an eyebrow. "As you wish, sir."

49

OFFUTT AIR FORCE BASE
OMAHA, NEBRASKA

COFFEE CUP IN HAND, Jack Hedges stood at the window and stared out at the broad, flat parade grounds that lay just beyond the trees. Since relocating to Offutt Air Force Base, he had taken over one of the duplexes on General's Row, a section of historic homes reserved for general officers. President Hedges and his wife occupied one side of the house. The security detail and essential staff took the other. He was waiting that morning in the downstairs study of the residence for a briefing.

As he gazed out on the parade grounds, he thought of other times and other places, when life seemed certain and the future was something he could count on. Now, after the explosion, nothing seemed certain at all. Even the basics of life—like running water and electricity—could no longer be taken for granted. And that turned his mind to the people living in the eastern half of the country. He took a sip of coffee and shook his head at the thought of what they must be enduring. *Even my grandparents didn't live like that.*

Outside, three black SUVs came to a stop at the curb in front of the house. Doors opened and the national security staff appeared. Lauren Lehman, the Secretary of State, stepped out of the first car. With her were Carl Coulliette, Secretary of Defense, and Russ Williams, National Security Adviser. Hoyt Moore came from the second car. Hedges had a wry smile. *Cabinet officers and senior advisers. Coming to tell me what I already know.*

Just then there was a tap at the door. Hedges glanced over his shoulder to see his chief of staff, Braxton Kittrell, enter the room. "They're here, Mr. President."

"Can we meet in here?" Hedges gestured to the room where they were standing.

Kittrell quickly surveyed the area. "Yes, sir. I think this will work. I'll get some chairs."

Out the window, a third SUV came to a stop. The passenger door opened and the Treasury Secretary, Charlie Fiskeaux, stepped out. "This ought to be interesting," Hedges grinned.

Kittrell appeared, bringing a chair into the room. "Did you say something?"

Hedges gestured with the cup he was holding. "Charlie's here."

Kittrell grinned. "Think he can sit in the same room with Lehman without getting into a fight?"

Hedges turned away from the window. A desk sat nearby. "I like Charlie. He's tight with the checkbook." Hedges took a final sip from the cup and set it on the desk. "We need a tightfisted Treasury Department. Now more than ever."

In a few minutes they were all assembled in the study. Hedges sat behind his desk. The others were seated before him, some in upholstered chairs from the living room, others on straight-backed chairs scavenged from around the dining table.

Lauren Lehman began. "Mr. President, as I think Russ already informed you, a Coast Guard reconnaissance plane located the *Amazon Cloud* off the Virginia coast."

"Yes," Hedges nodded. "Russ told me about that earlier. Do we know any more about it?"

"A Navy SEAL team boarded the ship," Lehman continued.

"They secured the vessel and found a Shahab-3 missile. It was loaded on a mobile missile launcher."

Hedges had a quizzical look. "Shahab—this was an Iranian missile?"

"Yes, sir, Mr. President."

Hedges turned in Coulliette's direction. "Carl, we think the Iranians are the ones who hit us with the first missile?"

"We need a little more data to confirm it," Coulliette replied. "But it looks like it, sir."

"More data?" Hedges frowned. "We have the telemetry. What additional data do we need?"

Lehman spoke up. "We'd like to see an analysis of the material from the warhead before we recommend any action."

"Do we have material from the first missile?"

"NEST is working on it."

"Tell NEST to work faster," Hedges suggested. "What kind of warhead did this second missile have?"

"Nuclear, sir."

"Was it armed?"

"No, sir."

Hedges shook his head. "And they couldn't launch it because of the electromagnetic pulse from the earlier detonation?"

"Yes, sir."

"Amazing," he sighed. "Do we have any way of connecting the first missile with the second?"

"We're working on that right now, Mr. President."

"And how are we doing that?"

"NEST sent a team to upstate New York," Moore explained. "They recovered snow samples with extremely high radioactive content. They're analyzing that now to see if they can determine a signature. Hopefully, that will tell us whose reactor supplied the material for the first warhead. If we can determine a signature for that material, we can then compare it to the warhead we seized from the *Amazon Cloud*."

"Snow samples?" Hedges looked puzzled. "I know it's autumn, but they already have snow in upstate New York?"

"Mount Marcy, sir. It's about a mile high at the top."

"And going up there was NEST's idea?"

"Yes, sir," Moore replied. "Pete Rios sent them."

"Was the missile that was launched against Israel a Shahab missile, also?"

"The telemetry we have seems to indicate that," Coulliette answered, "but the Israelis haven't said."

"Do they know?"

"After they shot down the missile," Lehman added, "they sent teams into the field to look for debris. Their search teams located pieces from the exploded missile and they have recovered the warhead. I assume they know."

"Have we asked them what they found?"

"I don't know, sir," she responded. "We've been concentrating on threats against our own country. I have not issued a request for information. The report about what the SEAL team found on the *Amazon Cloud* just came in. We thought it was important to brief you on it as soon as possible."

"I appreciate your promptness." Hedges' voice was tense. "But let's ask the Israelis what they know about the missile that was launched against them. If it was the same, and Iran is behind this, we will want to coordinate our response with the Israelis."

"Yes, sir, Mr. President."

"But we'll have to move fast because the Israelis won't wait around. Once they know for certain who lobbed that missile at them, they'll hit back and hit hard."

Charlie Fiskeaux had a frustrated scowl. "I think we ought to consider the effect this will have on the economy."

Hedges looked perplexed. "What do you mean?"

"Well, Mr. President, this won't be an isolated incident."

"You think it will affect our economy, even though they were unable to launch the missile?"

"I think knowing that there was a second missile is one more thing the markets will factor into trading activity."

Russ Williams added, "He's right. It's one more thing that will influence our citizens. They will know there was another missile. The attackers not only had the ability to send one missile, but now everyone will know they had the ability to send two."

"If they weren't scared before," Lehman added, "they're surely going to be scared now. That will affect what little economic vitality we have left."

"Well, I'm not certain we can do anything about it," Hedges said. "The people have a right to know and I intend to tell them."

"The eastern half of the country is still in the dark," Moore offered. "They won't know for a while."

"Maybe that will help, but we can't keep this from them," Hedges declared, "and we can't undo what someone else has already done."

"No, Mr. President," Fiskeaux countered, "but we can anticipate what it might mean."

"What are you talking about?"

"He's talking about the pending quarterly debt refinancing," Russ Williams said.

"Yes," Fiskeaux agreed. "We need to come up with a contingency plan for our quarterly debt refinancing."

"Do we have a contingency plan?"

"Not really."

"Well, come up with one and we'll consider implementing it."

"Yes, sir."

"There's one obvious option," Lehman suggested. "We could always postpone it."

Fiskeaux bristled at the notion. "We've never defaulted on our debt before."

"We've never been hit with a nuclear bomb before, either."

"We could alter the way we do it," Williams suggested. "We could refinance the domestic portion of the debt now, early. If we spin it right, it could look like a positive thing, like we are in such a strong position we're holding the auction early."

"Could make us appear desperate, too," Lehman groused.

"We are desperate," Williams added.

"I like the idea," Hedges responded. "Charlie, see what you can do about it. Russ will help you."

"Yes, sir, Mr. President."

50

OFFUTT AIR FORCE BASE OMAHA, NEBRASKA

ON MONDAY MORNING, Jenny arrived at the office early. Burke's comment the day before about having David interview the crew of the *Amazon Cloud* was stuck in her mind. Something about the way he said it let her know that he already knew David had left the base at Kings Bay. When she reached her desk, she switched on her monitor and logged on to the CIA system. She checked to make certain David had reached Germany, then glanced at her watch. Germany was eight hours ahead, which meant it was already afternoon. She picked up her cell phone to place a call, then thought better of it. *Maybe I should wait for him to call. No telling what he's doing.*

An hour later, Peter Burke appeared at the doorway to Jenny's cubicle. Her heart dropped into her stomach. He was the last person she wanted to see, but he was there and she forced herself to confront the issue. "We need to talk," she said, as forcefully as she could.

He seemed not to hear her. "Anything further on the *Amazon Cloud*?"

"Not yet." She tried again. "Look. About the other day. I—"

"No," he interrupted. "I know. It's awkward."

"I wanted to tell you—"

"It's okay." He stepped to her desk and rested his hand on her shoulder. "We'll work it out. People do this all the time. Office romance. It's okay. We haven't violated any regulations.'"

"There isn't any 'office romance,'" Jenny protested. "And I don't want to 'work it out.' There's nothing to work out."

"We can make—"

"Peter," Jenny cut him off. "There isn't anything to work out."

"What do you mean?"

"I shouldn't have let you kiss me."

"It wasn't just a one-way deal." There was an odd smile on his face. "You kissed me back."

"I know." She looked away. "I shouldn't have done that, either."

His arm still rested on her shoulder and he used it to give her a hug. "We'll figure it out." He smiled at her. "It'll be okay."

"No." She grabbed his arm and lifted it from her shoulder. "I told you before. I don't want to work it out."

"You're just feeling guilty," he frowned. "You don't have to feel that way."

"Peter." Jenny stood. "I don't feel guilty. There isn't anything to work out. Whatever happened before should have never happened."

"Okay," he said, softly. "We'll get through it." He turned away. "I'll check on you this afternoon."

When he was gone, Susan appeared in the doorway. "Well, that wasn't exactly what I expected. But at least you made your point."

"You were right," Jenny groaned.

"How's that?"

"He isn't a man who listens well."

"No." Susan gestured with her fist. "He's the kind you have to hit over the head to get his attention."

51

BERLIN, GERMANY

HOAG ARRIVED AT BERLIN CENTRAL Station early in the morning. A taxi took him to the Brandenburger Hotel, where he showered and changed clothes. After a brief nap, he rode to the International Conference Center.

At the lobby entrance, he made his way to an information booth and browsed through a stack of brochures. In them he found a schedule for the conference. Schroeder's address was being delivered at Hall Three on the far end of the main level. Hoag checked his watch. If the event began on time, Schroeder still should be at the podium. He picked up a building map from the desk and started toward the Hall.

When Hoag reached the far end of the building, he found the doors to the hall were closed. Even so, he could hear Schroeder's voice as it filtered into the hallway. Plainclothes agents manned the entrances. Armed guards patrolled the corridors. With no way to get inside the room, Hoag took a seat on a bench in the lobby opposite the doors and waited.

While he sat there, he studied the schedule and the building map. A press conference was slated for Hall Six, immediately following Schroeder's speech. Hoag checked the building map and smiled. Schroeder would have to pass by his position to get to the briefing.

In a few minutes, the doors to the conference room opened and Schroeder emerged, flanked by bodyguards and assistants. Hoag moved in front of him and blocked his path. "Hermann Schroeder," he called, thrusting out his hand with a smile. "David Hoag."

Instinctively, Schroeder grasped Hoag's hand to shake it. "Good to see you." He tried to push past. "I am on my way to a press conference."

Hoag walked with him. "I thought maybe we could talk about a couple of cargo containers loaded from the port at Bremerhaven."

Schroeder stopped short and glared at him. "What are you talking about?"

"The *Panama Clipper*. New York City. A Shahab-3 missile."

"You should see the officials at the docks." Schroeder started forward again. "We do not handle freight inspection."

A bodyguard tried to block Hoag's path, but Hoag moved closer to Schroeder and kept talking. "These cargo containers were inspected by a couple of your men."

"Oh?" Schroeder's voice had an imperious tone. "And what makes you so sure of that?"

"We have fingerprints."

Once more, Schroeder came to an abrupt halt. "That would be a serious allegation." He looked Hoag in the eye. "Are you raising this issue in an official capacity?"

"I've talked to the people who were there. They told me what happened."

"I assure you, Mr. Hoag, we would never allow such a thing to happen. No cargo of the kind you have described would ever be allowed onto a ship in our port, regardless of where it was being sent."

"It was loaded with your specific approval."

An assistant came to Schroeder's side. "Sir, we need to keep moving."

"I've talked to several people," Hoag insisted. "And I know what happened."

"I will look into it."

Schroeder started forward. One of the agents took Hoag by the arm. "I will show you to the exit"

Hoag shrugged free. "I can find it on my own."

"Then make certain you do."

52

PODGORICA, MONTENEGRO

NASSER HAMID ARRIVED AT THE AIRPORT and was cleared through customs without incident. He took a taxi downtown to the Apart Hotel, where he paid cash for a room. After a shower and a change of clothes, he returned to the lobby and stepped outside. The air was crisp and cool. To the north, the snowcapped peaks of the Dinaric Alps rose into the bright clear sky.

A taxi was parked near the front entrance but Hamid ignored it and walked the short distance to Moskovska Street. He turned left at the corner and three blocks later came to a modern high-rise building. A sign on a brass plate near the front entrance identified it as the central office of Banka Montenegro. He pushed open the door and made his way inside to a teller.

"I am here to see Zoran Tadic."

The teller smiled pleasantly. "Is he expecting you?"

"Perhaps," Hamid replied. "Tell him Olek Kamati would like to speak with him."

The teller stepped away from the window and disappeared through a door at the far end of the counter. A few minutes later, an assistant came to the lobby and escorted Hamid upstairs. He found Tadic seated at his desk in a large corner office.

"I wondered when I would see you," Tadic said when they were alone. He came from behind the desk and embraced Hamid with a kiss on both cheeks. "You are well?"

"Yes," Hamid nodded. "I am well."

"Good." Tadic gestured to a chair. Hamid took a seat. Tadic sat in a chair beside him. "I assume you have come to see us about your account."

Hamid had a satisfied look. "The money arrived?"

Tadic moved behind the desk and checked the monitor that sat near the telephone. Account information appeared on the screen. "It is here," he smiled.

"I would like to move some of it."

"You have the information?" Hamid took a small scrap of paper from his pocket and laid it on the desk.

Tadic glanced at it, then back to Hamid. "This is the amount?"

"Yes."

"This is a large transaction."

"Is it a problem?"

"No." Tadic shook his head. "But these transactions are cleared through Rome."

"What are you saying?"

"Someone will notice a movement this large."

"Will they halt it?"

"Not without a reason."

"Do they have a reason?"

Tadic smiled. "I do not think so."

Hamid thought for a moment. He had moved the money in large transactions for the sake of speed. Smaller transactions would attract less attention, but they took longer. He had a small window of opportunity. The more time he took, the greater the chance someone would find him. Even now he was certain the Israelis had located the launch site. They had been following him for several years, always a few steps behind. With the information they had obtained already, they might close the gap. His mind told him Tadic was right, they should break the transaction into smaller amounts, but his intuition told him time was more important. Finally, he shook his head. "Send it all at once."

"Very well." Tadic turned to a keyboard and entered a series of commands. He studied the screen a moment, then initiated the transfer. A few minutes later, he received a confirmation. "It is done." He took a small piece of paper from the desk, scribbled an amount on it, and handed it to Hamid. "This is your current balance."

"Excellent," Hamid nodded. "Now, if you could help me. I need to make a withdrawal."

"In cash?"

"Yes."

53

FRANKFURT, GERMANY

JOSEF MUELLER ARRIVED at the Messe Frankfurt convention center in the afternoon and made his way through the exhibition hall. A trade show of agricultural equipment filled the center. The halls were packed with visitors. Mueller paused for photographs at several sites, then quietly moved to a conference room off one of the ancillary corridors. There he met Andre Pierlot, the Belgian foreign minister.

A steward served them coffee and pastries, then retreated from the room. When he was gone, Mueller looked over at Pierlot. "Thank you for seeing me on such short notice."

"My pleasure," Pierlot replied. "I enjoy coming to Frankfurt."

Mueller took a bite of pastry. "You have no doubt been following events in America and Israel."

"Yes." Pierlot gestured with his coffee cup. "And we are glad for your leadership in such a time of crisis."

"I am glad to be of service," Mueller smiled. "We Europeans all face the same calamity—a world without American consumption to prop up our prices."

"But unlike many, we are in strong financial condition. Belgium holds very little U.S. debt."

"A wise move."

Pierlot paused to take a sip of coffee. "This crisis gives us a great opportunity to shed our dependence on America. Perhaps now we can finally take charge of our own destiny, without pressure from American politicians."

"Yes," Mueller nodded. "That is what I wanted to speak with you about."

"You have some specific ideas?"

Mueller set aside his coffee cup and leaned back in the chair. "I am wondering whether it is time for the European Union to take charge of its own defense."

"Military defense?"

"Yes."

"A truly European army?"

"Yes." Mueller had a serious look. "Apart from membership in NATO."

"You are, of course, talking about a withdrawal from NATO, correct?"

"I am indeed."

"You have no idea how long I have prayed for such a day."

Mueller struggled to suppress a grin. "You have not enjoyed the protection of the Americans?"

"Protection, yes," Pierlot nodded. "But I have not enjoyed being made to feel like a penniless servant in the process." He set his cup on the table. "What did you have in mind?"

Mueller leaned forward. "I am wondering if the European Union could not simply take over the NATO bases and military hardware, and send the Americans home."

A wide smile spread across Pierlot's face. "Just like that?"

"Yes. Just like that."

"And what of the Americans?"

"We do not need them. They are in no position to help us now anyway, and will not be for a very long time."

"And they are in no position to resist our decision."

"Exactly."

"We are strong enough to take care of ourselves. NATO was designed to counter the threat of a Soviet invasion. That threat no longer exists."

Mueller nodded in agreement. "We are long past the issues that plagued the 20th century. Now we face an entirely new set of challenges."

"The Union would have to vote on such a decision," Pierlot countered. "And the individual member states would have to ratify any decision the Union makes."

"That could prove to be a lengthy process."

"Perhaps we could find a way around that process," Pierlot suggested. "But first we must test the water. Find out whether the others would support such a move. How would we even make such a proposal?"

"I am not sure." Mueller shifted positions on the chair. "If I, as EU president, raise the issue, it will become instant news to the public, and the other members will see it as an attempt to impose a top-down decision."

"Yes. I see your point." Pierlot gave him a knowing look. "Should I poll the other chiefs privately? See what they think about the idea. Low-key, just raising the idea. That will give us an indication of where we stand without forcing them to take a public position."

"Good idea." Mueller had a satisfied expression. "I was counting on you to know what to do."

54

TEHRAN, IRAN

JIANG SHA SAT IN A CAR near a hangar at the east end of Mehrabad
Airport. Off to the west, the sun glinted off the wings of a Learjet as
it made its final approach toward the runway. Slowly, it descended
and touched down. It stopped short at the first taxiway and turned
toward the hangar. A few minutes later it rolled to a halt on the
tarmac fifty yards from where Jiang sat.

As the plane's engines whined to a stop, the door opened. A
stairway extended from the jet's fuselage and a man appeared in the
doorway. Jiang took a pair of binoculars from the seat beside him and
focused the lens.

"Franz Heinrich," Jiang whispered, as the man came into view.

Heinrich adjusted the sleeves of his jacket and started down the
steps. Before he reached the bottom, a Mercedes sedan came from the
opposite side of the hangar and rolled to a stop near the plane. The
driver hurried to the passenger side of the car and opened the rear
door. Heinrich stooped to enter and disappeared onto the backseat.

Moments later, the car moved away from the plane and turned
onto a service road twenty meters from Jiang's location. He waited
until the Mercedes was beyond the hangar, then started the car and
backed it from its parking place.

For the next thirty minutes, they wound their way through the

crowded streets of Tehran, the Mercedes always ahead, Jiang following at a safe distance. Finally, the Mercedes turned into the drive at
Laleh International Hotel and came to a stop beneath the canopy
outside the lobby entrance. A doorman rushed forward to greet
them. The trunk lid flew up as bellmen converged on the car.

Jiang continued past the hotel and parked behind a Dumpster in
an alley down the block. He hurried on foot back to the hotel and
entered through a service door. He made his way past the kitchen to
the freight elevator and arrived undetected in a room on the fourth
floor. Shikai Ma and Fan Wei were already there when he arrived.

A table sat in the corner directly opposite the door. On it was a
tape recorder, its large reels turning slowly as the tape wound from
one side to the other. Wires from the recorder snaked across the floor
and down through a hole behind the air-conditioner. Fan Wei sat at
the table listening through headphones. Shikai Ma glanced in Jiang's
direction as he entered. He placed his finger to his lips and gestured
for quiet. "They are in the room now," he whispered.

"That was fast. What are they saying?"

Ma handed him a set of headphones. "Listen for yourself." Jiang
fit them over his ears and listened to the conversation coming from
the room below.

Ardakan spoke first. "Mr. Heinrich, I trust you had a safe trip."

"Yes," Heinrich replied. There was no mistaking his German
accent. "It was a most uneventful trip."

"Good." There was the sound of a chair scraping the floor. "Shall
we sit?"

"I understood this was to be a meeting with President Kermani."
Heinrich's voice sounded reserved, almost hesitant. "It was previ-
ously arranged. Will he be joining us?"

"I am sorry," Ardakan replied. His words were apologetic, but his
voice gave no hint of reticence. "President Kermani had a scheduling

conflict. I am authorized to speak with you on his behalf. Please, have a seat." There was the sound of another chair against the floor. "I assume this is not merely a courtesy call."

"In light of the recent attack on the United States and Israel," Heinrich began, "we thought it a good idea to meet with you to discuss the situation. Rumor has it that the missile used in both attacks was a Shahab-3." He paused a moment. "The only question remaining is whether the Iranian government was involved directly with these attacks."

"I know of no such rumor. We attempt to live at peace with all peoples." There was a rustling sound. "Has anyone produced proof to substantiate these rumors?"

"Sources tell us the Israelis have recovered debris from the missile used in the attempt against them."

"Mr. Heinrich, we have no sources inside Israel, as I am certain you already know."

"But we both know what happened."

"Yes," Ardakan answered. "We know what happened in New York City, and we know what happened in Israel. And we know what happened in the German port of Bremerhaven."

Jiang gave Ma a questioning look. "What is he talking about?"

"I do not know," Ma shrugged. Wei waved his hand in a gesture for silence.

In the room below, Heinrich continued. "I see you have sources in *some* countries."

"Yes," Ardakan replied. "But how are these attacks a threat to Germany? I would rather suspect they present you with a golden opportunity. America is no longer an economic superpower. Germany is now the financial leader of the West. I am certain you are taking steps to make the most of it."

"That is why I am here. We would like to purchase your entire oil production."

"We already have many customers."

"You have one customer," Heinrich countered.

"We have contracts with that customer. Selling to you would require us to violate our agreements with them. And what would we gain from that?"

"A fair price. And protection."

"We need protection?" Ardakan seemed to bristle at the remark, as if he were being threatened.

"Israel will not remain silent long."

"The Jews are long on talk and short on action." Ardakan's voice had a dismissive tone. "Everyone thinks their Mossad spy organization knows everything. They know only what we want them to know."

"If they have your missile, then they have your warhead. It did not explode. We are certain they have it intact. The Americans will examine it and they will know which reactor produced the components."

"How could they know such a thing?"

"They have databases that go back over decades. They built one of your reactors. They supplied fuel for several of them. We built one. The Russians built one. All of that information is contained in databases that have been shared readily in the West. They believed in their theories of verifiable disarmament and they have disclosed this information among themselves for years. Israel may know already where the warhead material came from. In a few days, perhaps a week, the Americans will know. And then you will face the wrath of both countries. And you will face them alone."

"Unless we sell to you."

"We are prepared to offer you a defense against the Americans and the Israelis."

"And what is that defense?"

"The German Navy. And Germany's own land-based missile defense system."

"Your system can defeat American missiles?"

"Our system was developed precisely for that purpose."

"But what of the Chinese?"

"They are of no concern."

"No concern?" Ardakan's voice had a note of incredulity. "There is an army of three million lying just to the east of us."

"They have men, but they have no oil unless you sell it to them. We estimate—"

"And that is my point," Ardakan interrupted. "They have no oil. They will see our refusal to honor our contracts as a threat—even an act of war—and they will attack us to preserve their own security."

"We estimate their reserves at four months. It would take six months to deploy their army and reach Iran. By then, they will have run out of oil."

"And if we refuse this generous offer from Germany?"

"You go it alone."

"Or perhaps we turn to the Chinese for assistance."

"No," Heinrich replied. "I do not think so."

"What would prevent us?"

"Right now, the Chinese are assessing their options. If they wait until Israel or America attack you, it will be too late. Your oil fields will be worthless."

"What are you saying?"

"The only way China can preserve their supply of oil from you is to invade your country now. You should discuss this with President Kermani. Perhaps then he will make time in his schedule to meet with me."

Jiang slipped off the headphones. "We must report this conversation."

"Perhaps we should wait," Ma replied. "And see if he meets with Kermani."

"No," Jiang replied, shaking his head. "They know more about us than we realized. We must report this now."

55

TEL AVIV, ISRAEL

DREW POWELL STEPPED FROM A TAXI into the cool night air and
made his way inside the Café Noir. As he came through the doorway
he caught sight of Yorman Avital seated at a table in back. Avital, a
deputy minister of foreign affairs, was eating alone. Powell made his
way to the table and took a seat.

"Sorry I'm late," Powell began. "I came as quickly as I could,
without making it obvious."

Avital rested his fork on the edge of his plate and wiped his
mouth with a napkin. He reached inside his jacket, removed an
envelope and slid it across the table. "This will make it worth your
while, I think."

Powell took the envelope from the table and tucked it inside his
jacket. "We appreciate your help."

"Cooperation between our two countries is essential now."

"Yes," Powell nodded. "I agree."

Avital picked up a coffee cup. "Does the rest of your government
share that same sentiment?"

"I am certain they do. We are well aware of the precarious nature
of our situation."

"How are things in Omaha these days?" Avital took a sip of
coffee.

"They are well," Powell replied. "The government is functioning in all essential offices."

"I am sure things are difficult on the East Coast."

"Some places were harder hit than others," Powell shrugged. "But several of the agencies that remained in Washington are beginning to restore their services."

"That is good news."

A waiter appeared at the table. Powell waved him off with a gesture of his hand. When the waiter had gone, Powell turned back to Avital. "I understand you have located the debris field."

"Yes."

"Any determination yet on the origin of the missile?"

"Nothing official, but read the notes in the envelope." Avital paused for another sip of coffee, then set the cup on the table. "You will find what you need in there."

"I'll get right on it." Powell rose from his chair and started toward the door. Outside the café, he hailed a taxi and rode back to the U.S. Embassy. He arrived there a little before seven that evening. When he was seated at his desk, he opened the envelope. Inside he found two photographs.

The first was a picture of a man walking along a city sidewalk. He was slender, with olive complexion and dark hair. Dressed in a loose-fitting white cotton shirt and cotton twill pants, he wore a pair of tattered leather sandals that caught Powell's eye. He stared at them a moment, then turned the photograph over and found on the other side the name "Nasser Hamid" and the notation "Alexandria, Egypt."

The second photograph showed a missile reconstructed from pieces collected at the debris field. About fifty feet long and a little more than three feet in diameter, it was white with markings on the fins and nose cone. An Iranian flag decal was positioned at the opposite end near the point where the payload cone attached. A note on the back described it as an Iranian Shahab-3 missile.

Powell studied the photographs a moment, then lifted the receiver on the phone and called his assistant. When no one answered, he walked out to the hall and glanced around. Offices on the floor were empty and quiet. He checked his watch. It was almost eight. *But it's the middle of the day in Nevada. I need to get this to them.*

Through an open doorway he saw a woman seated at a desk in an office near the elevator. She worked in consular services, helping U.S. citizens who'd run afoul of Israeli law. She had a young daughter who liked to dance and a son who was a Steelers fan, but Powell could never remember the woman's name. He made his way toward her. She looked up as he approached.

"You're working late."

"Yeah," Powell replied. "I had a meeting."

"Need some help with something?"

He gestured with the photographs. "I need to transmit these to NEST. In Nevada."

"You can send them by delivery in the morning."

Powell shook his head. "Too slow. Do you know how to scan them?"

"Sure." She stood and came from behind the desk. "Do it all the time."

56

TEHRAN, IRAN

OLEG BATALOV CAME FROM his suite on the tenth floor of the Laleh Hotel. At sixty-five, he'd grown accustomed to certain things in life—a glass of wine before dinner, a cigar afterward—and he'd come to expect them in a punctual manner. Dinner, he felt, should be served promptly at eight each evening.

Batalov was born to a family of hardworking farmers who lived in the Ukraine. His father had been alive when the Communists took power and watched helplessly as the government seized his land. All his life afterward, he had dreamed of only one thing—getting back the family farm. That dream became his son's mission.

As a young boy, Batalov studied hard and applied himself at school, eventually gaining admission to the National Mining University at Dnipropetrovsk. He graduated with a degree in engineering and was put to work building roads for the Soviet Army. One of his closest friends was a young army officer named Vladimir Vostok.

When the government collapsed in the 1980s, Vostok left the army for an appointment in the emerging Russian government. He quickly became a key player in the Kremlin's economic policy division. Batalov formed his own construction company and went to work building roads and pipelines. Much of the business was sent his way by Vostok.

Ten years later, Batalov purchased the family farm and Vostok was the newly elected president of Russia. With Vostok's help, Batalov expanded his business to the Middle East where he landed contracts building pipelines to link oil fields with refining and shipping facilities. His latest deal involved a pipeline through Azerbaijan that would integrate Russian and Iranian oil production.

That day, at the Laleh Hotel, Batalov walked down the hall to the elevator on his way to dinner. He was joined there by his assistant, Andre Kanevsky. The two had spent the day negotiating terms of the new pipeline deal with officials from the Iranian Ministry of Petroleum.

"I thought our discussion went well today." Kanevsky pressed the button for the elevator. "They seemed to be ready to move forward with the project."

"We are far behind," Batalov complained. "We should have surveyors in the field already."

"At least they are still interested. I was worried they would be scared off by the trouble in America."

"I think they realize that Europe and Asia are their only markets now. Selling to Europe through Russia makes sense. That way, the two countries can maintain control over the distribution. They will be the world's largest suppliers."

"At a time when prices have skyrocketed."

"Yes," Batalov nodded. "The price is too high."

"It will come down."

"Perhaps," Batalov sighed. "But a few more missile attacks and the price of oil will be so high no one can afford it."

The elevator doors opened. Kanevsky and Batalov stepped inside. Kanevsky stood near the rear. "But they have plenty of money to pay us for our work."

Batalov chuckled. "They have plenty of that. For the moment."

Moments later, they reached the lobby. Batalov turned to the right and walked toward the restaurant. As he came to the corner, he stopped short. "Wait," he said, in a hushed tone.

"Why?" Kanevsky started past him. "What is wrong?"

Batalov took him by the arm and gestured with a nod. "You see that man? The one in the gray suit."

"Yes. What of him?"

"He is Franz Heinrich. That is Abadeh Ardakan with him," Kanevsky added. "What are they doing together?"

"I do not know." Batalov watched until the two men turned the corner at the far end of the hall. Then he nudged Kanevsky. "Come, we will follow them. I want to see where they are going."

Batalov hurried to the corner, then slowed as he made the turn into a hallway that led to a service area. Linen carts were parked there and an elevator was located just beyond them. As they turned the corner, Ardakan and Heinrich stepped into the elevator. Ardakan looked up as the doors closed. His eyes met Batalov with a look of surprise.

57

LAS VEGAS, NEVADA

PETE RIOS SAT IN A CHAIR propped against the wall of the NEST command center. Fingers laced together in his lap, head back, he dozed softly. A voice awakened him.

"Sir, we have received some information from our embassy in Tel Aviv."

Rios opened his eyes to find Jeff Howell standing over him. He rocked the chair forward and put both feet on the ground. "What is it?"

"Two photographs."

"Okay," Rios sighed. "Let's have a look." He followed Howell to the opposite side of the room.

Howell took a seat at his desk and opened an electronic file. An image appeared on his monitor. "This is the missile launched against Israel from the Egyptian desert. They reconstructed it from recovered debris."

The picture showed pieces of the missile placed together on a frame. There were holes from missing sections and not all the parts fit neatly together, but there was no mistaking its identity. "That's a Shahab," Rios observed.

"Yes, sir. A Shahab-3. Still has an Iranian flag on the side." He pointed to it in the photo.

"Okay." Rios backed away from the desk and glanced around the room. "The Israelis have confirmed the missile launched against them was an Iranian Shahab-3. We found a Shahab-3 missile on the *Amazon Cloud*. Any possibility these missiles were simply purchased from Iran by a terrorist group and loaded with warheads they obtained elsewhere?"

Richard Weavil answered. "It's possible, but not likely."

Rios turned toward him. "Why not?"

"They've never sold missiles of this kind to anyone."

Ken Aycock added, "Only Iranian missile sales we know about involved shoulder-fired missiles."

"Do we have a report from the team on those samples from upstate New York?"

"Not yet."

Rios turned to the operator at the console near the center of the room. "Get Owens on the phone. I want to know what he has. We need something, even if it's just an estimate."

Weavil continued. "Isn't it obvious who did this? These are Iranian missiles. Telemetry from the one shot at us confirms it. We have the missile from the *Amazon Cloud*. It's a Shahab-3 just like the one Israel shot down. Both of them were armed with nuclear warheads. This was an attack by Iran against us and against Israel. What more do we need?"

"We need to know for certain about the one they launched against us."

"Why?" Weavil stood. "They did it. We don't have to wait for a direct hit before we strike back. We're dealing with nuclear weapons. This isn't some guy with a car bomb in Times Square, or even a hijacked airplane. They're firing nuclear missiles at us."

"You're right," Rios calmly agreed. "This is nuclear war. And when we respond, cities will be leveled. Millions of civilians will die." He took a deep breath. "And before we do that, we need to be certain."

"Sir," the operator interrupted. "Jim Owens is on line two."

Rios picked up the phone. "I need your analysis of those samples."

"I'm just finishing it now."

"Good. Send it." Rios hung up the phone and turned to the operator. "What do we have on—"

Howell spoke up. "Sir, there was a second photograph from the embassy." Rios moved back to Howell's desk and leaned over his shoulder. An image appeared on the monitor. "According to the caption on the back," Howell explained, "this is a photograph of Nasser Hamid. It was taken a few days ago in Alexandria, Egypt. He was on his way to a café where he purchased a U.S. passport."

"Alert the State Department. Put a hold on any passports using his known aliases or likeness. And ask Interpol for help. We need to find him."

Madeline Lewis, an analyst seated to the left, broke in. "Sir, we have the report from Owens. It's a preliminary draft, but he doesn't think the final results will change."

Rios leaned over her shoulder to read from the monitor. A chart appeared on the screen. He scanned it quickly. "Gamma ... beta ... promethium ... strontium. Where's the conclusion?" She scrolled down the screen. Rios read the last sentence. "These findings are consistent with a determination that material in the samples was produced by Reactor Three at the Bushehr Nuclear Power Plant in Bushehr, Iran." Rios looked over at Weavil. "Now we know enough to act."

Rios turned to the operator. "Call the president's office. I need to brief him."

58

TEL AVIV, ISRAEL

EFRAIM HOFI SAT OUTSIDE the prime minister's office and waited. On his lap he held a large manila envelope. His knees bounced nervously, causing the envelope to jiggle against his trousers. An assistant looked up from her desk.

"A little nervous, sir?"

Hofi was puzzled. "What?"

She pointed to his lap. Hofi let his feet rest flat on the floor. "Sorry," he smiled. "Excess energy."

"It will not take long," she assured him. "They are concluding now."

Five minutes later, the office door opened and an aide appeared. He smiled courteously at Hofi. "He will see you now."

Hofi rose from the chair and stepped quickly toward the doorway. The aide moved aside to let him enter, then closed the door behind him. On the far side of the room, David Oren, the prime minister, sat at his desk. "Sorry for the delay." A file lay open before him. Oren made notes in it while he talked. "I was already in a meeting when you called. So…" Oren glanced up at Hofi. "You said it was urgent. I assume this is about the missile."

Hofi stood in front of the desk. "Yes, Mr. Prime Minister."

Oren looked back at the file on his desk. He gestured with the pen in his hand. "Then by all means, tell me."

Hofi opened the manila envelope and slid a photograph from it. "This is a picture of the missile that was launched against us."

Oren laid the pen aside and looked up from the file. He took the photo from Hofi and let his eyes scan over it. "We have reassembled all the pieces?"

"Most of them." Hofi pointed. "You can see the Iranian flag."

"You are certain this is an Iranian missile? It would be tragic to learn later that it was merely a missile made to look like one of theirs."

"It is an Iranian missile, sir," Hofi assured him. "We have confirmed the identity with multiple factors."

"What about the warhead?"

"We are analyzing it now, but initial reports indicate it is Iranian, also."

"And the Americans?" Oren laid the photograph on the desk. "What about the missile that was launched against them?"

"They have not made any public statements about its identity. But they have recovered a Shahab-3 missile from a second container ship. The *Amazon Cloud*."

Oren's forehead wrinkled in a frown. "Another missile with a nuclear warhead?"

"Yes, Mr. Prime Minister."

"And the telemetry confirms this identity as well?"

"Yes." Hofi took a seat in front of the desk.

"That would make three missiles in total. All of them armed with nuclear warheads. These people must be stopped. But I want to be as certain as possible where these came from before we respond."

"That is why I am here."

"There is more?"

"Mr. Prime Minister, the Americans sent a team to upstate New

York hoping to find traces of radioactive fallout from the detonation over Washington."

"What did they find?"

"They took samples from snow on one of the mountains. Mount Marcy. They have confirmed high levels of radiation consistent with fallout produced by material from the reactors at Bushehr."

Oren sat up straight. His eyes were alert. "You are certain of this?"

"Yes. According to the analysis, the material in the bomb that detonated over America came from Reactor Three at Bushehr."

"An Iranian nuclear attack on the United States," Oren sighed. He sagged back in his chair and put his hand to his mouth. "This is unbelievable," he whispered. His eyes darted back to Hofi. "Have they prepared a response?"

"Not yet." Hofi shook his head. "I am told they are just now briefing the president."

Oren sat up straight once more. "Then we must be ready to act."

"Will you need me to brief the cabinet?"

"I will telephone you when they are assembled."

59

BEIJING, CHINA

MING SHAO SAT IN THE REAR of a Hongqi limousine and looked out through the window at the shops and houses as they passed by. The car was a tight fit for the narrow streets of the oldest section of the city, but Ming enjoyed visiting the neighborhood and did so at every opportunity. Seeing the traditional wooden buildings gave him a sense of the past and reminded him of the ancient heritage that was his. He was one of a long line of presidents, party chairmen, and emperors stretching back over thousands of years. Unlike his counterparts in other countries, Ming's predecessors were ruling millions at a time when Europe was still inhabited by uncivilized hordes and North America was home to none but roving bands of hunters and gatherers.

The telephone in the car sounded, interrupting Ming's thoughts. His assistant, Yong Shu, answered it. After a brief conversation, he hung up and turned to Ming. "Quan Ji would like to brief you."

"When?"

"As soon as we return to the office."

"Has something happened?"

"I did not ask."

"You should have asked." Ming was irritated by the call and the obvious change in schedule it necessitated. "How else will we know if it is urgent?"

"Even if I had asked," Yong countered, "he would not have told me. Are not all of Quan Ji's briefings urgent?"

Ming smiled. "I see your point."

The car continued down the street and wound its way back to the Zhongnanhai compound. Twenty minutes later, Ming climbed from the car and walked through the entrance to the presidential office complex. Yong Shu brought his briefcase and followed.

They entered the office suite from the rear. Ming took a seat behind the desk and straightened his jacket. When he was ready, Yong Shu opened the door for Quan Ji to enter.

"Mr. President," Quan bowed and began. "I am sorry to interrupt your day." He moved quickly from the door and stood in front of the desk. "But this could not wait."

Ming gave him a tight smile. "There are new developments?"

"Yes." He took a seat across from the desk. "At your direction, our operatives followed Franz Heinrich during his trip to Tehran."

"And what did we learn?"

Quan looked grim. "It is as we suspected."

"They wish to divert Iran's oil production to German control?"

Quan nodded. "Their entire production."

The muscles in Ming's jaw flexed. "It is bad enough that the Russians are trying to steal it." He took a deep breath. "How did they convince the Iranians to do this?"

"They expect retaliation from Israel or the United States, or both," Quan explained, "and they are prepared to offer the protection of the German Army."

"The German Army," Ming scoffed. "They have no protection to offer from American ICBMs."

"They told Ardakan they have a missile defense system which they are willing to deploy."

"They have an American missile defense system. They are worried only about the Americans and the Israelis?" Ming's voice belied his growing anger. "They do not fear reprisal from us?"

Quan shook his head. "Heinrich told Ardakan we are not a threat to the region."

Ming's eyes were ablaze. "And on what basis did he make such a preposterous claim?"

"Germany thinks we have oil reserves that will cover only four months of consumption. And that we cannot reach Iran with ground forces within that time."

"Idiots!" Ming screamed. "They lied to me." He banged his fist against the desktop. "Mueller and Heinrich both lied to me." He looked over at Quan. "Who else knows of this?"

"You, me, General Hu, the operatives on the ground. And our analysts who prepared the written report."

"We should discuss this with General Hu." Ming pressed a button on the telephone panel. A moment later, the office door opened and Yong Shu appeared. Ming looked up at him. "Ask General Hu to come to my office."

"Yes, Mr. President." Yong slipped out and closed the door.

When he was gone, Quan continued. "You were right, Mr. President." He slid forward in his chair and leaned closer to the desk. "Your assessment of the German position was precisely correct."

"I would have preferred to be found totally wrong," Ming muttered. "How long will our current supplies last?"

"Iran supplies twenty percent of our oil. Loss of their production would inhibit availability throughout the country. Everyone would feel the effects of a shortage. But if we tap our strategic reserve we can survive a year without encountering severe economic consequences."

Ming had a questioning look. "Depleting the strategic reserve?"

"Yes," Quan nodded. "Maintaining consumption at current levels, without imports from Iran or some other source to replace them, would deplete the strategic reserve in twelve months."

"So," Ming mused, "we have twelve months to find alternative sources."

"That is correct."

Ming looked away. "Those Germans are treacherous," he seethed. His voice was low, his eyes cold. "They made promises which they had no intention of keeping."

"Even if we find alternative sources, Germany will control Iranian oil production. Their fuel costs will drop, while our own costs will soar."

While they were talking, General Hu had entered the room. He joined the conversation as he came to the desk. "And worse still," he added. "We will be purchasing oil from the Germans and funding their economy at our expense." He stood near Quan's chair. "Our annual growth will be severely limited."

Ming turned to him. "You share Quan Ji's pessimism about our situation?"

"We must strike at once, Mr. President."

Ming nodded. "You are moving forward with planning?"

"Yes," General Hu smiled.

"How much time do you need to finish your plans?"

"Three days."

"Too long," Ming replied in a resolute tone. "We shall reconvene the Commission in two days. I shall expect a complete plan at that time."

"Yes." Hu bowed. "We shall be ready."

60

OFFUTT AIR FORCE BASE
OMAHA, NEBRASKA

PETE RIOS STEPPED FROM THE GULFSTREAM jet and surveyed the flat Nebraska plain. A hangar stood directly ahead him. Nearby were rows of warehouses and utility buildings. But straight ahead, beyond the hangar, he could see all the way to the horizon. He'd been there before, in this exact same spot with the same incredible view, on the day terrorists flew airplanes into the World Trade Center in New York and the Pentagon in Washington, D.C. He'd flown out to brief the president on that horrible tragedy. Now he was back again. He would have preferred to spend the day right where he was, enjoying the view and the cool breeze that occasionally tousled his hair, but he had a duty and no choice but to press forward.

He held a leather satchel, the same one he'd carried to the briefing on September 11. Tattered and scuffed, it had been a graduation gift from his father when he completed law school. He'd carried it with him ever since. The flap at the top was held closed by two leather straps that buckled against the side. There was no lock or coded latch for security—just Rios' hand wound tightly around the handle. He liked it that way. In a world where information moved at the speed of light, carrying briefing documents in that simple, well-worn leather satchel reminded him that historic decisions were entrusted to the intellect and emotion of humans. Destiny rested on the shoulders of mankind, not on data spit from a machine.

With the satchel firmly in his grip, he walked quickly to a black SUV waiting on the tarmac just off the base's main runway. Ten minutes later, the SUV came to a stop outside the president's residence on General's Row. An aide met him at the door. Braxton Kittrell, the president's chief of staff, ushered him into the first-floor study. President Hedges was seated at his desk.

"Mr. Rios, I wish I could say I'm glad to see you." Hedges stood. "But I'm not sure any president is ever glad to see the director of NEST." The two men shook hands.

Rios smiled politely. "My sentiments exactly, Mr. President."

"Have a seat." Hedges gestured to a chair near the desk. "Can I get you anything? Coffee? A bottle of water?"

"No, sir. I'm fine."

Hedges looked past Rios and caught the aide's eye. "Tell them we're ready." The aide left the room. Hedges took a seat at the desk. "I have invited the national security team to join us."

"Certainly." Rios took a seat and did his best to relax. "No reason not to brief everyone at once."

Kittrell sat in a chair to his left. "Having everyone out here in the same location has changed the process. Since they're here and easy to reach, we thought we might as well make the most of it."

Hoyt Moore entered the room. He was followed by Lauren Lehman, Carl Coulliette, and Russ Williams. They brought chairs with them and sat around the desk. Rios was caught off-guard by the informality.

"It's okay," Hedges assured him. "We don't have room to keep enough chairs in here all the time, and we don't have the staff to move them in and out for us."

"Besides," Moore spoke up, "folks on the East Coast are living a sparse life. Carrying our own chairs is a small reminder of what they face."

"So," Hedges looked over at Rios. "Tell us what we need to know."

"Mr. President, as you've already been told, in the days following the detonation over Washington, we asked the Coast Guard to deploy their aircraft from Florida to patrol along the eastern seaboard in an attempt to capture and track airborne radioactive fallout from the explosion."

"Yes," Hedges nodded. "I signed the order approving that action and I've been briefed about the *Amazon Cloud*."

"We also sent a team into the mountains of upstate New York in the hope that we could find radioactive fallout in the early snowfall. We were hoping to find enough to allow us to ascertain a signature for the material used in the bomb—characteristics that would allow us to determine its point of origin."

"And you found what you were looking for?"

"Yes, sir. The team took samples from the southern face of Mount Marcy. Our analysis of those samples indicates the material in the bomb that was detonated over Washington, D.C., was produced by Reactor Three at the Bushehr Nuclear Power Plant in Bushehr, Iran."

Everyone in the room took a deep breath. Hedges leaned forward. He propped his elbows on the desktop and laced his fingers together. His eyes were focused on Rios. "You are certain of this?"

"Yes, Mr. President."

"Who did the analysis?"

"Jim Owens."

"I know him," Russ Williams interjected. "Good man. Works at MIT."

Hedges' attention was still focused on Rios. "Can we get a peer review of Dr. Owens' work?"

"Yes, sir ... I suppose." Rios had not anticipated any skepticism about the finding. "Jim Owens is a man of worldwide renown. His credentials are impeccable. His reputation is above reproach."

"I'm sure he's well-qualified, but we can't afford a mistake."

"I think we need to consider options," Lehman suggested, "assuming we can verify Dr. Owens' evaluation."

Hedges glanced in her direction. "What kind of options?"

"Whether we strike back, or—"

Kittrell interrupted. "I think we're beyond any discussion of whether we strike back. The only question is what we hit and how hard."

"Are we certain we know who attacked us?" Lehman argued. "Certain enough to launch a nuclear counterstrike?"

Kittrell pulled his jacket closed in the front. "As certain as—"

"Mr. President," Rios continued, ignoring the argument developing around him, "we have verified that the missile onboard the *Amazon Cloud* is an Iranian Shahab-3 with a nuclear warhead. The Israelis have determined that the missile launched against them was the same kind. Telemetry from the missile launched against us is consistent with a Shahab, also. And, we have analysis linking the warhead fired against us with a reactor in Iran. There is little doubt where these weapons came from."

Hedges leaned back in his chair. "But we still don't know if the attack was done with the direct involvement of the Iranian government."

Lehman gave a heavy sigh. She turned sideways and leaned against the arm of her chair. Rios reached inside his satchel and took out a photograph. "Mr. President, this was taken a few days ago in Alexandria, Egypt." He laid the photo on the desk. Hedges leaned forward to look at it. The others rose from their chairs and gathered around.

"Who is this?"

"This is Nasser Hamid," Rios explained. "The Israelis have been tracking him for some time. He came to our attention several months ago."

Moore elaborated. "We believe he's the mastermind behind a number of attacks against our embassies, and several other key sites that were hit over the last two or three years. He has links to key Iranian government officials."

"His primary relationship," Rios continued, "is believed to be with Adnan Karroubi, a powerful member of the Assembly of Experts and a friend of Hamid's father."

"So, he is working with the support of the Iranian government," Hedges said, thoughtfully, "but not as an official representative."

"Correct," Rios nodded. "We believe they fund him and that he has procured essential components for their nuclear program, but he is not an employee."

"Sounds like the CIA," Lehman said with a snide tone.

"Or the State Department," Kittrell chided.

Williams shook his head. "Doing nothing is simply not an option, Mr. President. We've been hit by a nuclear bomb. Someone fired a missile at us and took out the eastern half of the country. If we're not going to respond to this attack, is there any attack we would respond to?"

"Not responding will show the world we are weak," Lehman added. "That we have capitulated. That we are no longer the world's only military superpower."

"We are weak," Hedges said, softly. "But there is more at stake here. The world's markets are already fragile from what has happened. If we launch a nuclear strike against Iran—and that's what we're all talking about here—leveling Tehran. If we do that, it will disrupt markets for everyone, and not just the oil market. The entire world economy could collapse." He pointed to the photograph. "Do we have any way of capturing this guy ... Nasser Hamid?"

"We have not been successful following him on our own," Moore replied. "All of our intelligence about him comes from other sources, primarily Mossad. The FBI has a few agents in the region who have some information. The office in New York had a file on him, but no one knows where he is right now."

"And there's one more thing," Rios added. "The Israelis believe he has purchased a U.S. passport."

Hedges frowned. "He's coming here?"

"Perhaps."

"Why would he purchase a U.S. passport if he wasn't coming here?"

"It makes travel much easier," Kittrell suggested. "An American passport carries with it the reliability of our certification process. People instinctively trust it as an authentic document."

"We'll tag it and shut him down," Lehman asserted.

"Our office has already warned State," Rios said. "And we've asked for Interpol's help."

Lehman glared at him. "You can do that without asking us?"

"I'm the director of NEST," Rios said, calmly. "I can draw on any resource I deem necessary."

61

BAVARIA, GERMANY

LATE THAT AFTERNOON Josef Mueller sat in an upstairs parlor in the main house at Blomenburg, an estate in the Bavarian countryside that had been owned by his family since the time of the Holy Roman Empire. Mueller used it as a retreat from the hectic pace of life in Berlin and as a location for private meetings.

Dressed in brown wool slacks, a white shirt, and tan cardigan sweater, he relaxed on a sofa and sipped from a cup of tea. He checked his watch. Andre Pierlot, the Belgian foreign minister, was due any minute. If Pierlot's report was good news, Germany might soon be free of its NATO shackles. The thought of that sent a smile across Mueller's face.

NATO, the brainchild of Roosevelt and Churchill, had been foisted upon Europe at the end of World War II when no one on the continent had the will or power to resist. German leaders, cowering in fear of Soviet domination, were all too eager to embrace America's offer of protection. Germans found consolation in America's promise of defense, but they paid for it with their national pride and their wealth. With the signing of the NATO treaty, the economy and foreign policy were chained to the whims of America's own best interests. Germany was reduced to little more than a pet on the lap of American consumerism.

Mueller was certain that Hitler had been right—Germany was destined to rule the world. But Hitler had been wrong to think fascism could produce that result, and he'd been a fool to waste time on ethnic cleansing. Jews were not the enemy of the German state. They represented one of Germany's best assets. "They should not have been forced to labor in concentration camps," Mueller would say when he'd had too much to drink. "They should have been let loose to make money. And then we'd all be rich."

From outside, Mueller heard the sound of a car approaching in the driveway below. It came to a stop near the side entrance to the house and a car door opened. Voices filtered in through the window, then there were footsteps in the hallway.

An aide appeared in the parlor doorway. "Mr. Pierlot to see you, Mr. Chancellor."

"Show him in." Mueller rose from the chair and straightened his sweater. Pierlot's footsteps echoed in the hall. Then he was at the door.

"Chancellor Mueller," he called as he entered the room. "What a wonderful house you have."

Mueller crossed the room toward him. "Yes. It is a great place to get away." The two men shook hands. Mueller gestured toward a chair near the sofa. "Come. Have a seat."

When they were seated, a butler appeared with tea and cakes. They ate while they talked.

"I have good news, and not so good news," Pierlot began.

"What did you find?"

"The original six—Belgium, France, Italy, Luxembourg, the Netherlands, and Germany, of course, would all follow your lead. The others are split. Half of them are undecided, the other half are adamantly opposed."

Mueller smiled. "That makes it workable."

"Yes." Pierlot nodded. "Six votes in favor, with a split of the others, means the vote would carry."

"What is the bad news?"

Pierlot turned serious. "The United Kingdom is prepared to withdraw at merely the suggestion of such action."

"They are withdrawing now?"

"Not now." Pierlot shook his head. "But if the issue is raised formally for a decision by the European Parliament or the Council, they will withdraw from the Union."

"They were never very much a part of us anyway."

"My sentiments exactly. It would be worth the trouble to raise the issue for no other reason than to move them out."

Mueller lifted the teacup from its saucer. "The ones who are adamantly opposed, will they stay if we vote to withdraw from NATO?" He took a sip.

"I am not sure." Pierlot sat back in his chair. "Poland, Romania, and Slovakia are worried the most. They fear that without NATO they will come under Russian domination almost by default."

"They may be right," Mueller nodded. "But none of them are pro-American in their response?"

"Only Spain, Sweden, and Ireland. But that is more from a sense of moral obligation. Privately, they understand the situation."

"And what is their understanding of the situation?"

"They think an American response is only a matter of time. And when it comes, it will draw all of the NATO nations into a war in the Middle East—one that will very quickly put them on the opposite side of a conflict with China."

"China?" Mueller had a puzzled frown. "They are worried about China?"

"Yes."

"They think China will respond to an American move against

Iran?"

"They think China will have no choice but to protect its access to Middle Eastern oil," Pierlot explained. "And when the Chinese make that move, they will attempt to occupy the entire region. A NATO obligation would force European countries to support the Americans."

"So, Spain, Sweden, and Ireland are prepared to side with the United States?"

"No. You misunderstand," Pierlot corrected. "When asked about the possibility of withdrawing from NATO, they expressed a pro-American position. They identify membership in NATO with support for America. They are willing to defend the United States, and that would be their public position, but privately, they fear that doing so would put them at odds with the Chinese."

"You agree with that assessment?"

"I agree that China is a problem."

"I am not so sure," Mueller replied with a sly grin.

62

BERLIN, GERMANY

THE LEARJET CARRYING FRANZ HEINRICH home from Tehran touched down at the Berlin-Schönefeld Airport and rolled to a stop at a private hangar. Heinrich alit from the plane and made his way to a Mercedes sedan parked just beyond the tip of the wing. A driver held the rear door open as he slid onto the backseat.

When he was in place, the car started slowly across the tarmac. Before they were past the hangar, Heinrich's cell phone rang. The call was from Hermann Schroeder.

"I hope your trip was successful."

"It went as well as might be expected."

"We need to talk."

"So, talk."

"There is an ALDI Nord warehouse down the runway from where your plane is parked. Have your driver bring you there. We will talk in private."

Heinrich leaned forward and gave instructions to the driver. They arrived at the warehouse a few minutes later. Schroeder was seated in a car parked near the building. Heinrich joined him. "What is so urgent?"

"I received a visit from David Hoag."

"I am sorry," Heinrich replied. "I am not aware of such a person."

"He is an American," Schroeder explained. "Officially listed as a professor at Georgetown University. Actually, he works for the CIA."

"What did the CIA want?"

"He was asking about the container that was loaded onto the *Panama Clipper*." Schroeder looked across the seat at Heinrich. "This is the problem I wanted to discuss with you before you left."

"This is not a problem." Heinrich shook his head. "This is one man asking questions."

"How can you be certain?"

"If it were a problem, they would have raised the matter another way."

"I think it is a problem," Schroeder sighed.

"Do you know where he is staying?"

"The Brandenburger Hotel."

"Leave it to me. I will take care of it."

"You are certain you want to be directly involved?"

"I was directly involved in the problem." Heinrich reached for the door handle. "I might as well be involved in the solution."

Schroeder grasped his arm. "We must stop this before it goes any further."

"I am well aware of that."

"If you do not end it, I will have to."

"I understand." Heinrich opened the door and stepped from the car.

—— (((——

After the meeting with Schroeder, Heinrich rode to the Chancellor's office. He waited outside the door while Mueller completed a meeting. A few minutes later, Max Brody, the president of Bundesbank, emerged from the office followed by Raimund Geerken, the finance minister. They both appeared grim and worried. Heinrich looked up as Brody passed.

"Max," Heinrich offered in a friendly voice, but Brody barely acknowledged him as he brushed past.

When they were gone, Heinrich rose from his chair and walked into the office. Mueller stood at the window. Heinrich crossed the room toward him. "What is wrong with Max?" He gestured over his shoulder. "He and Geerken looked rather glum."

"They always look that way." Mueller turned away from the window. "How was your trip?"

"Good. No problems at all."

"Oh?" Mueller looked surprised. "All went well? They agreed?"

"Just as you requested." Heinrich had a questioning look. "Is something going on?"

"No. Not really." Mueller's eyes darted away. "I have been tending to business. You saw Kermani?"

"No," Heinrich said, shaking his head. "I met with Ardakan, the foreign minister."

"Oh." Mueller arched an eyebrow. "And what did he say?"

"They will agree to sell their entire production to us for one Euro per barrel more than spot market prices." Mueller raised an eyebrow. "Yes," Heinrich nodded, acknowledging Mueller's response. "It is a high price. But we got the deal we wanted."

"You told them we would take it?"

"Yes. Was that not what you wanted?"

"Anything to keep it out of the hands of the Chinese—at least for now. Is there a formal agreement?"

"Not yet. But the oil is moving our way now. Our traders are executing buy orders."

"Good."

Heinrich was still concerned. "Are you certain all is well? Brody and Geerken did not seem themselves."

"It will be fine," Mueller reassured him. "Let me tend to them."
He took a seat and propped his feet on the desk. "You spoke to
Schroeder?"

"Yes."

"He told you about the problem in Bremerhaven?"

"You should not get involved with that," Heinrich cautioned.

"We took care of it."

"We?"

"Hermann," he shrugged. "I do not know the details."

Anger swept over Heinrich. He had told Schroeder to leave this
until he returned. Instead he had gone ahead with it, and involved
the chancellor as well. Heinrich took a deep breath and did his best
to hide his emotions. "You handled it? All of it?"

"Except for the American."

Heinrich wondered what more they had done but he let the issue
pass and focused on the matter at hand. "Leave the American to me.
I will take care of it." He shook his head. "You should know nothing
of this."

"You were gone," Mueller said, sheepishly. "I had to take care of it."

"It could not wait until I returned?"

"We cannot afford any leaks. No one must know of our plans."
Mueller's eyes bore into Heinrich. "Germany is about to achieve her
destiny—her rightful place as the head of all the nations. Do you
believe that?"

"I believe we are a great people," Heinrich said, slowly.

"Now is our time," Mueller's eyes still focused on Heinrich. "Are you
coming with me, Franz? Are you with me on these things I must do?"

"Yes," Heinrich nodded. "As I told you before, I will come with
you."

"Good." Mueller grinned. "I have always counted on you."

63

TEHRAN, IRAN

ADNAN KARROUBI SAT AT A TABLE in the corner of Khayyam Restaurant, a traditional café located near the bazaar. Dressed in a gray robe and turban, he sipped tea alone and listened to the conversations around him. The restaurant was crowded and busy. No one paid him any attention.

In a little while, Hasan Dirbaz entered and made his way to the table. He took a seat across from Karroubi. "He has arrived in Podgorica," Dirbaz said flatly.

"Did they follow him?"

"Yes. He went to the Banka Montenegro."

"Were they able to seize the account?"

"No." Dirbaz's gaze shifted. "They were not successful."

"Why not?"

Dirbaz looked troubled. "Zoran Tadic was there."

Karroubi's eyes were wide. "Tadic is in Montenegro?"

"Yes."

"And working at a bank?" Karroubi was incredulous. "How could this happen?"

"Apparently, they do not know his background."

"And apparently neither do we." Karroubi's tone was biting. "Where is the money now?"

"The transaction cleared through Rome. It was briefly in a bank in Madrid, then it was transferred to Andorra and now we do not know where it is."

"It is lost," Karroubi sighed. He banged the table with his fist in frustration.

A waiter hurried to his side, looking nervous and worried, apparently well aware of Karroubi's identity. "You wish something, sir?"

"No. It is nothing."

"Actually," Dirbaz spoke up. "I would like some coffee."

"Yes." The waiter bowed. "Right away."

When he was gone, Dirbaz looked over at Karroubi. "They are awaiting instructions. What shall we tell them?"

"Finish it," Karroubi said in disgust. He wiped his mouth on a napkin and tossed it on the table. "Tell them to finish it. If they fail, tell them not to return." He scooted back his chair and stood. "Enjoy your coffee," he growled.

64

MOWCOW, RUSSIA

OLEG BATALOV SAT QUIETLY in the rear of an Audi sedan as the driver maneuvered it through the evening traffic. Seated next to him was a young woman less than half his age. Unlike some the agency had sent, this one was truly an escort. She smiled all the time and when she laughed it sounded genuine, even infectious. He would ask for her again, he was certain—if only he could remember her name.

Thirty minutes later, the car came to a stop outside Fabrika, a popular Moscow nightclub. Batalov stepped from the car and offered the young woman his hand. She took it and moved effortlessly from the seat to the sidewalk. Men loitering outside the club stopped and stared at her. Batalov felt his chest swell with pride as he led her toward the door. *I am paying for an evening with her. I might as well act like we belong together.*

The event that evening at Fabrika was a party held in honor of Rolan Lebedeff, a producer and key player in Russia's burgeoning motion picture industry. He was celebrating the completion of his latest film. His wife, Marina Kedrova, a celebrated Russian actress, was one of the stars of the movie, which featured many of the country's best actors. A Russian power couple, any party where Lebedeff and Kedrova were present was sure to bring out the wealthiest of Moscow society. Batalov had built much of his business following the party circuit. He hoped to make new contacts this evening through which he could obtain additional clients.

Inside the club, he made the rounds with his escort, greeting familiar faces and meeting new ones. As the evening wore on, the music grew loud and the dance floor began to fill. Batalov relinquished his date to the company of younger men and found a table near the bar. He was on his third drink when Anatolyn Luzhkov wandered past. Luzhkov was chief of staff to Vladimir Vostok. He and Batalov had worked closely together.

Luzhkov took a seat at Batalov's table and ordered a drink. "Oleg, how is business?"

"I am doing well. Thanks to you and my friend Vladimir." He raised his glass in a toast. "To the president."

"Yes," Luzhkov chuckled. "To the president." He took a sip and set the glass on the table. "I hear you are working on that project in Tehran."

Batalov nodded. "I returned from there yesterday."

"Everything is going well?"

"I was meaning to ask you about that." Batalov scooted his chair closer. "While I was in Tehran, I ran into Franz Heinrich." Batalov leaned closer and lowered his voice even more. "Now, I want to know—am I going to have competition for the new pipeline contract?"

"I ... I do not know," Luzhkov stammered. "I have not heard of—"

"If I am, I can lower my bid." Batalov's eyes danced playfully. "Perhaps sweeten it for some of the officials."

Luzhkov looked concerned. "You think Heinrich was in Tehran because of the pipeline?"

"I do not know," Batalov shrugged. "I assumed he was. He was meeting with Foreign Minister Abadeh Ardakan. It must have been important. They appeared rather serious."

"You are certain it was Franz Heinrich?"

"Oh, it was him, all right. I do not know him, personally. We have never met. But I know who he is and I have seen photographs." He took a sip from his glass. "It was him."

"Interesting." Luzhkov pushed back from the table. "Will you excuse me?"

"Certainly." Luzhkov stood. Batalov called after him, "You will find out about the competition?"

"I will see what I can do about it."

Batalov took another sip from his glass and watched as Luzhkov made his way past the dance floor to the exit.

65

BERLIN, GERMANY

IN SPITE OF THE LONG DAY and the late hour, Franz Heinrich returned to his office to catch up on details he'd missed while away in Tehran. The office was dark and quiet when he arrived. He switched on a lamp at his desk and logged on to his computer. Using an access code available only to system administrators, he entered the Bundesbank Web site and scrolled through Max Brody's email account. Then he switched to the Finance Ministry's site and checked an account for Raimund Geerken. Buried in a deleted file he found a draft of a statement written for Geerken.

Heinrich skimmed through the message and read it to himself. "Consistent with our obligation to provide a secure banking and financial system ... we are announcing today ... suspending acquisition of further U.S. debt. Henceforth, we shall not participate in this month's U.S. Treasury auction." He scrolled through the files and found three more versions of the same statement.

This is what they were talking about today in Mueller's office. This is why they were so upset.

Since the attack on the United States, speculation had grown about what would happen when current U.S. debt instruments matured and came up for renewal at auction. Heinrich had tried to broach the subject with Mueller but had gotten nowhere. Now he knew why. They were going ahead with the agreements reached in earlier meetings with Russian and Chinese officials. Those meetings had addressed the notion of no longer supporting America's need to borrow, but they had been held before the ...

Heinrich's eyes opened wide with a look of realization. *He knew they were going to attack. Mueller knew it. He was not surprised that the cargo container with the missile inside was passing through Bremerhaven. He was surprised that someone found it. He was not merely maneuvering Russia and China to flank American monetary policy, he knew the attack was coming and wanted to be in position for this very announcement.*

If Mueller knew in advance about the attack on America, then it could mean only one thing. The German chancellor was in league with Muslim radicals to bring down the United States. He ran his fingers along his jaw. *And they can do it, too. This is all the Muslims need—a legitimate government that goes along with their insane ideas. That is why he asked me if I was with him. He is assessing the liability and wondering if I can be trusted.*

A chill ran up Heinrich's spine. For the first time, the full weight of what had happened fell on him. And he was afraid.

The deal he'd just negotiated with Iran would cut off China from one of its major oil suppliers. It would also end Russian plans to transport Iranian oil by pipeline to Europe. *China and Russia will see this as an act of war.* Suddenly Heinrich realized the earlier agreements Mueller reached—to inject cash and support Russian and Chinese losses, to support the price and availability of oil, and now the lack of support for U.S. debt—were all part of a plan to destroy not just the United States economy, but the economies of Germany's major rivals. It was a strategy that would leave Germany as the lone economic superpower. *But it will never work. If I figured this out, someone in Russia and China will, too. And when they do, they will not sit by and watch it happen.*

Lost in thought, Heinrich stared at the monitor and tried to think of a way to stop events now set to unfold. If he confronted Mueller, he would do as he'd done before—simply ignore his warning. Then he would send Hermann Schroeder to dispose of him, as they had tied up the loose ends in Bremerhaven. "Schroeder," he sighed. Then he remembered the conversation they'd had earlier that day about David Hoag.

Heinrich sat up straight and moved his chair closer to the desk. If Schroeder was right, and David Hoag worked for the CIA, perhaps Hoag could help him.

Still in the system as an administrator, he accessed the Federal Police site and searched their files for information about David Hoag. What he found confirmed Schroeder's earlier statements. Hoag did indeed work for the CIA. But Heinrich also found something else even more alarming.

Schroeder's archives were loaded with files taken from several top-secret CIA sites, along with emails to and from Peter Burke at a CIA address. Heinrich was astounded. *The two systems are not compatible for that kind of access. You cannot get to those sites without accessing the CIA system with a CIA user name. You have to...* And then Heinrich remembered.

Several months earlier, he'd been scheduled to travel to Santiago, Chile, for a conference. Mueller met with him shortly before he departed and noted that the Americans were sending Peter Burke from the CIA to the same meeting. Mueller suggested he make a point of meeting Burke as "a useful contact we might need in the future."

Heinrich and Burke had met briefly, just before the conference ended. Burke, it turned out, was friends with Schroeder and asked Mueller to deliver an envelope to him. It had seemed an odd coincidence at the time, but Heinrich did as he was asked. Schroeder was giddy with excitement when Heinrich told him about the meeting. So excited he showed Heinrich the contents of the envelope. "A smart card," he'd announced, holding it up for Heinrich to see. "It generates a new electronic password each time you use it. With this," he gloated, "I can access the secrets of the world, and no one will ever know I was in the files." At the time, Heinrich had dismissed the remark as simply more Schroeder hyperbole. Now he was certain it was far more serious and he was sure Peter Burke was a German mole in the CIA.

Shaken and worried by what he'd found, Heinrich switched off the lamp on his desk and made his way to the corridor outside his office. Rooms on the floor were deserted and as he walked to the elevator he felt his heart rate quicken. When the doors opened at the parking garage, he stood motionless at the back of the elevator and listened intently for the slightest hint that someone was lurking just around the corner. His eyes focused on the walls, searching for the faintest traces of a shadow. He let the door close, then pressed a button to open it again. As the doors moved apart, he found himself staring at his driver. Heinrich's heart skipped a beat.

The driver looked worried. "Is everything all right, Herr Heinrich?"

"Yes, fine," Heinrich sighed, relieved to see a familiar face and glad to find the threat existed only in his mind. He followed the driver to the car and rode in silence across the city to his home.

Nadja was fast asleep when he stepped into the bedroom. He slipped off his suit and hung it on a clothes rack in the corner, then crawled in bed beside her. She awakened as he pulled her close.

"You are back," she said, her voice groggy.

"Yes, I am back."

"How was your trip?"

"Long." He nestled his face in her hair. "How was your day?"

"Good, but lonely."

"I am sorry you were alone."

"It is all right now."

"Did anyone call?"

"Just a wrong number," she said sleepily, "and several hang-ups."

He held her close, listening as her breathing slowed to the measured, rhythmic cadence of sleep. Finally he rolled on his back and looked up at the ceiling. Once again, his thoughts turned to Mueller and the events that were about to unfold. Somehow, someway, Mueller had to be stopped. His mind raced as he struggled to figure out how.

66

MOSCOW, RUSSIA

VLADIMIR VOSTOK WALKED PAST the iron gates and into the portal beneath the eastern wing of the Kremlin Senate building. Commissioned by Catherine the Great, the building had been constructed as a home to the Russian legislature. Later, it was converted to office space. Since the collapse of the Soviet Union, it housed the official offices of the Russian president.

As Vostok made his way across the inner courtyard, Anatolyn Luzhkov, his chief of staff, came to his side.

"Good morning," Vostok smiled at him. "How was the party last night?"

"Very good, until I met your friend Oleg Batalov."

"Oh? What happened? He had too much to drink?"

"Not when I left, but it was early."

"You look worried about something," Vostok chided. "What are you worried about?"

A guard opened the door at the main entrance. They stepped inside the building. Luzhkov pulled Vostok into a room to the right. "Oleg has just returned from Tehran."

"He got the contract," Vostok beamed. "That is good. We should ask him to employ a few of our people."

"Not now." Luzhkov waved his hand in frustration. "While Oleg was in Tehran he saw Franz Heinrich."

"Heinrich?" Vostok had a puzzled frown. "What was he doing there?"

"He was meeting with Abadeh Ardakan."

Vostok's expression turned serious. "You are certain of this?"

"Yes. Oleg saw him in the hotel. Oleg asked me about it because he thought Heinrich was there to discuss the pipeline he is bidding on. Heinrich was worried the Germans might underbid him. He wanted to know if I knew anything about it."

"Why was Heinrich really there?"

"I spent half the night trying to find out, and I still do not know. But I think we must find out quickly."

"Do you think they will try to interfere with our arrangement for the sale of Iranian oil?" Deep furrows creased Vostok's brow. "Are they bold enough, or stupid enough, to try to cut us off?"

"I think if Heinrich was in Iran it could only be for the purpose of discussing energy. Either nuclear or oil."

Vostok's countenance brightened. The muscles in his face relaxed. "Ask Gennady Panova what he knows about this. He is our ambassador to Germany. Let him earn his pay." Vostok patted Luzhkov on the shoulder. "Perhaps he can meet with the chancellor to inquire about our oil contracts. Their guaranteed purchases from us were part of the reason we wanted the pipeline."

"Do you think they know we were planning to flood them with Iranian oil?"

"I do not know, but I have never trusted the Germans. They have always dealt poorly with us."

"If they suspected we were trying to take advantage of them, they might see it as an attempt to sabotage their economy. Especially in light of market conditions now. Everything is more fragile. Everyone is on edge."

"Relax," Vostok smiled. "I am certain it is nothing." He turned to leave, then glanced back over his shoulder. "But check it out, just to be sure."

67

BERLIN, GERMANY

THE FOLLOWING MORNING, Franz Heinrich awakened with a sense of dread. Josef Mueller, his lifelong friend, was embarked on a plan that would plunge the world into chaos, all for the sake of achieving the long-awaited German national destiny.

As he lay quietly beside Nadja, his mind ran back to a time when he and Mueller were boys. They were walking to the theater on Saturday morning, just the two of them. As they made their way up the sidewalk, Avishai Geffen, a boy about their age, came running toward them. Mueller took Heinrich by the arm. "Do not tell him where we are going."

"Why not?"

"I do not want that stinking Jew tagging along with us."

As it turned out, Geffen said nothing of coming with them. He only wanted to tell them he was going to a soccer match with his father. Heinrich and Mueller kept walking and Geffen ran back to his house. "Stupid Jew," Mueller giggled. "How does he know he even has a father? They breed like rats." Mueller's racial slurs had stabbed Heinrich in the heart, and though he kept quiet at the time, he had thought of that moment often since.

As the childhood memory faded from his mind, Heinrich's eyes wandered across the bedroom to a photograph in a frame on the dresser. A man wearing a suit with a broad-brimmed hat was standing next to a woman wearing a cotton dress and heavy overcoat. Both of them were holding small suitcases. They were Amos and Milli Lerner, and they were Heinrich's grandparents. Standing behind them was a German soldier in full regalia, a broad smile on his face.

The picture had been taken in November 1937, as Amos and Milli were leaving for what they had been told was "resettlement in a new and better place." Transportation had been arranged by the German government. They were being moved "for their own protection and to ensure a successful future for all," but they were permitted to take only one suitcase each. That new and better place turned out to be Buchenwald, one of the earliest Nazi concentration camps. The resettlement trip was a journey from which Amos, Milli, and millions of other Jews never returned.

"History is repeating itself," Heinrich whispered.

Nadja rolled on her side to face him and draped her arm over his side. "What are you saying?" she mumbled.

"Nothing." He kissed her. "Go back to sleep."

When she was once again asleep, Heinrich gently lifted her arm aside and slid from the bed. He took a robe from the chair in the corner and slipped it on, then padded down the hall to his study.

A large armoire stood along the wall to the left. Made of walnut, the finish was smooth and dark from years of use. He opened the doors and spread them wide apart. A tallit hung inside, its long fringe dangling near the bottom of the cabinet. Heinrich lifted it carefully from its place on a hook and draped it over his head, letting the ends fall across his shoulders and down his chest.

From a shelf he took a Hebrew prayer book and opened it to the reading for the *Shacharit*—the morning prayers. He began with the blessings, then read a passage from *Torah*. Then he read from *Psalm 100*. The last few lines resonated with his spirit. "For the Lord is good and his love endures forever, his faithfulness continues through all generations."

"God is faithful," Heinrich said aloud as he completed the readings. "He is good, and he is faithful. I must be faithful, too."

When he was finished, he closed the prayer book and set it on the shelf, then lifted the shawl from his head and returned it to the hook in the cabinet. As he closed the doors, he bowed his head. "Lord, give me the strength to be faithful to what you have shown me."

68

BERLIN, GERMANY

AS HE HAD DONE EACH MORNING since arriving in Berlin, David Hoag left his room at the Brandenburger Hotel and rode the elevator to the lobby, then made himself conspicuously visible in the café, the hallway, and at the bellman's desk. He was sure his escapade with Hermann Schroeder would have produced a response by now, but so far no one had tried to contact him. If that didn't happen soon, he would be forced to return to Nebraska.

In the lobby, Hoag made his way past the front desk and started toward the main entrance. As he drew near the doors, a man came from behind him and took him by the elbow.

"Someone would like a word with you," he said, pointing to a car parked outside. A bellman opened the hotel doors as they approached.

Parked at the curb was a black Mercedes. The rear door of the car opened and inside Hoag saw Franz Heinrich sitting in the backseat. Hoag climbed in beside him and closed the door.

"Sorry for the abruptness." Heinrich smiled and offered his hand. "Do you know who I am?"

"Yes." They shook hands.

"Good." Heinrich caught the driver's eye in the rearview mirror, then looked back at Hoag. "I am glad we could spend this time together." The car started forward. Heinrich kept talking. "We both share a common problem."

"Which is?"

"We know far more than others, and we can share it with almost no one."

Hoag feigned ignorance. "I have no idea what you're talking about."

"Come, Mr. Hoag. I am special assistant to the chancellor of Germany. You can speak frankly with me. I know who you are. I read your file with the German Federal Police."

Hoag was taken aback. "My file? The German Federal Police has a file on me?"

Heinrich tilted his head in a thoughtful pose and recited, "Graduate of Harvard University. Dating Jenny Freed. Friends with Dennis Kinlaw." He cut his eyes toward Hoag in a mischievous look. "A penchant for taking the president's Chris-Craft boat for a ride on the Potomac."

Hoag grinned at the last comment. "Then tell me about the cargo container that passed through Bremerhaven."

The car came to a stop. Heinrich pointed to the door. "Let us walk."

Hoag opened the car door and stepped out to find they were at the entrance to a city park. Iron gates that guarded the entrance were open and a sidewalk led past them to a manicured lawn. He followed Heinrich in that direction.

"It is true," Heinrich continued the conversation. "A dockworker discovered higher than normal radiation levels coming from one of the cargo containers. He reported it to his supervisor. They called the Federal Police. Agents responded and entered the box." He glanced over at Hoag with a piercing look. "You talked to two of the men."

"They found a launcher with a Shahab-3 missile," Hoag protested.

"And they reported it to Schroeder, who contacted me."

"And it wasn't intercepted." Hoag did little to hide his growing anger.

"No." Heinrich shook his head slowly. "It was not intercepted."

"And we were never notified."

They reached the center of the park and turned to the right. Heinrich continued to talk. "It was loaded onto the *Panama Clipper* and sent on its way to New York."

Hoag's eyes were ablaze. "You let it pass?"

Heinrich nodded. "Yes, I let it pass."

"But why?"

"Because I had orders."

"Orders from whom?" Heinrich had a knowing look, but said nothing. "Who gave you the order?" Hoag insisted.

Heinrich had a tight smile. "Who do I work for, Mr. Hoag?"

Hoag's eyes opened wide. "The chancellor," he whispered.

"And," Heinrich continued, giving Hoag little time to respond, "as troubling as that may seem, that is now the least of your worries."

Hoag was puzzled. "The least of my worries? The German chancellor allowed Muslim terrorists to attack the United States with a nuclear bomb, and that's the least of my worries?"

"Shhh." Heinrich gestured for Hoag to lower his voice.

"What could be worse than that?"

"Your great American Treasury notes are about to become worthless."

Hoag looked perplexed. "What's new about that? They've already lost most of their value. Only thing keeping them afloat at all is trading by speculators."

"They have lost their value." Heinrich raised his index finger in a pointed gesture. "Now they are about to lose their credibility."

"What do you mean?"

From across the park, lights on the car flickered. Heinrich paused. "I am afraid I must go now."

"But I need to know what you're talking about."

"We will talk more later." Heinrich patted Hoag on the shoulder. "I must go now." He started toward the car.

"When?"

Heinrich paused and turned back to face Hoag. "Perhaps you should visit the Pergamon Museum. The crowds are not too large around ten in the morning. Tomorrow would be a good day. They have an excellent section on the Ancient Near East." He called over his shoulder as he walked away, "You can get a taxi at the corner to take you back to your hotel."

69

BERLIN, GERMANY

GENNADY PANOVA, THE RUSSIAN AMBASSADOR, looked out the window of his Audi sedan. The Brandenburg Gate came into view. When the car was directly opposite it, they slowed and turned onto Linden Avenue. A few minutes later he arrived at the Chancellery and was ushered into Mueller's office.

"Mr. President," Panova said, bowing. "So good of you to see me on such short notice."

"I am always glad to accommodate you, Gennady." Mueller gestured to a chair near his desk. "Please, have a seat." Mueller moved behind the desk. "How may I help you?"

"President Vostok wanted me to ask you about the oil contracts Germany has signed with Russia."

"What about them?"

"In light of recent developments, President Vostok wanted your reassurance that Germany would still follow through on the commitments contained in those agreements."

Mueller's eyes narrowed. "Is there something we have done that has made him think we would not?"

"I believe he was merely referring to the current situation with America and the effect that has had on the markets. Nothing is the same as it once was."

"I see," Mueller replied slowly. "You tell Vladimir we intend to honor our agreement to buy Russian oil, and we expect Russia to honor her agreement to sell."

"You will not find another supplier?"

Mueller paused, for the first time realizing why Panova had raised the question. They knew about Heinrich's visit to Iran. "We have an agreement, we will honor it." He stood. "All our arrangements with Russia were made with the current situation in mind." He looked Panova in the eye. "Make certain you tell him those exact words. All our arrangements were made with the current situation in mind."

Panova was puzzled. "Those exact words? How could you have anticipated an attack on America?"

Mueller came from behind the desk. Panova stood. Mueller escorted him toward the door. "Use those exact words," he said once more. "He will know what it means."

70

BERLIN, GERMANY

NOT FAR AWAY, THOMAS GUMPERT, an electronic information security specialist, sat at his desk two levels beneath the Interior Ministry building. A computer monitor on his desk was filled with messages. He scanned the message at the top, deleted it, and moved down to the next.

According to security protocol, each time a person attempted to access an Interior Ministry electronic file, the computer system initiated a verification procedure. That procedure was designed to determine whether the person accessing the file possessed a valid security clearance that allowed them to view the material in the file, and a job assignment that established a need to know the information. Both criteria—security clearance at or above the level of the file and a specific need to know—had to be met. The need-to-know aspect was determined by use of a specific code word assigned to both the person and the file. Users were required to enter both before the file could be viewed. If the system could not electronically verify that both the clearance and the code word were assigned to the user, it denied access to the file. But some system administrators had file-access privileges without the use of a proper code word. Each time they accessed a file without using a code word, the system automatically notified the security compliance officer. Those messages were posted on Thomas' screen for manual review.

The system generated hundreds of messages each day. Clearing them was boring work, but it was a crucial part of system security. Thomas sipped from a cup of coffee and methodically worked through the list of messages that had been produced the night before. Halfway through the list he came to a message that caught his attention.

According to the automated system monitor, an administrator with a user name registered to Martin Graf accessed files at Bundesbank, the Finance Ministry, and the Federal Police. Security clearance files authenticated the name as having a sufficient security clearance and verified the user had access privileges beyond "code word only." When Thomas tried to manually access the file for Martin Graf to verify the administrator status, he encountered a security block that read, "Access Denied. Thuringia." After repeated attempts to bypass it, he contacted his supervisor, Arno Freihof.

"He has clearance for the content," Thomas explained, "but the files were accessed without reference to a code word. When I checked the user name to verify his administrator status, I ran into a block that indicated his user information was part of something called 'Thuringia.'"

"The Kingdom of Thuringia," Freihof chuckled.

Thomas was puzzled. "You know about this?"

"I know about Thuringia." Freihof smiled. "An ancient Germanic kingdom. It was crushed in the sixth century by the Franks."

"I do not think that is the meaning."

"I know what it means. I will take care of it."

"Sir, I work in system security. I thought we had access to everything."

"Almost. Do not worry about it. You told me. I know what to do. Write it up as resolved and move on."

Thomas grumbled something about following procedures as he left the room. When he was gone, Freihof picked up the phone and called Hermann Schroeder. "We've had some unauthorized access to your files."

"By whom?"

"Franz Heinrich."

Schroeder was silent for a moment, then said, "You are certain it was him?"

"Yes. The access was automatically flagged by the system. One of our security specialists attempted to clear the message from the log. To do that, he had to access the user information. An information block identified the user information as part of Thuringia."

"I will take care it," Schroeder said briskly, and ended the call.

71

BERLIN, GERMANY

AN HOUR LATER, HERMANN SCHROEDER left his office through the side door and took the elevator to the parking garage below the building. A BMW was parked three spaces away. He got behind the steering wheel, slipped on a pair of sunglasses, and drove away.

Twenty minutes later, he arrived at O$_2$ World, an indoor ice arena. He took a seat in the empty stands and watched as members of the Berlin Eisbären, a professional hockey team, practiced on the ice below. The clatter of the sticks hitting the puck echoed through the building, punctuated by the occasional shout of a team member.

Ten minutes later, Erich Giering appeared at the end of the row where Schroeder was seated. He made his way over and sat down. Schroeder talked without taking his eyes off the practice. "You followed the American?"

"Yes."

"Where did he go?"

"Nowhere unusual yesterday. Sat in the hotel lobby most of the day. Walked across the street and sat on a bench. Went to a restaurant in the next block for dinner. This morning, Franz Heinrich picked him up at the hotel. They drove to the park, went for a walk."

Schroeder continued to watch the hockey team. "What did they talk about?"

"I could not hear after they got out of the car."

"What did they say while they were in the car?"

"Heinrich asked if Hoag knew who he was. Hoag said he did. Heinrich told him he had read his police file."

Schroeder glanced in Giering's direction. "Heinrich admitted reading our file?"

"Yes. He told the American he had read it and then he told him details from the file." Giering hesitated. "You showed Franz Heinrich our file?"

"Never mind about that." Schroeder gave a dismissive flick of his wrist. "What else did they say?"

"The American said, 'Then tell me about the cargo container that passed through Bremerhaven.'"

"Did they talk about it?"

"I suppose, but that is when they got out of the car. After that, I could not hear."

A grin slowly spread across Schroeder's face. "Heinrich is smart. You are listening to Hoag's phone in the hotel?"

"Yes, but he never uses it. Except to order room service."

"I want you to stay with Heinrich."

Giering looked puzzled. "You mean the American."

Schroeder shook his head. "Heinrich. I will get someone to cover the American."

Giering did not immediately respond. Schroeder glanced over at him. "Is there a problem?"

Giering had a troubled look. "Franz Heinrich reports directly to the chancellor."

"As do I," Schroeder replied, his voice curt. "What is your point?"

Giering cleared his throat. "The chancellor authorized us to fol-low Heinrich?"

Schroeder turned in the seat to face him. "I want you to follow him." He tapped Giering on the chest with his index finger. "Tell me where he goes, who he sees, what he says."

"Very well." Giering took a deep breath. "How do I get in touch with you? Shall I call your office?"

Schroeder reached in his pocket and took out a cell phone. "Use this." He handed the phone to Giering. "My number is already programmed in it." Schroeder stood. "Tell me everything he does." He moved down the row of seats to the aisle and disappeared through the corridor entrance.

72

LAS VEGAS, NEVADA

PETE RIOS GLANCED OUT THE WINDOW of the Gulfstream jet and watched as the treeless desert landscape gave way to the cluttered urban sprawl of Las Vegas. A few minutes later, the Strip came into view with its glittering hotels and casinos. Life seemed pretty much normal there, except for the empty streets. With the country in disarray, tourist traffic had nearly ground to a halt.

As he watched the city move beneath the plane, his mind replayed the briefing he'd given President Hedges a few hours earlier. Hedges appeared shaken by the news that the nuclear bomb detonated over the nation's capital was made with material from a reactor in Iran. But rather than moved to action, he seemed reluctant to respond. That hesitancy was reflected in the opinions of his deeply divided national security staff. Asking for a review of Jim Owens' analysis might appear prudent to a politician afraid of making a mistake, but to Rios it seemed like an act born of fear. They already had two missiles in their possession, both from Iran, both carrying nuclear warheads—one discovered onboard a ship off the U.S. coast, the other shot down over Israel just minutes before it would have obliterated Tel Aviv.

The plane banked and slowed as the wing flaps extended. Moments later, Rios heard the landing gear drop and lock into position. Within five minutes, the plane touched down and taxied to a stop inside a secure hangar. Rios exited the plane and crawled inside an SUV.

He arrived at the NEST command center to find the room buzzing with activity. Richard Weavil spoke up as Rios entered. "We have a location on Nasser Hamid."

"Good." Rios slipped off his jacket and hung it over the back of a chair. "Where is he?"

"He's in Kolasin, Montenegro," Weavil answered with a note of triumph.

"Checked into the Bianca Resort & Spa," Jeff Howell added, "using an alias, Olek Kamati."

"We've confirmed the alias is his?"

"It's him."

Rios was puzzled. "Why did he go to Montenegro?"

"Tourist-friendly," Aycock suggested. "And no extradition treaty with us."

"Bianca Resort & Spa is a ski resort," Weavil added. "Great time of year to be there, too."

Rios moved near the operator at the center of the room. "Do we have any assets in the area?"

The operator checked her monitor. "The Army has units in Italy. CIA has teams in Bosnia. There's a Marine expeditionary force off the coast of Greece."

"Montenegro is located on the Adriatic Sea," Howell chimed in. "We can mobilize someone from one of our bases there. Fly them over in a matter of hours. Bring in anything we need."

"We don't have time to do all that." Rios rubbed his eyes. "See what else is in the area. Somebody must have something we can use. We need a quick 'snatch and grab.' Get in, get him, and get out. The Israelis think this guy was the mastermind behind the whole operation."

"Marines can take him. They're not that far away."

Rios looked around the room. "We need him, but we need him alive. No Marines this time."

"Sir," the operator suggested. "The CIA has a Counterterrorism Pursuit Team in Podgorica."

"How far away is that?"

"Forty, maybe fifty miles south of the resort."

"Okay." Rios sighed. "I don't like using them, but get them working on this." He was talking fast now. "I want them to find Hamid, take him into custody, and get him out of the country. And don't let them get cute with it. Get him and get out."

"We're kidnapping him?"

"Do we care?" Howell called out. "We're snatching him off the street. We're rolling him out of bed. We're stuffing him in the trunk of a car."

"Call it whatever you want," Rios added. "Just tell them to get moving on it."

73

KOLASIN, MONTENEGRO

DRESSED AS A BELLMAN, Avner Shalev crossed the lobby at the Bianca Resort & Spa. Working on assignment from Mossad, he had arrived at the hotel a week earlier, posing as an Israeli expatriate in need of work. They hired him that same day.

A few paces ahead of him, Nasser Hamid turned the corner and entered a restaurant. Shalev continued past the restaurant and pressed a node on a wire that was hidden beneath his jacket. "He is in the restaurant."

A reply came immediately through a tiny bud embedded in his ear. "I have him."

Shalev continued to the end of the hall and stepped into the service elevator. "Let me know the moment he leaves."

Shalev rode up to the fifth floor and stepped out to the hallway. He walked quickly to a room at the corner and took a master key card from his pocket. He inserted it in the slot beneath the doorknob. A tiny green light glowed. He opened the door and stepped inside.

Directly opposite the door was a window that looked out on a courtyard below. To the left was a bed. A dresser sat along the wall to the right. Shalev checked the drawers but found them empty. A suitcase rested on a stand in the corner. He carefully opened the top and looked inside. Beneath the clothes he found a laptop.

Working quickly, he lifted the screen on the computer and waited as it booted the operating software. When it was up and running, he inserted a flash drive in the USB port and loaded a tracking program onto the hard drive. Two minutes later, a note appeared on the screen indicating the program had been installed. He removed the flash drive and closed the screen, then returned the laptop to the suitcase.

A telephone sat on the nightstand beside the bed. He lifted the receiver and popped off the mouthpiece cover. With the microphone exposed, he took a tiny transmitter from his pocket and placed it inside, then replaced the cover and snapped it closed.

When he was finished, he pressed the node beneath his jacket. "How are we doing?"

"Sipping a cup of coffee."

Shalev moved to the door and stepped out to the hallway. As the door clicked closed, a guest came from around the corner. Shalev acknowledged him with a nod and moved toward the service elevator. As he stepped inside, he pressed the node once more. "It is done."

74

JERUSALEM, ISRAEL

EFRAIM HOFI SAT AT THE CONFERENCE TABLE across from David Oren. Gathered at the table with them were the ministers from Israel's most important departments. Together, they formed the National Security Cabinet, a concentrated group of government leaders that functioned as an executive committee of the Knesset, streamlined to make quick decisions on matters posing an imminent threat to the country's security.

Oren called in a loud voice, "We should begin." The room grew quiet. "I called this meeting of the National Security Cabinet to address a grave situation. Most of you already know the details, but I have asked Efraim to brief us to make certain we are all on the same page."

Hofi stood. "As you are aware, two days ago our satellites detected a missile launched from the desert south of Gaza on a path that would hit Tel Aviv. Because of the advance alert, our missile defense batteries were able to shoot it down. After we confirmed that it was down, we deployed search teams along the flight path and located a debris field in a neighborhood near Gedera. With the help of the Army and civilian volunteers we collected enough pieces of the missile to reassemble a large portion of it. We have determined the missile was an Iranian Shahab-3."

General Grossman, Chief of General Staff for all Israeli Defense Forces, spoke up. "What about the warhead? Was it located?"

"Yes, what about that?" someone added. "There are rumors. Some say yes, and some say no."

"We found it," Hofi replied. "Damaged slightly, but intact and with no major radiation leakage. It fell in the backyard of one of the homes."

"Thank heaven no one was hurt."

"It took some time to remove it," Hofi continued, "but we have now examined it and determined that the material in the warhead came from Reactor Three at the Bushehr Nuclear Power Plant in Bushehr, Iran."

"We suspected this," Grossman nodded.

Emile Dayan, the Minister of the Treasury, looked puzzled. "This is the first time it has been confirmed to me."

Simon Epstein, the Foreign Minister, raised his hand. "What about the one that hit America?"

"NEST has now determined," Hofi answered, "that the bomb detonated over Washington, D.C., was comprised of material from the same reactor."

"That was a high-altitude detonation." Grossman had a quizzical look. "How did they make such a finding?"

"A team of scientists recovered radioactive fallout from snow samples collected atop a mountain in upstate New York."

Grossman shook his head. "I am not sure I would have thought of doing that."

"Ingenious," someone added.

Hofi picked up where he left off. "The missile that struck the United States was launched from a cargo ship a few miles off the New York coast. They found the ship and recovered a Russian-made launcher onboard."

"Do they think the Russians were involved?"

"No." Hofi shook his head. "They understand it was the type used by Iran to launch their Shahab missiles. Using trajectory data for the missile launched against us, our forces entered the Egyptian desert and located the launch site. We found a similar launcher at that location."

Rony Herzliya, the Minister of Defense, caught Hofi's attention. "Has Egypt responded?"

Oren glanced down the table. "To the launch or to the troops?"

"They issued a statement condemning the launch," Herzliya noted. "I was asking about the troops. I know they had not said anything about it as of this morning. I was wondering if we had heard anything new."

"They have made no mention of our troops entering their territory," Oren replied.

"I have almost finished," Hofi continued. "U.S. forces located a second ship drifting in the Atlantic Ocean near Virginia. It had been disabled by the electromagnetic pulse of the first explosion. A Navy SEAL team boarded it and found a Shahab-3 missile sitting on a launcher, apparently ready to launch."

Grossman looked puzzled. "I have heard a report of this, but no one has explained how it happened. What prevented it from launching? Is not the electronics system on the Russian launcher shielded from this sort of thing?"

"Apparently not," Hofi smiled, "and the laptop they were using to program the missile was an older one, purchased from a retail store. The pulse ruined the circuitry."

Grossman leaned back in his chair, shaking his head. "This is such a coincidence, it must be divine intervention."

Epstein spoke up. "What kind of warhead did that missile have?"

"A warhead identical to the one we shot down."

"And the missile launched from the Egyptian desert was aimed at Tel Aviv?"

"Yes."

"You have confirmed it?"

"Yes," Hofi answered. "We have checked and rechecked the trajectory."

"Using only our satellites, or others?"

"We used data from our own sources, and information supplied by the United States."

"They are in a position to supply accurate information?"

"Their satellite capability has been unaffected by these events." Hofi shifted his weight to a more comfortable stance. "NORAD is fully functional. The eastern half of the United States is nonfunctional, but their military remains fully capable and effective."

"Thank you, Efraim." Oren glanced around the table. "I think we are all confident these attacks—the one against the United States and the one against us—involved the use of Iranian equipment. The question we face is whether it was an act of war by the Iranian government, or an act of terrorism by an unaffiliated terrorist group."

"Has the United States formulated a response?"

"As far as I know, they have not."

"Should we wait for them?"

"We are an independent country. We make our own decisions based on what is best for our people. That has always been our position. It should not change now."

"If we go forward and launch a nuclear strike against Iran, the world will condemn us."

"The world already condemns us simply for who we are."

They continued to debate the issue for the next hour, exploring the connection between Nasser Hamid, Adnan Karroubi, and other key Iranian leaders, and then Oren brought the discussion to a conclusion. "I think we are in agreement. Based on the evidence we have developed connecting Nasser Hamid to Iranian officials, and the use of Iranian equipment that could not have been obtained other than with the explicit participation of the Iranian government, we shall formulate our own response and move forward. If the Americans approach us with a plan, we shall of course listen to them, but we will make our own decisions." He turned to General Grossman. "How long will it take to plan a nuclear strike against all military targets in Iran?"

"We have twelve preselected targets, which include their most essential facilities. Coordinates for those targets are already programmed. The missiles are ready. They can be launched within the half hour."

"I do not want to hit merely the essential places. Do we have the ability to hit all of their known military targets?"

"Yes, but I must warn you, civilian casualties will be enormous."

"I understand." Oren looked around at the faces gathered before him. "We are invoking the Samson Option—an all-out nuclear attack on every known military target in Iran. I will not risk the possibility of a counterstrike from them." He stood. "General, get me your plans by morning."

75

MOSCOW, RUSSIA

VLADIMIR VOSTOK WAITED in the dining room down the hall from his office. He stood near the doorway, slowly pacing back and forth. He thought of his conversation with Luzhkov, his chief of staff, and remembered again the report he'd given of Oleg Batalov's visit to Tehran. He replayed it in his mind, turning it over and over. Batalov had been his friend since childhood, but life had a way of changing people and he wanted to make certain Batalov was not playing them against the Germans to enhance his own bargaining position. But no matter how he turned the words, he could not find a way that indicated Batalov meant anything other than the straightforward statement he'd made—Franz Heinrich was meeting with Abadeh Ardakan.

The door opened, interrupting Vostok's thoughts. Luzhkov entered with Mikhail Mirsky, the Foreign Minister. Luzhkov escorted him to Vostok. "Gentlemen, I shall leave you to your private discussion."

"No," Vostok replied. "I would prefer you stayed."

"Fine with me," Mirsky added.

"Very well," Luzhkov nodded.

They took a seat at the table. A waiter brought lunch. When the plates were served, he stepped from the room. Vostok looked over at

Mirsky. "Panova met with Mueller?"

"Yes."

"What did he learn?"

"They say they intend to honor their agreement. Mueller said to tell you, 'All our arrangements were made with the current situation in mind.' He instructed Panova to deliver the message in those exact words." Mirsky gave Vostok a questioning look. "Do you know what it means?"

"I think he is trying to say that when he made the agreement with us, he already knew what was going to happen."

"He already knew? But how?"

"I do not know the details," Vostok smiled. "But I am certain that is what he means."

"If that is so, could we ever trust him?"

"How do you mean?"

"They are allies of the United States. If they knew an attack was coming, they had a duty to warn the Americans. Not warning them would be a breach of friendship, not to mention the hundred or so treaties between the two countries."

"Do you think Mueller is telling the truth?" Vostok reached for a drink of water.

"You do not think he knew?"

"I think Mueller wants to be a player in the world oil market. He plans to use the present uncertainty to the Germans' advantage. And he will say anything that makes him look good."

"They have done well so far. Prices have risen sharply. Our contract with them is now priced well below the market."

"If Germany made a deal with Iran, they must know the price will rise. And perhaps they know why." Vostok swallowed a bite of food.

"How would they rise?"

296

"What do you think about the Chinese?"

"They get roughly twenty percent of their oil from Iran."

Vostok gave Mirsky a questioning look. "If Germany made a deal with Iran, would it impede that supply?"

"For that to happen, Germany would have to buy Iran's complete production. They would never be able to fund it—certainly not with their current obligations to us and to China. And who would they sell it to?"

"How long would it take China to deploy its army to the Middle East?"

"Two months. Three at most."

"And how far would they get before they encountered someone strong enough to slow them down?"

"Turkey."

Vostok nodded thoughtfully. "And by then, they could control the entire Middle East."

76

BERLIN, GERMANY

IN THE MORNING, DAVID HOAG left his room at the Brandenburger Hotel and took the elevator to the lobby. At the front entrance, the bellman hailed a taxi for him and he rode to the Pergamon Museum.

Built over a twenty-year span, the museum was constructed to house antiquities recovered under German supervision from archaeological digs in the Middle East. Most of the artifacts came from the ancient Greek state of Pergamon. Hoag wandered among the exhibits, then took a seat on a bench opposite a giant marble bust of Attalus I.

A few minutes later, Franz Heinrich took a seat beside him. "We have little time."

"What's happening?"

"On Friday," Heinrich said softly, "the chancellor will announce that our government will no longer purchase U.S. Treasury notes. The governments of China and Russia will follow our lead."

Hoag felt the blood drain from his head. "That will force a default."

"Yes," Heinrich nodded. "It will."

"They want the U.S. to fail?"

"Some do," Heinrich shrugged. "But for most, it is not so much that America fails, as it is that Germany triumphs. They would not mind that you succeed so long as Germany is in a superior position."

"Why are you telling me this?"

"It seems the German government has become something quite different from what we expected."

Hoag frowned. "This was the chancellor's idea?"

"These plans have been in process for some time, even before the election. I did not see it until now."

"If the Treasury auction is going to fail, then I have to tell somebody. The president has to know. I can't keep quiet."

"If you call they will hear you."

"They? Who?"

"The Federal Police. Perhaps others."

Hoag was skeptical. "Even from my cell phone?"

"Yes, most certainly from your cell phone."

"Or the phone in my hotel room?"

"That phone probably has an area device planted inside it. I suspect they are listening to your phone calls and everything that happens in your room."

"Then I'll use a phone at the embassy," Hoag replied. "I can get someone there to let me inside."

Heinrich shook his head. "All transmissions from the embassy are monitored."

Hoag was incredulous. "They monitor our embassy?"

"Yes. For quite some time now, it seems."

"Phone calls and cables are scrambled, encoded, and encrypted," Hoag argued. "No one can read those without—" His eyes opened wider.

"Correct." Heinrich had a knowing look. "To listen to those communications, one would require the encryption codes and software."

"You have someone on the inside."

"A mole, I believe you call it." Heinrich rested his hands on his thighs. "I have said too much already." He checked his watch. "We must be leaving now." He took Hoag by the elbow. "Come with me."

"What's wrong?" Hoag glanced around, his eyes scanning the room. "Where are we going?"

"Out of the building." Heinrich's voice was low but stern. "Remain silent!"

Hoag followed him across the gallery to a hallway that led to the South Wing. They walked quickly. As they moved past, a man came from an intersecting hallway. He was wearing a black leather jacket and he stared at them as they moved past.

"Do not make eye contact," Heinrich whispered. He tugged at Hoag's arm. "Come this way." They turned right toward an alcove, then left again. A door faced them. Heinrich thrust out his hand and pushed it open, revealing a stairway. He quickened the pace even more.

Hoag hurried to keep up. "Who was that?"

"I have no idea. Which is why I'm worried."

At the bottom of the steps they reached a door that opened onto the street. Heinrich's car was parked nearby. A taxi waited for a fare across the street. Heinrich stopped near the rear bumper of his car and turned to Hoag. "You see the taxi?"

"Yes."

"Take it back to your hotel. Do what you must with what I have told you, but remember, they are always watching and they hear everything." He opened the rear door and slipped inside. As the car sped away from the curb, Hoag started across the street.

77

BEIJING, CHINA

CHINESE PRESIDENT MING SHAO sat at the conference table and listened as General Hu presented detailed plans for action against Iran. Easels with charts and maps stood around the room. Seated at the table were the members of the Central Military Commission.

"To summarize," Hu said, "we propose to reposition eight Group Armies. Three from the Jinan Region, one from Nanjing, and two from Guangzhou. These regions are farthest away from the border, but they are also the most stable regions with the least potential for problems while the units are deployed."

Li Chengfei, commander of the Second Artillery, was doubtful. "That is only six units."

"Yes," Hu replied. "As we move forward with deployment, we will also reposition the 38th Mechanized Group Army from Beijing and the 21st from Lanzhou."

"This will be a major undertaking," Ming observed.

"This is what you asked me to prepare."

"It seems much larger now that we put it on paper."

"This will be an invasion unlike the world has ever seen." Hu pointed to one of the maps. "Units will assemble here, at Khunjerab Pass." He tapped the map with a pointer. "And here, a little to the northeast. Those at Khunjerab Pass will move quickly through

Pakistan and into southern Iran. The other group will sweep through Afghanistan and into northern Iran."

"Avoiding the Americans?"

"If at all possible."

"Do you expect resistance?"

"Not in Pakistan. And I do not think we will meet with much in Afghanistan. The Americans will know they are outnumbered." Hu looked over at Ming. "Perhaps when we are ready you can inform the Americans of our purpose and give them the clear option of avoiding us. Or assisting." The group chuckled.

"That would be interesting," someone observed.

Hu continued. "Iran will be unable to stop us—short of using nuclear weapons on itself—which they may not have and even if they did they would not do."

Jin Ping spoke up. "We need to capture the oil fields intact."

"That is the whole point," Chengfei added.

"So," Ming asked, "how many troops?"

"As we discussed before, at least half a million initially, which is what we have proposed with the designated units. More will follow after that."

"How soon can you begin the repositioning?"

"We can begin assembling our forces at the border immediately and have five hundred thousand men there in two months, at the most. After that, we will need a continuous stream of reinforcements to bring our total force to one million men by the end of the first six months."

"You are ready now to begin?"

Hu nodded. "We are ready now to begin assembling troops in the Xinjiang Province."

"Does that give us enough lead time to get the reserve units prepared?"

"Yes."

"Once we start," Chengfei cautioned, "we cannot stop. We can cloak much of our deployment, but eventually American satellites will detect our movements. We must be moving forward from the border by the time that occurs."

"We have less than a year to complete this operation and get the oil flowing back to us. Otherwise, our supplies will be exhausted, prices will rise, and the Germans will have won without firing a shot."

Hu laid aside the pointer. "That is our plan, gentlemen." He turned to Ming. "Do we have your approval?"

Ming hesitated, then slowly nodded his head. "Yes," he said confidently. "You have my approval. Begin repositioning our troops. Do not advance beyond the border until I give the order. And do not change our alert status. We want to draw as little attention as possible."

"And if someone notices, what shall we tell them?"

"Military exercises. That we are merely conducting military exercises." Everyone laughed.

"But what of the Americans?" Quan Ji asked. "Their Treasury auction is merely days away."

"We have no choice," Chengfei shrugged. "The Germans expect us to side with them by not participating. If we purchase our usual portion, they will know we are not with them."

"We need the element of surprise to maintain our advantage," Hu insisted.

"But if we do not support the U.S. auction," Quan Ji argued, "the value of our present holdings will collapse."

"It is a necessary result," Ming sighed. "We cannot have both. We shall announce with the Germans that we are no longer purchasers of U.S. notes."

"But," Chengfei added, "only after Germany makes its position public."

"Yes," Ming nodded. "We will delay our statement until they have made theirs. And keep them unsuspectingly in the cat's paw."

78

KOLASIN, MONTENEGRO

SABEH GOUDARZI MADE HIS WAY across the deck behind the Bianca Resort & Spa and worked his way through the crowd that was gathered near the lift. As he came past the snow fence, he caught sight of a man standing near a stone fire pit not far from the walkway. Something about him seemed out of place. Goudarzi glanced around. At first, he saw only tourists dressed for the slopes. Then he saw a woman sitting at a table outside the bar. He turned away and moved into the crowd. As he did, he took a small radio from his pocket. "We have company," he said quietly.

"I know."

"Tell Majid to get in place."

"You have seen him?"

"He will be out in a moment."

Goudarzi stuffed the radio in his pocket and made his way through the snow to the fire pit. He passed near the man he'd seen earlier and let his eyes scan him, taking in every detail at a glance. His shoes were like those of any other. There was nothing out of the ordinary about the pants or shirt, either. But there was no mistaking the look—the way he stood, the shade of his skin. He was an American. Trained to handle himself physically, but not a professional boxer. A runner, but not competitively. And his eyes, alert and always watching. Goudarzi quickened his pace.

Just then Hamid emerged from the hotel. The radio in Goudarzi's pocket buzzed. He took it out and answered, "Yes?"

"He is here. Turn around."

Goudarzi spun on his heels, once more letting his eyes scan across the crowd. The woman seated outside the bar raised her hand to her mouth. Her lips moved as if she was talking, but he couldn't hear her voice. The man near the fire pit glanced in her direction, then his eyes focused on Hamid. His head turned as they followed him through the crowd. Hamid saw them, too, and moved quickly among a cluster of skiers.

"He is waiting in the lift line," Goudarzi said.

"I see him."

The chair lift rattled. A girl a few feet away laughed. Someone nearby was talking loudly. People moved back and forth in every direction, but through it all Goudarzi saw the man just three meters from Hamid. He had an olive complexion and dark black hair. Goudarzi snatched the radio from his pocket and put it near his lips. "Mossad is here. And the Americans. Take the shot."

Without warning, Hamid's head exploded. Blood gushed forward in a thick, red stream and splattered onto the snow. His chin flew up as his head snapped back, then he crumpled to the ground.

79

BERLIN, GERMANY

AT THE PERGAMON MUSEUM, Erich Giering threw open the door and rushed from the stairwell to the street. He spotted Franz Heinrich's car as it neared the corner. Across the street, a taxi drove away from the curb. Through the side window he saw David Hoag seated in back.

As the cars moved away, Giering ran to a gray BMW parked a few spaces down the street. He jerked open the door and climbed in behind the steering wheel. He put the car in gear and placed a call on his cell phone to Hermann Schroeder.

"He is leaving the Pergamon." Giering's voice was loud and he spit out the words between gasps.

"Calm down," Schroeder cautioned. "You sound as if you have been running."

"I was," Giering gasped. "Down the steps."

"What was Heinrich doing at the museum?"

"He met the American."

"Did they see you?"

"Yes."

"Are they together now?"

"No. They split up. Hoag took a taxi. Heinrich is in his car."

"Stay with Heinrich."

Giering switched off the phone and pressed the gas pedal. The car surged forward.

80

KOLASIN, MONTENEGRO

JASON WRIGHT, A MEMBER OF THE CIA Counterterrorism Pursuit
Team, stood near the stone fire pit outside the Bianca Resort & Spa
and watched as the crowd scattered. Their frightened shrieks filled
the air as they ran toward him, obscuring his view. He pressed the
node on the wire to his radio. "What happened?"

Before anyone answered, the crowd parted and he saw Hamid's
body lying facedown. Steam rose from the gaping hole in his head.
Blood turned the white snow to crimson slush. A voice crackled
through the earphone in Wright's ear, "Get to his room."

With practiced discipline, Wright turned away from the confusion and calmly entered the hotel. He walked quickly across the lobby
to the stairway and charged up the steps, taking them two at a time.
When he reached the landing on the fifth floor he paused to catch
his breath, then eased open the door and glanced down the hallway.
A housekeeper's cart sat just past the elevator, between his position
and the door to Hamid's room in the corner. He heard the sound of a
vacuum cleaner from one of the rooms, but there was no one in sight.
He pulled the door open farther and stepped into the hall.

A master key card dangled from a lanyard that was draped over
the handle of the housekeeper's cart. He snatched it up as he passed.
When he reached the corner of the hallway, he inserted the key card

into the slot in Hamid's door, then twisted the handle. The door opened and he stepped inside.

Directly opposite the door was a window. To the left was the bed. The dresser sat along the wall to the right. Wright pressed the node on the wire to his radio. "How much time do I have?"

"Police are on the way," a voice replied through his earphone. "Hotel security is trying to identify him. Get moving."

A suitcase rested on a stand in the corner. Wright moved it from the stand and set it open on the bed, then turned to the dresser. The top drawer held clothes and a toiletry kit. He scooped them up in his arms and dumped them into the suitcase. In the bathroom he found nothing but damp towels, a toothbrush, and a used tube of toothpaste. He wrapped the brush and tube in a dry hand towel and brought them to the suitcase.

He pressed the radio node once more. "What's happening?"

"They're still trying to figure out who he is. Keep moving."

Wright closed the suitcase and clicked the latches in place, then grasped the handle and lifted it from the bed. He made one last sweep of the room, then stepped to the door and made his way into the hall. As he moved past the housekeeper's cart, he draped the lanyard with the master key card across a stack of clean towels. A few feet past it he reached the elevator.

While he waited, the stairwell door opened and two men appeared. One of them was dressed in a bellman's uniform. The other was dressed like a maintenance man. They glanced up and down the hall, their eyes alert. The bellman's gaze focused on Wright and he started toward him. Just then the elevator bell dinged and the doors opened. Wright stepped inside and was gone.

81

BERLIN, GERMANY

FRANZ HEINRICH SAT IN THE REAR SEAT of the Mercedes and glanced anxiously out the window. The driver made the corner, then steered the car through traffic. Suddenly they lurched to a stop. Heinrich looked up to see pedestrians in the crosswalk. He glanced at the driver and was about to say something when he caught the reflection of a gray BMW in the rearview mirror. Trapped two cars behind them, it was just sticking out from behind a delivery truck, but Heinrich could see the windshield. The driver in the car wore a black leather jacket. Heinrich was certain he was the man from the Pergamon Museum.

The Mercedes started forward, but now Heinrich wasn't interested in returning to the office. He glanced to the right and spotted a Karstadt department store in the next block. He pointed in that direction. "Pull over here."

The driver seemed puzzled. "Are you certain, sir?"

"Pull over. I want out."

The driver brought the car to a stop at the curb. Heinrich threw open the door and stepped out to the sidewalk. He slammed the door closed behind and hurried to the store entrance. Inside, he walked down the center aisle past the men's section and cosmetic counter before reaching a doorway to the food court. He paused there and glanced around.

Behind him he saw two men. One of them was a store clerk, the other a customer. Their eyes were fixed on him. Above them, a security camera swung in Heinrich's direction. Then the man with the leather jacket appeared.

Heinrich turned away from the food court and squeezed in between four women who were walking together. He moved with them, chatting about directions to the lingerie section, then darted from their midst to the escalator and rode down to the U-Bahn station beneath the store. A train was just arriving. He timed his pace to the voice on the loudspeaker and stepped into a train car at the last moment. Once inside, he moved to the center of the car and grasped a handhold. As the train pulled away, he stared out the window and saw the man in the leather jacket standing on the platform.

82

LAS VEGAS, NEVADA

AT THE NEST COMMAND CENTER, Pete Rios stood near the operator's console and stared up at a screen on the wall. Arms folded across his chest, his eyes were focused on an image from the Bianca Resort & Spa. "Where's the laptop?" When no one responded, he turned to look over his shoulder. "Does anyone know what happened to the laptop?"

"The CIA took it."

"Are we certain? Has anyone confirmed that our people took it from the hotel?"

"No, sir."

"Then find out what happened to it." Rios' voice was loud and demanding. "I want that laptop. It's the closest we can get to reading Nasser Hamid's mind now."

"We're working on it," Richard Weavil answered.

"That laptop is the key," Rios continued. The veins in his temples pulsed. "The notes. The information. We can't let it get away from us. Who has it?"

"We're checking."

Ken Aycock spoke up. "Do we want to know who killed Hamid?"

"Do we care?"

"We know who killed him," Rios replied. "Get me that laptop."

"We know who killed him?"

"An Iranian sniper team got him."

"That wasn't Mossad?"

"No." Rios shook his head. "The Iranians did it."

"Back to the laptop," Jeff Howell said, changing the subject. "Is it so bad if Mossad has it?"

"Yes," Rios shouted. "It's no good if they have it. We need that information. We don't want the Israelis to analyze it."

"Why not?"

"Because I want our people to do it." Rios kicked a chair and sent it spinning across the room. "Our people. I want them to see it first. I don't want the sanitized version of what was found. I want the raw information."

"I thought the Israelis were our allies."

"They are," Rios snapped, "but they have a habit of making their own decisions about things." He moved across the room past Howell's desk. "I don't want to run the risk of them withholding something because of some internal political issue." By then he was at the door. "Just get me that laptop." He jerked open the door to the hallway and disappeared.

83

BERLIN, GERMANY

THE TAXI CAME TO A STOP in front of the Brandenburger Hotel. Hoag paid the fare and stepped out to the sidewalk. A bellman recognized him and turned to get the hotel door. Hoag waved him off and started up the street. He needed a moment to clear his head, to think about what Heinrich had told him.

A default by the United States on its Treasury notes would not be a critical financial blow. Those instruments were already trading for pennies on the dollar. From a financial perspective, a default would only memorialize what had already happened. The United States had been dealt a serious setback by the attack. It would be years before the economy recovered, but there was more to the situation.

Since declaring its independence from Great Britain, no U.S. central government, regardless of how or when it was formed, had failed to meet its debt obligations. There was a renegotiation of interest in 1790, when the federal government assumed responsibility for debt of the former colonies. And in 1933, obligations requiring payment in gold were amended to require payment in currency, but America always met its payment schedules. A default now would relegate the United States to the financial status of a developing nation. It would reduce the U.S. to a par with countries that still only had one airport. It would be a major blow to national pride, which would affect

American consumption. The U.S. economy thrived on consumption.

Hoag had information vital to U.S. interests. He couldn't keep it to himself. He had to call someone. Get the news to them about the German plan. *But the Germans are listening—assuming Heinrich is telling the truth.* He thought about that a moment. If Heinrich wasn't telling the truth, why would he tell him anything at all? *I think he's telling me the truth. But if I call from the embassy, they'll hear. And if I call on an unsecure phone, it'll be like broadcasting the news to the entire world.* His eyes lit up. *That's exactly right.*

If he simply placed a phone call from an unsecure phone—better yet, an unsecure cell phone—every major intelligence network would pick it up. They would all hear what he had to say. It wouldn't be a secret any longer.

Two blocks from the hotel he came to a retail kiosk near the steps to an underground U-Bahn station. He purchased a prepaid cell phone and dialed Jenny's number. It took a few moments for the call to get through. She sounded excited when she heard his voice. "David, are you all right?"

"Yes, but I have to tell you something."

"Okay. Are you sure this is a good time for this conversation?"

Normally, with that response, he would have assumed there really was a problem between them and he would have ended the call right there, but nothing about his situation was normal and she was the only person who would take him seriously. "Don't hang up."

"Okay." Her voice sounded hesitant, almost timid.

"I need you to listen to me and hear me all the way out."

"If this is about what I said the other—"

"Jenny, it's not about that. The Germans are going to announce on Friday that they will not purchase any more U.S. debt."

"They won't do what?"

"The Treasury auction. The Germans are not going to participate."

"David, why are you telling me this?" She sounded genuinely worried. "This isn't a secure line."

"Don't hang up." His tone was harsh and he softened it. "Please. Just listen. Berlin is seven hours ahead of Washington. That makes them eight hours ahead of you. If they announce on Friday afternoon here, it'll be sometime before the Treasury auction there. The United States Treasury auction will fail. The United States will be forced to default on its debt. U.S. Treasury notes will be worthless."

"Are you sure you're okay?" Now the officious Jenny appeared—the one that tried to right every wrong and solve every problem. Hoag knew she would never hang up now. "Do you want me to call someone for you?"

"I have this from a very high source in the German government," Hoag continued. "For the first time in history, the United States of America will be forced to default on its sovereign debt."

While he talked, he tried to think of every word that could be flagged by NSA's computers. The Germans might be listening, but so was everyone else. Towers in Lisbon, Paris, and London would catch the signal from the phone call. Computers at each of those facilities were programmed to trap communications that included key words and phrases.

"This is a matter of national security," Hoag continued. "President Hedges must hear this. You have to get word to him. Tell Hoyt Moore. Anyone at Offutt Air Force Base who will listen. This is bigger than anthrax."

Jenny chimed in, "Do you realize you have just broken half a dozen laws?"

"We are talking about a threat larger than any nuclear bomb ever considered by Al-Qa'ida, Hamas, or any other terrorist cell."

"You. Are. Out. Of. Your. Mind! If anyone at NSA or Menwith Hill is listening, this man is an American citizen. He is not a terrorist."

"This is financial terrorism and it's happening this Friday." Hoag was serious about the call but he found it difficult to keep from laughing at the sound of their conversation.

"Sir, you are discussing classified information on an unsecure phone connection. This information is protected. It cannot be accessed without a Level One SCI clearance. This is code word information requiring a single scope background investigation. And you've just now disclosed it to anyone with a shortwave radio."

Hoag grinned. *Jenny understands.* "The U.S. Treasury auction is the most important sale of sovereign debt in the world. Germany's refusal to purchase that debt will have repercussions for China, Russia, and the European Union."

Jenny whispered, "This will be worse than anything done by the *Panama Clipper*, *Amazon Cloud*, or the *Santiago*."

"Larger than the nuclear bomb that hit Washington, D.C."

"Or the one aimed at Tel Aviv."

"And when Germany makes its announcement, there won't be—"

Suddenly the phone call ended. Hoag checked the message screen and saw he had no service. *At least the Germans were listening. Let's hope everyone else was, too.*

He opened the back of the phone and took out the battery, then pried loose the SIM card. A trashcan stood nearby. He tossed the battery in it and put the SIM card in his pocket. On his way back to the hotel, he threw the remaining pieces of the phone down a storm drain.

84

NORTHERN IRAN

HERMANN SCHROEDER LAY IN A KING-SIZE BED at the Hotel Adlon Kempinski. His cell phone rang. He picked it up from the nightstand and answered the call.

"I lost him," Giering panted, out of breath.

"Where?"

"He went into a Karstadt store. Now he is on the U-Bahn. Got on at the station in the basement."

"Idiot." Schroeder's voice was biting. "How could you be so stupid?"

"He was good at it."

Schroeder ended the call abruptly and scrolled down the contacts list for a number. When he found it, he placed a call and moved the phone to his ear. Someone answered on the first ring. "Heinrich recognized us."

"You are certain?"

"Yes, I am certain," Schroeder snapped. "Would I call you otherwise? We were following him. He bolted from the car and lost us in the train station."

"What shall we do?"

"Take some men to the house. Search the study."

"His wife will be at home. It is already late afternoon."

"I do not care about his wife. See what you can find. The woman is of no consequence." There was no response. "You have a problem with that?"

"No."

"He was meeting with the American. Search his study. We must determine if he shared any information. This is a matter of treason."

Schroeder switched off the phone and laid it back on the night-stand. *If Heinrich's wife gets in the way, she dies.*

85

LAS VEGAS, NEVADA

PETE RIOS WAS LOST IN A DREAMLESS SLEEP when he felt a hand on his shoulder. "Sir," a voice said, rousing him. "We have something you need to hear." Rios opened his eyes to find Jeff Howell standing over him. "Sir," Howell repeated. "I think you'll want to listen to this."

Rios blinked his eyes and looked around, trying to remember where he was. The walls were bare. A table sat beside the bed with a small lamp. Across the room was a sink with a mirror above it. He sat up and rubbed his hands over his face. Then slowly, it came to him.

After more than a week in the command center, he was exhausted. Sleeping in a chair, resting his head on the desk, drinking lots of coffee, had gotten him only so far. Finally, he had given in and walked down the hall to one of four rooms equipped for overnight stays. He'd been asleep five hours when Howell awakened him.

"You let me sleep too long," Rios grumbled.

"Nothing much happened until now."

"What is it?"

"NSA intercepted a conversation from Berlin. They think it's a phone call from a CIA employee named David Hoag."

"Where'd they hear it?"

"An NSA listening post in London picked it up. He was calling someone named Jenny Freed."

"Who is she?"

"A CIA analyst. She and Hoag are working out of Offutt."

"What were they talking about?"

"The upcoming Treasury auction."

Rios frowned. "What about it?"

"Hoag told her the Germans were not going to participate."

Rios pushed himself up from the cot, reached for his jacket, and followed Howell back to the command center. Howell nodded to the operator. "Give us the audio on that intercept." The conversation played through the speakers.

When it was finished, Rios gestured to the operator. "Play it again." He listened once more, then glanced around the room. "What do you think?"

"Sounds like they wanted someone to hear," Weavil suggested.

"This was a cell phone call?"

"Yes," Howell replied. "A throwaway phone purchased in Berlin."

"The call ended abruptly. What happened?"

"The cell phone tower relaying the call was shut down," Aycock offered. "I guess the Germans were listening, too."

Weavil spoke up again. "But is it real?"

"You mean, is it accurate?"

"Yeah," Weavil said. "Is this reliable information?"

"What do we know about Hoag?"

"Grew up in Ohio," Howell offered. "Earned a degree in Near Eastern history from Yale and a law degree from Harvard. Recruited by the CIA. Proficient in Arabic. Worked as a field officer in Istanbul, London, and Paris. Placed on loan to Georgetown. Part of a team working under Winston Smith tracking Nasser Hamid before the explosion. He and Jenny Freed were sent to Offutt just a few days ago. Hoag's most recent assignment was to interrogate the crew from the *Panama Clipper*."

"How did he get to Berlin?"

"Took a CIA Gulfstream from Kings Bay to Bremerhaven. Flight was arranged through Winston Smith's office. I suppose he got to Berlin on his own."

"And we can assume he found something at Bremerhaven that piqued his interest," Rios mused. "What's the connection?"

"That was the *Panama Clipper's* last port before sailing to New York."

"Has the CIA responded?"

"No." Howell shook his head.

"Do they know about the call?"

"I don't know. We just received it."

"Send this conversation to the CIA," Rios ordered.

"This is an NSA file," Weavil warned. "Their general counsel's office requires us to check with them before passing it on."

"Send it," Rios ordered. "We are way beyond covering ourselves now." He hesitated a moment before continuing. "As a matter of fact, send it to everyone. Work it up in a report, include a transcript of the call, and send it out to CIA, DIA, Treasury, the president ... any other cabinet-level agencies you can think of. And send it now."

"It'll be mostly raw information. We haven't had time to give it much analysis."

"They need the information immediately. The quarterly auction is just days away. Where's this Hoag guy now?"

"Not sure," Howell responded.

"Find him."

"Shouldn't we ask the CIA about it? He's their employee."

"No," Rios said, his voice terse and decisive. "Let's find him ourselves. Ask NSA what they have for a location on the call. Find someone to get in there and locate Hoag."

"You think he's in trouble?"

"I think the Germans heard that call and turned off the cell tower to shut him up. Which means what he was saying is probably true. And if that's so, then the Germans are out there right now trying to find him. We need to find him first."

"This is crazy," Weavil said. "All of this over one phone call? Why would Germany fail to support our auction?"

"Haven't you been paying attention?" Rios shouted. "The value of our bonds has plummeted and isn't likely to recover. We are half the nation we once were. Germany is at the height of its economic power. Josef Mueller sees a chance for Germany to recover its former glory, and he's taking it." Rios paused and ran his fingers through his hair. "Find Hoag. Just find him."

86

BERLIN, GERMANY

HEINRICH CAME FROM THE SUBWAY TRAIN and stepped onto the platform at the Charlottenburg station. He glanced around warily checking the crowd as best he could. When he saw nothing suspicious, he moved to the exit and walked up the steps to the street. As he reached the top, his cell phone rang. The call was from Nadja, his wife.

"They are here, Franz." Her voice trembled. "In the house."

"Who?"

"Federal Police! They are searching your study."

He couldn't believe what she was saying. He never thought Schroeder would go this far. "Why?"

"They did not tell me."

In the background, Heinrich heard someone banging on a door. "What is that?"

"They are trying to get in," she shouted.

Heinrich's heart raced. "Where are you?"

"In the bathroom," she sobbed. "They are—"

Heinrich listened, waiting for her to continue. When she did not, he became frantic. "Nadja?" he shouted into the phone. Still there was no response. "Nadja!" he shouted again. Then the phone beeped, indicating the call ended. He shoved it into his pocket and ran to the corner to hail a taxi.

As he rode toward the house, he called Hermann Schroeder. "Your men are at my house," he shouted. "Searching my study. Are you out of your mind?"

"Relax, Franz."

"My wife is terrified."

"I have talked to them. She is okay."

"What are you doing?"

"What did you think would happen, Franz? If you associate with Americans, you can expect us to ask questions."

"They are searching my study."

"You have something in there to hide?"

"Pack your personal effects," Heinrich seethed.

"What are you talking about?" Schroeder chuckled. "You sound like a madman."

"When the chancellor finds out about this, you will be looking for a job. Pack your personal things from your office. And call your attorney."

"How dare you try to dismiss me," Schroeder scoffed. "Besides, the chancellor knows. He ordered the investigation."

Schroeder's words struck Heinrich hard. He felt the energy drain from his body. His mind reeled as he tried to make sense of it. Josef Mueller—his lifelong friend—ordering an investigation? This could not be true. The sound of Schroeder's voice continued from the phone, but Heinrich had no desire to listen any longer. He switched it off and looked up at the driver. "Turn on Seeling Street."

The driver tried to argue. "It is quicker to go by—"

"Seeling Street," Heinrich snapped. "And stop at the alley in the center of the block."

The taxi made the turn at the corner, then slowed in the middle of the block. "Stop here!" Heinrich shouted as he threw open the door and jumped from the backseat. He tossed the driver forty Euros and slammed the door.

Heinrich made his way up the alley and came quickly to a spot near the backyard of his house. Through a hedgerow, he watched the windows for any sign of movement inside. After a moment, he crept farther up the alley where he could see past the corner of the house to the street. Satisfied no one was there, he made his way across the small backyard and went inside.

"Nadja! Where are you?" There was no reply. He darted from room to room downstairs, then hurried up the steps to the second floor.

From the top of the stairway he could see into his study. The desk was turned on its side and papers were strewn in every direction. The door to the hall bathroom hung precariously from a single hinge. The doorframe was cracked. Splinters of wood littered the floor. With two long strides he reached the doorway. What he saw made him gasp.

On the far side of the bathroom, Nadja lay motionless in the tub. Her arms and legs were sprawled to the side. Her eyes were open wide, frozen in a look of terror.

Heinrich rushed toward her and gently lifted her by the shoulders. Her head flopped back against this arm. "What did they do to you?" He brushed the hair away from her face. "Nadja," he cried, "what did they do?" Then he saw the bruises on her neck. Blood dripped from the back of her head and trickled across his forearm, and he realized she was dead. He slid down the side of the tub and sat with her resting across his lap. Tears streamed down his face as he rocked her gently in his arms. "Why?" he sobbed. "Why did they do this?"

87

OFFUTT AIR FORCE BASE
OMAHA, NEBRASKA

PRESIDENT HEDGES SAT IN THE BACKSEAT of a Cadillac limousine and stared out at the Nebraska landscape. An early flight that morning with whirlwind stops in Memphis, Jackson, Atlanta, and Charlotte left him drained. Devastation in the East seemed overwhelming. No one had any solutions that were feasible and it all seemed hopeless. Outside, leaves were falling from the trees and the grass was turning brown. Winter was fast approaching and with it more hardships would follow. Right now they were trying to put their lives back together, but in a few weeks they would be struggling to stay warm.

The car rolled quietly down the street and came to a stop at the presidential residence on General's Row. Braxton Kittrell, his chief of staff, met him there. "We have a situation, Mr. President."

"What is it now?"

"Rony Herzliya, the Israeli minister of defense, gave an interview."

"What did he say?"

"A reporter asked if cabinet members wanted to retaliate with nuclear weapons. He said it was tragic that preserving life for some should come at the expense of 'life as we know it' for others."

"Sounds like a veiled threat. Can't they control themselves for one day? Just one day," Hedges shouted. "That's all. One lousy day."

He followed Kittrell into the house and across the first floor to the study. Kittrell replayed the defense minister's statement from the DVR. Hedges watched it in disgust. "We have to get them to hold off," he said when it was finished. "Send somebody to see them. We don't want them dictating the terms of our response."

"They have legitimate security concerns. They were attacked, too."

"This is a bigger issue than them. We'll protect them. They ought to know that. We gave them the missiles that allowed them to protect themselves. We'll continue to support them. Offer them replacements for the missiles they used. Offer them upgrades to the systems they're using. Do we have upgrades?"

"Yes, Mr. President," Kittrell nodded. "We do."

"Then offer it to them. Tell them we're on their side. Tell them anything, but get them to hold off. We need more time to prepare our response."

"Yes, sir."

Hedges reached up with both hands and tugged at his hair in frustration. "So much of this is coming at us all at once—"

The telephone rang, interrupting him. Kittrell answered. He spoke for a moment, then hung up and turned to Hedges. "Sir, there's been another development." Kittrell looked pale.

"What now?" Hedges had a worried expression.

"It's about the Treasury auction on Friday, Mr. President."

"What about it?"

"Charlie Fiskeaux is on his way. NSA has intercepted a conversation. Hoyt Moore will be here in a moment with the transcript. I'll let them give you the details."

88

BERLIN, GERMANY

INSTEAD OF RETURNING TO THE HOTEL after the phone call, Hoag walked up the street to a small café in the next block. A waiter seated him at a table with a view through the front windows. While he sipped from a cup of coffee, he noticed a man standing on the opposite corner. Dressed in a business suit, the man stood near a bench at the bus stop, but his eyes were fixed on the window where Hoag sat. Then he noticed pedestrians passing by on the sidewalk. They slowed to stare at him, then hurried away.

As he watched them, he saw in the reflection of the window across the street three uniformed policemen standing near the front door of the café. Moments later, one of the officers entered the dining room. He spoke to the waiter but pointed in Hoag's direction. The waiter came to a nearby table and whispered something to the people seated there. They got up and moved to the far side of the room.

Worried now, Hoag glanced around for an exit. Along the back wall there was a door that led from the dining room to the kitchen. He rose from the table and started in that direction. "You!" the officer called. "You there!" Hoag ignored him and walked faster, weaving around tables and chairs as he made his way across the floor. By the time he reached the rear of the café, he was moving at a run and burst through the door into the kitchen.

Beyond the door, a line of stoves stood to the left. Stainless steel tables sat to the right. Cooks were hard at work and didn't seem to notice the intrusion. There was another door straight ahead on the far side of the room. Hoag squeezed past the kitchen staff and ran toward the door. He reached it in full stride and shoved it open with his forearm. The door flew back with a bang.

To his relief, it opened into an alley. He stumbled outside, banging his shoulder against a Dumpster. He recovered his balance and turned toward the street at the end of the alley, then broke into a run once more. Behind him, the kitchen door opened again and he heard footsteps coming toward him, but he kept his eyes focused on the street fifty yards away.

At the corner, he raced up the sidewalk, away from the alley. He was still moving fast but his legs were growing tired and heavy. Sweat trickled down his back. Then a Mercedes came alongside him. It slowed to a speed that matched his pace and the front window lowered. Through it he saw Franz Heinrich seated behind the steering wheel. "Get in," Heinrich called.

Hoag was wary, unsure whether Heinrich was as friendly as he seemed. While he tried to decide, there was a shout from behind him. Then a woman cried out. Hoag glanced over his shoulder and saw a policeman coming from the alley. A man dressed in a business suit hurried from the corner. Up ahead, two more policemen were coming toward him from the opposite direction. Hoag realized he had little choice. He leaped into the street, jerked open the rear door of the Mercedes, and dove inside. Heinrich pressed the gas pedal. The car shot forward and picked up speed.

He pulled himself up to a sitting position and turned to look out the rear window. "How did you know where to find me?"

"Your cell phone call changed everything," Heinrich said in a terse manner.

"They heard?"

"Yes. And they are very upset."

"They cut off my call."

"They had little choice." Heinrich gestured with his hand. "It was heard by the entire intelligence community."

"Good," Hoag nodded. "Now everyone knows."

"Yes. They know." Heinrich pointed at himself. "And now they are after me."

"You?"

Heinrich's eyes went cold. "They killed my wife."

Hoag was startled. "What?!"

"Schroeder found out I was in the computer system. That's how I knew most of what I told you. And he knows I met with you."

"And now he knows you were my source."

"Yes," Heinrich nodded.

"I'm so sorry."

"Nothing is the same now."

Hoag looked out the rear window again. A BMW followed with three men inside. "This isn't good." Heinrich pressed the gas pedal. The Mercedes sped forward. The BMW gave chase, swerving left and right, in and out of traffic, trying to keep up.

Just then a door opened from a car parked along the street. The Mercedes struck it with the right fender. The door ripped loose from its hinges and flew through the air. People on the sidewalk screamed.

At the corner, a pushcart filled with produce crossed the street. Heinrich sounded the horn and the vendor ran to the curb for safety. Heinrich jerked the steering wheel to the right. The Mercedes swerved, narrowly missing the cart. The BMW, unable to change directions, struck the cart, shattering it to pieces.

Just past the crosswalk, Heinrich turned the steering wheel to the left. The tires skidded against the pavement as the car made the turn. Then the rear wheels broke loose and the back of the car came around. Heinrich lifted his foot from the gas pedal. The tires brushed the curb and caught traction, but the car slowed enough to allow the BMW to catch them.

Heinrich glanced in the rearview mirror. "They are right behind us. See what you can do."

"Like what?"

"I do not know. Throw something at them."

"There's nothing back here!"

"Let down the seat. Look in the trunk."

Along the top of the rear seat Hoag found a button. He pressed it and folded down the back, then crawled into the trunk. It was dark inside but light filtered through the opening and he felt around with his hands.

Suddenly, the trunk lid flew up. Hoag peeked over the edge to see the BMW just inches away. The driver was frantic, bobbing his head left and right in an attempt to see past the flapping trunk lid. A wrench lay on the trunk floor. Hoag grabbed it and threw it at the BMW. It glanced off the hood, struck the windshield, and ricocheted over the top of the car. The driver braked and ducked to the side in a reflexive action. The car swerved. The Mercedes surged ahead but the BMW recovered and quickly caught up.

In the meantime, Hoag located the spare tire. He released it from its holder and lifted it to his lap, then shoved it out the back. The driver's eyes were wide with fright and he threw up his hands to cover his face as the tire banged against the hood, then smashed into the windshield. Suddenly the car shot to the right, jumped the curb, and plowed through a sidewalk café. Patrons leaped to the left and right. Plates and cups went flying.

The car careened to the opposite side of the street, bounced off a parked van, and rolled into the street. Just when the driver seemed about to get it under control, a delivery truck backed from an alley and blocked the street. The car screeched to a halt inches from the truck's rear wheels.

Hoag shouted, "Did you see that?" As the Mercedes pulled away he crawled back inside the car and shoved the rear seat in place. "They looked like—"

A bus crossed the intersection in front of them. Heinrich jammed on the brakes but they were going too fast to stop. At the last moment, he turned the steering wheel sharply. The car slid sideways and slammed to a stop against the side of the bus. The force of the impact threw Heinrich against the window on the passenger side. His head struck the glass with a resounding blow and he flopped over in the seat.

Hoag glanced out the window to see the men from the BMW hurrying toward them. Frantic to avoid being captured, he climbed over the front seat and shoved Heinrich's limp body out of the way. He slid behind the steering wheel and pressed the gas pedal, but nothing happened. He stomped it with his foot but still the car didn't budge. A quick check of the gauges told him the engine had stalled. He moved the shifter to park and turned the key. The engine made a noise but didn't start. He tried again and again. "Come on. Don't quit now." He turned the key once more and the engine came to life.

By then, one of the men from the BMW had reached the car. He jerked open the driver's door and ducked his head inside. "Get out of the car," he demanded.

Hoag stiff-armed him, holding him at bay with the heel of his left hand pressed against the man's forehead. With the other hand, he put the shifter in gear. It clicked into place and he pressed the gas pedal to the floor. The Mercedes shot forward, knocking the man to the ground and slamming the door closed. Hoag steered the car away from the bus and sped down the street.

89

OFFUTT AIR FORCE BASE
OMAHA, NEBRASKA

JACK HEDGES SAT AT HIS DESK, head back, eyes closed. From outside, he heard a car door close. His eyes opened and he looked at Braxton Kittrell. "Is that them?"

Kittrell stood near the window on the opposite side of the room. He pushed back the drapes and looked out. "Yes, Mr. President. They're here."

The front door opened and the sound of footsteps approached. A moment later, Charlie Fiskeaux appeared. Behind him was Hoyt Moore.

"Mr. President," Fiskeaux began. "We have a problem."

Hoyt Moore elbowed his way past Fiskeaux and stepped toward Hedges with a document in his hand. Kittrell intercepted him. "I'll take that." He took the document from Moore, quickly scanned it, then handed it to Hedges.

"Sir," Moore began. "NSA intercepted a telephone conversation between David Hoag and Jenny Freed."

"Freed." Hedges frowned. "Alex Freed's daughter?"

"Yes, sir."

"She's out here with us," Hedges continued. "I saw her the other day. When we were in the situation room."

"Yes, sir," Moore replied. "Both she and Hoag were reassigned here after the attack."

Hedges had a concerned look. "What did they say in the conversation?"

"Apparently, Hoag made contact with someone in the German government. According to the contact, Germany will announce on Friday that they are not going to participate in the Treasury auction."

"Not going to participate?"

"Yes, sir," Fiskeaux spoke up. "Hoag says the Russians and the Chinese won't, either."

Hedges focused on Moore. "How did we intercept this call? Don't we have secure lines in Germany?"

"He was talking on a cell phone he must have purchased from a kiosk."

"Where are they now—Jenny and Hoag. Where are they?"

"Freed is here," Moore explained. "We aren't sure about Hoag."

"Has anyone talked to Miss Freed?"

Moore nodded. "We're doing that now."

"What does she say?"

"Hoag was sent to Kings Bay to interview the crew of the *Panama Clipper*. A lead from those interviews took him to Bremerhaven. Something he learned there led him to Berlin. We have a report that he confronted Hermann Schroeder, the head of the Federal Police, earlier this week at a conference, and he was seen with Franz Heinrich."

Hedges was surprised. "The chancellor's assistant?"

"Yes, sir."

"So, this could be credible information."

"Yes, Mr. President," Fiskeaux blurted. "Which is why we're here. We need to figure out what to do. We can't wait until Friday to formulate a plan."

Hedges held up his hand in a calming gesture. "The first thing we're going to do, Charlie, is not panic." He looked back to Moore. "Do we know for certain the two people in the conversation are actually our people?"

"Yes, sir."

"Okay," Hedges nodded. "Get Miss Freed in here. I want to talk to her."

Fiskeaux raised his hands in a gesture of frustration. "But what about the quarterly refunding?"

"Charlie," Hedges began, "we can't really force the Germans to buy our bonds. You want me to put a nuclear missile to their head and force them to do it?"

"But the U.S. will default."

"Is this about the country, or your reputation?"

Fiskeaux was taken aback. "Sir?"

"Are you worried that people will remember you as the Treasurer who presided over the first U.S. default?"

"No, Mr. President." Fiskeaux argued. "It's not about me or my reputation. It's about the reputation of the country." He clenched his fist. "And it's about the Germans."

"Forget Germany," Hedges said, waving his hand. "And anyone else who doesn't want to participate. They know what a decision like this will do. They know the consequences." He paused and took a deep breath. "This is a quarterly refunding, right?"

"Yes, sir."

"We're not refinancing the entire debt, just the portion due now."

"That is correct."

"How much are we looking at?"

"About 450 billion."

"That's the total?"

"Yes."

"How much of that represents debt owned by American citizens and institutions?"

"About fifty-five percent of that amount," Fiskeaux shrugged. "Roughly 245 to 250 billion."

Hedges placed his hands on his hips as he thought. Slowly, a resolute expression formed on his face. "We can do that," he nodded thoughtfully.

Fiskeaux looked puzzled. "Sir?"

Hedges looked up with a smile. "We can refinance that much ourselves. The Russians did it once before. And not too long ago, as I recall."

The frown on Fiskeaux's forehead deepened. "Which part of the debt are you talking about?"

"The part held by United States citizens and institutions." Hedges tapped the desktop as he spoke. "American individuals. Domestic corporations and institutions. We can refinance that part."

"How?"

Hedges looked over at Kittrell. "Get the president of the Federal Reserve for me." Kittrell backed away from the desk and stepped toward the door. Hedges looked over at Fiskeaux. "The Fed can buy that much on its balance sheet."

Fiskeaux groaned. "We'll have inflation." There was a note of resignation in his voice.

"We're going to have inflation anyway. But in the meantime we'll protect our own people."

"What about everyone else?"

Hedges looked him in the eye. "We take care of our citizens and our domestic economy first. That's what the people elected us to do. We'll worry about the others later."

"If we refuse to pay," Fiskeaux offered, "they'll never loan us anything again."

"Yes, they will. They'll loan to us. Money always chases the best return. Might cost us more, but they'll loan to us." He paused for effect. "We cover our own people."

Kittrell returned to the room. "I have the Fed on line one, Mr. President. You still want to see Ms. Freed?"

"Yes." Hedges took a seat at his desk. "Find her and get her in here. Let's see what she knows about that phone call."

90

BERLIN, GERMANY

THE MERCEDES RACED DOWN THE STREET with Hoag at the wheel. He had no idea where he was headed, but he knew they had to keep moving.

Gradually, Heinrich regained consciousness. He reached up with his hand and touched his head. "What happened?"

"You hit the window."

"Must have knocked me out."

"Yeah."

A few blocks later, the street split to the left and right. Hoag looked over at Heinrich. "Which way do we go?"

Heinrich glanced out the window. "Left." He pointed. "Go left." Hoag jerked the steering wheel to the left. Tires squealed as the car made the turn. "Now right," Heinrich shouted.

Hoag was startled. "What do you mean?"

Heinrich pointed out the window to an expressway entrance ramp. "Go there. Go there."

Hoag steered in that direction and pressed the gas pedal. The car raced up the ramp and merged into the right lane. He tucked in behind a delivery van and checked the rearview mirror. "Did they follow us?"

Heinrich turned sideways in the seat and looked out the rear window. "I see no one."

Hoag checked the mirror again. Five cars behind them he caught sight of a police car. Its blue lights flashed as it weaved through traffic. "Oh, no," Hoag groaned. "They're coming."

Heinrich glanced over his shoulder, then turned to look out the windshield. "We need to get off this highway."

Hoag pressed the gas pedal closer to the floor and changed lanes. They closed fast on a trailer truck. He cut over to the far left and sped around it. Behind them, the police car was trapped in traffic.

Up ahead, an exit sign hung from an overhead bridge. Heinrich pointed in that direction. "Get off here."

Hoag checked the mirror once more and turned the steering wheel. The car shot across three lanes, narrowly missing the truck they'd just passed. Car horns blared but Hoag ignored them and kept his eyes focused on the exit. They scraped the guardrail, bounced, and then recovered. Hoag's stomach dropped as the Mercedes plunged down the ramp.

A narrow paved road appeared at the bottom. He jammed his foot on the brake and looked to the left to check for traffic. A Mini Cooper sedan moved past. Hoag timed their arrival to slide in behind it. He slowed the car more and checked the mirror for the police.

"Think we lost him?"

"I do not know. But keep your eyes on the road." Heinrich pointed out the window. "We dare not attract attention here."

The road ahead was narrow and winding. Hoag lifted his foot from the gas pedal and did his best to calm his racing heart.

91

OFFUTT AIR FORCE BASE
OMAHA, NEBRASKA

LONG AFTER THE CALL WITH HOAG HAD ENDED, Jenny sat at her desk and wrestled with what she should do with the information he had given her. She thought about telling Peter Burke, but an inner sense told her that was not the right thing to do. *He'll never accept it. Not coming from me and certainly not from David.*

Finally, she rose from her seat and walked down the hall to Susan Todd's cubicle. She leaned through the doorway. "Got a minute?"

"Sure." Susan leaned back in her chair. "What's up?"

"David called a few minutes ago."

"You look worried. How is he? Everything all right?"

"He said the—"

Just then Tom Benton, the president's personal aide, appeared at Jenny's side. "The president would like to see you."

Jenny was puzzled. "Are you sure he wants me? Jenny Freed?"

"Yes, ma'am," Benton replied. "The president is waiting for you at the residence." He gestured over his shoulder. "I have a car waiting outside."

"I'll be just a minute."

"No." Benton took her by the elbow and guided her away. "We need to go now." He escorted her down the hallway toward the exit.

As they drew near the end of the hall, the door burst open and

Peter Burke appeared. He had an angry scowl on his face. "Get in here," he fumed, pointing toward an empty room to the left.

"I don't think so," Benton responded. "She's on her way to see the president."

Burke ignored him and pulled Jenny aside. "Are you out of your mind?" He spoke in a hoarse whisper. "What were you thinking?"

She jerked her arm free. "What are you talking about?"

"That phone call with David Hoag." Her eyes opened wide. Suddenly she knew why the president wanted to see her. "That's right," Burke continued. His voice had a sarcastic tone. "It's every-where. NSA, CIA, DIA … they all have it."

"He called me," Jenny protested.

"You know better than to discuss information like that on an unsecure phone line."

"I'm sure David had his reasons." She squared her shoulders. "And I'm sure he was telling the truth."

"There are proper channels for reporting that sort of thing. We have people who can verify whether information like that is true." Burke glared at her and gave a heavy sigh. "You should have told me as soon as it happened."

Benton motioned for her. She stepped past Burke. "I have to go. The president is waiting."

Burke looked stricken. "If you tell him about the call, you'll be admitting to a violation of federal law."

Jenny paused at the door. "I'll tell him whatever he wants to know."

"This will be the end of your career."

"No." She turned away. "I don't think so." Then she followed Benton out the door and down the steps.

92

LAS VEGAS, NEVADA

AT THE NEST COMMAND CENTER, a message on Jeff Howell's monitor flashed green and red. He clicked on it and a link opened to a page from NSA. "We're getting something," he called. Everyone turned in his direction. "NSA has a radio feed from the German Federal Police."

"Put it on the speaker," Rios replied. Seconds later, chatter from a police radio played in the room. They listened as the police talked back and forth. Rios looked over at Howell. "We need a translation. Do you speak German?"

"I do," Aycock offered.

"Start talking."

Aycock listened attentively, then began. "He's looking for a car. A gray Mercedes."

"Who is this we hear?"

"Berlin police." A second voice came from the speaker. Aycock paused. "That's someone else. That's the Federal Police there." He paused a moment. "Now we're back with Berlin. He has a report of a car matching that description. License plate AG-7932."

"Do we know for certain whose car they're talking about?"

Weavil spoke up. "It's a gray Mercedes from the German motor pool. Assigned to Franz Heinrich."

"How'd he rate a Mercedes?"

"Special assistant to Chancellor Mueller. He probably can have any car he wants."

"Why are they after him?"

Aycock continued, "Suspects are wanted in connection with an ongoing investigation."

"He's Hoag's source," Howell suggested.

Rios looked at him. "You sure about that?"

"I got a hunch."

"Can we locate him?"

"They have a second sighting," Aycock called out. "Someone saw the car near Teupitzer See."

Weavil spoke up again. "That's a lake. South of Berlin. Straight down the highway from Berlin."

Rios folded his arms across his chest. "Are the Germans responding to that report?"

"Not yet."

"That's curious," Rios mused. "What do we have in the area?"

"CIA station in Berlin."

"No," Rios said, shaking his head. "Not the CIA. Not again."

"Then what?"

"We have a base at Wiesbaden," the operator suggested.

"Good," Rios nodded. "Notify them to put a Special Missions Unit on alert. Have them ready to go."

"We can't send in the Army," Weavil protested. "This is Germany."

"We have to get to Hoag and Heinrich before the Germans do," Rios countered. He turned back to the operator. "Tell that SMU to get ready."

93

OFFUTT AIR FORCE BASE OMAHA, NEBRASKA

TOM BENTON USHERED JENNY INTO President Hedges' study at the residence. Hedges was seated at his desk. Fiskeaux and Moore stood to the left. Kittrell stood to the right. Hedges rose as she entered the room. "Miss Freed," he said politely. "Good to see you again. We met at a Georgetown party not too long ago."

"Yes, sir," she nodded. "Dr. Hamilton's retirement reception."

"Have a seat." Hedges gestured toward a chair in front of the desk. "I understand you received a phone call from David Hoag."

"Yes, sir. He called me earlier today."

"And he told you the Germans were not going to participate in our Treasury auction."

"That is correct."

"You were at that retirement reception with Mr. Hoag. Are you seeing him ... socially?"

"Yes, sir."

"If I may, Mr. President," Moore spoke up. Hedges nodded his approval. Moore turned to Jenny. "Any reason why he called you, as opposed to his supervisor, Peter Burke?"

"We have a long relationship," Jenny replied. "And I think he knew I would believe him."

"Did you believe him?"

"Yes, sir," she nodded. "I believe he was telling me what he learned."

Hedges continued. "You've found him to be trustworthy?"

"Painfully honest." She remembered the conversation they had before he left, and another they had months before at a café overlooking the Potomac River. She and Hoag hadn't always seen eye-to-eye on everything, but she had never known him to lie and as she remembered him now, a flood of emotions swept over her. She longed with all her heart to see him.

"This was a breach of policy," Kittrell added. "Discussing matters of this nature on an unsecure phone is forbidden. You were aware of that?"

"Yes, sir."

"Do you think he was aware of it?"

"I'm sure he knew it was unsecure. But from the way he was talking, I think he wanted to be heard. If you've listened to the call or read the transcript, I think you'll agree." Kittrell started to say something else, but Jenny interrupted. "And, if I may. The information he gave me on the phone was not classified information. It was sensitive and important, and we have policy in place that forbids discussing it that way, but he was not divulging information to which our own agencies had assigned a status."

Hedges and Moore exchanged a look. Moore grinned.

"That may be so," Fiskeaux argued, "but we need to find out if he has been compromised by someone. We need to determine the reliability of his sources."

"Charlie." Hedges had a wry smile. "We'll find out about all that in a few days, won't we?"

"Sir?"

"When we hold the auction. If the Germans buy, we'll know it was a false alarm. If they don't, we'll know he was telling the truth."

"Yes, sir. I suppose so."

"Meanwhile, you'd better get with the Fed and work out the details of our plan. I talked to them. They're ready to go." Hedges looked across the desk at Jenny. "Miss Freed, I appreciate your cooperation. Your parents were in New York when the missile struck?"

"Yes, sir."

"Have you heard from them?"

"Yes, Mr. President. They're fine. Thank you for asking."

"Tell Alex I said hello."

"Yes, sir."

Hedges glanced over at Moore. "Hoyt, you'll see that this doesn't cause her any problem?"

"Yes sir, Mr. President." Moore flashed a smile at Jenny. "She does good work. I think you saw her analysis of the ships."

"Yes, I did." Hedges nodded approvingly. "Keep it up."

94

TEUPITZER SEE
TEUPITZ, GERMANY

HOAG TURNED THE MERCEDES from the highway onto a narrow two-lane road. A few miles farther, the road curved sharply. Outside his window was a commanding view of the lake with its dark water set against a gentle shoreline. Hoag glanced at it as they went by, but Heinrich pointed out the windshield. "Keep your eyes on the road. Tourists always watch the lake. Then they drive into it."

Five kilometers beyond the curve, they passed a farmhouse on the left. "Slow down. We must make a turn." Heinrich pointed. "At the next road."

"Which way?"

"To the right."

Hoag followed Heinrich's directions and brought the Mercedes to a stop in a parking area down the hill from a rambling lake home. Situated on a hillside, it was constructed on one level with a deck that ran all the way around. Steps led from the deck down to a path that wound through a stand of trees to a dock with a small boathouse. Hoag switched off the engine and sat quietly, listening to the sound of the water lapping at the shore and the whisper of a breeze blowing through the tops of the trees. "Peaceful," he smiled.

"Yes," Heinrich nodded. "Which is why the house is here." He opened the car door. "Come. Let's go inside."

They made their way up to the door and stepped into the house. Hoag collapsed in an overstuffed chair near the fireplace. Heinrich went to the kitchen and put on water for tea. When it was ready, they sat at a table near a window and drank while they talked.

"They were serious about catching us," Hoag began.

"Yes," Heinrich nodded. "I would say so."

"All of that over a simple phone call?"

"You touched a nerve."

"Perhaps." Hoag took a sip of tea. "Sure there wasn't more to it?"

"Oh," Heinrich nodded. "There is more to it, all right."

Hoag was puzzled by the answer. "What more?"

"Mueller has made secret deals. Before the attack against America."

"Secret deals? With whom?"

Heinrich took another sip of tea. "First with the Chinese." He rested his hands on his lap. "To induce them to refrain from buying any more U.S. debt."

"The Chinese agreed to that?"

"Yes," Heinrich nodded. "As did the Russians."

Hoag felt like he'd been hit in the stomach. "So, China and Russia won't participate in the Treasury auction, either?"

"No." Heinrich shook his head slowly. "I am afraid not."

Hoag leaned back from the table and stared into space. "Well," he said finally. "That's the end of it, then."

"It is not so bad," Heinrich shrugged.

"No?" There was a note of disdain in Hoag's voice. "Why not?"

"Your bonds are already devalued. No one other than speculators wants them now."

"But they decided not to buy them before this happened."

"True." Heinrich took a sip of tea.

"What else is there that I don't know about?" Heinrich looked away. Hoag pressed the point. "Tell me."

"Before the attack on your country, Mueller agreed to purchase oil from the Russians, both as an inducement regarding the agreement to forgo buying U.S. debt, and to assure the availability of oil after your bonds collapsed."

"So," Hoag mused, "not only would we be forced to default on our debt, what little capital that remained would be spent chasing the price of crude oil."

"Exactly. But the latest situation makes things a little worse, still."

"How?"

"Mueller has now convinced Iran to sell Germany their entire production."

"All of Iran's production? That's impossible."

"Not really. We have the financial reserves for it and the deal is really structured as a marketing agreement. Germany is essentially acquiring the right to sell Iran's oil to the rest of the world. Anyone who wants it will have to see Mueller."

"Arrogance."

"No," Heinrich said, shaking his head. "It is an act of strength. With America no longer financially viable in the world markets, Germany is the most financially sound country in the world."

"How did he convince Iran to do that?"

"He sent me to see them," Heinrich said, confidently.

"You negotiated the deal?"

"Yes," Heinrich nodded. "I negotiated it."

"How will they handle the Chinese? Iran is their largest foreign supplier. Did you tell the Iranians what to do when the Chinese come knocking on the door?"

Heinrich gave him a knowing look. "That is the question. Mueller has been propping up the Russian ruble—as he promised.

Not as rigorously as they would wish, but he has been able to support their markets."

"But not the Chinese?"

"He will, as you Americans say, leave them hanging out to dry."

"Not a drop of oil."

Heinrich shook his head. "And they will have nowhere else to go for it, either. With Mueller's deals in place, Germany controls Russia's access to the world's capital, and Iran's access to the world's oil market."

"The Chinese won't like it."

"But what can they do about it?"

"Invade the Middle East," Hoag suggested. "Take the oil."

"They could never do that. They are strong, but not that strong."

"It wouldn't be difficult. They already have a defense arrangement with Pakistan. They could move their army through the passes, swing around to the west, cross into Iran from southern Pakistan."

"But what of the hundred thousand men you still have in Afghanistan?"

"That would be scary."

"Indeed."

Conversation lagged and they sat in silence, each of them staring out the window. Finally, Heinrich spoke again. "There is one more piece of the puzzle."

Hoag shook his head in disbelief. "What is that?"

"You have a man in your CIA who has been very helpful to Schroeder and the Federal Police."

Hoag had figured as much when Heinrich first told him the Germans were monitoring communications from the embassy. They couldn't do that without help from someone on the inside providing the access codes. He looked across the table. "Who is it?"

"You expect me to give you a name?"

"You wouldn't have brought it up if you weren't going to tell me. Who is it?"

"Peter Burke."

Suddenly Hoag felt very vulnerable and he realized Jenny could be in danger. "Peter Burke helped them do it?"

"Helped us do it."

"You were in on it?"

"I was the contact. We could not risk having something like that connected to our highest officials."

"But you are the chancellor's special assistant."

"Yes, and I am expendable," Heinrich shrugged. "If there was a problem, I could be fired or … whatever."

"You would do that? You would have risked your life for it?"

"I would have then," Heinrich nodded.

"But not now?"

"Things have changed. Nothing is as it once was." Heinrich had a faraway look in his eyes. "Perhaps it was never what I had imagined it to be."

Hoag took another sip of tea and turned to the window. "How did you know about this place?"

"It was my grandfather's." From the tone of his voice, he welcomed the change of subject.

Something near the lake caught Hoag's attention—a reflection or a movement—he wasn't quite sure, but he studied the shoreline of the lake. Then a man leaned from behind a tree. He held a rifle that he pointed toward the house.

"Duck!" Hoag shouted as he dropped to the floor.

A bullet shattered the window and lodged in the wall on the opposite side of the room. Heinrich slid from his chair and together they crawled beneath the table. Hoag glanced over at him. "How many people know about this place?"

"Everyone knows about this place."

"We have company. I wondered how we got up here without much trouble."

Heinrich raised his head to see out the window. A second shot struck the window to the right. Shards of glass peppered his hair. He dropped to the floor once more. "Come. We must get out of here." He crawled on his hands and knees across the room.

Hoag followed. "Where are we going?"

"Many people know the location of this house." They reached a door at the far side of the room. Heinrich reached up for the knob and opened it. "But few know its secrets. I will show you some of them." Beyond the door was a stairway that led into a basement. Dank, musty air greeted them as they crawled past the door and onto the steps. "Come with me," he motioned. "We must hurry." Heinrich stood and led the way into the basement.

95

TEUPITZER SEE
TEUPITZ, GERMANY

DIRK FEDDER LEANED AGAINST a pine tree behind the house and took a cell phone from his pocket. He checked to make certain the phone had service, then placed a call to Hermann Schroeder.

"They are here. We have them surrounded."

"You have not taken them?"

"No. We had a clean shot, but missed."

"Have you been spotted?"

"They saw us when we took the shot." Fedder glanced around, checking. "But no one else knows we are here."

"Take them."

"This could get messy."

"Then do it quickly."

The call ended. Fedder signaled to his team. They tightened the circle around the house, then started up the steps to the deck.

96

TEUPITZER SEE
TEUPITZ, GERMANY

HOAG LINGERED NEAR THE BOTTOM of the basement steps while Heinrich groped in the dark. "Can you see where you're going?"

"I can feel my way along," Heinrich's voice was remarkably calm. "There is a shelf over here. I am looking ... Here it is." Hoag heard a click and then a shaft of light appeared from a flashlight in Heinrich's hand. He waved it like a wand. "Not sure it would still work," he smiled.

With the light in hand, Heinrich led the way to the uphill side of the basement where a row of wooden shelves lined the wall. He grabbed the end of the shelves and pulled it away from the wall.

A thud from upstairs rattled the floor. "What was that?"

"They kicked in the front door," Heinrich whispered. Footsteps plodded across the floor above them, but Heinrich calmly pushed back the shelves a little further, revealing a door along the wall behind them. He pushed it open and shined the light into a small room. "Get in." Hoag stepped inside.

Heinrich reached out through the open doorway and pulled the shelves back in place, then closed the door. "We must hurry."

"What is this?"

"A safe room. My grandfather built it before World War II." Heinrich shined the light in front of them as they made their way across the room. "He used it to smuggle Jews."

"Your grandfather was a Jewish sympathizer?"

"My grandfather was Jewish."

"Wow." Hoag glanced around, trying to think of what it must have been like that long ago. "How long can we hide in here before they find us?"

"We are not staying in here."

"Where are we going?"

"Follow me. I will show you." On the opposite side of the room was a curtain. Heinrich pushed it aside to reveal a tunnel.

Hoag stopped short. "We're going in there?"

"It is our only choice." There was the sound of a door opening. Heinrich gestured overhead. "That was the basement door," Heinrich smiled. "What shall it be?"

Hoag gestured toward the tunnel. "Let's go." And he followed Heinrich inside.

Twenty minutes later, they emerged from the tunnel into a clump of bushes on the backside of the hill that rose behind the house. Hoag glanced around to get his bearings. Through the trees he caught a glimpse of the lake, but saw nothing else familiar. "Where are we?"

"Less than a kilometer from the house." He gestured over his shoulder. "That is the hill behind the house."

"Won't they see us?"

"The hill will hide us from view." Heinrich dusted off his pants. "Come. We must get to the road."

As they started down the hill, Hoag picked up the conversation where they'd left off at the table. "We need to prove Burke was involved."

"That would be difficult. Not impossible, but difficult."

"You could come back to America with me."

"I am afraid that is out of the question. They would never let me leave the country. Not even sure we can get you out." Heinrich glanced back at Hoag. "But there is a way to prove he did it."

"How?"

"Burke gave me a smart card to pass to Schroeder."

"You actually met with Burke?"

"Yes. As I told you, I was his contact. We met on a trip in Chile. You know about these smart cards?"

"Yeah. Generates a password that lets you into the CIA's system. From there you can get to anything."

"Well," Heinrich said, arching an eyebrow. "That is what we did. We accessed your system."

"You know where the smart card is now?"

"It is in Schroeder's desk drawer at his office."

"Great! We get to break into Schroeder's office. Think we can do it?"

"I think so."

A few minutes later they reached the road. Heinrich straightened his jacket and snugged his tie beneath the collar of his shirt. He cut his eyes at Hoag. "You look like you just walked through the woods. Brush your shoulders."

Hoag dusted off his shirt. "You think we can get a ride?"

"I am certain someone will stop."

"But will they give us a ride?"

"Of course they will. I have been coming here my entire life. I am their neighbor." A car appeared in the distance. "Here comes someone now." Heinrich held up his hand to wave. "I think I know this person." The car slowed to a stop beside them.

97

BERLIN, GERMANY

THE NEIGHBOR WHO BROUGHT HOAG AND HEINRICH in from the lake dropped them off at the train station. They took a taxi from there and rode to the Interior Ministry building. It was dark when they arrived.

Through a window on the first floor they saw a guard at a desk in the lobby. Security scanners stood near the door. Hoag glanced over at Heinrich. "How are we going to get inside?"

Heinrich reached in his jacket and took out a building access card. "I think this still works."

"But the guard will recognize you."

"We will try the back."

They slipped around the building to a door near the loading dock. It was a simple steel door secured by a magnetic lock with a card reader. Heinrich swiped the access card in the reader. A moment later, the lock clicked. Hoag followed him inside.

Moving quickly but quietly, they made their way upstairs to the fourth floor and emerged from the stairwell near the elevators. Schroeder's office was at the end of the corridor. With Heinrich in the lead, they crept past the receptionist's desk and entered Schroeder's office suite. The door was open. Hoag lingered there while Heinrich moved behind the desk.

He opened the drawer and reached inside. "Here it is," he

whispered. He held the smart card for Hoag to see. "This is it."

"Okay. Let's get out of here before someone sees us."

Heinrich came from behind the desk and handed the card to Hoag. "Guard this with your life." Hoag took it from him and slipped it into his pocket.

They retraced their steps from the office to the receptionist's desk and stepped out to the corridor. Schroeder was standing near the elevator. Hoag felt his heart sink. "We're done," he whispered.

Heinrich turned his head in Hoag's direction. "Get ready to run."

Schroeder stepped toward them, his eyes fixed on Heinrich. "Did you think you could avoid us, Franz? We need to talk."

"Chasing me around the city is no way to hold a conversation."

"Yes, well, sometimes a phone call is not the best way, either." Schroeder glanced over at Hoag. "Who is your friend?"

"I think you know who he is."

"I suppose I do," Schroeder smirked. "The one with the cell phone."

Heinrich's face went cold. "You killed my wife."

"It was an accident. A tragic accident."

"Right."

Schroeder cocked his head at an imperious angle. "You doubt me?"

"I saw your men at the house." Heinrich lunged for Schroeder and grabbed him by the throat. "Run!" he shouted.

Hoag ran toward the stairwell. Schroeder moved to cut him off, but Heinrich wrestled him to the floor. While they thrashed at each other, Hoag threw open the stairwell door and hurried down the steps.

Hot and gasping for breath, he finally reached the bottom. He paused there a moment to regain his composure, then eased open the door. Through the opening he saw the guard seated at a desk near the center of the lobby. *Great! How do I get out of here?*

Just then a phone rang at the desk. The guard answered it, said something in German, then ended the call and reached for his radio. He held it to his mouth and spoke in an excited voice.

They're after me. No time to wait. He pushed open the door and ran for the exit.

As he came from the stairwell, the elevator bell rang and the doors opened. A second guard stepped out. "Halt!" he shouted. "Halt!"

The guard ran after him, but Hoag had a head start. Before the guard could catch up, he squeezed past the security scanner and raced out the door. With the guard still behind him, Hoag ran down the steps and across the sidewalk to the street. An Audi screeched to a halt, narrowly avoiding Hoag's leg. The driver sounded the horn and shouted out the window. Hoag ran around the car and opened the door. "Get out," he ordered.

"You are crazy," the driver retorted. "I am not giving you my car."

Hoag grabbed him by the collar and pulled him from behind the wheel. By then the guard was at the sidewalk. He reached for his pistol as Hoag shoved the driver into the street and climbed behind the steering wheel. He put the car in gear and started forward. A shot rang out. The bullet struck the rear window. Glass exploded through the car. Hoag shifted gears and kept going.

Up ahead, a police car approached from a side street. Blue lights atop the car cut through the night and the siren wailed. Hoag pressed the gas pedal. The Audi's engine whined as he raced to beat the oncoming car.

The police car sped up and shot into the street in front of him. Hoag swerved, but the right fender of the Audi clipped the nose of the car and spun it around. Still he kept his foot on the gas pedal and his hands on the steering wheel.

Behind him, sirens wailed. He glanced in the rearview mirror. A block away, another police car raced toward him but there was no choice now. He had to keep going. At the end of the street he turned left. The Brandenburg Gate loomed ahead. He shifted gears again, pressed the gas pedal and raced toward it.

98

INTERIOR MINISTRY BUILDING
BERLIN, GERMANY

BACK ON THE FOURTH FLOOR, Schroeder gained the upper hand in the fight with Heinrich. He slipped his arm free and wrapped it around Heinrich's neck. Then he stood to his feet and squeezed harder, pinning Heinrich against him in a headlock. With Heinrich unable to wriggle free, Schroeder started toward his office, dragging Heinrich with him.

When he reached the desk, he threw Heinrich into a chair. Heinrich sprawled against the armrest, exhausted and unable to lift his arms. "You are pathetic," he grumbled.

"But I whipped you," Schroeder growled. He drew back his fist and struck Heinrich on the jaw. Heinrich's head snapped back and his eyes closed. His body went limp and slid to the floor. "And I whipped that pitiful excuse of a wife you had, too." He stepped over Heinrich's legs and made his way to the chair behind the desk. There he picked up the phone and placed a call to the security guard downstairs. "Did you get him?"

"No, sir. We did not locate him until you called and then he eluded us."

"Eluded you?" Schroeder screamed. "You are fired." He ended the call and placed another, this one to the guards at the gate in back. "Did he come through there?"

"No, sir. He commandeered a car from someone in front of the building and fled."

"What car?"

"An Audi. Black. We're searching the tapes now to see if the cameras caught the license number."

"Which way did he go?"

"Toward the Gate."

Schroeder pressed a button for another phone line and called the command center downstairs. "Close the airports and the train station. Put out an alert for David Hoag. Inform Berlin, too. I want every available unit searching for him. He's driving a black Audi. Guards in back think they have a license number. Check with them. I want him found, do you understand me?" Schroeder slammed down the receiver and wiped his hands over his face. "CIA analyst," he scoffed. "He will never see morning alive."

Heinrich rolled over and raised himself up on his knees. He caught hold of the desk and pulled himself up from the floor, then dropped onto the chair. "You will never find him," he groaned.

"I will find him, all right," Schroeder boasted. "And when I do it will be the end for both of you." He took a pistol from beneath his jacket and laid it on the desktop, then leaned back in the chair and closed his eyes. "I am not letting you or some CIA analyst beat me."

"He is smarter than you." Heinrich took a deep breath. "Smarter than either of us."

"Maybe so. But he is not meaner."

"That is true," Heinrich nodded. He glanced in Schroeder's direction to make certain his eyes were still closed. "Very true." He eased forward in the chair. "But you are not that mean." With uncanny quickness, Heinrich reached over the desk and snatched up the pistol.

Schroeder grinned. "What do you think you are doing?"

Without a word, Heinrich pointed the pistol at Schroeder and squeezed the trigger. A shot rang out, ripping a hole in Schroeder's chest. Blood spattered on the desk and oozed down the front of Schroeder's shirt. He stared at Heinrich, his eyes wide, his mouth open.

"That was for my wife," Heinrich said. He raised the pistol once more and took better aim. "This one is for me." He squeezed off a second shot that struck Schroeder between the eyes.

99

LAS VEGAS, NEVADA

THE INCREASED RADIO CHATTER from the German Federal Police caught Pete Rios' attention. He turned to Ken Aycock in the command center. "Do they have Hoag?"

"No, sir. They're still searching for him in Berlin. Security guards at the Interior Ministry building saw him leave in a black Audi."

"Interior Ministry? What was he doing there?"

Jeff Howell spoke up. "That's where the Federal Police has its headquarters."

Rios was perplexed. "Did he go there on his own, or did they take him there in custody?"

"I doubt they had him in custody," Howell replied. "It's an office complex. Not a working police station. They don't have a detention facility there."

"What about the man he was with? Franz Heinrich. Any information on him?"

"No, sir," Aycock answered. "Looks like Hoag left the building alone. But they're serious about finding him. Federal Police have closed the airport and train station. Berlin police have patrol cars on the street looking for him."

"Where's the Special Missions Unit from Wiesbaden?"

"En route."

"Check that," Weavil corrected. "They're on the ground at the drop site. Picking up the van now."

"Great," Rios replied. "Now all we need is Hoag's location."

"Sir," the operator interjected. "We have an E-8 airborne command aircraft in the area. Maybe they can help."

"This is going to get out of hand quickly," Weavil warned. "First an SMU, and now JSTARS. We're conducting a military operation on German soil."

Rios turned to the operator. "Tell the Air Force to find Hoag." He cut his eyes at Weavil. "I don't care what the Germans think about it. They can file a complaint with the UN."

100

BERLIN, GERMANY

A BLOCK PAST THE BRANDENBURG GATE, Hoag turned right. Two
blocks farther, he glanced in the rearview mirror and saw a police car
coming toward him. Seconds later, another unit appeared behind it.
Before long, there was a line of cars chasing after him. Hoag pressed
the gas pedal. The Audi picked up speed. He ignored the lights flashing in the mirror and focused on dodging traffic.

At the next corner, he turned right, then made a hard left across
oncoming lanes and turned into an alley. He sped down the alley
toward the cross street. When he reached it, he bounced into the
street and kept going into the alley on the opposite side. He switched
off the lights and drove in darkness. Behind him, the police cars
reached the street and stopped to wait for traffic to clear. By then,
Hoag had reached the cross street at the end of the next block. He
made a hard right from the alley to the street, shot through the next
intersection, then made another hard right into an alley, doubling
back in the direction he'd just come. Off to the right, sirens blared as
more police cars rushed to join the line that snaked through the city.

Still without headlights, he drove through the dark alley toward
the cross street but slowed the car to an idle. "If I did this right," he
said to himself, "I can turn left at the street and drive quietly away."
He moved the shifter to a lower gear and prepared to stop.

Suddenly, a Berlin police van screeched to a stop on the street in front of him, blocking his way. Hoag brought the car to a stop and shifted into reverse. The side door of the van opened and six men jumped out. Dressed in black, they wore hoods over their faces. Only their eyes peeked out from beneath. They spoke in muffled voices but carried assault rifles, which they pointed straight at him.

"Hands in the air," the first man shouted. "Hands in the air, now!"

Hoag slipped his foot from the clutch and pressed the gas pedal. The Audi lurched backward, but before it moved ten feet shots rang out, flattening all four tires. Hoag moved the shifter to neutral and raised his hands.

One of the men came to the passenger side of the car. Another appeared at the driver's door and opened it. He grabbed Hoag by the shoulder and helped him from the car. "Let's go," the man said, quietly. "We gotta move quickly." The sound of his voice seemed not at all German and it caught Hoag by surprise.

"Who are you?"

"Get moving," the man said, and he shoved Hoag toward the van.

The other men followed and hustled him inside. The last man pulled the van door closed and called to the driver, "Let's go." The van started forward, blended into traffic, and turned at the corner.

Hoag sat on the floor, unsure what to do next. When they stopped him, he was certain the men in the van were Federal Police. Now he wasn't so sure. Then he noticed they were armed with M-16 rifles. Each of them carried a Glock pistol as a sidearm. Finally, one of the men pulled off his mask. "Good evening, Mr. Hoag," he smiled. "First Sergeant Buford Young. United States Army. Are you okay?"

A sense of relief swept over Hoag and a lump formed in his throat. "Yes. I'm fine." He blinked back tears.

"Good." Young slapped him on the back. "Sit tight and we'll have you out of here soon."

"Where are we going?"

"We're going back to the base at Wiesbaden. But you're going home."

A radio crackled. Young turned his attention to the driver. "What was that?"

"Berlin police."

The others gathered near the front of the van. There was more radio traffic. "That's Federal Police," someone suggested.

"They saw us," another added.

"Keep driving," Young ordered.

"They know we're on this street," the driver replied.

Young glanced out the windshield and pointed. "Turn right."

The driver turned the steering wheel. Tires squealed as the van careened around a corner. He pressed the gas pedal and the van picked up speed, weaving in and out of traffic. They darted around a delivery truck, then swerved hard to avoid a car in the center of an intersection.

A siren wailed. One of the men looked out the back. "They're after us," he shouted. "Two blocks behind."

Young pointed again. "Turn here." They made a left. "Now here," he pointed to a sign for an expressway on-ramp. "Take the highway."

The driver swerved onto the ramp. They zoomed up the incline to the merge lane and blended into traffic. "Slow down," Young ordered. "Drive normal." The driver squeezed the van in between two trailer trucks and kept pace with the vehicles around him. Young called over his shoulder, "See anything back there?"

"Not yet."

"Let me know if they follow us."

A few minutes later, Young shouted again, "Anyone back there?"

"Still clear."

Young pointed once more. "Here we go." A sign for the airport hung from a rack above the highway. He glanced down at the driver. "Take it."

"This isn't the right one," the driver argued.

"It'll work. Take it. We can't risk being found."

The driver changed lanes and merged into the exit. He watched through the rearview mirror, then a smile turned up the corners of his mouth. "I think we're clear."

101

JERUSALEM, ISRAEL

DREW POWELL STEERED THE CAR from the street into a parking lot at the Botanical Garden in Jerusalem. He chose an empty space near the visitors' center and got out. A path led from the lot down to a lake a hundred meters away. He followed the path to the water and waited. A few minutes later, he was joined by Yorman Avital, his contact at the Foreign Affairs Office, with whom he had met earlier. They walked along a path by the lake while they talked.

"Thank you for meeting me," Powell began.

"You said it was urgent."

"We have information that indicates you are preparing to respond with a strike against Iran."

"I am not at liberty to discuss that issue."

"Sources tell us your response will include an all-out attack against every known nuclear site in the country."

"We are now certain the attacks came from Iran. Both the attack on Tel Aviv and the one on New York."

"As are we," Powell replied. "But we need time to formulate a response."

"What more is there to consider? We know the perpetrators. They have stated their resolve to wipe us from the earth many times. And they have made similar threats against the United States. To delay a response any longer would be a sign of weakness."

"This situation is bigger than Iran. Bigger than Israel. Bigger than the U.S."

Avital frowned. "What do you mean?"

"I can't discuss the details right now. We just need you to hold off responding for a little longer. Give us time to complete our analysis of the situation."

"What more is there to know? Our adversary attacked us. We know who it is. We must respond." Avital glanced at him. "You must tell me, if you want me to discuss this with my superiors. I must be able to give them some reason for the delay."

"Okay," Powell sighed. "You have received the report on our upcoming Treasury auction?"

"Yes," Avital nodded. "Most alarming. But is it reliable?"

"From all that we know right now, that report is accurate."

"This is a second attack, not with missiles but an attack nevertheless. An attack on your credibility and an attack against the global financial system."

"And that is our point," Powell countered. "If that report is true—and we believe it is—then Germany is involved in ways we don't yet fully understand. Perhaps Russia and China, as well."

"What involvement do the Russians and the Chinese have with the attacks?"

"That's what we're trying to determine. We think they may have agreed not to participate in the auction, too. We'd like to understand the nature of that involvement and determine if they actually participated in the missile strikes before we respond."

"We would like to make certain no further attacks occur."

"As would we," Powell responded. "But there is still another ship out there."

"Where?"

"We aren't certain. It left China bound for Los Angeles. We've tracked it as far as Singapore, but it has disappeared. Without knowing where it is, an attack on Iran would be an open invitation for them to use that third missile against us."

"Your satellites cannot locate it?"

"No." Powell shook his head. "At least not yet. It's not on the open ocean, but we don't know where it is."

"And it is no longer in Singapore?"

"No."

"Then it must be in Pakistan. That is where the company that owns it is located."

"Perhaps, but we haven't been able to confirm that." Powell looked over at Avital. "We just need more time."

They reached a bench at the water's edge. A path led to the right, away from the lake toward a second parking lot. Avital paused there and turned to face Powell. "The forces of evil are closing in on us. Both of us." His voice had a professorial tone. "And the world has a short memory. Before long, other developments will turn their attention elsewhere and make our response to Iran seem unwarranted and disproportional."

"We just need a little more time."

"I will pass on your request." Avital turned away and started up the path. A security guard appeared at his side and escorted him from the garden.

102

BERLIN, GERMANY

THE VAN CARRYING HOAG and the Special Missions Unit turned from the road onto a street that wound around the perimeter of the Berlin airport. A few minutes later, they reached a hangar on the far side of the runway. A Gulfstream jet was parked inside. The fuselage door was open and stairs extended to the ground. The driver brought the van to a stop alongside. One of the men in the van opened the side door. Sergeant Young said something, but the sound of the jet's engines made it difficult to hear.

Hoag turned toward the door, but Young grabbed his arm. He leaned close, his lips all but touching Hoag's ear. "Wait. Let them get out first."

The men climbed from the van and lined the path to the foot of the steps. When they were in place, Young tugged at Hoag's arm. "Now we go, sir." He hustled Hoag from the van, past the soldiers, and up the steps toward the fuselage door. As Hoag's feet hit the steps, a second soldier came behind him, arms spread wide, shielding him from view.

At the top, Hoag ducked his head and moved inside the plane. Young leaned into the cockpit and looked over at the pilots. "He's all yours."

"Thank you, Sergeant," one of them replied.

Young glanced back at Hoag. "They'll have you home soon." Then he stepped out the door and was gone.

Hoag moved down the aisle and settled into a seat near the wing. An attendant closed the fuselage door and pressed a button to retract the steps. Before the stairs were all the way up, the plane was moving forward. Hoag glanced out the window and watched as the soldiers on the ground climbed into the van and drove from the hangar. Once again a lump formed in his throat. *They risked their lives to find me and get me to safety. So many to rescue just me.*

As the plane came from the hangar, he saw a police car approach. With lights flashing, it came to a stop in front of the van. Two officers jumped from the car, pistols drawn. Moments later, a second car arrived, then another.

Still the plane kept rolling and turned onto the taxiway. Hoag rose from the seat to look out the opposite side of the plane. Through the window he saw the soldiers, weapons ready, in a standoff with policemen who were outnumbered and overmatched. He wondered how long they would stare at each other before someone was killed.

At the end of the taxiway, the plane turned sharply and rolled to the center of the runway. Then, without stopping, it turned again. The engines powered up to full throttle.

One of the police cars started across the tarmac in front of the hangar, racing toward the runway. It crossed the taxiway a little ahead of the plane and cut through the grass, angling for a line that would intersect their path and cut them off, but it was too late. Hoag felt his backbone pressed against the seat as the jet roared down the runway. Out the window he watched the police car reach the edge of the pavement just as they zoomed past. Moments later, the nose of the plane lifted and they were airborne.

103

CHINESE BORDER WITH PAKISTAN

COMMANDER LUO LI-JEN STOOD ATOP A HILL and watched as a convoy of trucks approached on the road below. Standing next to him was Kang Rongji, the unit's chief logistical officer. Below their position, the convoy slowed and turned into a grove of trees. They rattled to a stop and men climbed down. Working together, they unloaded crates of supplies. Within the hour, a tent compound began to take shape.

Luo nodded approvingly. "What time will the next unit arrive?"

"In two hours," Kang replied. "They were scheduled to allow time for each unit to get their tents in place before the next one arrives."

"They will require additional space. Nothing ever goes exactly according to plan. You are prepared for that?"

"There is a field three kilometers down the road. We will put some there. If that is not enough, we can convert the woodlands."

"No," Luo said, shaking his head. "I would prefer expanding the camp in that direction," he said, pointing toward a grove of trees.

"It will take time to prepare the area. Not all of the heavy equipment has arrived yet."

"No." Luo was indignant. "Were you not in the planning sessions? We must leave the terrain as natural as possible. That way, we can use the landscape to help obscure our numbers."

"It will be more cumbersome for the men."

"It will not seem so cumbersome to them if it keeps them alive. Let them pitch their tents beneath the trees."

"We cannot hide them forever. The Americans still have satellites. Eventually they will see us. Especially as our numbers grow."

"Then we must hope for a diversion," Luo said with a wry smile. "To take their eye from us while we become too strong to resist." A truck rolled by on the road. Dust drifted through the air. Luo folded his arms behind his back. "Do we have water trucks?"

"Sir?"

"We need to dampen the road," he said, "to hold down the dust."

Kang nodded. "I will assign a crew to it right away."

Luo smiled confidently. "By doing many little things, we shall succeed in achieving much larger objectives."

104

OFFUTT AIR FORCE BASE
OMAHA, NEBRASKA

THE GULFSTREAM JET WITH HOAG aboard touched down and rolled onto a taxiway. A few minutes later, it came to a stop inside a secure hangar. Hoag stepped out hoping to see Jenny waiting for him. Instead, he was met by a broad-shouldered man of medium height with olive skin and curly gray hair.

"Mr. Hoag, my name is Pete Rios." They shook hands. "I'm the director of NEST."

"NEST?" Hoag was puzzled. "Why are you here?"

"We were tracking you in Germany." He turned toward a black SUV parked nearby and gestured for Hoag to follow. "We're the ones who got you out."

"Thank you."

"Just doing our job."

"The soldiers who picked me up had a little trouble at the airport. Are they okay?"

"We're taking care of it." They reached the SUV. Rios opened the door. "If you'll get in, we can be on our way."

Hoag climbed inside and slid to the opposite side of the backseat. Rios got in next to him. He closed the door and motioned to the driver. The SUV started forward. Rios turned to Hoag. "I think we should talk now, before things get crazy."

"I work for the CIA. Shouldn't they debrief me?"

"I haven't told them where you are."

"Okay," Hoag said slowly. "Why is that?"

"I'm skeptical of the agency. They burned me once or twice. I prefer to collect my own information. Run my own show."

Hoag had a quizzical look. "How did you know where I was?"

"NSA in London picked up your cell phone call."

"Good," Hoag smiled. "Then you know about the problem with the Treasury auction."

"Yes," Rios nodded. "But before we get to that, I'm curious. Why did you go to Germany in the first place?"

"Investigators at Kings Bay found fingerprints on the missile launcher recovered from the *Panama Clipper*. The FBI refused to release the identity for three of them. I had someone go around the FBI and found out the prints belonged to three officers from the German Federal Police."

"They were inside the cargo container while it was still at Bremerhaven?"

Hoag nodded. "They knew the missile was there and that it was headed for New York."

"And they let it go anyway."

"Yes."

"Who made that decision?"

"The chancellor actually gave the order, but all communication about it came from his assistant, Franz Heinrich."

"We should have expected as much."

"The Germans have bought up Iran's oil production."

"I don't think so." Rios shook his head. "That would be a huge financial transaction. They could never pay for it."

"Prices have skyrocketed."

"Still," Rios argued, "it's a big transaction."

"I don't know about the financial terms, but Iran has agreed to sell it to them. Germany controls access to Iran's oil."

"And the Chinese? What do they plan to do about the Chinese?"

"You tell me. Have we been monitoring China's military activity?"

"I don't know."

Hoag frowned. "Why not?"

"We've had all we could do just figuring out who was behind the missiles and keeping Israel in the loop … and taking care of you. Who was your source about the auction?"

"Franz Heinrich. The Russians and the Chinese won't participate, either. They had it all worked out long before the attack. They had already decided not to buy any more of our debt."

"Is Heinrich reliable? I mean, he's pretty cozy with the chancellor. And if he's the guy who let the missile go to New York, is there some other reason he's telling us about the auction?"

"I don't think he and Mueller are that cozy anymore." Hoag arched an eyebrow. "The German Police killed his wife."

Rios looked surprised. "Why?"

"Trying to get her to talk."

"About what?"

"About what Heinrich was telling me, but we have a bigger immediate problem."

"What could be bigger than all this?"

Hoag had a knowing look. "We have a mole."

Rios looked away. "Who is it?"

"Peter Burke. Works for the CIA."

"Heinrich tell you that, too?"

"Yes. And he gave me this." Hoag took the smart card from his pocket and held it up for Rios to see. "He took it from Hermann Schroeder's desk."

"Schroeder is head of the Federal Police. How did it get in his desk?"

"Burke passed it to Heinrich at a meeting in Chile. Heinrich gave it to Schroeder. It was part of Mueller's plan. They've been in our system for months. Do you know Burke? He's Deputy Director for Middle East Analysis."

"I've met him a few times. You can prove he was involved? Other than by what Heinrich told you?"

"I think so," Hoag replied. "But I need to get to my office."

105

JERUSALEM, ISRAEL

FROM HIS MEETING WITH DREW POWELL at the Botanical Garden, Yorman Avital rode to the Foreign Ministry office. Simon Epstein was waiting when he arrived.

"What did the American say?"

"They want more time."

Epstein shook his head. "We cannot give them more time."

"I told him as much, but I said I would pass along the request."

"Well, you have passed it on."

Avital pressed the point. "Will you inform the prime minister?"

"It would be useless."

"Useless?" Avital's voice was firm. "The Americans are our ally—perhaps our only ally. Should we not do them the courtesy of at least considering their request?"

"The Americans do not live with their enemies on their borders."

"And we cannot hope to survive without them."

"Our plans are already in place."

"Plans can be changed."

Epstein looked at him. "You agree with their request?"

"No." Avital shook his head. "I do not agree with them. But that is not the point."

"Then what is the point?"

"They are our friends. We should extend to them the same courtesy we would expect to receive. The courtesy of due consideration."

———— (((————

In spite of his reluctance, Epstein passed the American request to David Oren's office. Oren called an emergency meeting of the Israeli Security Cabinet to address the matter. "I wanted to inform you of a request from the United States asking us to delay our response to Iran."

"Delay?" General Grossman was indignant. "Why do they want us to delay? And why should we consider their request? We are our own country. We make our own decisions, based on our own information."

Oren ignored Grossman and gestured to Epstein. "Simon, you know the details."

Epstein stood. "The Americans have learned that German police discovered a Shahab-3 missile in a cargo container while it was still on the loading dock in Bremerhaven. They allowed it to be loaded on the ship that carried it to the American coast."

"That is preposterous," Grossman blurted. "The Germans would never do such a thing."

Epstein looked him in the eye. "You have forgotten our history?"

Epstein continued. "The Americans have also learned that before the attack on their coast, Germany, Russia, and China had agreed together to refrain from purchasing U.S. debt instruments. This was apparently part of a coordinated plan."

Oren spoke up. "Coordinated with the attack?"

"That is what the Americans would like to find out."

Emile Dayan, the treasury minister, added, "The market has already collapsed. No one will buy their debt now anyway."

"But this was an agreement reached before the attack."

Grossman leaned forward. "They think if we do not attack they can find someone to loan them trillions of dollars?"

Epstein cleared his throat. "They think the attack on America and on us was part of a much bigger plan. They would like time to learn more about it before we respond to Iran."

Grossman turned to Oren. "Mr. Prime Minister, if we do not respond now, we will never be able to do so. An attack later will not be seen by the world as us defending ourselves. It will be seen as a second unrelated attack and they will attack us in response."

Dayan nodded in agreement. "And if we do not respond, the Iranians will see it as a sign of weakness. Their puppets in Lebanon and in Gaza will be emboldened to move against us on the ground."

Oren looked down the table at Efraim Hofi. "What do you think?"

"We must go now," Hofi said, quietly. "I do not like the prospect of what the world might be afterward, but I like even less what the world will be if we do nothing."

Oren glanced around the table. "All in favor of going forward with the response to Iran signify your vote by standing."

Grossman leaped to his feet. Dayan scooted back his chair and slowly stood. Then, one by one, everyone in the room rose from their seats.

"Very well." Oren sighed. "We should review the targets."

106

OFFUTT AIR FORCE BASE OMAHA, NEBRASKA

THE SUV CAME TO A STOP OUTSIDE the Adams Office Annex. Hoag climbed out and started toward the front entrance. Rios followed. Neither of them said a word as they walked down the hall to Hoag's cubicle. It was early. Offices were empty, the building was quiet.

Hoag took a seat at his desk and logged on to the computer system. Then he took the smart card from his pocket and located a serial number on the back. Rios stood at the doorway and watched while Hoag found the system access site.

A check of the number indicated the card had been assigned to James Mann. Hoag clicked on the name to verify Mann's location but was denied access to the files. Rios came from the doorway and stood behind him. "What's wrong?"

"The card was originally issued to someone named James Mann, but I can't get in the file."

Just then Susan Todd appeared. "David," she exclaimed. "You're back."

"Yes," Hoag whispered. "But keep it quiet."

"Have you seen Jenny?"

"No, I came straight from the airport."

She glanced at Rios, then the monitor. "What are you two doing?"

Rios gave her a polite smile. "I'm Pete Rios. Director of NEST."

"Oh really," Susan quipped. "And I'm the First Lady."

Rios took out his wallet and flashed his identification. "Rios," he said, tapping the photo. "NEST."

Susan glanced down at the agency information on the card, then looked over at Hoag. "Is this for real?"

"Yes. It's for real."

She backed away. "I better get Burke."

"No," Hoag barked. She gave him a startled look. His face softened. "Not yet. I need your help."

"What are you trying to do?"

Hoag gestured toward the smart card. "I'm trying to find information about the person to whom this card is assigned. It says it was given to James Mann, but I can't get into his file."

"Let me see." She leaned over Hoag and entered a command. A file appeared on the screen. "That's because he's dead."

"Dead?"

"Died three years ago." She pointed to a number on the screen. "That's the code for it right there." She moved to a different screen. "He was listed as deceased, but the card was never retrieved or canceled."

"Can you find the log that shows the first time it was used?"

She switched screens and scrolled down to the bottom. "Wow."

"What?"

"This thing has been used on a nonsystem computer almost the entire time." She scrolled up the screen toward the top. "There." She pointed to an entry. "That's the first time it was used. It was logged in almost four months ago on our system." She checked the identifying data. "It was used by ... Peter Burke. But after that, it was used by someone else." She looked over at Hoag. "After Mann was supposed to be dead."

"That's what we needed to know," Hoag grinned.

Rios spoke up. "Can you preserve this file?"

"I can code it so no one can delete it."

"Do it."

Hoag slid back his chair from the desk and stood. Susan took a seat and entered a command to re-code the file. "Jenny will be here in a few minutes."

Hoag checked his watch. "I don't think I can wait." He turned away and started up the hall.

Susan called after him, "She'll be upset you didn't wait."

Hoag hesitated, then stepped into Jenny's cubicle and scribbled a note. Rios leaned through the doorway. "We gotta go." Hoag laid the note on Jenny's chair and turned to follow Rios.

107

DIMONA, ISRAEL

YIGAL ARI SAT AT HIS DESK and stared out at the hills in the distance. He had been sitting there since the call came an hour earlier. Now, the moment had arrived. Building security had phoned to let him know General Khoury had been cleared through the front gate.

There was a knock at the door. "Yes," he answered.

Anat Einik, his assistant, peeked inside. "He is here."

"Very well. Show him in."

Anat stepped aside as Khoury entered. He held a large blue envelope. Ari stood. "General Khoury," he said, doing his best to keep his voice under control. "I have been expecting you."

Khoury had a face of stone. "You are aware of the Cabinet's decision?"

"Someone in the prime minister's office called an hour ago to notify me. But no one in authority has issued an official order."

"You will receive the Emergency Action Memo after you have targeted the missiles."

"The missiles all have preloaded targets. They are ready to go."

"The Cabinet has some changes."

Khoury dropped the envelope on the desk. Ari opened it and reviewed the information. He frowned as he read it. "There are twenty new targets here."

"Yes."

"This will delay our launch time."

"By how long?"

"Two hours," Ari shrugged. "Perhaps a little longer."

"I will inform them of the delay. Add the sites."

Ari pointed to entries on the pages in his hand. "You realize two of these sites are in Tehran."

"Yes."

"Striking those sites will obliterate the city."

"Yes."

"Many civilians will die as a result."

"Yes."

"Women and children."

"I know what will happen," Khoury replied in a curt tone. "Just do as you are ordered."

"Very well." Ari moved from behind the desk. "I will have the technicians begin at once."

108

OFFUTT AIR FORCE BASE OMAHA, NEBRASKA

HOAG WALKED UP THE HALL with Rios at his side. Rios straightened the lapels of his jacket. "Are you ready?"

"Yeah. I think so."

At the end of the hall they turned and came to Burke's office. A secretary's desk sat in an alcove near the door. She hadn't arrived yet. Rios moved behind the desk. "I'll wait out here. You set him up."

The door to Burke's office was closed. Hoag tapped on it and pushed it open without waiting for a response. Burke was seated at his desk when Hoag entered. He looked up with a scowl. "Didn't I tell you to—" He stopped short when he saw the intruder was Hoag. "Where did you come from? And what were you doing talking on that cell phone?" Burke snapped. "You work for me. You're accountable to me."

"Right," Hoag nodded. "I think we're—"

Burke kept going. "If you had something to report, you should have sent it to me. You should have never used an unsecure line for it. And what were you doing in Germany? I never approved travel for you."

"We have a bigger problem to address," Hoag said, finally wedging a few words into the conversation.

"I set the agenda around here. You don't tell me what to discuss in my office."

"Well, set it around this." Hoag took the smart card from his pocket and held it for Burke to see.

"What is that?" Burke reached for it, but Hoag moved away.

"This is the card you gave to Franz Heinrich when you met him a few months ago in Chile."

"What are you talking about?"

"I'm talking about a smart card, issued to James Mann, who's been dead three years, but somehow his user status was left unchanged in the system so you could pass the card to Hermann Schroeder."

"You aren't making any sense at all." Burke gestured with his hand. "Where'd you get that?"

"From Franz Heinrich."

"I have no idea who you're talking about. I don't know anyone by that name."

"Yes, you do," a voice said from the doorway. Hoag turned around to see Jenny. She held a photograph. "You met him in Chile." She laid the photograph on the desk. Burke's face was ashen. "I found the photograph while looking for the other ship. The *Santiago*." Her eyes met Burke's. "Also a city in Chile, where you met Heinrich."

"You two will never make this stick," Burke sneered. "It'll be my word against yours and some photograph."

"Except for one thing." Rios appeared in the doorway. "I heard every word." He turned his head aside and called over his shoulder, "We're ready now, gentlemen."

Two men dressed in gray suits stepped into the office. "Mr. Burke," the first one said. "We're with the Secret Service." He moved to the end of the desk. "If you'll stand and place your hands on the desk, please."

"You aren't going to cuff me!" Burke protested.

"Sir," the agent continued, "this will be much easier if you cooperate." Burke rose slowly from his chair. The agent nudged him. "Lean forward, sir, and place your hands on the desk."

Burke propped his hands against the desktop and looked over at Hoag. "You haven't heard the end of this," he hissed.

"Sir." The agent pulled Burke's right arm back and fastened the handcuff around his wrist. "You have the right to remain silent. If you give up that right ..." The agent continued as he slid the cuff around Burke's other wrist. When he was finished, he led Burke from the office.

As they stepped into the hallway, Donna Bynum appeared. "Mr. Rios, they need you in the situation room."

Rios looked puzzled. "What's happening?"

"I think there's been a development in Israel."

Rios glanced at Hoag. "You better come, too."

109

DIMONA, ISRAEL

IN THE DATA CENTER, YIGAL ARI checked the printouts to make certain coordinates for the additional targets were correctly loaded into the guidance system. When he was certain the information had been entered, he checked to see that it had been accepted by the target acquisition computer for each of the twelve Jericho missiles. It was a tedious process, but one made necessary by the last-minute changes the Security Cabinet ordered.

With three independent warheads per missile, they were about to strike thirty-six targets, all of them inside Iran. Nuclear reactors, centrifuge facilities, missile sites, air force bases, and two major oil fields. A shudder ran up Ari's spine. *Millions of people will die. Thousands more will be burned and maimed, their bodies covered with* … He pushed the images from his mind and did his best to focus on the task at hand.

Once he determined the information in the system was correct, he came from the data center and walked down the underground corridor to the launch control room. A biometric system guarded access to the door. He pressed his palm against the screen and waited while it scanned his prints. When the scanner finished, a green light on the panel blinked. He leaned closer and spoke his name. The lock on the door clicked and a guard inside pushed it open. Ari stepped inside.

A panel of electronic instruments lined the wall to the left. Two weapons technicians monitored it. Three workstations extended across the room. Launch control officers sat at either end. Yosi Gavriel, the launch commander, was seated between them. General Khoury stood near the back wall, arms folded across his chest, eyes watching every detail.

As Ari entered the room, Gavriel turned in his direction. "All is in order?"

"Yes," Ari nodded. "The targeting information has been confirmed and accepted."

An alarm bell rang, catching Ari off guard. He jumped at the sound of it, then glanced around to see if anyone noticed. Khoury had noticed. "So many training exercises and still you jump?"

"I hope I never get used to it," Ari replied. He moved behind Gavriel and stood near Khoury.

Gavriel and the launch control officers sat at the ready, pens in hand, notebooks open on the desktop. Moments later, a voice came over the loudspeaker.

"Stand by for an Emergency Action Message." There was a pause, then the voice continued with letters from the Hebrew alphabet. "Kaf, tet, zayin, qof, dalet ..."

As the message continued, each of the men wrote the letters on a page in his notebook. When they finished, the launch control officers swapped books. Seconds later, the message repeated and they wrote the code again. When the message ended, the three compared what they had written. Then Gavriel turned to Ari. "They all read the same."

Ari glanced over Gavriel's shoulder at the notebooks. He studied them a moment, then nodded. "I concur. The emergency message has been accurately received."

With that, the launch control officers rose from their desks and stepped to a safe located along the wall behind where Ari and Khoury were standing. They unlocked the safe and took out an authentication card. One of them handed the card to Ari.

About the size of a credit card, a series of letters was written across the front. Ari checked to make certain the letters on the card matched the first letters of the message they'd just received. "They match," he agreed. Then he handed the card to Gavriel.

Gavriel repeated the process, carefully checking the letters on the card against the first few letters of the emergency message. "I concur. The letters are the same. The message is verified." He handed the message to one of the technicians monitoring the electronic panel.

The technician turned to a keypad near the center of the panel and entered a series of letters and numbers taken from the emergency message. Red lights atop the panel turned green. The technician turned to Gavriel. "The missiles are fueling."

"Very well," Gavriel replied. "By designation in the Emergency Action Message, which has now been verified and confirmed, missile launch is ordered to commence in thirty minutes." He pressed a button on the panel at his workstation. A digital clock appeared on a monitor before him. It began with nineteen minutes fifty-nine seconds, and slowly counted down.

At the sight of it General Khoury took a deep breath. "Soon we shall see the wrath of God visited upon our enemies. They have slaughtered our women and children, and have sworn an oath to offer us as a sacrifice to Allah. And now they shall see! Now the world shall see," he laughed harshly. "Nothing can stop us now!"

110

OFFUTT AIR FORCE BASE
OMAHA, NEBRASKA

WITH RIOS LEADING THE WAY, Hoag and Jenny hurried across the street to the central office complex. A guard opened the door for them as they approached. Inside, they darted across the lobby and made their way downstairs to the situation room. The room was packed with officers and cabinet officials. Rios squeezed past them to stand beside Hoyt Moore. Hoag and Jenny wedged their way in between an Air Force colonel and two men from the Treasury Department.

Hoag leaned close to the colonel. "What's going on?"

"NORAD has detected Israeli preparations for a missile launch."

Hoag was concerned but not surprised. "What kind of attack?"

"Nuclear."

"Did we know this was coming?"

"Apparently not," the colonel shrugged.

"What are the targets?"

"Iran."

"Which sites?"

"All the sites."

"They're hitting every nuclear installation in Iran?"

"No." The colonel shook his head. "Every military site." He looked grim. "They're hitting them all."

Jenny took Hoag's hand in hers and squeezed it tightly. Her palm felt clammy. He glanced down at her with a nervous smile.

President Hedges was near the operator at the console in the center of the room. He paced back and forth. "Is he on yet?"

"Yes, sir," the operator replied. "Mr. Oren is on the line."

Hoag looked over at the colonel. "Who's he talking to?"

"The Israeli prime minister."

"How's it going?"

"Not too well right now. They've been at it for a while."

"Mr. Prime Minister." Hedges' voice was firm but tense. "I thought we had agreed to delay a response."

"Mr. President." Oren sounded tentative. "I'm in the midst of important—"

"I know what you're doing, David," Hedges countered, making no attempt to hide the irritation in his voice. "That's why I called. I need you to stop the countdown."

"They have sworn to wipe us off the map," Oren replied.

"I know. We've been following developments closely. But I need you to—"

"They tried to do that very thing. If they had succeeded, millions in Tel Aviv would be dead now. Would you still be urging restraint if they had succeeded?"

"I understand the threat, David, but you stopped them." Hedges' face was red, his fists clenched as he fought to keep his emotions in check. "We worked together, we stopped them. Your people, our missile system. It worked. The world knows what happened. And right now, Iran is the villain. If you hit them with missiles, you'll be the villain."

When there was no immediate response, Hedges leaned near the operator. "Is he still on?"

"Yes," she nodded.

"David? Are you there?"

"I am here, Mr. President. Perhaps you are right, but our people demand a response."

"We are not puppets, Mr. Prime Minister. We are heads of state and we have been placed in our positions to exercise the wisdom given to us. This is a time for wisdom, not vengeance." Hedges paused to take a breath. "Give us time to respond to what is really happening. We will work with you. We will respond together to eliminate our real enemies, not just the ones who show their faces in public."

"You have information that you wish to share?"

"Yes, but I can't give it to you on the phone. Stop the launch sequence and I'll have someone brief you with details."

There was a noise in the background. Voices shouted. Hedges glanced around, an anxious look on his face. "What was that?" There were more voices shouting in Hebrew.

Someone in the Situation Room spoke up. "Sounds like they're going forward with the launch." A collective gasp went up. Murmuring wafted across the room.

"Shhh!" Moore held up his hand for silence. "Mr. President, I believe they're actually standing down."

The Prime Minister returned to the phone. "Mr. President, I have ordered the IDF to suspend our launch sequence."

"Great," Hedges beamed. "Thank you, Mr. Prime Minister."

"You will have someone brief me immediately?"

"Yes. We'll send them within the hour. And the Secretary of State will be in Jerusalem by morning."

"You and I need to talk."

"Yes. Secretary Lehman will arrange a meeting."

The call ended. A cheer went up from the room.

111

OFFUTT AIR FORCE BASE
OMAHA, NEBRASKA

HOAG AND JENNY LEFT THE SITUATION ROOM and walked outside. As they came down the steps, Hoyt Moore caught up with them. "Good work."

"Thank you," Hoag replied. "Did they tell you about Peter?"

"Yes. And I must say, I wasn't surprised."

Jenny had a look of amazement. "You knew about him?"

"I didn't know he was a mole, but I knew what kind of person he is. It was only a matter of time before something like this happened."

"Good thing we found out now," Hoag nodded.

"I hope you feel that way at the end of the day."

Hoag was puzzled by the remark. "What do you mean?"

"I'm designating you to take Burke's place."

"Will that need approval?"

"The president already signed off on it. As of now, you are Deputy Director for Middle East Analysis." Moore shook Hoag's hand. "Be in my office in an hour. We have a situation developing in China that will affect your area of responsibility." Moore turned away and walked toward an SUV parked nearby. Hoag stared after him.

Jenny took Hoag's arm. "Just like that?"

"I guess so." He watched as Moore got inside the SUV and drove away. "What does a director do?"

"I think you'll figure it out." She tugged on his arm. "Come on. Walk with me. We never got to finish that conversation we started on the plane."

"What conversation?"

"About *Revelation* and the prophecies." He gave her a questioning look. She continued. "You know. The locusts."

"What about them?"

"If the terrorists are the locusts, what happens after that?"

"War."

"Armageddon?"

"I don't think so. There's a war at the end of chapter nine. It's not the war of all wars, but it's one so awful that when it's over, no one wants to see it repeated and they take drastic steps to see that it doesn't happen again."

"What kind of drastic steps?"

Hoag came to an abrupt halt and turned to face Jenny. He put his arms around her waist and pulled her close. "We need to talk. About us. And if we don't do it now, we'll never get to it."

"Okay." She pulled away from him and folded her arms across her chest. "We need to talk." She looked up at him. "But me first."

The response startled him. "Okay." He gestured for her to continue. "You go first."

Jenny looked him in the eye and smiled. "I will."

"You will what?" Hoag gave her a blank stare.

"I will marry you." He grinned and reached out to pull her close. She slipped an arm around his waist and looked up at him. "But we still have to talk."

"What more is there to say?"

"There's something I have to tell you."

"Okay." The smile on his face melted. "Tell me about it."

She took his arm. "Let's talk while we take a walk. We have an hour before you have to be back."

"What's troubling you?"

"We haven't found the *Santiago*, that missing ship. We're still searching, but ..."

112

DIMONA, ISRAEL

AS THE CLOCK AT GAVRIEL'S WORKSTATION reached four minutes thirteen seconds, an alarm sounded. Everyone in the control room looked up at the speakers mounted on the wall. Then a voice spoke. "Standby for an Emergency Action Message."

Gavriel and the launch control officers took out their notebooks and pens. Moments later, the voice continued. "Lamed, ayin, resh, ayin, gimel, gimel, bet, qof ..." They dutifully copied down the text and swapped notebooks.

When the repeat broadcast concluded, Gavriel checked the pages, and then turned to Ari. "Sir, they read the same."

Ari glanced over Gavriel's shoulder at the notebooks, then nodded. "I concur. The Emergency Action Message has been accurately received."

As they had done before, the launch control officers unlocked the safe and removed a second authentication card. Ari compared the letters on the card to the first few letters of the message they just received. "The message is authentic," he nodded.

Gavriel took the card and repeated the process. "Yes," he nodded. "The message is confirmed." He reached across his desk and handed it to the technician. "Quickly," Gavriel snapped. "This is an order to stand down."

Before the technician could grasp the message, Khoury stepped forward and snatched it away. He held the message in one hand and drew his automatic pistol in the other. "Move this way. Both of you," he said, gesturing to the technicians with the pistol. "Step away from the panel."

As they stepped aside, Khoury moved to the center of the room. "Now, this is what we are going to do. We are going to stay right where we are and wait while the missiles launch. And if everyone does as they are told, we will all get to go home at the end of the day." A broad grin spread across his face. "And then we can watch while the few Iranians who survive try to figure out what hit them."

"You cannot be serious," Ari shouted. "We have orders to stand down."

Khoury shook his head. "I do not know anything about any orders to stand down. All I know is those worthless Iranians want to destroy us. Only now, we have the chance to destroy them. And we are going to do it."

Ari moved to the right. "This will never work."

"Of course it will work. I may have to shoot you, but it will work. The launch sequence has been initiated. Computers are in charge now. Nothing can stop them but human intervention." He wagged the pistol. "And I am going to make certain that will not happen."

One of the launch control officers spoke up. "There are six of us, and one of you."

Khoury held up the pistol. "I have fifteen rounds. That is two each. Do you want to be first?"

By then Ari was at the end of the workstation. "You will never get away with this." He came around the end and moved toward Khoury. "You will be tried and executed."

Khoury stepped forward quickly and grabbed Ari around the

neck. "Perhaps you are right. Perhaps I will die. And if that is true, why should I care what happens to you?" He pressed the muzzle of the pistol against Ari's temple. "How brave are you feeling now?"

From the corner of his eye, Ari caught a glimpse of the countdown clock. Fifty-nine seconds and counting ...